Hos

'Toby Litt is awfully goo
new every time he writes' Muriel Spark

'A really gifted storyteller' *Guardian*

'Litt is equally adept at building tension and coming up with a haunting phrase. Perhaps most impressive of all, though, is the richness of his imagination. This is a writer who doesn't quail at taking big risks and who possesses the talent to bring them off' *Daily Telegraph*

'Litt is rare among younger novelists in having published nothing except good work'
Literary Review

'One of the most inventive and original writers around' *Sunday Mirror*

'Prolific and precociously gifted' *Marie Claire*

'For bravery and bravura, Toby Litt takes the biscuit' *Financial Times*

'One of the country's most talented young novelists' *Red*

'Toby Litt is that once-in-a-lifetime blind date who goes on to give you the time of your life'
Julie Burchill

By the Same Author

Adventures In Capitalism

Beatniks

Corpsing

deadkidsongs

Exhibitionism

Finding Myself

Ghost Story

Hospital

A Dream-Vision

TOBY LITT

HAMISH HAMILTON
an imprint of
PENGUIN BOOKS

HAMISH HAMILTON

Published by the Penguin Group
Penguin Books Ltd, 80 Strand, London WC2R ORL, England
Penguin Group (USA) Inc., 375 Hudson Street, New York, New York 10014, USA
Penguin Group (Canada), 90 Eglinton Avenue East, Suite 700, Toronto, Ontario, Canada M4P 2Y3
(a division of Pearson Penguin Canada Inc.)
Penguin Ireland, 25 St Stephen's Green, Dublin 2, Ireland
(a division of Penguin Books Ltd)
Penguin Group (Australia), 250 Camberwell Road, Camberwell, Victoria 3124, Australia
(a division of Pearson Australia Group Pty Ltd)
Penguin Books India Pvt Ltd, 11 Community Centre, Panchsheel Park, New Delhi – 110 017, India
Penguin Group (NZ), 67 Apollo Drive, Rosedale, North Shore 0632, New Zealand
(a division of Pearson New Zealand Ltd)
Penguin Books (South Africa) (Pty) Ltd, 24 Sturdee Avenue, Rosebank, Johannesburg 2196, South Africa

Penguin Books Ltd, Registered Offices: 80 Strand, London WC2R ORL, England

www.penguin.com

First published 2007
1

Set in 12/14.75 pt Monotype Baskerville
Typeset by Rowland Phototypesetting Ltd, Bury St Edmunds, Suffolk
Printed in Great Britain by Clays Ltd, St Ives plc

A CIP catalogue record for this book is available from the British Library

ISBN: 978-0-241-14280-6

For Mic

Acknowledgements

The author would like to thank: Mic Cheetham; Simon Prosser, Juliette Mitchell, Sarah Day, Amelia Fairney, Julie Duffy, Anna Ridley, Laura Hassan, Jeremy Ettinghausen; Richard Thomas; Ali Smith; Lawrence Norfolk; Kate Colquhoun; China Mieville; Niall Griffiths; Ian Sansom; Julian Grenier & Caroline Volans; Rachel Holmes; Dr Crawford; Nurse Heidi Wilson & Paul; John O'Connell; Jenny Colgan; Ben Moor; Peter Dixon; Melanie Angel; the many Dr Litts. For research: Dr Ian McCrea, Henry R. Swindell, Tolulope Ogunlesi. For their diagnoses: Dr Alex Warwick & Dr David Cunningham. And most of all Dr Leigh Wilson.

www.tobylitt.com

19:59 hrs

Chukka-chukka-chukka-chukka.

Swooping out of the late evening sky, the Dauphin XTP3000 plunged down towards the hospital.

The boy felt his stomach get left behind in the air above: if only.

On the hospital roof, the H of the helipad glowed brightly in its circle of halogen.

Paramedic Bill "Zapper" Billson spoke into his helmet-mic: 'He's fading fast.'

The patient was bagged, and Billson was doing what he could to keep oxygen flowing to his brain – keep the brain alive.

'I'll be landed in another minute,' replied chopper pilot Hank "Cowboy" Smith.

The boy wanted to open his eyes, to look out the window, but the pain from his stomach was too great.

'He hasn't got much longer than that,' replied Zapper, his voice devoid of panic. He'd signed off on two arrests already this shift and had no intention of making it three in a row.

'Trauma team's there,' said Cowboy, who could see the group of them standing by the door. Down-draught from the rotorblades pressed their green and yellow uniforms against their bodies.

A figure with two fluorescent orange paddles stood on the H and waved Cowboy in. He didn't need help – he'd done this thousands of times. Easy on the old stickeroo.

The boy felt the chopper bounce slightly on the concrete.

As soon as they were down, before the rotors stopped, Trauma team swarmed onto the helipad.

'Give us the weather report,' said the authoritative voice of Sir Reginald Saint-Hellier.

'Bloody pissing it,' replied Zapper. He enjoyed their shorthand, from drizzle to thunderstorm.

'Specifically.'

'What we have here is an unidentified Caucasian male, mid thirties, found in the local park having lost consciousness and fallen to the ground – looks like he was out for a run.'

The boy lay there quietly, trying not to draw attention to himself. He knew the medical people had a more urgent patient to deal with.

Cowboy sat back in the cockpit, doing post-flight checks. He felt mildly curious about whether this one would live but wasn't going to let it ruin his evening.

'I think he's going to arrest soon,' Zapper said.

'Why don't you let us take it from here?' said Sir Reginald.

'My pleasure,' said Zapper, then, more quietly, so only Sir Reginald could hear, 'See you later, sir.'

The older man gave Zapper a wink then helped slide the unconscious body onto the waiting gurney.

The boy, too, could sense he was being lifted out of the helicopter. He tried one last time to open his eyes, failed. Where was his mother? He needed his mother.

Nurse Gemma Swallow took the man's hand. As soon as they were away from the din of the rotor-blades, she began her questions. 'Can you hear me?' she asked. 'What's your name? Can you tell me your name? I am Nurse Swallow. My first name is

Gemma.' She knew the man wasn't going to answer, might never speak again. But this was the job Sir Reginald had given her when she joined Trauma team, was it only four weeks ago? 'It helps, sometimes,' he had said. 'Patients need to be spoken to, even when they can't hear. They're human, we need to keep them as such by treating them that way. Also, it reminds the team that they aren't just symptomology.' And so Nurse Swallow continued, 'You are at the hospital now. They brought you here in a helicopter. We're going to look after you. We're going to find out what's wrong with you.' Then she said again, but with variation, 'You're in Hospital.'

In through the doors – shoom – which part without being parted and along a short corridor with bright striplights scrolling overhead and round a tight corner with a slight jolt from uneven flooring and – bang – into the Emergency Medicine department, doors swinging shut swinging swinging shut behind them.

Nurse Swallow kept up – her stethoscope banging unnoticed against her breastbone, where she always had a few faint, saucer-shaped bruises.

The Trauma team wheeled the gurney up to the examining table and then gently, on a count of three, transferred the body from one to the other.

'Alright,' said Sir Reginald, and repeated Zapper's exact words: Caucasian male, mid thirties. Then he added his gloss: 'Glasgow Coma Scale 3. Pupils pinpoint. No motor responses, no response to pain, not much of anything. So, we have precious little time. I want him intubated asap. 100 per cent oxygen. I want saline. Type and cross-match 6 units packed cell CBC. Chem-7.'

As the great man reeled off his requirements, Nurse Swallow kept self-consciously speaking calm and clear words into the man's ear. She stood to his right, holding his right hand. 'You're in the best place, now. We're going to do everything we can for you. The other voice you hear is Sir Reginald Saint-Hellier's. He's Consultant in Charge of Intensive Therapy. You're in very good hands. Can you tell me your name?' The body, of course, gave no reply.

Around Nurse Swallow, the Trauma team was moving smoothly into action. To her left, bending over the patient's held-open mouth, anaesthetist Sarah Felt slid a breathing tube down into the trachea. Patricia Parish, one of the most senior team-members, inserted a cannula into a vein in the left forearm, then attached the long plastic tube flowing out of a transparent saline bag. Other nurses moved swiftly in and out, bringing things, removing them.

Opposite her, standing back a little, Surgeon John Steele looked calmly on – it was not yet his time.

The boy, his eyes screwed tight with pain, could hear the doctors very near by, talking about the other patient, saying medical things. He was jealous, angry, wanting them to be discussing *him*, saving *his* life.

Most of all, he could hear the woman at his side, speaking sweetly into his ear, asking his name. He wanted to tell her what it was, but two things were stopping him: he couldn't speak and he couldn't remember.

Not being able to speak was the worst thing, for it meant he couldn't tell her what was wrong – the appletreeseed. He had swallowed an appleseed, by mistake, and it had started to grow.

With eyes still closed, the boy could sense that his

other senses, while not heightened, were easier to focus upon. Around him was a near-constant clatter: things banged into other things, but that's what they were designed to do; without damage. And then there were the beeps, a whole thick forest of electronic information. And also the smells, some acrid and eye-stingy, some balmlike and NutraSweet. The floor had been almost-corrosively washed, and the breathing-space above it wasn't soon going to forget; monitoring equipment was cooled as its work heated it up, giving the dual scent of circuitry; patients with open wounds were swabbed to disinfect – a grazed-knee smell, of mending and *that didn't hurt so much* and *be a little soldier* and *what would you like as a treat?*; air-conditioning took away certain viler smells, but their absence was haloed there quite clearly: vomit, shit, blood (a difficult scent to ignore once noticed); the sweat of those long on shift and the deodorants of those just arrived (the close-up voice smelt light, floral, scented but not perfumed).

The pain inside him increased. It was unbearable – as if something were actually going to break.

'And I'm now going to remove your clothes,' said Gemma Swallow.

She went across and fetched the angled scissors, then began to cut off the man's white cotton T-shirt.

Next came his gray tracksuit bottoms and black cotton underpants.

She left his socks and trainers on – a twisted ankle was the least of the man's problems.

Until Gemma was finished, the nurses worked around her; then, when she had carried the clothes away, they formed a tight circle around the body.

At her previous hospital, Gemma would have been

there among them. For a couple of quiet shifts, Sir Reginald had recognized this by allowing her to join in. However, mostly, she had been assigned to the lowly knee and shin areas, where life-threatening discoveries were almost unheard of.

The only things she had come across were previously unnoticed cuts, bumps, scrapes, grazes and bruises on the broken bodies of Road Traffic Accident victims. She was by now more than used to the variations involved with Man *vs* Truck and Child *vs* Motorbike.

So far, her most glamorous announcement, apart from the usual broken and shattered and pulped bones, had been of splinters of glass from a car window in the calves of a poor twelve-year-old girl who had been texting a friend while she crossed the road.

It made no difference – the delicate, broken little thing had died a few hours later, on the operating table of Mr John Steele. But Nurse Swallow knew he had done all he could, fought death every millimetre of the way, and she didn't blame him at all.

This evening, however, she was reduced to going through the man's pockets in search of any clue to his identity.

The left one contained a handkerchief, clean, wrapped around a set of keys; the right felt empty at first, but the fabric against Gemma's knuckle was unusually stiff.

Putting her hand in again, she encountered the soft edge of something – which, when she pulled it free, turned out to be the plastic-coated photograph of a girl. She was pretty.

Just then, Gemma heard an all-too-familiar sound: a harsh, unbroken wail from the ECG. Across the bottom of the monitor, she knew without seeing, flatline in lime-green.

'He's crashed,' said Sarah. 'Why's he crashed?'

'Get the defibber,' called Steele.

The tight circle broke open, and Gemma – still holding the girl's photograph – got a proper look at the patient. They looked alike, girl and man; he must be her father.

'Tension pneumothorax,' she said, almost before she had taken in the subtle signs: only the left side of the man's chest was moving, and the veins in his neck were distended.

No-one had heard her, so she had to shout it. 'Tension pneumothorax!'

By this point the paddles were almost charged, hovering in Sir Reginald's hands just above the man's body.

'Really?' Sir Reginald asked.

Gemma became aware that all eyes – most especially Steele's – were upon her.

Then Sir Reginald looked down, and his vastly experienced eye took in the symptomology.

'Well,' asked Sarah Felt, as if deliberately to make things worse.

Time seemed almost to stand still, and Gemma felt at that moment as if her very fate hung in the balance.

Of course, of all those eyes upon her there was only one pair Gemma really cared about, one pair whose glance deeply affected her heart.

What a terrible humiliation it would be to be proven wrong in front of Steele! But she wasn't doing this for him – if she'd had her way, she wouldn't have needed to say anything at all.

'Look, we should just zap him,' said Steele. 'He's been under for –'

'She's right,' said Sir Reginald. 'I need a 14–16G intravenous cannula.'

The circle closed again, though not before Gemma had caught Steele's eye – and been terrified by what she saw there.

Sir Reginald calmly performed the needle thoracotomy – a quiet hiss of air proving that Gemma had been completely right.

Almost immediately, the man's heart spontaneously started up again; no need for the defib machine.

With the smooth, relaxed movements of a professional, Sir Reginald stepped away from the body. 'You were wrong,' he said to Steele, quite gently but with definite intent. 'I think you owe Nurse Swallow an apology.'

She felt a deep deep anguish for the brilliant surgeon – that she had caused him to be humiliated, even in such a small way, and in front of the whole Trauma team! He was such a proud man, and by doing what she'd done she had wounded him.

'Nurse Swallow,' she heard him gruffly say, 'I apologize for questioning your clinical judgement.'

Her throat felt far too tight to talk, but she managed to croak out, 'That's quite alright, Mr Steele.' She was just about to add, 'We all make mistakes,' when she realized what a fatal thing it would be to say – fatal to her hopes. But more fatal than the humiliation she'd already inflicted? Perhaps not.

Looking anywhere but at Steele, Nurse Swallow caught the eye of Patricia Parish, who gave her a little wink. 'Well done,' it said.

*

For the next few seconds they worked in a rare pocket of silence, angel passing. Gemma could hear Steele's breathing, powerful, fast and just slightly ragged. He was annoyed – probably more with himself than with her.

Sir Reginald was Steele's mentor, and everyone knew how much Steele hated to do anything that diminished him in his eyes. Gemma was aware, though, that reacting badly to a situation like this would be far worse, in Sir Reginald's view, than admitting to a hasty mistake and taking the time to think about it afterwards.

Gemma gathered the man's clothes and placed them in a transparent plastic bag, with the photograph of the girl on top. This would accompany him wherever he went.

'Well,' said Sir Reginald, bringing the tense silence to a close, 'I suggest we get this brave soul down for a CT as soon as possible. As I don't think we've got anything particularly urgent coming in, Mr Steele, Nurse Swallow – I hope you two can take him. Everybody else, enjoy a few precious moments of leisure while you can. Splendid work, by the way, especially from Nurse Swallow.'

Embarrassed beyond belief, Gemma avoided Patricia's wicked eye as she helped to push the trolley with all its tubes and cables down the corridor. Steele was steering, and she dared not go in any direction other than the one he chose.

Almost before she knew it, so flustered was she, they were in the special high-speed lift travelling down through Hospital.

When she forced herself to look up from the patient, she was relieved to find that Steele was staring impatiently at the bright numbers counting down above the door. Never had he seemed so magnificent to her as he did then, his square jaw tight with anger and wounded pride. Then, somehow, he sensed her eyes upon him. 'I shall have to watch out for you in future,' he said.

Of course, Gemma was mortified; she felt she must be blushing to her roots. How terribly he must hate me now, she thought. It was all she could do to keep from crying.

Gemma and Steele wheeled the unknown young man into the scanning unit, then he briefed the radiologist on what Sir Reginald wanted done. The full-body CT scan would take about ten minutes, after which it would be their job to take the patient to the Intensive Care Unit or perhaps, if things were as bad as Gemma feared they were, straight into theatre.

Gemma was readying herself for an awkward wait, in Steele's infuriated company, when he seemingly casually said, 'Shall we go and try and find a coffee while we've got time?'

This was quite bizarre. She could only think that he sensed her embarrassment, and wanted to prolong it so as to teach her a lesson she wouldn't forget. She hardly dared look at his face, fearing she might find a sarcastic expression there. When she did catch his eye, it seemed unironic enough, though she had always, ever since she started at Hospital, found him the most inscrutable of its inhabitants.

'That would be, um, good,' she said, not quite sure what she had just agreed to.

'Good,' he said.

Waking up, the boy found his pain had almost all gone – for the moment, at least. The voices were quiet; the squeaky-feet, too.

Slowly, he opened his eyes and looked around him. The room he found himself in was, yes, completely empty of people.

There were pieces of equipment surrounding him, but not one of them was turned on. He recognized the green grid where his heartbeat would have been displayed. It disappointed him not to have a chance to see what it looked like.

Turning his head, he took in the other machines, gathered as if they and not trained doctors and nurses had been attending to him. It was only then that the boy noticed a pale white shape lying on his chest and legs, which turned out to *be* his chest and legs. Until he'd seen himself, it was as if he hadn't been there. But that wasn't the most important thing. Help, no! – he hadn't got any clothes on – help!

Although there was no-one to see, his hands jumped to cover his willy.

There was a twinge inside him, a quick reminder of the pain he'd felt in the helicopter.

He needed to get something to wear. It didn't matter if all the doctors and nurses had already seen him naked – he needed *clothes*.

The boy swung his legs off the table, still keeping his hands cupped between them.

A little jump was needed, off and backslide, before his feet touched the floor.

Where had they put his clothes? He looked around for any likely places, saw none.

He stepped out of the circle of machines, and immediately felt even more naked; they had given him a reason (illness) for being like that.

Running quickly on light feet, he reached a yellow screen-on-wheels. Part-hidden behind it, he made a more considered examination of the room – which seemed to contain nothing he could put on to cover himself.

This was an emergency. No time to make a plan. So, the boy immediately skipped across to the nearest double doors and, on tiptoes, peered out through the porthole of reinforced glass.

He saw a short corridor leading up to a pair of identical swing doors – through which a woman immediately walked. A glance was enough to see that she was heading in his direction.

With only a few seconds to act, the boy sprinted back behind the yellow screen.

As the double doors banged open, he picked himself up onto a chair so that his feet, too, would be hidden.

'Hello?' asked the woman. The boy almost puked with fear: she knew he was there, she'd seen him. 'Anyone?' she asked. Then muttered to herself, 'Good.'

There was a phone just the other side of the screen, and to this the woman went. The boy could sense her, centimetres away, breathing, being a grown-up woman; he could even smell her perfume – what if she smelled him? Smelled his fear? Smelled, somehow, his nakedness?

He kept his breath ultraquiet and listened to her fingers dialling the touch-tone, crunchy beeps coming out of the ear-piece.

Her perfume was strong, heavy. At other times, if he'd smelled it, he would have gone bleugh and coughed. Now it was a matter of life and death and horrible embarrassment that he kept absolutely totally silent.

'Yes, it's Patricia,' the woman said. 'We're meeting at a quarter to. Yes, just as planned. Exactly as planned. It's all set. Yes, all. Usual routine. Sorry. I know. But we don't want to mess this one up. *Someone* will be very angry if we do. See you.'

The phone went klick, and the boy heard her dial a second time. The conversation was almost identical, except she said, 'I know, it's so exciting, isn't it?' A third call brought the comment, 'You're not going to back out now, are you? You're the star of the show . . . Good girl. Good.' A fourth and final conversation added nothing new.

When she was finished, Patricia looked quickly around the room and then went back out the way she'd come in.

The boy blew air out from puffed cheeks, though he wasn't really out of breath. It was just a way of saying phew, close one.

He wasn't sure whether it would be worse to be caught naked by a woman or a man. A man, he thought, might be better – as long as he didn't laugh.

A quick check through the porthole showed the second room as empty, Patricia gone.

But, when he got in there, he found nothing to wear and – what was worse – nowhere to hide. Better be quick, he thought.

This porthole revealed a longer stretch of corridor with wooden doors off to left and right.

The boy thought for a moment about going back and trying the other way out of the first room. But that might be just as exposed as this. He changed his mind then changed it again.

A slight twinge in his stomach refocused him on the dangers. All those doctors and nurses could return at any moment.

He pushed through and raced along the corridor.

Senses heightened, the boy noticed everything around him: the cleanish white floor reflecting the long striplights back up at themselves. Ceiling tiles over his head with randomly repeating stippling on them, some with punched-out corners revealing a cardboard-like undertexture. On the walls were noticeboards in blue felt covered with pinned-up sheets of photocopied paper.

Feeling nakeder than before, the boy reached the next set of doors – and saw through the porthole a stocky bald man coming towards him, only a few paces away. Unable to do anything else, the boy stepped to one side and waited, praying.

The bald man bashed confidently through, letting the doors swing shut behind him.

Standing to the left, the boy was completely exposed to the man's back as he walked on. The grey hair above the man's ears curled upwards, like horns.

Steele and Gemma were just starting off down the corridor when who should step out of the lift but Sarah Felt – and not just any old lift, but the superfast emergency lift. It was highly irregular for her to be using this. Almost exclusively reserved for life-or-death cases, the emergency lift was sacrosanct.

Sarah smiled at Steele, ignoring Gemma completely. 'Ah,' she said, 'I'm glad I caught you. Sir Reginald would like a word with all the senior members of the team.'

Gemma was just thinking she might say something about the lift when, astonishingly, Steele said it for her: 'Why didn't you just bleep me? And what the hell were you doing clogging up the emergency lift?'

Sarah Felt was quite unfazed. 'There was nothing on – I checked. Things are very quiet at the moment.'

Not in Gemma's heart they weren't. But even in the midst of her confusion, she examined her rival anew. Sarah Felt was twenty-six, willowy, with long blond hair which hung far down her shoulders when loosed from the tight paper cap that held it captive most of the working day, or night. A natural athlete, the brilliant young anaesthetist was a competition-level snowboarder – always jetting off to Klosters or wherever to pick up gold and silver medals. Steele, too, was into winter sports, though Gemma had learned from Patricia that cross-country skiing was more his thing. In despair, she remembered that ice-skating at her local rink was the closest she'd ever come to winter sports – and even then, she'd spent most of the time on her very wet btm!

Gemma noted that Sarah had not answered his question about why she had come in person, when a message to his bleep would have got him back twice as fast. She just stood there, maddeningly confident, arms crossed, smile on her pretty face.

'I'm sorry, but, you know –' said Steele, and Gemma realized he was speaking to her.

'One of the other nurses will come down to assist you with that patient,' said Sarah, interrupting him. Then why, thought Gemma, hadn't that replacement come down with the original message?

'Duty calls,' said Steele to Gemma.

'Come *on*,' said Sarah, and dragged him off.

Gemma was left to watch them heading towards the non-emergency lifts, and to wonder to herself what exactly had just happened.

After a moment's thought, she could find no other explanation than that Sarah had wanted to send her a warning; the *get your filthy claws off him* message could hardly be any clearer.

The bald man with the funny horns of grey hair strode swiftly down the corridor. It was obvious to the boy, even in his terror, that this was a confident and important personage. He wore hospital-working clothes, yellow and green.

As the distance between them grew, the threat of discovery seemed to increase – and it would somehow be worse, the boy felt, to be spotted from further away. The man, even from the other end of the corridor, would be able to see him there, hiding, naked. Perhaps there would be a small chance of outrunning him; that depended on how fit the man was and what was on the other side of these swing doors.

The broad back of the man seemed sensitive, as if it had already seen the boy and was just deciding whether it could be bothered to inform on him.

But no –

At a door on the right, the man stopped, turned and, without knocking, entered.

That was it. Safe, for the moment. Although the man could have gone to fetch something and be coming straight back out, now.

The boy peeked through the porthole – should he go on? He needed to make a decision quickly.

Two women came into view, then three men, and soon the corridor seemed to be full of grown-ups – and all of them were walking in his direction.

No decision needed now, he sprinted back towards where he'd started from – only slowing when he reached the door the man had gone through. The boy didn't stop running, but went on the very tips of his toes; lightly, rapidly. He looked at the door and the name on it was Sir Reginald Saint-Hellier. Then he sped up again, slap-slap-slap went his bare feet, and he listened through the footfalls for the first laugh of a man or shriek of a woman.

Ten metres to the door, five, three, one – and he was gone from sight.

A look through the porthole showed him an empty corridor. Perhaps the men and women hadn't been coming this way, after all; perhaps they'd headed off into another corridor.

Then Sir Reginald came out of his office and turned in the boy's direction. He might easily have seen the top of the black-haired head, peering out of the circle of metal and through the reinforced glass. But he was distracted by the sheaf of papers he was flicking through.

The boy ran. No point trying to hide behind the screen again. If the room were to fill up with people, they'd soon find him there. His best chance was out the door at the far end – he took it.

It was a storeroom, full of exciting equipment. Some of the machines looked to the boy like those which had recently been gathered around him. These must be their back-ups and replacements. The shelves were stacked neatly with row upon row of multicoloured cardboard boxes: drugs, needles, tape, scalpels.

The boy had stopped running but he kept a swift pace. There was no guarantee this room was unoccupied – but somehow it felt like it was; the silence was that of *empty* not of *keeping quiet.*

Soon, he came to the far end – a door, a fire door. It was the only way out; there had been no other exit visible, to left or right. Neither had the boy seen any clothes, though even a doctor's white coat would have done – covering him probably down to his knees; a little too obvious, perhaps: not a good disguise for moving unsuspiciously around Hospital.

At the far end of the storeroom, Sir Reginald entered with Patricia. They did not come any further; just stopped there and spoke to one another in sharp whispers. The boy, who had immediately ducked back behind a shelf and crouched into a ball – the boy couldn't hear a word they were saying. But they were physically there, and that meant he couldn't get out *that* way.

The storeroom was colder than the corridors; it might even have been slightly refrigerated. The boy did his best not to shiver. He was tough, and cold didn't affect him in the way it did other, softer people.

The psst-psst conversation ended, and the two dangerous doctors went back out of the storeroom. As the doors closed behind them, the boy could hear a hubbub of activity which told him, for certain, that he had no choice but to use the fire door.

This was a big risk. The words ran yellow on black across the aluminium push-bar: IN EMERGENCY ONLY. An alarm might go off, and the boy had no idea what was behind the door; maybe he would find himself outside, on a fire-escape high off the ground, naked; or maybe, naked, he would stumble into a room full of nurses drinking coffee and reading gossip magazines or whatever they did on their breaks. It didn't matter – he had to take the chance; if he didn't, he'd just get caught where he was.

The first downward pull didn't budge the bar. A second try, and it took all the boy's jumping-staying weight (not much) to crack the resistance and open the door.

As feared, an alarm bell began to ring immediately, very violently. The boy felt almost as if its clapper were banging against his heart.

Slightly dazed, Gemma went in quest of the nearest coffee machine. Fulfilling her promise to the radiologist of one black, two sugars at least gave her something to do.

This floor of Hospital – the 8th – was still largely terra incognita to her. The H-shape of the hospital building, and the fact that all four corridors leading off from the central stem seemed to mirror one another, made it a particularly perplexing place to try to find your way around.

As she went, Gemma thought about Steele. What chance did she stand? He was a respected surgeon, of five years' standing in Trauma – devilishly handsome. She, a lowly nurse who had started on the job only a month ago. Gemma wasn't without *some* confidence in her looks: delicately freckled skin, strawberry-blond bob. But Steele seemed to have come from a different universe, as far as sexual magnetism went.

There had been a little scene between them, early on – before she'd even begun her first day's work. She remembered arriving at Hospital and feeling, right away, quite overwhelmed. The sight of the towering building had been a little too much for her – so much had happened in her first placement, so many small mishaps and miracles, tragedies and triumphs. And here she was again, starting at the bottom. The thought of it had drawn from her a solitary sob.

Almost immediately, she had looked round to see if anyone had noticed – and someone had.

Steele was just that moment striding past her, having parked his silver sports car in his specially reserved spot.

As it was her first day, Gemma hadn't yet been issued with a uniform.

Steele stopped and addressed her. 'Are you visiting someone?' he asked, his voice full of genuine concern.

'No,' she had replied. 'I'm starting work here today.'

'Oh,' he said. 'Which bit?'

'Trauma,' she said.

There was a definite pause as he looked her up and down. She had taken him in already, at a shy glance: dark curly hair, tall, energetic, muscular but not beefed up – his most remarkable feature were his dreamy eggshell-blue eyes.

He started to say something but just as he did his bleep went off loudly. Gemma caught only a few of his words, '. . . couple of weeks . . .' Then, before she could reply, Steele had turned away from her and was dashing in through the ambulance bay.

A couple of weeks. I give you a couple of weeks – that's what she immediately became convinced he had said.

Even now, it was only with deep shame that she could think of her weakness in letting her feelings out so freely, and within sight of Reception!

Yet, simultaneously, she felt a little glow of pride. A couple of weeks? She'd lasted twice that already.

But the scene in the carpark had only been a prelude. It was when, a couple of hours later, after going through all the office-visiting and form-filling of a new job – it was when she walked into Trauma for the first time and caught sight of Steele standing looking at the whiteboard that she realized what deep trouble she was in, both professionally and emotionally. He was gorgeous *and* efficient, a surgical whizz *and* the most handsome man she'd ever seen – and she was going to be working in close proximity to him, day and night.

When he'd gleaned what he needed to know, Steele turned round and spotted her, standing by the door.

'Aha,' he said, so everyone could hear. 'I believe this is our new nurse. And her name is . . . ?'

Gemma realized she was meant to fill the gap.

'Swallow,' she had said, as confidently as she could. 'Gemma,' she added.

'Welcome to Trauma,' Steele announced. 'May your stay here be a long and happy one.'

The others standing around – consultants, anaesthetists and nurses – seconded this, a little embarrassed.

Only Gemma caught the irony – how could it be long and happy and only last a couple of weeks?

From then on, she was very wary of Steele – doing her best never to draw unnecessary attention to herself. As his name might suggest, he had a clean, sharp edge to him; Gemma didn't want to get cut.

She had settled in, so she thought, pretty well. Sir Reginald said he was content with her work, and that was what mattered most.

After his sarcastic comments of the first afternoon, Steele had seemed to ignore her completely. It wasn't even clear he remembered the carpark incident – which made it both better and worse.

Two weeks passed, at the end of which she was still securely there, but he gave no acknowledgement, even grudging, that she had crossed any Rubicon – a Rubicon *he* had set up for her.

Gemma was furious and entranced.

Yet what did she have about her to make her stand out from the crowd? Other nurses had confided to her their own attraction towards Mr John Steele; he had quite a little fan club, and he was crushingly aware of it. There was a running flirtation between him and at least three other Trauma nurses. And yet, from all she gathered, and she gathered a great deal, Gemma had never yet heard of it going any further than flirtation.

Her time in her previous job had taught Nurse Swallow that the best place to pick up on all the gossip was with the smokers – here at Hospital, they shivered just round the corner from the ambulance bay. Gemma was impatient – if only she had been prepared to give it a couple of months, see what information came her way in the usual course of things. But she was young and just a little reckless – allowing her wayward heart to lead her where it would. Steele was single *now*, in that all accounts agreed: at least, he wasn't *actually* married. If she waited too long, another woman might come along and snap him up for herself. Strangely, it wasn't the nurses with whom Mr John Steele flirted that worried her as her main competition. Her chief rival, so it seemed to Gemma, was Sarah Felt.

There was no flirtation between the anaesthetist and Steele, or not on the obvious bubbly level as with the other nurses – all of them except her! No flirtation, but a definite intimacy and, what was perhaps even more dangerous, a sense of teamwork and camaraderie and mutual professional admiration. Steele flirted with the nurses but it was Sarah Felt that he would make a point of thanking, after a particularly taxing case. Toleration was what he radiated towards the others, toleration and *occasionally* good-humoured liking; but Sarah Felt he *admired*; he thought quite obviously that she was *his* kind of anaesthetist. (And most anaesthetists were men.)

From what Gemma had observed, Sarah Felt did what Steele asked, most of the time. She employed his favourite sedatives and in doses amicably agreed between them. But, now and again, she would suggest an alternative course of action. 'Don't you think we might be a bit heavy-handed if we use blah-di-blah – the side effects are more extreme, and recent research has shown that recovery times are 15 to 20 per cent longer.' And to Gemma's dismay, Steele, without exception, followed Sarah Felt's advice.

The tender-hearted young nurse stopped and looked around her. This corridor seemed to go on for ever. She was lost, again.

Behind the fire door was a staircase leading both up and down. The number 24 was stencilled in glossy black paint on the whitewashed wall.

The boy let the door shut behind him and then, quick as he could, began to make his way downwards.

Each stair was a light gray-green colour, and edged with ridgy metal. He could feel the harsh texture on the balls of his feet.

The naked boy felt horribly exposed: better get out of this place as soon as I can, he thought.

On the 23rd floor, the fire door looked impossible to get through – no handle, probably a push-bar on the other side. The boy tried it anyway, fearing that at any moment the sound of pursuing feet would stop being only imaginary. And it moved, the door, and it opened – into what proved to be another storeroom, this one with the lights off, very dark.

The boy stepped through and let the fire door close itself behind him. For the first time since waking up, he felt just a little safer.

Was it worth the risk of turning the lights on? Probably not. There was a low green glow from the FIRE EXIT sign behind him; by this, he saw a layout identical to the floor above. At the very far end were two round portholes, monster-eyes full of dim yellow light. The boy set off towards them, passing more shelves, more little boxes of supplies; too dark to read the labels.

He was about halfway when he began to hear the sound coming from behind the door. It was a long low moaning groaning keening weeping – maybe humans were making it, but animals, too, could quite easily have been the terrible cause: slaughterhouse-bound cattle who hadn't yet started to panic but knew something was very wrong.

The boy almost turned back; a big part of him didn't want to find out what kind of illness made men and women sound like that. But where there were people, there were clothes; embarrassment overcame terror, and he carried on.

By the time Gemma handed it over, the coffee was lukewarm.

'I'm really sorry,' she said.

Bunty Hardwick, the radiologist, couldn't hide her annoyance; she put the paper cup to one side without taking a sip.

'We're used to it by now,' she said.

Dressed in a crisp white labcoat, she was a pony-tailed young woman with green tired-rings beneath her eyes. But the light from her screen wasn't exactly flattering.

Gemma, wanting diversion, looked through the large thick-glass window to where the final quarter of the man's body was disappearing slowly into the huge metal doughnut of the scanner; head and torso already done.

'Was Steele called away?' asked Bunty Hardwick, resurrecting the dead conversation. 'I thought he went off with you.'

Gemma had forgotten that Sarah had only spoken to them once they were out in the corridor. 'Oh,' she said, 'he had to go and see Sir Reginald.'

'What a *shame*,' said Bunty. 'He always adds a certain something to my day – if you know what I mean.'

Not *another* one, thought Gemma.

Bunty took a tiny sip of coffee, then winced. She was waiting for Gemma to reply, so that they could get into a bit of girly gossip about who they fancied, among the doctors and surgeons. 'Well . . .' Gemma said, with no idea how she was going to continue.

But just then, Sarah Felt herself swept in through the door.

'Finished?' she asked Bunty, without a word of preamble.

'Another . . .' the radiologist checked her screen '. . . two minutes.' She didn't react to Sarah's abruptness.

Sarah then turned to Gemma and said, 'This is my punishment – for using the lift, I mean. Steele told Sir Reginald as soon as we got up there, the dirty whistle-blower. So while they discuss important issues of the day, I'm down here lugging trolleys around like a bloody porter.'

Gemma was too astonished to speak. When they had gone off together, of course she'd assumed Sarah was being proprietorial over Steele because there really *was* something going on between them. Sarah had certainly done her best to give that impression. For a moment, Gemma was delighted: Steele had been perfectly right to report Sarah for using the lift. What if a patient – this patient? – had gone into arrest whilst she'd been occupying it? But then Gemma realized that Sarah's jealousy and Steele's response were exactly the sort of behaviour long-term, and slightly embittered, lovers get up to in a work environment – animosity being the cover they use for their secret affair. They were an item, Gemma concluded. (It was the best explanation.) This was a depressing thought – and more than depressing, disheartening.

They sat there in silence, both impatient for Bunty to finish her work. But it was really the scanner which was taking the time, as it had to – mapping inside-out the brain and body of the man.

'Almost done,' Bunty said, sensing the tension in the room but not yet guessing its explanation. At least, thought Gemma, the radiologist hadn't tried to mention Steele again.

The CT machine reached the end of its cycle. With a slight sigh, Bunty stood up and went through into the scanning room. The patient was regurgitated by the doughnut, a sight that always fascinated Gemma. Sarah was sitting on a nearby chair, examining her perfectly manicured nails.

With the machine's assistance, Bunty placed the young man back on the trolley. 'Can you give me a hand?' she called. Both Gemma and Sarah automatically moved to help, but it was Gemma who – standing to begin with – got there first.

Bunty spoke: 'Tell Sir Reginald the results are in

the computer now, whenever he wants to look at them. But it's a subarachnoid haemorrhage, definitely – just as he thought.'

Bunty had picked the clipboard off the end of the trolley and was writing the usual reference codes on the form.

'We're going straight to theatre,' said Sarah.

'Oh, then give my love to Mr Steele,' Bunty said, showing that she'd finally worked out what was going on between the two other women.

In silence, they wheeled the patient out into the corridor.

It was the Burns Unit. There was a sign on the door, which was stupid because anyone in the storeroom would know where they'd just come from. But the boy could also tell because the patients he could see were wrapped head to toe in bandages, just like in a cartoon.

He watched at the porthole for a few minutes – saw no nurses. The room was a long vision, very dark, with an atmosphere all its own – of pain and more pain and the control and management of pain and the terrible unfairness of pain; the end of pain, also. The curtains on the window were blackout, tightly drawn; the unit was lit almost entirely by the screens of monitors and one or two anglepoise lamps. It would be easy to hide, so through the door he stepped.

But even his lightest footfall had been heard by one of the blinded listeners-out. 'Nurse?' he said, in pathetic hope. 'Are you there?'

Along the ward, the word began to echo; others joined the chorus, wanting. 'Nurse!' – 'Are you a nurse?' – 'I need more morphine.' – 'Where have you been? I've been buzzing for a quarter of an hour. This man needs water.' – 'Come to me. Come over here.'

In the first section, off to the right, there were six beds; six more to the left. The air smelled as if someone had been frying bacon in there; the boy began to salivate – he felt his mouth filling with wetness just as he realized the bacon had been human flesh, and the cooking burning. He spat into the palm of his hand then wiped the wetness down his bare leg.

'Just something to drink,' said one of them, 'whoever you are. A little water in my mouth.'

All the men had suffered burning in quite different ways, and their skin had reacted accordingly. The first of the beds, going clockwise, was occupied by an Ethiopian man, Akliku Lij, who had been attacked at a wedding. Vodka had been poured over him and cigarettes flicked at his face; it had been half a joke, half because he was black and had danced with one of the groom's daughters from a previous marriage.

The second man, Patrice DuChamps, had been involved in trying to rescue his wife from a chip-pan fire: almost all the burns were up his left-hand side; he was left-handed.

The third, Andy Woods, had been caught in a chemical fire: a lorry had overturned on the motorway in front of him. His van had been immediately surrounded by a runny substance very similar to napalm. He had tried to reverse but behind him cars and lorries were blocking the way. In the end, as his car got hotter and hotter, more and more likely to explode, Andy Woods had pulled his jacket over his head and made a run for it.

In the next bed, to the boy's right, was Bob

Packard, a fireman who had fallen through the glass roof of a skylight and into a blazing school kitchen. Because he was wearing protective clothing, he had been less badly burned than the others, but the burns were all over his body – unconscious for several minutes before his mates got to him, he suffered blistering not charring. His arms and legs wept beneath head-to-foot bandages.

To the fireman's left was a man called Mohammed Mohammed who had set himself alight outside the embassy of a country which, he firmly believed, kept his people in oppression and servitude. A friend had filmed his moment of glory. The pictures were replayed for Mohammed, in the camera's viewfinder, as they went along in the ambulance. 'Be careful,' he had croaked, 'don't erase it by mistake. I don't want to have to do it again.' In the week since then, his friends had been pleased but a little underwhelmed by the media response. It got five minutes on the early evening bulletins but had gone by the time the main news came on – replaced by a story about the drummer in a rock band.

The last man, Arnost Svoboda, was unconscious and only an hour or two away from death; third-degree burned in a house fire started by his daughter's boyfriend's crack-pipe.

It was by now clear to the boy that none of the bandaged and movement-restrained men could get out of bed; also, if no nurse came in response to their cries and button-pushing, no nurse would come just because of him: he was safe, therefore, to search around for clothing.

'It's not a nurse,' said Bob Packard, the fireman. 'I can see it's not.'

'What you seeing, man?' Akliku Lij asked.

'Nurse!' called Andy Woods.

'I said it's not a nurse,' said fireman Bob Packard. 'It looks more like a child.'

'Child?' said Mohammed Mohammed, whose English was limited – and who hadn't, as a consequence, been able to give satisfactory interviews to the national press.

'Perhaps he can help,' said Patrice DuChamps. 'Hey, he wants some water. Get him some water.'

'I'm so thirsty,' said Bob Packard. 'It's been hours . . .'

The boy didn't like being discussed, even if the thirsty man couldn't see well enough to have noticed his nakedness.

'Where's the water?' he asked.

'It *is* a child,' said Andy Woods. 'You're right. I heard its voice.'

'There's a water fountain in the middle of the ward, on the left.'

'Are you a girl?' asked Akliku Lij. 'What are you doing here? Is your father here?'

But the boy was already hurrying away.

'It's not visiting time,' said Andy Woods.

The boy walked quickly past the other beds, other burned men. One or two noticed him and tried to call out. No clothes – none that he saw. He reached the water fountain; no plastic cups in the dispenser bit. Hunting about, the boy spotted a glass on the bedside table of a sleeping man opposite: no sooner seen than stolen – he'd get another easily. After filling it as full as he could, the boy scampered back to the thirsty man.

'Oh, God,' Bob Packard said, 'Oh, in my mouth – pour it in my mouth. I can't move my arms.'

'Are you a girl or not?' Akliku asked again.

The burned fireman drank all the water. 'Ah,' he said, 'you're an angel, that's what you are.'

'Yes,' said the boy, in a high voice, 'I'm a girl.'

'What are you doing here?' asked Bob.

'Your father, is it?' asked Akliku.

'It's a bit late for visiting,' said Andy.

'I'm going – I'm going home,' said the boy, remembering to sound like a girl, to confuse them. 'Goodbye.'

They all protested, but within a couple of seconds he was safe once again in the dark of the storeroom.

Never before had Nurse Swallow had to endure such an excruciatingly awkward lift ride – even the one down with Steele had been nothing compared with this. Sarah Felt, however, seemed quite content to let it pass in embarrassed silence. Her message to Gemma delivered, the cool anaesthetist had nothing further to say. But it would take more than frostiness to make Nurse Swallow give up on their being if not friends then at least civil to one another. 'What do you think?' she asked, indicating with a nod the young man on the trolley.

Sarah's reply was immediate and vicious. 'We never talk about that sort of thing within the patient's hearing. Research has shown that even in the deepest states of coma, they are often capable of absorbing information from around them – particularly if that conversation includes their name.'

'But I deliberately didn't –'

'This has a proven negative effect on their chances of a recovery, either full or partial. But I don't expect you to know anything about that.'

Gemma thought it more dignified not to reply. She felt a little guilty at having used a probably-dying patient as a conversational opener or re-opener, but it was the only thing she'd been able to think of. It had been a mistake, one that had put her, for the moment, at even more of a disadvantage with Sarah.

When the boy came within earshot, he could hear that the alarm was no longer ringing. This probably meant that it was safe to go back into the stairwell, but when he stuck his head through the door it was still very very tentatively. What he heard wasn't silence, too echoey for that; no footsteps, though – no shouts or anxious talking.

The boy scampered down another flight, and found the next fire door propped open with a metal bucket, the bottom of it filled to a depth of five centimetres with cigarette stubs.

Skipping over this, the boy found himself in another storeroom. The lights were on but it seemed uninhabited, at the moment.

The boy strolled with increasing confidence towards the doors which almost certainly, he knew, led into another ward: what would this one be? How horrible?

The layout, once he'd recce'd it, was almost identical to that of the 23rd floor: beds grouped in sixes to left and right off a long corridor. He couldn't see whether their occupants were bandaged or women or what else. No nurses came past, so he snuck through and hid himself behind the first curtain he found. From here, he could see – and sense – more.

Old; the people here were very old: some of them were asleep, some looked dead, and yet others smelled dead. The nearest man was one of these last. The boy went to have a closer look, and then he saw it – hanging over the visitor's chair beside the end of the bed: a tartan dressing-gown. Saved.

In these circumstances, it was better to be quick and quietish rather than deadly slow and completely silent; confidently made sounds, the boy's experience told him, were less noticeable than terrified half-noises.

The boy picked up the gown, which smelled very powerfully of the man in the bed – whose face seemed to be made of hairy holes: one big one, which was the mouth, two smaller ones the nostrils, two tight slitty ones the eyes, two long-haired ones the ears. He seemed, so loud was his snoring-out and breathing-in, to be respiring through all of them at once. Hole-man was called Marsh Blunt.

Fascinated and disgusted, fascinated by his disgust and disgusted by his fascination, the boy let himself watch for a while.

Like flaps of flesh, the apertures in the head opened and closed – air going in odourless and coming back as after months underwater in a swamp.

The boy put his hands to his mouth but, doing so, brought the dressing-gown up to them: closer, this had a different and an entirely worse smell.

Once or twice, the boy had been taken by his father into pub toilets, when there was nowhere else to go – this was *that* smell, softened a little by the musty cloth but still unmistakable.

The boy put the gown straight back down on the chair, not even bothering to make it look as if it hadn't been touched. What happened here later on wouldn't matter ('Someone's been mucking about with my dressing-gown!') – he would be far away, out of Hospital.

Turning away from the hole-man, the boy bumped

straight into a tall figure. He tried to escape but felt his arm being grabbed, hard.

Despite being high-speed, the lift seemed to take an inordinate amount of time travelling even one floor.

As the doors finally opened, Sarah announced, 'It's right and right again.' Gemma gritted her teeth and said nothing. Other floors might confuse her, but she knew her way around Surgery, by now. 'Steele likes to work in Theatre Seven, whenever he can.' This, too, Gemma had learned in her very first week. There were very few details of Steele's likes and dislikes she hadn't, she felt, been able to pick up, here and there. His preference for Cutmeister-Pro-9 high-gloss blades. Coffee, black one sugar. Tea, strong, white no sugar. Nurses: short hair and not too much make-up, and definitely no strong perfume . . .

Gemma was due on a break as soon as she was done, and she could hardly wait – she needed to get out of the building, take a few breaths of fresh air, perhaps even cadge a cigarette if there was someone there she wanted to talk to.

The whiteboard gave her a small revenge on Sarah: Theatre Seven was already occupied, so Steele had been shunted into number Nine.

With some haste now, they rolled the trolley down the wide corridor and in through the double doors.

'A foot has no dignity, listen to me. What kind of knowledge is it, the knowledge gained by a foot? I'll tell you. It is a dark and vegetable knowledge.' The man, luckily, was whispering, not shouting. He gripped the boy from behind and sent hot breath into his right ear. There were things he needed to say; he had a story. If his voice was nasal, then that nose would easily be a metre long. 'Once upon a time, before the invention of shoes, we feet knew everything – dryness as well as moistness. Yes, we risked stones and cuts and divots, but we also loyally served and informed the brain upstairs. As we walked, the brain upstairs showered the light of its gratitude upon us. Now, we are kept stupid – all our potentialities are still here, within us. Listen, even now I can speak English and not sound ridiculous like a speaking foot. My name is Proudfoot; Proudfoot is my name. But I am just one foot on its own, a solo non-performer, and I need to be in-tandem. You and I, my friend, together we could strike out for the horizon. I know at first it would be embarrassing for you, being seen by all the young girls escorting or rather being teamed up with a big, veiny, hairy foot. After a while, though, once we were a little closer to the horizon and a little further away from this place – by then you'd have got used to life with me. As feet go, I'm not so smelly. I can shut up – you might not believe it from me now, but I know that a boy's thoughts are often of special, private boy-things. I will leave you silence for thinking-time; you will allow me to go off and visit ladies of the night. No questions will be asked, either way. It will be good.' The man took a nasal breath, then continued: 'Forgive me if this is a bit abrupt. I'm a foot – I've spent my life in leather uppers; they never taught me manners. Of course I'm blunt – the only time anyone ever paid any real attention to me was when I stubbed myself into a bed-leg or a kerb or the heel of my twin. And then what did I get? Thanks for the thousands of miles of trudging? Gratitude to the jumper, the twister, the loyal upholder? Not a bit of it. Entirely taken for granted. A foot has no dignity. And we have our pride, we feet. Before he was amputated, my lovely twin – forgive the tears – he was my companion, and he said a lovely thing, he said, "Fuck this world and fuck everyone in it, the fuckers." That's what he said to me, day after day for most of his life, and then, finally, in his very last few hours, he said it again, twice. You've probably had time to consider, now. Am I sweating? Do I smell cheesy to you? Don't worry, the moment we're out again on the open road I'll stop seeming grotesque. We'll travel such distances, westwards – towards the sinking sun. There's miles of life in me yet – but all I need is the chance to prove it. Don't go. Don't leave me here, paralysed. You are the one I need – you're just the right size, not too big. Strap on and strike off, otherwise it's all just shite and onions. I'll have you in harness and together we'll be free!' In his excitement, the man's grip momentarily weakened. This was the chance! With as much force as he could, the boy jammed his heel down on the man's bare toe: he felt a gristly contact and knew that a decent amount of pain had been inflicted. Mr Proudfoot's grip around his neck loosened; a jab backwards with the elbow, and the hands fell away as if they'd never been there.

Superquick, the boy ran out of that cubicle and back into the storeroom – where he saw a figure at the very far end, silhouetted, closing the fire door.

Turning again, the boy dashed past Mr Proudfoot's outstretched hands and sped along the corridor until he came to the fourth group of six and six beds. A nurse was now in sight, further along, talking to someone behind a curtain. The boy looked quickly around and saw that these men, too, were asleep.

There were no dressing-gowns, but maybe he could find something in the bedside lockers.

The first one contained nothing but a can of lemonade, empty; the second, a pair of Wellington boots and some woollen socks; the third was full of books and magazines. The next three were just as useless.

After a quick check on the nurse, gone from sight, the boy crossed over to the opposite six beds.

Suddenly, though, there were footsteps! Was it Mr Proudfoot, trying to catch him and be mad again?

Only one hiding place presented itself: beneath the bed at the far right – the bed next to the window.

In a second, the boy was curled up there, his back against the cold wall and his arm touching the bedside cabinet.

Matron Kettle – the kindest matron in Hospital – had just briefed Nurse Martha Castle, discreetly, about the various old gentlemen currently in residence.

Nurse Castle had been away on holiday, so quite a few of the patients were new to her.

This wasn't her favourite ward to be on. She found old men harder to deal with than old women: many of them took age very personally, and thought they had become old after losing concentration for a moment – they fretted constantly over *when* that moment had been. Ageing had been a battle of wits between them and some invisible force, and now they were definitely losers, and they didn't take the defeat any better than one at poker, football, golf or love. Some put up a final defiance, flirting relentlessly and grotesquely; it was necessary for the female nurses on the Geriatric ward to tolerate and sometimes slightly encourage this, as long as it didn't turn to out-and-out bum-grabbing. Fantasized rivalries kept the men talking among themselves (as to which nurse fancied them most – or which of them was fancied by most nurses) and made the men's sallies a little more tactical and infrequent. It shut them up, in other words. *Shutting up* was what it was all about – hence the nightcap, i.e., sedatives – especially for the demented.

As she went round the beds, checking notes and making sure the men were comfortable, Nurse Castle remembered what Matron Kettle had said:

Yi Qu, 66, Chinese and doesn't speak a word of English apart from thank you (fang-queue); hasn't been visited by any relations in the four weeks he's been here; has emphysema from lifelong smoking of cheap cigarettes; joins the ward poker game, if it's going; wins.

Herbert Hoof, 98, a host of age-related illnesses, too many to count; fought in the First World War and remembers it far more clearly than yesterday; still wakes up screaming with nightmares of gas attacks; lovely placid old gentleman, in-between times; lost hearing in left ear when a shell went off that side of him, and has had a loud ringing like a wind-up alarm clock going off ever since, poor fellow; if only they were all like Herbert.

Harold Upward, 82, cancer of the liver, moss-green eyes, thick white hair, with a prostate that's been shot to billy-o; naval man, he'll tell you, *not a dirty squaddie*; used to getting up, as he puts it, *au crack sparrowfart*; wants more than anything to go home – just to be at home to die; says, 'If I can make trips to the wazzer by myself, use the old bumpf to clean up, I'll be fine on my ownsome, won't I?'; likes very much to dress in women's clothes and doesn't care who knows it; 'No-one's going to tell me what's sissy or not. I did nine years at sea with the buggers – rum, bum and tiddly-um-pum-pum – if I'd wanted it, I'd have got it, I can tell you. Plenty of it.'

The boy, hiding beneath Harold's bed, watched the nurse's white-shoed feet come close. She might hear his breathing at any moment.

Billy Stickers – yes, he really is called that – 69, cancer of the just about everything; minor British film star of the 1950s, comedies mainly; shouldn't really be on this ward; wants to go home; not a chance, not a chance in hell; plenty of visitors in elegant twin-sets and very well-cut suits with vaguely familiar Sunday-afternoon faces, under the wrinkles; age is an *especially* cruel thing to the once-beautiful, Nurse Castle.

Sukhveer Blenkinsop, 62, ex-postman, malnutrition; beriberi; diseases picked up whilst on an ashram in India, near the Himalayas; thinnest man I've ever seen; meditates cross-legged all day long and tries to teach those around him breathing exercises – even Yi Qu, who can't understand a word and can hardly breathe to begin with; won't eat if you don't watch each and every mouthful going in.

The Spaceman, late fifties; diabetes; hypertension; will only give his name as 'The Spaceman' and insists he is 'not of this planet' but will not tell us which planet he *is* of; when an earth-name was demanded of him he said Gene Cernan – but turns out this was an astronaut from a failed mission to the moon; refuses all 'earth-treatments' and says it's only a matter of time before the mothership returns to take him back to his home planet; sometimes speaks incomprehensibly up his pyjama sleeve; probably 1960s acid casualty; will go into detail, if asked, about the beauties of the Horsehead Nebula; very knowledgeable about astronomy and inquiries are proceeding along these lines; special diet which he must be kept to; gets along well with Sukhveer Blenkinsop, the other space cadet of the ward; very gentle but doesn't like to be touched on the head, he says this interferes with his signals; is perfectly sane otherwise; supports Chelsea FC and joins in the poker game.

The boy watched as Nurse Castle's feet moved away, to the six beds on the other side of the corridor.

Steele had finished scrubbing. When they came in, he was standing feet apart examining the CT scans up on a large computer screen to the side of the theatre.

'Mr Steele,' said Iqbal Fermier, a young trainee surgeon who would be observing, and only observing.

Iqbal Fermier was of course looking forward to this – Steele was a particular hero of his – but he couldn't help but feel terribly frustrated. It would be at least six months before he was allowed to assist; until then, it was all textbooks, cadavers and dreams of surgical glory.

Steele turned around. 'Patient the same?' he asked, all brisk business.

'Stable,' said Sarah.

'Good,' said Steele, monosyllabically. Gemma could see that he was already halfway off into the dreamworld of neurosurgical intervention. It was clear to her, too, that another anaesthetist – not Sarah Felt – was to be in charge of this operation. This was Sir Reginald's further minor punishment for her unauthorized use of the emergency lift. But he, as everyone knew, was not a vindictive man, and tomorrow Sarah's slate would be wiped completely clean.

With help, they wheeled the trolley until it was beside the operating table. On Steele's nonchalant count of three, they lifted the inert body across from one to the other. (Iqbal Fermier, to his further frustration, wasn't even allowed to help with this.)

Steele, of course, stood off to one side with his hands raised – he could not risk getting them dirty and infecting the patient.

'Right,' he said, 'let's get this show on the road. Thank you, Miss Felt, Nurse Swallow.'

Not wanting to risk another lift ride in Sarah's company, Gemma took off as fast as she could. Sarah, however, dawdled slightly, as if she had something still to do in the theatre.

'I saw you, young lad,' whispered a croaky voice. 'I'm not really kipping, just playing possum so I don't have to talk to that ruddy awful young nurse. I know where you're hiding. I saw you sneak under there. Don't sweat, I won't let the cat out. I know a fellow like you probably has good enough reasons for hiding.'

The boy said nothing.

'What's your name?' the old man asked. 'Mine is Harold. I'm very old and bloody ill.'

'I need some clothes,' whispered the boy.

'Well, there's a spare pair of pyjamas in my locker, if you want to take them. What size are you?'

'I don't know,' said the boy.

'Try them on,' Harold said. 'I've shrunk so much they're probably a good fit. There's certainly enough room for me in my trousers these days, if I could only get out of bed to put them on.'

After making sure the nurse wasn't coming back, the boy pulled open the locker door – still keeping low – and extracted a neatly folded pair of stripy pyjamas. Without wishing to offend the old man, he gave them a sly sniff: washing-powder was what they smelled of, not urine.

'Those are the ones,' said Harold. 'You put them on quickly. Then we can talk.'

The boy's relief at finally getting into some clothes was almost enough to make him cry.

'How do they fit? Will they do?'

'Excellent,' said the boy, who had to turn the legs of the pyjama bottoms up a couple of times; the top was perfect. 'Thank you.'

'Oh, I can easily requisition some more. Now, do you want to tell me what kind of pickle you're in?'

'I'm on my way home,' said the boy. 'I have to go home.'

'Good for you,' Harold said. 'That's exactly the right attitude. Get out of this Godforsaken hole as soon as you can. I only wish I could go with you. But you see I'm stuck here – quite bedrid. A crock – a complete chipped piece of old cracked pottery. And none of your porcelain, either.'

The boy was very grateful to the old man; he felt sorry that he was now so useless and weak.

'What did you say your name was, again?' Harold asked.

'I didn't,' said the boy. 'I can't remember it.'

'I have the same problem, sometimes,' said Harold. 'I can always remember my serial number, though. Strange how some things stick.'

The old man's voice was floaty, as if he were trying not to go to sleep.

'Goodbye,' said the boy, and walked away on tiptoes.

Steele took another look at the computer screen. The unknown man's brain was a Rorschach blot of black on white: an asymmetric, bent-inwards H-shape. In the middle, a massive subarachnoid haemorrhage. Beautiful. Textbook. Just as he'd predicted, up in Trauma. This poor bloke was in serious trouble.

'Right,' he said, 'is he under?'

The anaesthetist, Vaughan Piccolo, checked the read-outs again. 'Yes, sleeping like the proverbial.'

'Okay,' said Steele. 'Let's make this one quick and clean.'

The head had been shaved once the man was properly sedated. His skin was stained with the yellow of disinfectant.

Ready.

With his favourite brand of scalpel, Cutmeister-Pro-9, Steele made the first incision: a confident slice right across the top of the head.

He was happy now – very soon he would be in his element: the cerebral cortex and all its mysteries.

Iqbal Fermier stood back so as not to interfere; he might just as well have been watching the whole thing on television: dammit.

The boy found himself in a strange corridor, long and dark and smelling of rot. He had no idea how he'd got there. Water flowed down walls which, if there had been a decent amount of light, he was sure would have looked green, slimy; aquatic. His feet as he walked were wet, ankle-deep in something he hoped was as usual as water.

He continued to walk forwards, and the further he went the narrower the corridor became.

After a couple of minutes, he was able to touch the walls to either side of him with outstretched arms; another minute of progress, and the ceiling had come so low he had to stoop.

If it got much tighter than this, he would be forced to go back the way he'd come.

But the corridor was changing again. The walls and ceiling weren't closing in, but the edges were going. A square cross-section was turning into a circle. The corridor was becoming a pipe.

Determined, the boy kept going on.

The water began to rise. Harold's stripy pyjamas were soaked right up to the knees.

Illumination still appeared from somewhere, though there were no longer any striplights, enough glow to keep the corridor a steely perceptible gray.

The next change was the appearance at regular intervals of ridges – all around the circle of the wall. These tightened and became more pronounced, with each step onwards.

Now he felt as if he were crawling through the mid-section of a Chinese New Year dragon, a series of hoops connected by fabric.

He remembered a holiday-camp swimming-pool: the slide – long, enclosed, plastic.

And now the slimy tube, for it could no longer be called a corridor, began to dip down.

If he kept going – if it did not begin to rise again – he would start to slide; and then who knows where he would end up. Perhaps to starve wetly and die in an inexplicable pointless long sweeping dip of corridor-tube.

The only upside was a rise in temperature; the

water swilling past him, streamlike, seemed warmer – it also, a little disgustingly, was becoming thicker. Not yet at the point of glutinous: the viscosity of saliva.

But as he continued – he had decided, *whatever happened*, not to go back – the saliva became adrenalized: thicker still, tending to strings as when brushing one's teeth or trying to spit after a sprint. If it carried on like this it would eventually become spun sugar, snappable, friable.

The boy reached the tipping point, the point where crawl became unstoppable downward slide; he pushed onwards.

The brain lay open beneath his hands, minutely pulsing. Although in theory Steele still recognized it as a human thing, possessed of cultural value and crammed with personal memories, he had long ago grown accustomed to seeing it more as a clinical landscape. The twisting runnels and serpentine hillocks of the surface always enticed him to step further in; go for a real hike.

As a terrain, it was often one he visited in the aftermath of flood – in this case, *deluge*. With subarachnoid haemorrhage, a blood vessel in the brain burst. This could happen at any time, to any one of us. He had already mopped this leakage up, carefully draining off the excess fluid. Blackened blood sucked up a plastic tube, for later disposal by someone less skilled. The ruptured artery was now neatly cauterized. A good job. Splendid work. The worst damage, however, was usually caused in cases like this by the increased pressure within the dome of the skull. As the leaking blood took more and more intracranial space, the brain tissue compressed: oxygen starvation occurred; neurons were lost; memories died or were scrambled; people ceased to be people.

He hated comparing cerebral matter to anything else; people often asked; it wasn't pink blancmange or cooked cauliflower: the density and texture of it were quite unique, and different parts were different again from one another.

The unknown man's brain had been severely distorted over the course of the haemorrhage. Steele felt he had done all he could, for the moment. Best thing now was to sew the poor bloke up, give him a few days to recover (if he made it through the night) and then see what kind of neurological function was left, if any. Steele didn't hold out particularly high hopes. He'd seen worse, but not often.

Suddenly, and for no apparent reason, the ECG began to caterwaul. In between one contraction and the next, the man's heart had stopped beating.

'Strange,' said Steele, more puzzled than panicked.

Already the surgical team around him was springing into action: fetching across the crash trolley, squirting gel onto the defib paddles, turning the dials.

'Clear?!' called Steele, when everything was in place.

It was only when the boy had begun to accelerate and knew that, *whatever happened*, he would never be able to climb back up the way he was descending, that the light went completely.

He tried to stop himself screaming, failed.

The ridges did not abate – every few feet he received a bump, peristaltic.

The saliva-water rushed thickly along with him, warmer and warmer – almost bathlike, now.

He was falling violently, ridges bumping him up or out to hit the roof; this felt soft, though. The building felt as if it had become inside-animal.

Whatever happened; whatever? – he might die of drowning or starvation in this bizarre corridor.

The fall began to undulate with his gentle upward bashings from side to side. His face was brushed by outgrowths from the walls – these began by feeling like seaweed or riverweed.

He could grab, perhaps – he tried, and slowed minutely; it did not come away in his hand, none of the silky stuff – but it soon thinned to hair – hair in slime, flowing with him – and thickening slime, thickening all the time.

Before, he hadn't worried about suffocation; but now he realized he would die sooner from that than starvation.

Genuine terror, now – genuine fear of the imminent end.

The tube shimmied with a rhythm he could neither predict nor map once it had gone by: it had no regularity or beat – but as he was falling, the tube must be spiralling, or taking a kinky path down.

He fell faster, the hairy walls no longer impeding him.

How long had this been going on? He had been towards the top floor of Hospital when this began, when he set off down this corridor (snakes to the ladders); now, he must be approaching the lower floors – ground level. He *must*.

Finally, a rhythm developed to the bashes: the floor was meeting him again and again for longer and longer – the floor being the wall against his back, where gravity held. Around him, the hair was becoming thicker still – he did not know how much longer it would allow him to breathe: he brought his hands up to his face and cupped a gap in front of his mouth, just like in the shower.

Jerks knocked this away, banging heel of hands against teeth. Ow.

He grabbed a long breath, perhaps final.

'Come on, come on,' said Steele.

The man had been flatline for fully two minutes.

With the defibrillator now reset, the neurosurgeon gave the heart another jolt of electricity.

Steele was frustrated. He wanted to save this man's life, for whatever it might be worth – after further operations, physical rehab and everything else that could nowadays be done. But he also wanted to see how well his cut-and-paste job held up. If he found himself doing the postmortem tomorrow afternoon, not enough time would have passed; little would be learned.

These emotions weren't as selfish as they might seem: yes, Steele was ruthless in wanting to become a better brain surgeon, but he wanted to become a better surgeon so as to save more lives.

This heart was a stubborn customer.

Iqbal Fermier stood, willing the body back to life. Steele's work had been astonishing – so accurate, so neat – it would be a shame if it all went to waste.

'Again,' said Steele. 'We'll give him another twenty, this time.'

The tunnel ceased to be what was on either side of him, or ceased to be there (to touch) when he stretched or tried to stretch his arms out – he couldn't push them very far as what *was* there was hair, thick and getting thicker all the time.

He was falling through a mane, wet, with thick warm water streaming, waterfalling, alongside him; the wet-hair smell of wet hair, but not human or dog.

The hair all around him was suffocating him, catching under his chin in strands, giving him a mad upwards beard (his first) – the hair was slowing him. It felt slippy, as though it had shampoo on it – as if it were being washed, and now the not-doggy smell was replaced by the smell of cheap detergents: chemical names. The keeping of the hair slippy was, he knew, the keeping of him alive.

He waited – he fell and there was nothing more he could do: he waited as he fell as he drowned.

The water became warmer still, then hotter rather than warmer, then painfully hot: he was on the point of scald, inner boil.

He waited as he fell as he drowned as he was burned boiled scorched.

And then miraculously there was air, and the smell the true smell of earth.

He felt the hair thicken again, slowing him almost to a stop.

Again he waited, almost stopped, and what he waited for was the drowning to finish.

Then, with a shock, two shocks, he felt his feet connect with something hard and stop-capable: a floor, perhaps. But he'd lost the knack of standing, was at an angle in his approach. His knees connected, too, saved only from injury by a grab at hair slippy but grabbable tangleable to slow him up.

There was no air here at what must be the bottom, the lowest floor of Hospital; he was underwater – and the climb above him would be impossible even with infinite time.

His hands by themselves, with no thought from

him of trying to save himself (he was already dead – might as well be), searched through sheets of curtains of hair – and they *discovered* things: in all directions – to his surprise, hope. They found a wall, another thing a what must be is that a shelf? – a horizontal line which meant shelves above and below, and then a stick or pole beside the shelves and finally, still with no thought of anything but a panicked increase of pointless knowledge of the place in which he would die: a handle – a door-handle, which he turned.

Blip and the heart re-started.

Long-held air blew out through tightly clenched teeth.

'What a tease,' said Nurse Heidi Wilson, widely famed for her cheek. 'Playing hard to get like that.'

Iqbal Fermier tried not to snigger.

'How long, in total?' Steele inquired.

'Four minutes twenty seconds,' replied Nurse Fielder, whose job it was to keep track.

'Thank you all very much,' said Steele.

He took a moment to look down into the man's face. This was a lesson learned from his mentor. Whatever other eccentricities or failings Sir Reginald might have, he was spot-on in reminding staff that each patient was a person, was an individual (even undergoing amputation), was a soul of sorts. The unconscious face on the operating table was so vulnerable – no, that wasn't it. There was no sense of possible defence. The face was *vacated*. Not like the dead; corpses, in Steele's experience, usually put on a sly smile. Physiologically, this was explained by muscle-relaxation. But it was hard not to believe they were sending a signal back to everyone left-behind: *Look, we're in on the big secret.* Some old ladies came across as quite mischievous: *We've scoffed all the sweets.* Children, oh dear, beamed: *I've got wings!*

Steele examined the man's face for clues as to his life. Had it been happy, so far? There weren't too many harsh wrinkles, no laughter lines, either, but these always smoothed out under sedation.

Lifting one of the eyelids with his thumb, the surgeon gazed at the iris. It was a deep glistening grey, bright with the ringed battery of lights overhead.

'Let's get him up to ICU,' said Steele. 'Good job, everyone. Splendid work.'

He realized he'd just used one of Sir Reginald's catchphrases. In the past, this would never have bothered him. But now . . .

The boy gushed out, into a white and well-lit corridor just like the one in which he had begun; how long ago?

His lungs were like chicks in a nest, agape for worms; his lungs were a crowd of fists, reaching out of him to grab at the life that was air that was life. It was a wrestling match, for a few moments; each breath was a bodyslam – on the point of damage-causation, and then he knew he was alive and staying alive.

Some distance away a nurse crossed from a room on one side of the corridor to a room on the other, but without glancing sideways towards him.

The boy was wet and still breathing – yes, still able to breathe.

He looked into the hairy space – the door read CLEANERS' CUPBOARD. The pole which his dying hands had grasped was the handle of something, broom or brush or mop, which had fallen part-way into the corridor with him: it stuck now out of the curtain of hair – he did not want to pull it out to see what was on the bottom of it.

The cupboard hadn't changed; it was full of dangling hair – water was flowing out as it had flowed down with him; maybe not as fast as he would have expected.

Up and down the corridor he looked, all the long long way to where perspective should, somehow, be truer, but wasn't – he knew from having reached that point, from *not* having reached that point before: it was white and there were nurses, moving quietly as nuns, moving quietly as nurses. The water, after its initial first gush, was slowing, as if the wound-in-reality of the door was staunching itself. The water became thicker, like transparent glue; it was setting, and if he didn't get away, he might be stuck down here for ever.

The boy tried to shut the door of the hairy cupboard, but the glue was too thick. He got it halfway closed, the glue at the base rucking up like a carpet.

The glue-water was now over his ankles; a couple more minutes and he would be a living statue; to get him out maybe they'd have to amputate his feet – maybe they'd amputate him, and his feet would be the only part of him that kept living.

Lifting each foot high, the glue stringing out, he stepped as it dried through squidge and slick onto the unwet floor – where the residue on the soles of his feet was tacky but didn't stop him moving.

Disorientated by the long fall, he chose the opposite direction to the last nurse he'd seen, went.

The first door he passed said a man's name, DR F. U. BUNDY, and then some letters; the next was a meeting room and the one after that a woman's name.

There didn't seem to be any patients on the floor with the hairy cupboard.

Soft footsteps were approaching; he couldn't get away in time: it was a nurse, when she came into view, but a very unusual nurse.

'Porter's here,' said Nurse Heidi Wilson from beside the door.

'Already?' Steele said, surprised. 'In that case it must be the one and only . . .' And as a handsome man with shining black skin pushed a hospital bed into theatre, Steele said warmly, 'Monsieur Othniel Calixte.'

'*Ça va?*' said Othniel, smiling.

'*Ça va bien,*' replied Steele. It was their joke to converse entirely in bad French, except when someone non-French-speaking needed for medical reasons to understand what was going on. '*Très bien. Mais cet homme-là n'est pas bien. Il est très fragile. Veuillez transporter cet homme malade très vite à la ICU.*'

'*Avec grand plaisir,*' Othniel replied, although great pleasure was far from being his emotion right at that moment.

'*Merci, mon ami,*' said Steele. He sensed that the other man was more reserved than usual – his smile less infectious, his thoughts elsewhere.

The surgeon watched in silence as the body was transferred across to the bed, and Othniel, with his usual efficiency, checked that all the lines were unentangled and the monitoring equipment was ready to follow.

'*Au revoir,*' Othniel said, quietly.

'*A la prochaine,*' Steele replied.

After they were gone, he gave a moment's thought to the other man's troubles. What might they be? He had no idea.

*

This nurse was very tall and extremely, almost obscenely voluptuous. The gathering in of her uniform at the waist and above forced her breasts into a deep cleavage. Her long slender legs were exposed all the way up to the tops of her thighs – and though they were covered by the familiar white, the material was not that of normal tights or stockings: all down the side of her, where she caught the light, a squidge of shine shone, along the ridge and edge, a glint which looked as if it had been squeezed from a tube of toothpaste or white oilpaint. Her costume, all over, which looked more fancy dress than practical, was brightly agleam: she was definitely clean. When one leg passed the other, and when her arms touched this way or that the side of her ribcage, her uniform gave a gentle squeak: this nurse was dressed in rubber. On her feet were six-inch white stilettos, also coated in a gloss of rubber. Her hands wore white latex gloves (on top of rubber ones) which stretched up to the elbows; as she approached, before she saw him, she was engaged in pulling them tight (with a snap) and smoothing them flat (with a squeak). Behind her nurse's hat, her hair was a tangle of white-gold locks. This was the woman known as the Rubber Nurse. But, however unusual she looked, however unlike the other nurses, she would still catch the boy and take him back to Trauma.

A sharp pain from his stomach served to remind him why this would be such a terrible idea: he was dying.

'Hey you,' she said. 'Are you alright?'

The boy told her he was, began to explain why he was there – a lie about getting lost.

'Are you in pain?' the Rubber Nurse interrupted.

'No,' he said quickly.

'You wouldn't like me to give you a thorough examination in a nice private room, just to make sure that everything is still working as it should?'

'I'm fine,' the boy said. 'I'm just going to the toilet.'

'I could help with that, too,' said the Rubber Nurse. 'I'm a very adaptable girl.'

'I'm sure you are,' said the boy.

'You're cute,' said the nurse, who was slowly turning coy – her body language altering to that of an eleven-year-old girl, and not one dressed head-to-pointy-toe in fetishwear.

The boy had no idea how to respond to this humiliating compliment.

The Rubber Nurse's toes turned in, her hands interlaced behind her shiny bottom and as she spoke she swayed this way and that: 'What's your name?'

At this, the boy finally made his escape bid, turned and sprinted away down the corridor.

For a few moments he'd been paralysed by the adult (adult in so many and unexpected ways) presence of the Rubber Nurse. But then he had realized she would never be able to run in those absurd heels. And he was right: she just stood there and stared at him – wide-eyed, full-lipped, doll-faced, blond-haired – as he got further and further away.

'Come back here, you naughty boy!' she shouted, all trace of the little girl gone. 'If you don't come back, Nurse is going to be very angry with you. Very angry, indeed. And we *all* know what happens then. Nurse will find you, and when she does, she'll really make you suffer, you naughty naughty boy. Oh yes, she'll take you to her room and perform some particularly ticklish procedures. A naughty boy like you needs to be examined very thoroughly, from top to bottom, inside and out. Nurse gets very annoyed when her patients misbehave – it upsets her. Everything she does for them, however strange and painful it may seem, is intended to help cure them. Everyone is sick but everyone can be cured. Your cure can begin right here: step into the hairy closet with me.'

The boy had been ambushed by one of his fantasies – something like them, anyway; he was terrified, and ran.

His pyjamas felt dry, although only a few moments before they had been sodden; perhaps their material was one, he thought, specially scientific.

The first thing was to put some distance between himself and the Rubber Nurse; although she seemed less of a practical danger than any of the other nurses he'd encountered (she didn't seem to want to take him back to Trauma, but perhaps she had been intending to trick him), he still felt more threatened by her.

There had been something deeply unnerving about her – her height, the way she spoke and the things she said. She seemed to want something from him which he was pretty sure he didn't have.

Sarah Felt waited as Othniel Calixte pushed the bed into the lift.

The doors had almost closed when a shiny boot jammed itself in between them, and they rebounded to admit a fat white Security Guard: Pollard.

'Oh, shit,' he said, sighting Othniel and then, 'Hello,' as he noticed Sarah. 'Mind if I join you?'

He pushed the button for the 12th floor, where the Security Guards had their offices. Then he turned round to examine the comatose body. 'It must be funny,' he said to Sarah, 'not knowing who's touching you, and all that. Any old thing could happen.'

'We take very good care of our patients,' she replied.

Pollard glanced at Othniel, who stared back. 'It's not you I'm worried about, love,' Pollard said. 'You're not gonna do weird stuff to me while I'm unconscious.'

'No,' she said, 'and not when you're conscious, either.'

'Shame,' said Pollard, turning away. Then added, resonantly *sotto voce*: 'You could certainly use it.' He coughed the word *lezzer* into his fist.

Othniel and Sarah exchanged a brief look; each seemed intent on apologizing to the other.

Pollard let out a long squeaky fart then turned around, feigning surprise. 'Oh, so he's not dead just yet, then?'

A sour smell began to overtake the lift.

Othniel thought, Compared to this man, the dead smell of flowers.

'You're disgusting,' said Sarah.

Pollard turned around, bulky and annoyed. 'If anything stinks in here,' he said, eyes on Othniel, 'it's not fucking me.'

'I didn't mean your smell,' said Sarah.

The Security Guard was about to challenge her on this when the lift, luckily perhaps, arrived at his floor.

'See you around,' he said, and pointed up at the CCTV camera in the top corner of the lift: a shiny black upside-down dome.

The doors closed on his leering face.

As they began to rise again, Sarah said to Othniel, 'You must get that all the time.'

'It's very boring,' Othniel said, 'but Pollard is really a coward. Cropper is the psychopath. With Cropper, I am careful; with Pollard, I don't care.'

'Why do they have to employ such thugs?'

'Thugs make good . . .' Othniel said, 'uh . . . thugs.'

Sarah laughed, then quickly checked the monitor to see that the unconscious man's blood pressure and heart rate were still alright.

In sympathetic silence, the lift continued up to the 21st floor.

Sure now that the Rubber Nurse had given up her pursuit of him, if she'd ever bothered beginning a pursuit, the boy was desperate to find out which floor the long slide down the hairy corridor had brought him out on. It must, he thought, be a sub-basement area, deep beneath the hospital buildings. The thought of this annoyed him: he was surely closer to the front door, and to escaping, and to getting home, but the journey from now on might be upwards – upstairs. How many basement levels could there be? Four or five, perhaps – six at the maximum.

The boy walked until he came to a sign on the wall – really, he needed to get a map of the entire building; or at least a list of which floors the departments were on. He couldn't risk asking anyone; that would give the game away, the game which wasn't a game.

Walking past the open door of a ward full of old people (which, in itself, might have given him a clue), he saw something amazing: sky – the amber night sky of the city.

Most of the oldsters seemed to be asleep; the lights along their ward were out. The boy decided to risk going in.

He made his way unchallenged to the window and found, to his horror, that he was able to look down as well as across and up – down exactly, he counted them, twenty-two storeys. Up, another three, plus the helipad.

All of that fall, down and down and down through the fear of drowning, and he hadn't descended a single floor: he was in the same Geriatric ward. It was very difficult to understand, and as far as the boy could work out, not really worth the effort. Hospital was a weird place: the sooner he was out of it the better.

Sarah helped Othniel push the bed into the Intensive Care Unit. The patient was stable, and all that remained for her to do was sign him over to whomever.

Nurse Angela Dixon, thirty years old and with bright and brittle orange hair, came away from a comatose woman whose pressure sores she had been attempting to treat.

'We've been expecting you,' she said. 'Last on the right. Next to the fire door. Plug him in and I'll join you in a second.'

Following the familiar routine, Sarah and Othniel wheeled the unconscious body past the other unconscious bodies. Sometimes the nurses in attendance looked up to check them out, sometimes they didn't. Sarah loved the atmosphere of Intensive Care; it was so quiet and serene, compared with Trauma – compared with most of the rest of Hospital, in fact. There was an almost religious aura to the comatose and their carers.

The bed glided smoothly into the empty space. Sarah began transferring the equipment from batteries to mains. Last of all was the ventilator. Othniel watched – his job such that although he knew exactly what needed to be done, he would never be allowed to do it.

In the next bed along was a comatose man of

about thirty with two gunshot wounds, one to the shoulder, one to the gut. He knew nothing of what was going on all around him.

Angela Dixon joined them, as promised, and Othniel handed her the clipboard of notes. 'Thank you very much,' she said, gladdening Sarah's heart. Not everyone in Hospital was as loathsome as Pollard.

Sarah bent down and pushed the final plug into the wall-socket.

At ten o'clock exactly, Hospital, most of Hospital, was either asleep already or settling itself down to sleep. Many offices, busy during the day, were now empty or occupied by solitary figures trying to finish paperwork. Consulting rooms and the corridors outside them, waiting rooms with their rows of uneasy chairs – their televisions were off, their drinks machines and water-coolers unbothered. On the administrative floors, 13th and 14th, computers in gray and faun stood reflecting one another dimly in undusty screens. Here and there, a cleaner followed a questing vacuum-cleaner or a porter pushed a sodden mop. By now, Geriatrics patients were expected to have turned their bed-lights out, despite insomnia, night-terrors and pain of infinite variety. The newborn babies in Neo-Natal, lying in the suspended plastic trays of their trolleys, swaddled in soft blankets, were remarkably placid – a few only needed to be rocked by their mothers. On the Children's wards, Sisters had mostly established a calm of pre-slumber – broken sometimes by sobs or giggles. It was quiet, too, down in Pathology, where the day's corpses – zipped in bags – lay within their long metal compartments. But elsewhere the twenty-four-hour sounds continued: ululations from birthing pools, snickings and slurpings and classical music in operating theatres. Noisiest of all, just gearing up for its busiest time, was A&E on the ground floor. This was what some emergency medic, years and years ago, had nicknamed 'the Flood'. Chucking-out time from the pubs always brought with it an influx of cases, trivial and fatal. But the hour before closing was already an alcohol-lubricated rush of viciousness, clumsiness, stupidity and tragedy. Here came twisted ankles, dog bites, sprained wrists, broken fingers, flattened noses, reddened mouths, glassed faces, dislodged retinas, broken arms, knife wounds, ruptured spleens, gaping throats, broken necks, gunshot wounds. Here came, one after the other, chancers thrown out by bouncers and looking for an opportunity to sue for a couple of scratches, Munchausen's, contrite fathers, apologetic taxi-drivers, naughty nurses and cheeky devils from the hen-night-gone-wrong, dinner-jacketed palefaces from the stag-party-turned-nightmare, street preachers with their average visions of the Apocalypse, the lost and upset wanting directions from someone in uniform or to use a phone to say they've had their phone nicked and they'll be home late or that they're not fucking coming home ever fucking again, sobbing wannabe blood-donors, homeless looking for somewhere to get warm and have their kissy sores rebandaged. Here came the weeping girlfriends, weeping ex-girlfriends, weeping ex-girlfriends' best friends and weeping ex-girlfriends' ex-best friend's exes. Here, too, motorbike accidents by the score, failed and soon-to-be-successful suicide attempts, overdoses of both sorts, schizophrenics in need of more medication or silence or light or another head, old people with chest pains and breathing difficulties, policemen and women with facial abrasions (and abrasions on their knuckles, as well – scuffed toecaps, too), carpark footballers with groin strains, diabetic dwarves, men whose foldable bikes had folded while they were riding them, women who had walked into doors or fallen downstairs or been beaten semi-unconscious by someone they preferred not to name, kids – girls and boys – gone into toxic shock after inserting their first tampon, candidates for the rape kit. Here came fallen-off-garden-wall burglars, fish-fryers with worse-than-usual fat burns, chubby young women going into labour who hadn't even known they were pregnant, bloody-faced Asian boys surrounded by dozens of mates accusing the staff of racism for not seeing their friend fast enough, gone-wrong and got-stuck rectal insertions of all sorts (carrots, kiwi fruit, lightbulbs, staplers, mobile phones set to vibrate in plastic bags, even the occasional dildo). Here came all human life and death – the quiet night in gone amusingly or horrifyingly wrong, the no-babysitter children who managed to get into the garden shed, to get into the drinks cabinet, to get into the knife drawer. Here came the dying and the almost-dead and the dead.

Behind the reception desk, looking out across this routine carnage, sat Sister Agnes Day – watching through her one eye (the other was well-matched glass). Yet even though she'd seen, monoscopically, most of the possible varieties of human misery (often female) and stupidity (usually male), of violence and plain bad luck – even though she'd been doing this job for five years, things still happened, occasionally, to surprise her.

But not this youngish couple approaching now – her with her big bump, him with the overnight bags.

The woman, Mary Walker, gave a series of grunts. She was, she knew, just about to enter the second stage of labour.

'Come on,' said the man, James Walker. 'Let's try and not have them here, shall we?'

They made it to the desk. Sister Agnes Day wore horn-rimmed spectacles, and looked like a cross between a trout and a traffic cone. When she smiled, which was rarely, her sluglike lips seemed to copulate. But she wasn't an unkind person, not without good cause.

'We're back,' said the woman. 'My contractions are every three minutes. I'm going to have these babies very soon. Yes, two of them – *twins*. So you're not sending us away again.'

Sister Agnes Day hadn't been on shift the first time they arrived, but she apologized anyway. The woman, she thought, looked convincingly agonized. She would call for a porter with a wheelchair.

'Hey! Yeah! You!'

Sister Agnes Day was still sometimes surprised but, again, not by this young man coming towards her – him, she knew; him, she knew only too well – she could identify him by his walk, the junkie strut: carefree and desperate, a cocky, jerky, nervy hodge-podge of contradictory movements. Roll up those sleeves, drop those unclean pants and you'd see trackmarks, abscesses and, if you were unlucky, lesions that looked like vaginas in hardcore pornography.

Behind him came a skeleton carried by an ogre: at least, that's what it looked like.

The junkie and the ogre were shouting; the skeleton wasn't.

'She's ill,' he said. 'She needs fucking help.' As if he'd spoken once already and been ignored.

'Is she conscious?' Sister Agnes Day asked, trying to prioritize.

'Depends what you mean,' said the cocky junkie, whose given name was Magnus Avenir but whose streetname was Spanner.

'She's breathing,' the ogre said. His streetname was Case, short for Headcase, short for Total Fucking Headcase. His given name, long-forgotten, had been Colm McNaught.

'Shut it,' said Spanner. 'I'm dealing.'

'Excuse me,' said James Walker, the man with the pregnant wife. 'We were here first.'

'Are you dying?' shouted Spanner. 'Is she dying?'

'If you could all calm down, we'll deal with you much faster.'

'Look, I'm about to give birth,' said Mary Walker. 'How calm do you expect me to be?'

'I will call a porter to take you up,' Sister Day said to her. 'Please go and sit down.'

'Is there a fucking doctor here?' shouted Spanner.

'There are nurses and there are plenty of them,' replied Sister Day, aware this wasn't strictly true. 'And the calmer you are, the sooner I'll get one to look at your friend.' As she spoke, she speed-dialled the porters. 'Yes,' she said, when they answered. 'One to go up to Maternity, in a wheelchair.'

Throughout this brief call, Spanner had stood in front of her, snorting in a way that was meant to be intimidating. She'd dealt with worse – he looked as if he'd fall over if she coughed in his direction. In the ogre's arms, the skeleton was looking delicately bluish. Her name was Nikki Froth.

'I'll get you a nurse.'

'And not some fucking student, either.'

*

The boy's stomach was aching almost constantly, now. He thought of his mother (though that thought also gave him pain) – what she would have done?

Milk. A glass of milk.

And where to get that without being seen?

The kitchens.

In order to find them, he needed a map of the building. But maybe there was an easier way.

Continuing down the corridor, he eventually came to a right turn, which brought him into the lift lobby.

There was no-one around, so he pressed the call button and waited. If they asked he could say . . . he could say he was going back to the Children's ward.

A lift arrived, but occupied.

When the doors opened, a tall black man was standing there with a wheelchair: Othniel Calixte.

For an intense moment, they looked straight at one another.

'Up,' said the boy. 'I want to go up.'

The man smiled, unexpectedly. 'Well, I'm not stopping you,' he said.

Then the doors closed.

Without thinking too much about it, the boy pressed the call button again.

Another lift arrived, this time empty, and he got in, phew.

Faced with the buttons, he thought about pressing G for Ground Floor – but just then another pang smacked him right in the stomach. It was as if something in there was living: a leg.

Alongside the numbers for the other floors, Hospital departments were listed. The boy's finger descended past Rheumatology, Orthopaedics, Oncology/Haematology – descended all the way to the 6th floor and, yes, Kitchens.

The doors closed by themselves, and the boy was afraid the lift would start to rise, taking him back to Trauma.

Quickly, he pressed 6. And the lift began its controlled fall.

In case it stopped and someone came in, the boy assumed a casual pose, leaning against the metal bump-bar that went round all three walls. He was extra-glad of the pyjamas; they didn't fit too badly, and made him look like a proper patient.

Administration and Chapel. Security. Immunobiology. Tropical Medicine. John Keats Ward. Surgery.

Here the lift did stop.

When the doors opened, a nurse was standing there: NURSE HEIDI WILSON said her name-badge. She pushed the G and stood with her back to the boy, who looked even more casual than before. The lift descended.

Ping – the boy walked round the nurse and out into the lobby.

'Hey, you don't want –'

Nurse Wilson was speaking to him, but the closing doors cut her voice off – and they didn't reopen; the lift continued down.

This floor was smelly, not in a good way.

Gemma took the lift down to the ground floor and was just walking through A&E when someone spoke to her.

'Nurse?'

It was Sister Agnes Day.

'Nurse Swallow,' she said, reading Gemma's name-badge. 'Do you have a minute? I've seen you before. You work in Trauma, don't you?'

Gemma said that she did. Though, of course, it was obvious from her uniform.

'Well,' said Sister Agnes, drawing Gemma towards her with the quietness of her voice, 'we've got a slight emergency, and no-one around to deal with it. That girl there' – she nodded – 'is overdosing on something. Could you help out?'

'I really shouldn't,' said Gemma. Relations between A&E and Trauma were difficult at the best of times – if she was found to have been interfering . . .

'I'd do it myself,' Sister Day said, 'but I'm absolutely forbidden to leave my station. If she's unattended, there's a possibility she'll go into respiratory failure.'

The girl did look a little blue.

Gemma hated ethical dilemmas like this; she could get into real trouble, especially if something went badly wrong.

'Alright,' she said. Her job was saving lives; if she could do it, she would.

'Consulting Room Four is empty. Get that hulking brute to bring her in.'

Gemma had already noticed the blue girl's companions. Close up, they looked no more savoury.

'Please come with me,' she said.

Spanner stood up as well. 'About fucking time,' he said.

'Not you,' said Gemma. 'And he can't stay for the examination, either.'

Case carried Nikki with surprising tenderness (yes, he quietly loved her) into the consulting room, and then left entirely without the expected protest.

Gemma looked with pity at the girl lying motionless on the exam table. She was very young but had already lost almost all the looks she'd had – probably she'd been beautiful; now she was grey from skin to soul.

With her penlight, Gemma checked the pupils – which dilated normally. Then she took the girl's pulse and listened to her chest. For a moment, she was puzzled.

A quick alcohol-and-cotton-bud swab of the girl's forehead brought away a little blue colouring.

'Okay,' Gemma said, 'you can stop faking. What's this about?'

Nikki opened her eyes, which were green and unnaturally bright.

'Help me,' she said. 'Please help me get away from those men.'

Before Gemma could reply, an A&E nurse – Lisa Post – barged through the door; no knock.

'Thank you *very* much for your help,' she said. 'But we can take this from here.'

All the bitter and longstanding rivalry between A&E and Trauma was in Lisa Post's voice. Gemma, however, didn't want to see this frightened girl fall victim to that.

'Can I talk to you outside for a moment?' she said to Nurse Post – who groaned with impatience but joined her.

In a few words, Gemma explained what she thought the situation was.

'*Please* get someone from Social Services,' she said.

'Yeah, yeah,' said Nurse Post. 'It's nothing we haven't seen a million times. Cases don't have to arrive by helicopter for us to take them seriously.'

Gemma was unconvinced, but there was really nothing more she could do.

She popped her head back round the door, 'I'm handing you over –'

'To us,' said Nurse Post, pushing past.

'Don't go,' said Nikki Froth, all big green eyes.

Gemma hated to join the long line of people who had clearly abandoned this waif in the past.

'I have to,' she said, wrenched.

'Yes,' added Nurse Post, 'we're afraid she does.'

With her heel, the A&E nurse shut the door right in Gemma's face.

Gemma stood there for a second, considering making an issue of it – better not; better make the best of what was left of her break.

Othniel Calixte arrived in A&E five minutes after receiving the call. Sister Day pointed out the couple. Othniel approached them, giving the woman a bright smile – to make her feel better, to help.

Mary didn't appreciate it. 'Just get me upstairs. I have no sense of humour, and I don't want to flirt.'

James gave a look of apology over his wife's head.

Othniel took them to the lift, preoccupied with thoughts of that evening's ritual. How would it go?

His background reading, recently, had led him towards great fears. Hospital felt dangerous this evening.

All of the porters apart from him were direct from Haiti. He, however, had grown up in Midfordshire. There had been some debate about whether they should allow him in the Union, but when the spirits were consulted they had said yes.

To begin with, five years ago, Othniel had got everything wrong – spoken bad French, clapped at the wrong time, in the wrong rhythm, called out the last but one response.

There were some who thought his lack of culture

would affect the success of their rituals – most, though, were wary of disagreeing with anything the spirits had definitely shown themselves to favour.

Othniel was a very quiet chap, and was well aware of the resentments towards him within the Union. But he felt he had to overcome the doubters and rise, eventually, to be Head Voodoo Man, shaman, director of ceremonies and master of Hospital club.

In his spare time, he obsessively read books written by academics about the origin and development of voodun. His knowledge, over the past few years, had become immense – far outstripping that of any of the other porters, including Pierre Estime, the long-established Head Voodoo Man.

Part of his problem, although none of the others realized this, was that nowadays he saw the mistakes Pierre Estime was making, all the things he was doing which he shouldn't be – and Othniel couldn't help himself from trying to nudge things in a more authentic direction.

He wanted the spirits to be treated with far greater respect, as proper deities rather than cosmic bookies. It offended his sensibilities that so often the ceremony was merely an excuse to present them with a list of demands, instead of asking that their will be done. He knew that extremely powerful forces were pent up within Hospital, waiting to be liberated; he could feel them, he had glimpsed them.

They made it up to the delivery rooms within the space of three contractions – which were, as the wife had said, coming regularly every three minutes.

At the reception desk, Mary started with the words, 'Do you have something for us, now they're practically born, or are you going to send us away again?'

The midwife, Honey Hopeful, who was Jamaican, said, 'We get you straight in there, lady. No worry. We hope you understand . . .'

'I'm in serious pain. I was in pain before.' Another contraction began. 'You can . . .' But then Mary was unable to speak.

'I think Delivery Room Four be free, now. I go check. They cleaning it out, after the last baby.'

Another midwife, young and very beautiful, Zandra Pandit, approached them down the corridor.

'Room Four clear, you know?' Honey Hopeful asked.

'No,' Zandra Pandit said. 'I mean, no, I don't know.'

'Just go,' said the husband, then began massaging the small of Mary's back. 'You're doing really well,' he said in her ear. Midwife Honey Hopeful eavesdropped as she walked off – at an even, shuffle-footed pace – down the corridor. A screamer, she could tell. They go to all these classes, give you birth-plans ten pages long, and then, oh, when they feel that pain come up like the tide it's drugs-drugs-drugs, aren't drugs wonderful, darling?

Still, the woman was pretty advanced by now and, if they were lucky and she wasn't too much of a tightarse, they should even get the little buggers out well in advance of midnight.

Once she'd got them settled, she would give Henderson MacVanish a call. She knew he'd be glad to hear from her.

And Delivery Room Four was free.

Avoiding the eyes of junkie Spanner and ogre Case, Gemma walked through A&E and out of the main doors, then turned towards Smokers' Alley.

It still amazed Gemma how many hospital workers, even lung specialists, hadn't kicked the filthy habit.

Luckily for her, Patricia Parish was already there, so she didn't have to bum off a complete stranger. Always ready to welcome another member into their already oversubscribed club, Patricia handed over a high-tar cancer-stick. Gemma didn't really *need* to smoke. But it was a very useful way of getting to know the gossip.

'Gemma Swallow, Trauma's newest star, this is Linda Loos. She works in Oncology.'

'Oh, how's that?' asked Gemma.

'Don't,' said Nurse Loos. 'I'm on my break.'

The young nurse was too too thin with downy hairs all over her goosefleshy arms; bad teeth, too: classic bulimic.

'I was only asking,' said Gemma.

'See you later,' Nurse Loos said to Gemma, putting quite a significant stress on the word *later*.

When she had calmed herself down with a couple of deep, sinful drags, Gemma began to tell Patricia exactly what had just happened, not with Nikki Froth but upstairs with Sarah Felt. Patricia was her confidante – an odd-looking woman, slightly wonky-faced, her hair a pubic halo; an Afro, really, although she was very pale-skinned. Her figure was good, and Gemma had observed that she made the most of it when out of uniform. The fingernails on both Patricia's hands were bitten away almost completely; sometimes they even bled.

As Gemma was very wary about being overheard, they moved off a little to one side, though still under cover. It was raining.

Patricia seemed genuinely appalled. 'That's awful,' she said. 'The bitch.'

'I'm glad you think so,' said Gemma. 'I wasn't sure what to think.'

'I never realized what a total cow she was – or how irresponsible.'

'But do you think there's something going on between Sarah and Steele?'

Patricia took a long deep pull on her cigarette and then, taking even longer, let slow smoke out through her nostrils. 'Well, I'd never noticed anything before, or I'd have told you. But now you mention it, there always has been a certain tension between them. Perhaps you're right . . .'

'Come on,' said Gemma. 'I need to know. If I don't, I might end up making a complete fool of myself here.'

'I don't think there's much danger of that,' said Patricia. 'You're too much in control.'

'It doesn't feel like it,' replied Gemma, the last of anger's energy leaving her.

The boy knew the smell of kitchens from school: institutional food – it had a fitting weightiness, as if stodge could be inhaled as well as dumped onto scratchy-soft use-mellowed white plates.

He followed a series of arrows which pointed him right and right again to the KITCHENS. The doors were open; no-one was expected to be on this floor at this time.

After a quick glance round, the boy walked through; until he'd realized that eating was a possibility, he hadn't been hungry. But what he really needed was some milk to drink, to calm his stomach.

Metal worksurfaces reflected very dully the undersides of metal shelves. There was a vast dustbin just near by – when he looked inside it, he wasn't thinking of foraging. A piece of paper that looked as if it had been screwed up then pressed flat again, several times, rested on top of transparent plastic shapes and pieces of yellow maybe-hopefully-just-gristle:

Mains
Chick Tik Masla, rice
Lamb cutletts, new pots, runner beans
Steak n kidney pud, carrots
Fish n chips
Veg Lasagne

Puddings
Spotted DICK!!!, custurd
Rice Pud
IceCream, Choc or Strawb

The acoustic was echoey, though the boy kept quiet enough not to offer it the chance to demonstrate this. From the far side of the room, a low buzzing came – and he went across in anticipation of refrigeration.

Bingo, he was right: a pair of double doors, cold to the touch.

Thinking mostly of being locked in there and freezing to death, the boy opened them and passed through – into an alley of meat, beefsides hanging from frosty hooks.

He explored the whole fridge, going down further alleys, this time of cardboard.

The menu had given him a clue, but the cold store confirmed it: ice-cream was the only edible thing. Milk deliveries probably came in the morning.

He found a tub of vanilla, too heavy to lift, prised the lid off and went in search of a spoon.

Although this was the fulfilment of some sweet-toothed fantasies, the boy was unjoyful: he'd lost interest in confectionery a year or so earlier.

The ice-cream tub was a quarter of his body-weight; he had no desire to eat it all, just to freeze away some of his stomach pain.

When he went out into the kitchen, he sensed immediately that something had changed – and not for the better. The vast room sounded minutely different, more muffled but as if the air were crackling like brown paper. It was the realization that he *really* mustn't make a noise that gave the boy notice: it wasn't *something* that was different, it was *someone.*

Before he heard the first footstep, he knew that he was about to hear it – close up; too close; behind him.

Here was the reason the door had been left open.

One glance over his shoulder, and the boy had seen enough: dark-blue cloth with silvery buttons.

'Oi!'

It was a Security Guard, a huge Security Guard. He was carrying a bowl and spoon – heading for an iced snack of his own.

'Oi, you!'

The boy sprinted away as fast as he could. In his stomach, the pain increased, but this only made him go faster – and faster still, when he made it out onto the corridor.

Behind him the rubber-soled boots, every time they hit the floor, made a squeak as well as a thud.

They stood and finished their cigarettes, looking out through the rain. Then, all at once, Patricia seemed to reach some sort of decision. 'As far as I've heard,' she said, lowering her voice to a huskily intimate whisper, 'Steele has never become involved with anyone who works at the hospital.' Gemma's heart was getting ready to sing when Patricia added, 'Except, well . . .'

'Go on,' Gemma said.

Patricia looked at Gemma, hard, then at her watch, then took another few moments to light a cigarette. 'Have you heard,' she asked, 'of the Rubber Nurse?'

'No,' said Gemma, thinking, quite innocently, what a strange job description that was. 'Who is she?'

Gemma had noticed that Patricia tended to hiss her S-sounds, especially when the gossip, as now, was sizzling hot.

'No-one really seems to know – not that I've spoken to, anyway. She works in the hospital, but it's very hard to tell in which department. She kind of floats around from place to place, usually at night, like some sort of special consultant – but I don't think anybody calls her in. Everyone calls her the Rubber Nurse because of how she dresses – in very high heels and one of those sexy nurse outfits. Not a cheap one, though. Shiny and expensive. Very very tight-fitting.'

'And she works here?' asked Gemma, suddenly aware of her shapeless smock of a uniform and white rubber slippers, and that Patricia was only mentioning this creature because she had some connection with Steele. 'They let her work here wearing *that*?'

Patricia's tone, if possible, became even more confidential. 'As far as I know, it's part of her job.'

'Her job?' asked Gemma, completely confused.

'I think she's something like a stripogram,' Patricia said, 'with added extras. No-one ever talks about her – she's just one of the weird characters who turned up one night and never went away.'

'But what does this have to do with Steele?' Gemma asked, desperate.

'There have been rumours,' said Patricia, 'but, then, there have been rumours about the Rubber Nurse and most of the male staff in this hospital – and quite a lot of the female staff, too. And that's not to mention the patients.'

'Steele dated a stripogram girl?' Gemma asked, appalled. 'I don't believe it.'

'*Dated* isn't the word,' said Patricia – part of her, Gemma could tell, was enjoying this. Perhaps her confidante wasn't as nice as she seemed. Perhaps she enjoyed causing pain through gossip.

'Meaning?' Gemma asked.

'Like most of them, he was rumoured to have spent some private time in her company.'

'What exactly do you mean?' asked Gemma.

'She has a room.'

'Where?'

Patricia looked at her watch again. 'I have to be getting back.'

'*Where?*' Gemma repeated her question.

Patricia was smoothing down her uniform. 'Look, it's probably nothing to worry about. Like I said, there are rumours about most of –'

'Where?'

'7th Floor – somewhere in the south-west wing. But I didn't tell you that.'

'Thank you,' Gemma said.

'For what?' Patricia replied. 'For making mischief and shattering love's young dream?'

'No,' said Gemma, 'for being honest.'

Patricia turned and walked away, suppressing a smile. Honest? She didn't think so. As far as she knew, the delectable Steele had never had anything to do with the sexy and bizarre Rubber Nurse. But as for herself . . . Her smile changed to a different sort of smile. 'You,' she said to herself, 'are a *very* naughty girl.'

It was a straight dash towards the lifts; they were his first chance, but only if one was there, doors open, just about to go. Failing that, he at least might confuse the guard for a couple of seconds – had he gone left or right down the parallel corridors?

'Come back here, you little bastard,' the shout came, already slightly breathy; a good sign.

Every five paces, the boy strained to go faster, without overstriding.

'You can't get away.' The voice was quieter, the boots further back.

The boy risked a look, and saw he had maybe fifteen yards on his pursuer. Not enough. But as he kept going, he felt himself pulling away.

Round the corner into the lift lobby – none of the doors open. As he passed them, he tried to punch the call button: first one he missed but second was dead on.

Left or right? His momentum had already decided left; keep a smooth curve – so he sidestepped himself and swerved right, completing an S-shape.

Another long, empty corridor; featureless, without hiding place. He was going to be caught, unless –

Two toilets opposite one another, Ladies and Gents. It was pointless but better than turning around and giving himself up.

Into the Gents; sinks, mirrors, urinals, and eight cubicles in a long door-closed row. Eeny-meaningless-meany-miney – the fifth one: close door, flick lock, up onto the seat and squat.

Only then did he notice the lock was broken; the metal tongue went across but the catch-box had been smashed off. The red square saying OCCUPIED would give him away faster than anything, so he leaned forwards and flicked the small bolt back.

'I can hear you,' said the Security Guard, and laughed. He was already in the Gents; the snick of the loo-lock had been a gift to him.

Crouching barefoot on the black toilet seat, the boy felt terrified. When he caught him, what would this man do? There was a horrible, evil glee in that voice – and it was talking now:

'You're in serious trouble, young man. You picked the wrong person to run away from. Allow me to introduce myself. My name is Cropper. I am Chief Security Guard. This hospital can't have snotty little kids running around the kitchens helping themselves to whatever they like.'

The boy heard cubicle doors one, two and three open. He looked up to see if it was possible for him to climb through the gap at the top: too narrow, damn.

Even in his panic, he noticed something odd: a word written in black capital letters on the top left-hand of the cubicle: HELLMOUTH.

'I know you're in here somewhere.'

HELLMOUTH – the boy shut his eyes and screwed his fists up and, with anger and no hope, tried not to be where he was – tried to be invisible. Perhaps, like in films, the guard's radio would crunch and he would be called away to deal with an emergency elsewhere.

Door four opened and squealed shut.

'You can't hide,' said the guard.

The boy was screwed into the tightest, intensest knot he could make. *Please. I wish . . .*

*

James Walker felt curiously distanced from Mary. He looked around the place where his two children, a boy and a girl, should, if everything went well, touch wood, be born. Just another hospital room; no sign of all the other joyous and terrible events which had taken place here. It would be completely unbearable, James supposed, if it did show that. Better a neutral, clinical space. This wasn't like a dungeon or a torture chamber, with fingernail scratches up the walls and dried vomit in the corners and bloodstains on the flagstones and the zing of screams still ringing back off the walls. Since the last whatever, glory or horror or in-between, a cleaner had come in and done a thorough job of airing the place. The floor was dry but had been given a good going-over with a mop. New sheets on the bed.

All through the process of approaching parenthood, the walls of the hospital rooms they'd visited had been decorated with large photographs of flowers, opening. The delivery room was no exception: on the far wall was a chrysanthemum with petals half magnolia and half blood-crimson, to the right was a bunch of violets against a white, Mediterranean-looking stucco background, and to the left was a single white lily, its stamen crispy with egg-yellow pollen. The only exception to the flower rule had been the midwives' clinic. The walls in *their* waiting room were covered with photographs of the babies they had delivered, each accompanied by a thank-you note. More than anything else during the nine months – nine and a half months – these flashy-fleshly images had given them some idea of what to expect, the beauty and ugliness, domesticity and transfiguration of it. In the moment, posing for those first few snaps, mothers neglected to cover themselves up, and fathers, inured by the last few hours or days to exposed, stretched, split skin, forgot to exclude these areas from the frame. There was nothing on display quite so bad as a prolapsed uterus, but everything short of that was present. In the midwives' waiting room James and Mary hadn't merely waited. Fascinated and appalled, they had wandered around reading excerpts from the cards out to one another – and, more rarely, pointing out a particularly gruesome detail in a photo.

'Why don't they know?' Mary asked. 'You're not taking any photos of me looking like that.'

She pointed to a woman beamingly holding her baby for the first time in her arms; at the bottom of the frame was her vagina, looking like fresh roadkill. 'Enough,' Mary said. 'I don't want to look any more. Imagine that happening to me.'

'They all look very happy,' he said. 'And they've all got babies at the end of it.'

'The end of it what? Who knows what they went through? Certainly they've lost all self-respect.'

'I don't think that's really an issue.'

Door five opened and shut. Doors six, seven and eight, too.

Without daring to open his eyes, or untense, in case it broke the spell of invisibility or whatever, the boy listened.

'Fuck-bollocks,' said Cropper. 'Bollocks, where the fuck did he go? He can't of –'

There was a loud slam as the huge guard kicked one of the other doors open.

'He must've bloody –' he said, then ran out – no doubt to search behind the other doors of this corridor.

The boy let himself relax, enjoying the feeling; escape, impossible escape!

He opened his eyes and looked around the cubicle, hoping to see how the guard had missed him. The door was shut, unlocked – but it did have a lock! Disbelieving, the boy flicked it shut. How had that repaired itself?

He stood up off the toilet seat, and as he did so he caught sight of the black-pen writing: it should have said HELLMOUTH. But it didn't. This time it had been changed to GETWELLSOON.

Although he knew the guard had gone, the boy was as quiet as he could be opening the door and looking around the Gents.

A second before he saw, he understood – or realized: he had hidden in cubicle five; he had just stepped out of cubicle four.

As his only proof was the fact he was standing where he was, the boy caught hold of the sides of the doorway. Nodding his head, as if stupid, he counted again: no mistake – in five, out of four.

He thought back to the moment just before the guard should have caught him. There had been no sensation of movement, but, sure as sure, he had moved – though, in truth, it had felt much more like staying in the same place while the whole hospital shifted a metre to one side. That wasn't possible, he knew, but if he *had* passed through the inch-thick wall of the cubicle, it had been without any sensation of doing so.

The boy had no explanation – unless it was something a bit like the hairy tunnel in reverse: he'd slid and slid, down and down, only to find himself on the same floor. Perhaps this worked horizontally as well as vertically, only without a storeroom, without a doorway. Either that or he had special powers which only became apparent in moments of extreme crisis. He was a secret superhero – secret even from himself; could be – could indeed be. The only way of confirming *that* was to get in danger again – not something he wanted to do.

Now he had proved it, the teleporting, at least to himself, the boy let go of the doorway and went to inspect the other cubicles one by one.

Just as he'd thought, each of them had black marker in the same place. The other words, from one to eight, were: AUTOPSYTURVY, COW-JUMPED, ENDGAMER, FOLKTAILS, DIA-BOLICK and BABYLONDON.

How odd; they were half one word and half another, added up to make a new nonsense or sense. He looked around but the rest of the graffiti was nowhere near so intriguing. 'A&E IOU nothing' 'Babel was here' 'Polard is rasist scum! Croppa burn in hell you fucka' 'Time wounds all healers' 'Soon!' 'White fucking barsteads seen' 'I bin a norty norty boy an now I am GLAD.' There was a crude drawing of a woman who looked very like the strange nurse the boy had seen when he fell out of the hairy cupboard. Perhaps, if he got a chance, it might be worth checking in one or more of Hospital's other toilets. He would wait here for a while, though. Until he was sure he could be sure.

What a difference one hour had made to Gemma's view of the world!

The Nurse Swallow who went back up to Trauma was in a very different frame of mind to the one who'd come down such a short while ago. How devastated were her hopes! How altered her chances with Steele! Before, she had believed these chances almost non-existent. Now, she had reason to suspect they were improved, but Steele – the object of her affection – was terribly diminished. A vivid image of the Rubber Nurse had formed in her jealous head – one which, somehow, was remarkably accurate.

As she slowly walked away from her locker, Gemma hardly cared whether she was late back on shift. What did it matter now? The man of her dreams had just been revealed to be as base and sordid as all the rest of them. And the only way to find out the truth of the matter would be to go and confront this Rubber Nurse in her 7th-floor lair.

It was difficult for Gemma to go back to work opposite Steele. She was worried that her turbulent emotions would interfere with her ability to do her job properly – a mistake, coming after her excellent nursing earlier in the day, would be terrible; and, of course, might prove fatal for an innocent patient. Gemma was as meticulously caring as she could be, talking calmly to each of the four cases – two RTAs, one shooting and one suspected stroke. So involved was she that she didn't notice they had cleared the whiteboard again, and was completely taken aback, flummoxed and flutteringly unprepared when Steele stepped aside to ask her, 'So, how about that coffee, then? Or now that you're not trapped with me down in the bowels of the building, are you going to cruelly refuse me?'

'And you're paying?' Gemma found herself saying, flirtatiously, presumptuously.

'To apologize,' Steele said, with a laugh, '*again.*' It was only then that Gemma noticed the Trauma team hadn't broken up quite as quickly as she'd thought it had – a few of its members were still within earshot, and two of these, talking to one another, strangely enough, were Sarah and Patricia. She remembered the Rubber Nurse, Steele's liaison.

'Maybe another time,' Gemma said, quietly.

Steele was obviously a bit taken aback by her abrupt volte-face but he wasn't going to make a big thing of it. 'Well,' he said, 'the offer's there.'

Gemma knew, even as he was saying this, that she might never be able to accept his invitation again – might find things out about him that would make her hate even the idea of sitting down with him for an intimate tête-à-tête. That might be true, but it didn't stop her bitterly regretting chickening out this time.

With a quick smile and a surprisingly comical shrug, Steele turned and walked towards the door. 'Anyone *does* want to come for coffee?' he announced.

It wouldn't take a genius to predict that Sarah Felt was first in line. 'I'm gasping,' she said, and Gemma could see she was – in more ways than one.

With some desperation, Gemma's gaze met Patricia's – and her false friend immediately understood her alarm. Instantly, she acted. 'Me, too,' she said.

Gemma saw Sarah smile, and thought what a practised hypocrite she was.

She watched as the three of them went off together, just as earlier she'd seen Sarah on her own take Steele away from her. All this had happened and the shift was still not yet halfway through!

The boy heard someone coming into the Gents, and feared that it was the Security Guard again.

Luckily, he was still inside one of the cubicles so hadn't been spotted.

Footsteps shuffled to the next one along, closed the door.

A man's voice started to talk, gruff and Scottish; the boy listened to it for a while, without understanding.

'I have tried colonic irrigation on a number of occasions, as relief for my particular problem – and what these doctors, none of them, seem to realize is that I have a very *particular* problem. My bowels are not run of the mill at all. They are not, and never were, run of the *anything*. Trot or canter, amble or saunter – no, they were a crawl, on hands and knees, doubled up in agony, praying to my maker, begging for mercy, cursing him for such solid handiwork. Grunt. The foolish man builds his house on sand, and you can go to work on an egg. But you try keeping a typing pool of thirty stroppy secretaries, many of them lesbian and some Catholic as well – you try keeping your eye on that ball with an impacted colon. It's easier for a camel to pass through the eye of a needle than for me to . . . in fact, no, it's probably about the same. And that's what it feels like, too – Heavens to Betsy. Anyway, colonic irrigation was, I found, like hard drugs: the effect – the high, if you will – is less and less every time. You find yourself down some very seedy back-alleys, and the company you keep is all obsessed with just the one thing. There's nothing more boring than listening to other people discuss their digestive symptoms . . . Especially when their symptoms are so much less interesting than one's own. I try to keep TIM in order – that's what I call him, TIM, The Inner Man. First rough him up with some roughage, then curry favour with a vindaloo. You see, TIM's a hard bastard. Stubborn as you like. I'd be tempted to say

TIM's SAS quality, but they're noted for being in and out before you've noticed. No, he's more of a covert agent – years embedded behind enemy lines, sending brief coded messages to the outside world. A grey man. But tough, I tell you – able to withstand any interrogation without cracking. Grunt. I've often thought there must be etymological similarities between "defect" and "defecate". The exchange on the bridge over the misty river at midnight. Tiny splashes. But to get him out, what could I offer the Soviet bloc in return? One of their number? Their number two? They wouldn't do a deal, though. To each according to his needs, from each according to his whatjumacallit. That's socialism. So, what do they need from me? Inside information. They're their own little world – sealed off from everywhere else. Hardly any traffic between them and us. Of course, one hears the grumbles of the dissidents. Sometimes there's even the feeling of a force building towards reform. In the end, though, a few petty expulsions is all we get. Tits for tats among the diplomats. A drop in the ocean compared to the great yearning for freedom that one senses among the lumpen-proletariat. They will move as one, if ever they do move – that is why we call them the masses. Workers of the world, ugnn, untie! And they, the workers, certainly will – their solidarity at this moment is unquestioned. They are holding the party line with utmost firmness. There will be perpetual revolution! Grunt. All opposition forces will be repressed. Grunt. Once stick your head above the parapet, once show a desire for the greater ocean of internationalism – bang, you're sent for years into a deep internal exile. The gulag. I am in the gulag. The gulag is in me.'

Creaklessly, the boy opened the cubicle door and slipped out.

As he left the Gents, the voice was still grumbling on.

Nurse Linda Loos resented the zombies (her nickname for the groaning, vomiting Oncology patients), although her own grandfather had been the original reason she became a nurse. He, Arthur Root, had been bedridden for years; and when, as a shy nine-year-old, Linda had played at tending to him, bringing him cups of water (tea) and plates of Lego (biscuits), he had complimented her and told her, quite sincerely – he no longer made jokes – what a wonderful little nurse she was; that had been her clue: she *was* a nurse, a nurse already, wouldn't have to waste years of her life pretending to become one. Like most children, nothing had disgusted nine-year-old Linda more than the idea of years of schooling, and nothing excited her like instant achievement.

But, since qualifying, three years of night-shifts had done their damage: Nurse Linda Loos still quite liked helping people who she liked, even zombies, but she truly hated helping people she hated – and she hated Janet Dammers.

'Hell-o-oo,' said Janet. 'You-o-oo,' said Janet. 'Young lady,' said Janet. It was a rare moment when Janet said nothing. Right now she was saying, 'Could you get one of those nigger boys who are always around to fetch me a cup of tea? Make themselves useful, for a change.'

Nurse Loos assumed that Janet meant one of the porters. She herself had a black boyfriend, but she absolutely banned him from visiting her on the ward – or anywhere inside the building. The less the patients knew about her, the better. She had found out the hard way how they used any information they picked up. It was all too easy to imagine what Janet Dammers would say about Edward.

'I can get you another glass of water,' Nurse Loos said, 'but I'm afraid it's a little late for tea. You had some earlier, didn't you?'

'But I always have tea at this time. You know that. It quite unsettles me when I don't. At the home . . .'

Everything was better at the home – and there were no nigger boys there to spoil the view.

Nurse Loos had already reminded Janet Dammers, several times, that things were different here than in the home – of necessity. For a favourite patient, she would have managed something – a Coca-Cola, a contraband chocolate biscuit. But Janet would get the bare minimum, and slowly.

Once she'd made up her mind, it was hard for Nurse Loos to remember a time when she hadn't hated someone. The decision was usually made before they opened their mouths – she often took against people when they were post-operatively unconscious.

'Oh, well,' said Janet. Then, as if this had been a concession, she said, 'I hope tonight you'll be able to do something about Mr Froth's clicking jaw. I don't so much mind his snoring, that I can take, but it's that abominable clicking coming only ever so often. I'm sure it can't help him very much, either.'

Mr Froth, bowel cancer, heavily sedated, curtains drawn, was already fast asleep, and clicking loudly.

'Why don't you just try to settle down?'

'How can I? It keeps me awake – don't you understand?'

Janet Dammers would die, and Nurse Loos would

be glad – both of them knew this, both had decided to take this as a starting point.

'We will see what we can do about moving your bed, tomorrow.'

'You said that yesterday, and the day before, and –'

Nurse Linda Loos was soon out of range of Mrs Dammers' irascible memory.

Othniel was on an easy patient – Mr Proudfoot, an old man who had just tried to escape from Hospital.

The Security Guard in A&E, Shears, had caught him just as he was about to reach the exit.

There was no need for restraint, Mr Proudfoot wasn't a violent sort. Plus, he only had one real leg; the other was prosthetic.

Sister Agnes Day had called for a porter to wheel him back to Geriatrics.

As they took the lift, the old man muttered something about feet, about one of his feet.

Othniel didn't exactly ignore Mr Proudfoot, but he knew him listening wasn't crucial to what was being said, and so he allowed his concentration to focus elsewhere: the coming ceremony.

He was, he realized, far more nervous than usual.

Othniel respected Pierre Estime, Head Voodoo Man. He was able to call some powerful spirits down to ride him. Back home in Haiti his speciality had been the Iguana lizard, which he had once seen on a TV documentary made by the British Broadcasting Company. It had seemed a fearsome demigod to him, a little like David Attenborough, and well worth importing secretly into the festivities of his local voodoo branch. However, since starting work at Hospital five years ago, Pierre had encountered a monster of even more fearsome aspect – this was Mr Kissa, the health service manager in charge of the porters.

Kissa was the angry wrathful minor god who sat square in the power constellation of their small universe. Hated and feared, feared and hated, Kissa was the deity of the shift pattern, the Lord of Bank Holidays, the Archdemon of Sick Pay, the Magus of Time and a Half.

But even he wasn't the real trouble. No, what worried Othniel this evening was not Pierre Estime but Cyrille Delira. Cyrille Delira was Number Two – and quite incapable of hiding his ambition to become Head Voodoo Man asap.

He was a reckless man, cowardly but given to unpredictable moments of violence. Most often these came when he had someone at his mercy. In this way, he tried to cover his cowardice. Othniel knew for certain that Cyrille Delira had been cruel to patients, had stolen watches and jewellery from them. There were quieter, darker rumours: that Cyrille liked to visit the Intensive Care Unit at night, with a scalpel.

The lift arrived on the 22nd floor.

As Othniel wheeled Mr Proudfoot onto the ward, he heard the old man talking about the open road.

'And what have we here?' said Nurse Martha Castle, looking up from her desk.

It wasn't that Mary hadn't known anything this painful before – she just hadn't known anything this *incessantly* painful. Of course, there were peaks and troughs, waves and between-waves; she was doing her best to treat the contractions as a navigable sea. But she just needed a break, to be able to gather her strength together for the final agony; just half an hour would do, or fifteen minutes, even – fifteen good minutes. James was there, and he was doing his best, but really it was irrelevant. *Concentrate on your breathing*, he'd say, or, *You're doing really well.* She was afraid of her lack of strength – that was what terrified her most, the possibility that, when it came to it, and despite all the assurances of midwives and other women, she'd be the woman who *failed* – who failed to find those great secret reserves of strength she didn't even know she – oh no! – had.

'Where's the epidural?' she asked, for the fifth time. 'Is the anaesthetist coming?'

'He's on his way,' her husband said.

'Liar,' she said. 'You don't want me to have it.'

'If you want to have it, you can have it.'

'Before then,' midwife Honey Hopeful interjected, 'I think I'd like to have the doctor come in and take another look at you – see how dilated you are.'

'No,' she said, 'I want the epidural. I can't take any more. I'm really tired and I need help.'

The boy peeked out into the corridor; no Security Guard in sight, no footsteps to be heard. It was probably safest for him to stay inside one of the cubicles, but he was impatient – the tree was growing; he didn't have all that much time.

So, keeping his feet quiet on the shiny lino, he ran in the opposite direction to the lift lobby.

His logic was simple: better get off this floor as soon as possible, not using the lifts. The length of the corridor kept him exposed to sight for a long time, but eventually he made it to the fire exit.

Here, he took the staircase down – intending to keep going until he reached ground level.

Only five floors to go.

*

Gemma was thinking about going to have another cigarette when Sir Reginald came out of his office, strolled down the corridor and stood taking in, as he would have said, 'the state of play'. Satisfied everything was under control, Sir Reginald knitted his fingers together and stretched them above his head, uncricking his spine. Then he turned round with a grin to see if anyone else, like him, was at a loose end. 'Where's everyone gone?' he asked.

Gemma felt a little overawed but was quite equal to saying, 'Most of them are having coffee.'

'That might not be a bad idea,' said Sir Reginald. 'I don't think we're going to have much time later.'

Gemma took this statement very seriously: within Trauma, Sir Reginald was commonly credited with almost supernatural powers of prediction – at least as far as lulls and rushes of the seriously sick and horribly injured were concerned. 'Really?' Gemma said, as if Sir Reginald had been stating a fact.

'I think so,' he replied.

He stood there looking at her, and she, too, took him in as if for the first time.

Sir Reginald Saint-Hellier was a squat, energetic man in his mid fifties. He was mostly bald but two flukes of grey hair reached out towards one another from just above his ears – like the twisting vapour trails left by a taking-off fighter jet. Together, they had the effect of making Sir Reginald look as if he had a pair of grey fleecy horns. His teeth were bulbous, like over-inflated balloons, balloons about to burst. Although he might have been thin on top, he made up for this by being very, very hairy everywhere else. His arms were greyly forested all the way from the biceps to the knuckles. Hairs sprouted from his nostrils and both his ears, leaving Gemma (and many others) to wonder why he didn't trim them – they were so disfiguring, and he paid such close attention to detail elsewhere in his life. Perhaps it was because Sir Reginald was a widower. His wife, Heather, a respected consultant paediatrician, had died tragically a couple of years before, after being knocked over by a speeding ambulance (driven by Bill "Zapper" Billson). She had been on her usual route to work at Hospital when the accident happened. In a further irony, she was brought to Trauma and Sir Reginald happened to be on shift that day. He refused to step down, and succeeded quite brilliantly in saving her life. She had been making a good recovery, but a few days later she succumbed to a nosocomial illness. Sir Reginald was said to have been inconsolable. However, he took only a week's compassionate leave. 'Nothing for me at home,' he had said. 'Might as well be doing some good.' This, Gemma suspected, was when the nostril hairs had made their debut.

And now Gemma found herself heading down to the canteen with the great man himself. 'How are you finding things?' he asked. 'Are you happy here?'

'Very happy,' she replied, glad for once to be talking about work rather than her affections. 'It's everything I hoped it would be – and more.'

'More, eh?' said Sir Reginald, in a way that, from anyone else, Gemma would have taken as flirtatious. 'So you've managed to find somewhere to lay your head, all that sort of malarkey.'

'Not yet,' Gemma said. 'I'm in the nurses' dorm at the moment. But in a year or two I hope I'll have saved enough money to buy a flat.'

Sir Reginald couldn't possibly be interested in this, Gemma thought. But it seemed that he was – very much so. 'It is difficult getting started,' he replied. 'I remember it myself. But something unexpected always has a habit of turning up.'

Gemma agreed, a little unnerved to be going into details of her domestic arrangements with such a senior member of Hospital staff. She consoled herself with the idea that he almost certainly found time for a 'cosy little chat' with everyone, a month after they joined the team.

Whilst they were waiting for the lift, Sir Reginald got into conversation with another Hospital bigwig, Henderson MacVanish, Chief Obstetrical Consultant. Gemma was introduced, much to her embarrassment, as 'a bright and coming star' in emergency medicine. But then the two men began to discuss something regarding 'the extraordinary meeting' (those were the only words polite Gemma caught) they were due to attend later on that evening.

The lift arrived and the two men stepped inside. This, Gemma thought, might be a good time to escape. She turned to make her excuses to Sir Reginald but he put his hand out and gently grabbed her upper arm. 'Not quite so fast, my dear,' he said, pulling her after them. The young nurse stood there, blushing and feeling the after-impression of Sir Reginald's strong fingers.

She had only a moment or two to wonder, as Sir Reginald pushed the button for the 15th floor, whether he might be a dirty old lech. He had called her 'my dear' before, but never . . .

Their little confab over, Henderson MacVanish smiled at her and said something she didn't quite catch. He spoke with quite a posh Scottish accent, and a burr which fuzzed over his words. On the next floor down, he got out. 'I'll continue spreading the good word,' he said to Sir Reginald, then walked off into the Burns Unit. Gemma didn't have time to wonder what business a gynaecologist had in such a place – or what he'd been doing up in Trauma.

'So,' Sir Reginald said, 'how are you bedding down, overall? Everything alright?'

'Oh, fine,' said Gemma, annoyed with herself for having nothing more interesting to say.

'Good-oh,' he said, back to the familiar but not overfamiliar old Sir Reginald. 'I haven't moved job for a very old donkey's years. Seem to have been in this place since it was built – 1968, if you were wondering. The Trauma team can seem a very exclusive private members' club when you first join. I hope they've made you feel . . .'

The lift stopped at one or two floors on the way down, and people got in and out; Gemma hardly noticed them.

For the last few floors, they were alone, but Gemma was relieved to find that Sir Reginald kept the talk strictly professional.

WPC Melanie Angel and PC Peter Dixon strode into A&E. Both had been here before, many times – some nights, what with the assaults on staff and the general lunacy, they never seemed to get away. But this evening, for a change, they were visiting another part of Hospital: Intensive Care. WPC Angel, who had never been there, was looking forward to it; PC Dixon, who had been there often, was deeply anxious.

'So, anyway,' WPC Angel continued, 'I'll be at the DIY shop this weekend, picking out colours.'

They walked up to the reception desk – out of politeness as much as anything.

'Evening, Agnes,' said WPC Angel. 'How's it been?'

'Oh, the usual,' she said, light glinting off her glass eye.

'That bad?' said PC Dixon.

'No broken bones – no bones broken in here. Quite a bit of shouting. Death threats, etc.'

She looked around to where Spanner and Case had been told to wait. They were gone.

'How very dull,' said WPC Angel, not noticing the surprised look on Sister Agnes's face. 'But we're not here for that.'

'Not for the moment, anyway,' said PC Dixon.

'Unidentified male up in ICU,' WPC Angel said.

'Well, see you later,' said Sister Day, peering around the room.

'No doubt,' said WPC Angel.

They walked out of A&E and down a corridor of consulting rooms until they came to the lift lobby. As always happened, the space they passed through went defiantly quiet – a few characters avoided eye-contact, a few more made a point of making it. There was the odd familiar face, no-one to worry about.

As WPC Angel pressed the call button, PC Dixon tried to work out the odds of Nurse Angela Dixon, his ex-wife, being on shift in the ICU. On average, she worked about three nights in seven. He hadn't seen her in eighteen months.

'You've been there before, haven't you?' asked WPC Angel, crashing into his thoughts.

'A few times,' he replied. He knew he should probably say something in advance: all the nurses wore name-badges, and if Melanie noticed they both had Dixon as a surname, she was bound to mention it. But he didn't know how to bring up the subject. He and WPC Angel had only been partnered up for a couple of months, and despite several long nights on patrol together they'd yet to have a heart-to-heart of any sort. Then he remembered he was still wearing his wedding ring.

The lift arrived.

'Hello,' said a high voice. 'What's your name?'

It was a boy, about the boy's age, wearing a red baseball cap, a white dressing-gown and blue flip-flops. He had been standing at the window, staring out across the city.

'I said, what's your name?'

'What's yours?'

'You can call me what you like. Other people call me Chemo-boy, Chemo or just Mo, for short.'

The boy hated to copy, but saw no choice. 'You can call me what you like, too.'

Chemo took this as a serious responsibility. He looked the boy over, as if his choice of name would be adopted by the rest of the world. Then he became distracted. 'You aren't ill. Why are you here?'

The boy was pleased about this; he didn't want to have to mention the appletree growing – and that wasn't an illness. 'They brought me by mistake,' he said. 'I went in a helicopter. I'm going home.'

Seemingly having forgotten all about names, Chemo took off his cap. 'I've got no hair,' he said. 'I've got leukaemia.' He said these two things as if there'd been an exchange, and he'd swapped one for the other. 'If you really want to know, I've got several neuroblastomas. They're the worst kind of leukaemia. If the chemotherapy doesn't work, I've got three to six months. That means two months, really. You're not awake for the last bit. Do you want to come and see where I live? I've got chocolates which I'm not supposed to have but they're hidden.'

The boy was a little overwhelmed by this contradictory list of all Chemo's possessions. Chocolate might not be ice-cream or milk but at least it was something.

Chemo went across to the window and picked up a blobby cardboard bowl. 'It's for when I puke,' he said, and mimed splattering it full. 'I puke all the time. Do you like girls? It's mostly boys here.'

He pushed through the fire door, as if the boy had agreed to follow him towards chocolate.

James had been right. Self-respect was no longer an issue. Five or six men and women had now had their fingers inside her stretching vagina – she lost count around four. Also, four centimetres dilated, five, then five and a half, then five and a half again, had it stopped?, then seven, and the midwife with the ridiculous name, Honey Hopeful, saying she'd have the first baby by midnight and the second just after. Why did they say things like that? It didn't help. They were all so fucking stupid, and stupefied – they'd seen this so often, day after day, that they could no longer take anyone's pain seriously.

Honey Hopeful leaned in to Mary. 'I just hear about the anaesthetist. He right now starting another operation. An emergency, you see. Bad traffic accident, outside. He be at least a half-hour coming, now. Y'understand, lady?'

Mary was intending to have a good sob at this, but the next contraction overtook her. She leaned her sweaty head forwards against the metal bedhead and thought about how much she didn't want this to be happening. She was at the very centre of something but, because it kept going away, her pain, the focus of it, she also felt peripheral to it. She had divided herself from herself, and was afraid that to bring their babies to birth required a unity: all she was and had to give.

When the contraction was over, she leaned back and tried to assess her remaining strength – she didn't even have the strength to do this; the possibility that she was already empty was too much of a terror to allow. I'm a victim, she thought, I'm doing this to myself, but I'm the one that's suffering. No-one else in the room is suffering, so they don't have the *right* to say anything about what suffering is. They say you forget the pain, but I won't forget. *This too will pass*, she thought, *this too will pass.*

Spanner and Case were approaching the pharmacy, conspicuously.

'You sure you got it?' Case asked again.

'All in here,' Spanner said, and tapped his forehead with something amounting to violence.

'And we can trust him?'

'Shut it,' said Spanner. He was more than confident that the information provided them by Cyrille Delira, a hospital porter, was correct.

They had been dealing with one another for a couple of months now – ever since Cyrille had picked Nikki up from her usual spot and, as a bonus, asked if she knew where he could score.

Nikki hadn't been quite so fucked up, then – thin, but not the stick insect she'd become. The porter, who was Haitian, wanted a blonde. It was late. The light wasn't too good. Nikki brought him back to the squat which Spanner and Case were slowly burning to the ground.

Since then, Cyrille Delira had become a regular customer of Spanner's. Nikki, after that first time, he'd shown no further interest in.

During droughts, Cyrille was able to get hold of small amounts of methadone. In return for these, he was gradually working his way through every exotic drug and drug combination Spanner and Case could get hold of.

But he refused to steal for them directly from the pharmacy. If he was caught, he would lose his job – he seemed to care more about this than was natural. Spanner had never figured out why. A lot of other Haitians worked there – perhaps that was the reason. Brotherhood.

The pharmacy was run by Asians, said Cyrille. They were the only ones to deal directly with Hospital supplies.

Eventually, Cyrille got hooked on something, came around more and more often. And, one long night, Spanner – who already knew the layout of Hospital as well as its architect – had made him promise to find out the combination to the pharmacy.

'They watch it, man,' said Cyrille. 'The Pakis pay off the Security Guards. They watch like hawks.' He made his eyes bulge.

'I'm invisible,' said Spanner. 'Whenever I fucking feel like it.'

And he wasn't far wrong.

After losing track of the boy, Cropper had conducted a rapid search of the floor then returned to the security offices.

'I want you to look for a boy,' he told Pollard, who was lounging back on a swing-chair in front of a large bank of black-and-white screens. The control desk, for choosing camera angles, zooming in and out, recording and erasing, was much like that in a television studio.

Cropper described the boy. 'Forget everything else.'

'There're lots of boys,' Pollard said. 'And we've got to get ready . . .'

'You're staying here,' said Cropper. 'No argument.'

Pollard didn't even try.

Nikki Froth never wanted to see either of them again, although she would miss Case more than Spanner. When he hadn't been beating her up, on Spanner's orders, he had been very kind.

The consulting room downstairs had been required, she guessed for more consulting, so they had hustled her out of there and into the lifts.

After that, she got a bit confused. They had gone up, of that she was sure – up and up for quite a while. And now she was in a ward with lots of young girls.

The walls were pink, and the girls were only five or six years younger than her, but they knew *nothing*. They were here to have their tonsils out or because they'd lost too much weight. Their innocence made Nikki feel like crying.

Many things made Nikki feel like crying; very few actually made her cry.

The walls were too pink.

'Hello, there,' said the social worker, Helen Mugabe.

Nikki jumped – she hadn't seen her coming.

'Would you mind if I sat down?' asked Helen Mugabe.

'No,' said Nikki, who hadn't even noticed the chair beside her bed.

Asking to sit down – this one hadn't been in the job very long. Nikki was expert at many things, instant social-worker assessment not the least.

Helen Mugabe, by Nikki's guess, was about twenty-six; plump. Her face was brown with fat freckles. She wore reassuringly bright prints, as if happy fabrics could help make miserable people happy. In this, she wasn't wrong: Nikki knew she would feel better talking to her than to some whiny-weasly white man in a leather jacket and DMs.

'Why don't you tell me about it?' asked Helen.

And Nikki began to give her the edited version: she would admit to faking an overdose, but only so she could get away from her pimp; she would mention Spanner and Case, but that was all.

The lift arrived on the 21st floor.

'It's this way,' said PC Dixon, without having to check the arrowed signs on the wall.

'Know your way around, don't you?' said WPC Angel.

Unable to speak, PC Dixon walked on.

The lift ride had been nightmarish. With every increment in the red numbers above the door, he had felt dizzier and dizzier. It didn't help that he was slightly phobic of lifts – always thinking of the huge column of emptiness directly beneath his feet.

As they walked along the corridor, PC Dixon told himself that Angela wasn't the sort of woman to make a scene. Then he remembered that she was *exactly* the sort of woman to make a scene. That was one of the many reasons they'd divorced. If he was lucky, she wouldn't be there. And even if she was, he might get in and out of this horrible situation without WPC Angel's admiration of him being completely destroyed – her admiration meant quite a lot to him, and might come to mean a great deal more.

'Hello, Peter,' said Angela's voice, and at first he wasn't sure whether it was in his head or not.

'Hello,' he said, turning round.

His ex-wife had just come out of a side room, carrying a couple of transparent bags. PC Dixon knew enough to recognize them as saline drips.

'Oh,' said WPC Angel, 'so you two know one another?'

'Only too well,' said Nurse Dixon.

WPC Angel took this as slightly flirtatious. Then she saw the name-badge.

'He didn't tell me he had a sister.'

'He doesn't,' said Nurse Dixon. 'And I'm not his cousin, either. Keep guessing.'

'Angela was my wife,' said PC Dixon.

'Only for six months,' said Angela.

'We had been going out for four years, before that,' said PC Dixon.

'A fact I've done my best to forget,' Angela said, and smiled at WPC Angel. 'Are you his new partner?'

'Yes,' she said. 'We've come to do the unknown man. Are you dealing with him?'

'This-a-way,' said Angela. 'But you won't get much out of him. As a witty conversationalist, he's about as entertaining as Peter.'

They followed her down the corridor.

Dixon was hoping the worst might be over, but then Angela added: 'He's a *lot* more lively in bed, though.'

WPC Angel gave him a look – too fast for him to know what it meant, for him to estimate what damage had already been done.

*

'That's Orlando,' Chemo said, 'he'll live but with impaired liver function.'

Orlando was already asleep, curled up into a ball; his bed, the first bed along.

'This is Thomas. Say hello, Thomas.'

'Sister is coming back,' said Thomas. 'You'll get caught. You shouldn't – '

'Thomas is eight and he's going to die,' said Chemo. 'So I don't know why he's so afraid of *Sister*.' This last comment was for Thomas, who stuck his tongue out and said, 'I have a fifty-fifty chance.'

'A fifty-fifty chance of being a mong,' whispered Chemo. 'And a hundred per cent chance of being a whiny little boo-hoo.'

The boy laughed.

Thomas hissed out, 'You're so stupid, and you think you're so clever.'

'Mong,' said Chemo, matter-of-factly. 'Caroline isn't very well,' he whispered again, but in a different tone. 'I said goodbye to her yesterday, and the day before. Maybe I'll say goodbye tomorrow. It gets a little boring but she likes it.'

A girl with bright red hair lay flat on her back, only her chest moving.

'It's a wig,' said Chemo. 'She even sleeps in it. I liked her. She wasn't a *mong*!' And he said the word very loud, over his shoulder.

'Does she have what you have?' the boy asked.

'No, what I have is much worse, but they caught me early and caught her late. I think she knew. She's brave and keeps quiet. Her parents are getting divorced. Are your parents divorced?'

'No,' said the boy. At least he knew *that* for definite.

'If you get ill, they'll probably get divorced. It won't be your fault – it wasn't Caroline's fault, or mine – but it happens. That's Olu, who'll be okay because he had a bone-marrow transplant from his little sister. She's never going to let him forget that.'

'What?' asked another boy. 'Did you say "Sister"? I need some water.'

'Not that sister, stupid. This is Ahmed. He gets everything wrong. And his mother smells.'

'She does not,' Ahmed said.

'She smells of –'

'Don't say it,' said Ahmed.

'She smells of –'

Ahmed cupped his hands over his ears.

'And this,' said Chemo, 'is my bed. The one next door is empty. Lenny was in there until yesterday, and before that it was Kate and before her it was Montague – what a name.'

'Did they all die?'

'Pee!' shouted Chemo, who'd spotted that Ahmed's hands had dropped. 'She smells of pee!'

'I'll get you,' said Ahmed.

'Not with those tubes stuck in you,' said Chemo. 'Lie back and enjoy it.'

'Did Montague die?'

'Montague, no. Not here, anyway. I think he went to a private hospital.'

'Was he going to die?'

'No-one dies in a private hospital. Because if you're going to die, they turf you back here.' For some reason, this made Chemo laugh.

The boy, thinking about Montague, tried to join in.

'Kate died, loudly, all night – I didn't hardly sleep at all. Lenny was in remission. I liked Lenny. He gave me the chocolate.'

Chemo bent down under the bed, tugged at something, then came back up with half a bar of Dairy Milk. 'You could have that bed,' he said. 'If you wanted to stay tonight. It can be a bit noisy in here, with all the crying and groaning. My dad brought me these –' He was pointing to some big padded ear-protectors. 'They're what fighter pilots wear. Try them on.'

The boy did, and saw Chemo saying something. No words were audible. He made a guess – half lip-read, half getting into Chemo's world. 'Don't call me a mong.'

Chemo laughed hard, holding on to the bars at the top of the bed – as if, otherwise, he'd fall off.

'You're funny,' he said. 'Eat some chocolate. It makes me puke and then I have to hide the puke so Sister doesn't know I've been eating chocolate.'

The boy was just unwrapping the brown bar when a hiss passed along the ward: Sister.

'Really?'

'She's coming,' said someone.

'Under that bed,' Chemo ordered. 'She'll never look for you there.'

The boy took the chocolate with him but felt too scared to eat it – the crinkling of the tinfoil might give him away.

Someone had told James Walker that he would be able to tell when his wife was about to give birth because she would sound like a goat being tortured. He wasn't sure if this was either a good thing to have heard, or strictly accurate. Right now, Mary sounded like lots of animals being tortured, sometimes one after another – squealing rats, honking asses, jabbering cheetahs, knocking woodpeckers – and then sometimes all at the same time. Pain had made her capable of cacophony. And James wanted to leave the room. What stopped him, apart from love and other duties, was the thought that he himself *could* leave and Mary couldn't; the unfairness of it, the impossibility of sharing, made him angry enough to stay. In between contractions, Mary stopped being the jungle at whoop and was capable of speech – usually capable of demanding they bring the anaesthetist to her so she could have the epidural.

She no longer wanted anything to do with the bottom half of her body; it had betrayed her. There was no way, after this, they would be able to continue their marriage (Mary's top half and bottom half, not Mary and James – though probably them as well) – no way their cohabitation could carry on unchanged.

The balance of power, Mary sensed this rather than articulated it – the power-balance within her had shifted. She was, she felt, stronger than she had ever known herself to be, yet she wasn't nearly strong enough. And the distance by which she fell short was impossible to judge, as part failure was indistinguishable from total. How could she ever go back to using her legs for walking, her cunt for fucking, her anus for shitting? She had been reduced to a state of such abject stupidity that she needed someone to remind her to breathe. Over the past few months, they had done all the middle-class things – made a birth-plan, discussed creating a positive ambience, chosen music, practised hypnotherapeutic breathing, drunk raspberry leaf tea (even him). It was all shit. There were a couple of things inside her that were fighting to get out and, if necessary, they would kill all three of them in the attempt. And the things didn't even have a motive, just a load of hormones and other chemicals telling their muscles to tense, relax, tense, relax. In any other circumstances, the panic she was feeling would have had her running away; some of her movements, stupidly, were her trying to get out of her body. But as the labour got more and more intense she realized there was no way of separating her from her body – that was a comforting fiction (lie); *her* didn't exist, only *body* did; body and babies and babies not leaving body and body trying to get rid of babies so as to have babies and babies helping body so that body could have babies even though body *had* babies already, only in a way that was both greater and nothing at all. Body, in doing this, was the most intelligent thing in the world and the most stupid – simultaneously and also indivisibly. Body didn't want to learn what it was having to learn – it was abhorrent that it was capable of these inner movements. She felt as if she were all bowel, had never been anything other than a great big shitter – the toothpaste-squeezy peristaltic tube down which metaphysics entered the world. An image came to her: the first baby staying still as the fixed point in the universe and her trying, by pushing and squeezing and screaming and yes okay shut up *breathing*, to move herself away from the baby. Couldn't she keep them? She felt nostalgia for the period of her life that this experience was making her hate. Those nine months, though, had *never* happened, and were all that had ever happened. Body knew that she had always been all bowel and that bowel had always been shitting. Bowel shat or tried to shit first baby, and yet baby wasn't of shit, right now baby *felt* to her like shit, right now baby *was* shit, but baby born was baby changed, born baby changed everything, born baby made the world unshit, turning bowel into mother and breathe-breathe-breather into father.

Spasm of this moment, called contraction but really squeeze of all the universe and more besides.

James told her to pant for a bit; she hated him so much she tried.

As they came out of the lift and walked along the corridor to the canteen, Gemma tried to assure him – this man she so wanted to look up to and trust – that she'd found everyone very friendly. She did not mention Mr John Steele's initial coldness, or the recent sub-zero frostiness of Sarah Felt.

'Good good,' said Sir Reginald.

They entered the cafeteria. It was just before ten, and the room was almost empty. Twilight-shifters only.

Gemma, as discreetly as she could, looked round for Steele and the others.

She spotted the three of them immediately, sitting right beside the till at a table with six seats. Her relief was immense – surely she and Sir Reginald would *have* to join them; there would be no embarrassing and prolonged tête-à-tête.

They got to the coffee machine without having to queue. Sir Reginald didn't seem to have caught sight of the others.

Almost before she knew it, they had paid – or rather, Sir Reginald had paid – and they were looking for somewhere to sit down.

'Oh, hello there,' said Sir Reginald to Steele, Sarah and Patricia.

Gemma's heart lifted as Steele's eggshell-blue eyes met hers, in obvious welcome.

'Coming to join us?' said Sarah.

'No, no,' said Sir Reginald, quickly. 'I need to corner this one on her own for a while – find out what's *really* going on with my newest member of staff.'

Sarah wasn't going to issue the invitation a second time; the first had probably only been to keep in with Sir Reginald.

'Oh, come on,' said Steele. 'Can't you do that later? It's not often we all get a chance to sit down together.'

Gemma was astonished by this, but Sir Reginald was touching her arm again. 'This has to be *absolutely* private,' he said, and gave Patricia a wink.

'Oh yes,' Patricia said, 'I understand.'

Gemma was able to see nothing more – neither Sarah's pleasure nor Steele's annoyance – as Sir Reginald guided her towards the far corner. None of the tables here were occupied; they really *would* be quite on their own.

'We know very little,' said Nurse Dixon, addressing herself exclusively to WPC Angel, who took notes in a small black pad; PC Dixon did likewise. 'As I said, he hasn't spoken a word. That's probably because he has a very severe subarachnoid haemorrhage. Not that *some* men need that excuse for clamming up. He was brought in around eight this evening.' She explained the circumstances in which he was found. 'Keeping fit. Unlike some.'

They stood at the foot of the unknown man's bed. He was right next to a wall of floor-to-ceiling safety glass – and it was only through reflections in this that PC Dixon was able to snatch glances at his ex-wife. She looked slightly older, definitely harder. 'I'll give you his effects. They're bagged up in the office. I expect some of you lot took witness statements from those who selflessly went to his aid. It's a nice park. I used to go for lots of lovely walks there – on my own.'

'Any identifying features? Birthmarks?'

'I know what an identifying feature is, darling,' said Nurse Dixon. 'I've seen enough of them – some more sightly than others.'

Of all the vicious things his ex-wife had said, PC Dixon particularly resented this reference to the scorch marks all down his back. Aged five, he had pulled a kettle off the hob – and spent three months in the local hospital having his dressings changed. He was still very self-conscious about the long bumpy red mark that had been left behind by the steaming water.

'Leave it out, Angela,' he said. 'We're just trying to do our jobs, here.'

'And to think we met in circumstances not dissimilar to these,' said Nurse Dixon, speaking poshly. It was her impression of PC Dixon's mother, who, she thought, had airs. 'I was but a mere girl of twenty-one.'

'So, I can put down that he has no identifying marks,' said WPC Angel, now almost as embarrassed as her colleague.

'He seduced me,' said Angela. 'I love a man in uniform.'

'That's enough,' snapped PC Dixon.

'I thought he'd be strong, brave, trustworthy . . .'

'If we could just see those effects,' said WPC Angel. 'Then we can be on our way.'

'Don't let him take you in,' said Nurse Dixon, reaching over to touch WPC Angel on the sleeve. 'He can be very convincing when he wants to. But, in reality, he's a worm – a nasty little worm.'

Turning on her heel, she marched off towards the nurses' station. WPC Angel followed her, with PC Dixon tagging along behind.

'This is it,' said Nurse Dixon. 'Not much.'

She handed the baggie over to WPC Angel, who put it down on the desk and began to make a list of the contents: one white handkerchief, clean; one set of keys – probably house keys; one photograph of a girl.

Melanie looked closely at the face behind the laminated plastic. A dedicated dad, he must be, to carry this round with him all the time. The girl looked, what? Eleven? Perhaps a bit younger. This would definitely help identify him, eventually.

'He's going to die, you know,' said Nurse Dixon, interrupting WPC Angel's thoughts. 'He'll make it into tomorrow but he'll be very lucky to survive beyond that. One in a hundred chance. It's not murder – no-one bashed him on the head or anything. You'll just have to wait until someone phones up. Or advertise, if you can be bothered.'

'We know how to deal with missing persons,' said WPC Angel.

'This is more of a found person, wouldn't you say?' Nurse Dixon replied.

'I don't think there's anything else we need, is there?' said PC Dixon.

'Okay, you go off and make the streets safer for all of us. Maybe you can find a prostitute and try to save her from her life of sin, save her by shagging her – that's always a good one, isn't it? Well, Peter?'

'Come on,' said PC Dixon, utterly humiliated.

'Thanks for your help,' said WPC Angel.

They turned to go.

'Remember what I said,' Nurse Dixon called after them. 'Don't believe anything he says – he's a lying little shit.'

*

The keypad was there, the drugs were just behind it, but the combination – somehow, Spanner's mind had managed to misplace that. Eights were involved. Maybe two of them.

'You said you knew.'

'Shut it.'

'You said –'

'I know what I fucking said. Look, would you fucking keep it quiet, you twat. I'm trying to think.'

Something was bothering Spanner. He knew he hadn't written the combination down, but he also knew that he had taken measures to avoid forgetting it.

'Fuck,' he said. 'I'll just call the bastard.'

It was only when he pulled the mobile from his pocket that he remembered – the number was there, listed under Cyrille's name. Actually, listed under CYR2: Spanner was careful to be cryptic.

'No need,' he said.

8268.

He tapped the number in and, with a loud beep, the door unlocked itself.

'Welcome to Heaven,' said Spanner, then stepped aside to let Case go in first.

'Any living relatives?' asked Helen Mugabe.

They were doing forms.

'Look,' said Nikki, not wanting to be too difficult, wanting still to appear *nice*, 'are you gonna help me or not?'

'I need to know this, Nikki,' said Helen. 'I know these are a bit boring, but the sooner we're through them, the sooner we can sort you out somewhere to stay.'

'My grandad's all.'

'You mean your parents aren't alive?'

'Still see my grandad.'

'And you don't see your parents?'

'They're dead.'

'We will find out if they're not,' said Helen, gently.

'They might as well be dead, you get me?'

'Where do they live?'

'Not round here.'

'Yes, but where *do* they live?'

'Dunno. My grandad lives round here. I think he's in a home for the elderly.'

Helen breathed in and out; strongly perfumed.

'So, in conclusion, you don't have anywhere else you could stay?'

Nikki was aware that the girls in the next couple of beds were listening to every word. They would tell all their friends up and down the ward about her: a drug-addict prostitute, a real drug-addict prostitute.

'I need to get into a safehouse. Can you get me into a safehouse? That's all I need to know. Cos if you can't, I'm walking out of here – I'm walking right out of here, now. Can you fix it?'

Helen could see the girl's fear. She wanted to give her a definite answer but couldn't; chances were, Nikki would end up in a B&B.

'Nikki, I'm going to do my very best for you, I promise.'

'So you mean no?'

'So I mean I'll try.'

Nikki threw back the sheets.

'You can stay here tonight,' said Helen. 'I've already sorted that. It's better than nothing, isn't it?'

Nikki stood up. 'I'm going.'

*

Sister stopped short of Chemo's bed and began talking gently to another young patient. The boy could see only her ankles, which were sturdy. Her voice sounded middle aged. It must be difficult, thought the boy, talking all the time to children who are going to die. This was the second time he'd hidden under a bed. Was looking after children any worse than looking after old people who are definitely going to die?

Her conversation over, Sister passed down the middle of the ward telling everyone to put their lights out.

'I'll be disappointed if I have to come back and say it a second time. You all need all the rest you can get.'

The boy watched and listened as she went to the fire door, returned and kept going to wherever – the nurses' station, probably. Then she unexpectedly returned with a glass of water for Ahmed. Then she left.

'You can come out now,' said Chemo.

The boy handed him the chocolate. 'Thank you,' he said. 'I'm not hungry.'

'You don't have to be hungry to eat chocolate,' said Chemo, 'you just have to be alive.'

The boy didn't want to say, 'You need it more than I do,' though that was what he felt. His attitude to the chocolate had changed; Sister's appearance had had something to do with it. He wanted to get away from this ward as fast as possible. Even though he wasn't ill like they were, in the same way, this might be the place they put him, if they caught him. Especially if they didn't believe about the tree: it was just another sort of growth, maybe they'd think it was a rare cancer and treat him with the same hair-fall-out drugs. The sooner he got out of Hospital, the safer he'd be.

'Good luck,' he said to Chemo. 'I hope you don't die.'

'Don't go,' said Chemo. 'Everyone else is boring.'

'Huh, thanks,' said Ahmed.

'Correction,' said Chemo. 'Everyone is boring apart from mongs who are too mong even to be boring.'

That was the last the boy heard, as he was off at a run down the ward – passing the certain-to-die, the fifty-fifty and the maybe-to-live. He didn't want to have a percentage following him around; he wanted to keep living as long as he could, by bravery or toughness. Doctors were bad for people; his mother was what he needed, not them.

PC Dixon made it to the lift lobby but then excused himself. 'Just give me five minutes,' he said.

He caught WPC Angel's eye – she looked sympathetic. This made him feel worse, an object of pity.

Dixon dashed back to a men's toilet they had just gone past. The sobs broke from his chest even before he reached the cubicle.

It wasn't the humiliation which was making him cry, it was the memory of Nikki – the girl Angela had called a prostitute. Nikki Froth.

They had first met when he arrested her. The second time was when another copper brought her into the station. But it was the third time that had really made him notice her: he had been on a liaison visit to a sixth-form college, talking about what serving the community as part of the Metropolitan Police was like, day to day. The girl asking the most and the keenest questions looked familiar – and then he recognized Nikki. She looked so different without the tarty make-up. She looked beautiful.

Her story wasn't untypical, wasn't even rare. Both her parents were functioning alcoholics, he a stock-broker, she a management consultant. Nikki went on the game after watching a TV documentary which made it look bad and depressing but quite easy. 'Just stand around wearing a short skirt at night and it'll happen,' she had once told him. Her background was quite privileged, but she hated being dependent on parental handouts. Nikki wanted to buy her own clothes, pay for her own drinks. After the first arrest, her parents found out what she'd been up to. They did their best to sober up and deal with it, but she wanted to make it a really big issue. She flaunted herself in front of them, and invented things she'd done to tell them. When another woman on the game offered her a place to sleep, she left home.

Just as his ex-wife had said, Peter had tried to save Nikki. He hadn't been in the force all that long; he thought, maybe, he could make a difference – he thought he might as well try.

It wasn't sexual, not to begin with. Apart from anything else, he was wary of what diseases he might pick up from her. But then it happened, and had been very different from what he'd imagined. She was so tender, so in need of someone gentle.

What she ended up with was a pimp, one of the worst. Nikki tried to run away but she was always caught.

Dixon got some mates in the vice squad onto the case. They looked into it, then said there was nothing they could do. He suspected they were being paid off. They were no longer his mates.

The pimp worked Nikki mercilessly for six months

then swapped her for two younger girls from Moscow.

The last PC Dixon had heard of her, Nikki Froth was doing internet porn from a basement in Prague.

He closed his eyes and let the tears come.

In Oncology, Mrs Dammers was *still* awake – the clicking from Mr Froth's jaw had ensured that. Her internal monologue continued:

'I will *not* allow you the luxury of forgetting me. Not like you forget everyone else who lies here and dies in this bed – all apart from those one or two *especially touching cases* you tell your wife or girlfriends about when you get home, when you meet them at the hotel – the ones she'll maybe ask you about again a few weeks later. "Oh, I'm afraid he died," you'll say, or, "Oh, she's much the same" – but most of us, we're just bodies to you, bodies and information about bodies. I'm not memorable to look at, I know that well enough – and my cancer isn't anything out of the ordinary. It's not a fascinoma – isn't that what you call them? But I have my mind, a good mind, at least it used to be, double first at Cambridge, and I see things with my eyes, hear them if they're loud enough or close enough. I can see you – I can see that you are vain about your vocation. You were sure of it once, that's why you became a doctor; you felt it was the only thing in the world you could be – the only thing worth being: saving people, saving them from death! And I am dying – I *know* I'm dying – better than you – I feel every bit of it – but I will not be meek; I will not pass quietly away. I intend to leave my mark on everyone I meet, including you, Dr Mass Destruction – so that when I am dead, people will remember me. They will think, "Who was that horrible old witch?" They will think, "Why was she so vicious?" I will leave my mark on your consciousness, your memory, your soul. This comes out of hate for this world, and myself in it, not love, not regret. You can learn a lot of hate in eighty-three years, especially as a Jew – I'm a Jew, didn't you know? A very English Jew, who married a Gentile but didn't become a Jewish mother – I never had any children, none that lived. So remember me, then – I'm Janet Dammers, and I'm the one that told you, as they dragged me away to die, kicking and screaming, that your vocation was false from the beginning – false and a cruel lie, *told by the Devil*, to make you bring more cruelty into the world with your smooth hands and your slow voice. I see it all and I see through it all. You thought you were a good doctor but you were *mistaken* – and now you are beginning to suspect this – beginning to realize just how wrong you were. *Your vocation is false* – it always was.'

That's what she would say to him, Dr Mass Destruction, the moment she got his attention – and you only get their attention for a moment. 'And how are you feeling today Mrs . . .' look down, check chart, '. . . Mrs Dammers?' *Then* she would say it.

The consultant obstetrician, Henderson MacVanish, came through the door and asked if now would be a good time to perform a vaginal exam – or, as he said, with his strong Scottish accent, 'just have a wee lookie at you in there, now'.

Go on, she thought, and bring all the gynae students in – start the teaching seminar, film it for sex education classes. She was only *dying*, and they saw *that* all the time. They made jokes about it, bastards.

James knew this was the most difficult time, so far. It might prove to be the most difficult time of all, but he doubted that. He doubted, also, if there were anything he could truly *do*. Being physically present, he knew, was his main function; keeping his intact and unpained body in the room. Why? As marker of something – as a gross insult to his wife's agony, as a sentinel of the future when again and again he would learn the hard virtue of sitting helplessly by. There was a cramp in the fingers of his hand, from being squeezed. He couldn't say it hurt, though. The comparison, in this chamber of horrors, would be heinous not just odious. Mary bounced up and down on the balls of her heels. James was *bored* with giving massage – only three hours in, and he was bored. And this could go on for *so* long that it didn't matter when it ended – part of them would never leave this room. He readied himself for another contraction and the ritual of caring. He knew it was brutal but didn't believe in it entirely; not from the inside. 'Ooooh, ow-ow-aw-ow-w,' Mary had said, to begin with. Now she was ululating, her new skill-column of the throat going all the way down to her sternum, and resonating in the opening gap.

Henderson MacVanish performed the VE and told them that she was eight centimetres, which was good, he added, very good.

'Only another one to go. And the first few are always the painfullest. After you get going into the swing of things, it all whizzes by pretty fast. Right now, it may seem like it's for ever but once it's over the whole thing will seem to have gone by in just a wee flash.'

James was annoyed that the man knew what they were experiencing so exactly, and was able to voice it in such catastrophically banal language. But the clichés were true, fuck them.

James remembered the woman taking the NCT classes telling them that most obstetricians had never been present for a normal, healthy birth. By the end of this, he tried to console himself, he would be more experienced than the man just leaving the room.

Before he went, Henderson MacVanish nodded to the midwife Honey Hopeful. 'I'll be back, *if* you need me, dearie.'

Pollard hadn't been concentrating very hard on the CCTV screens. He was incredibly pissed off with Cropper.

Why should he be expected to miss all the fun, just because he was meant to be looking for some boy? What did Cropper want with a boy? He had seemed very serious when he radioed through, a while ago. 'Drop everything else,' he'd said.

And then, out of the corner of his eye, he saw him – small gray screen to the left: north-west stairwell, in between the 5th and 4th floors, heading down.

Stripy pyjamas, rolled up at the legs. Just as Cropper had described him.

Little bastard.

Maybe if they caught him quick enough, Pollard wouldn't have to miss anything.

Pollard radioed through to Cropper, who had gone off to the locker-room to get changed.

'I'll be right with you,' Cropper said. 'Don't take your eyes off him.'

Gemma sat facing the great man and took a sip of black coffee to steady her nerves – it was scorchingly hot, and she had to spit it back out again into the mug. Luckily, Sir Reginald, busy tearing sugar sachets and pouring them into his own milky cup, hadn't noticed. Gemma's tongue touched the roof of her mouth; it was definitely burned and would be sore for several days. She just hoped it didn't blister badly – what a stupid mistake!

A second glance at Sir Reginald caught him looking intensely back at her whilst stirring his coffee. Gemma found herself unable to break his gaze, which had something powerfully hypnotic about it.

'So,' he said, starting again, 'now that I've finally got you to myself . . .' Sir Reginald's usual bassoon-boom had sunk to a confidential burr. Gemma didn't feel comfortable with this tone at all. 'I'm glad to hear you've settled in.' Yes, yes, thought Gemma, we've had that twice already, get to your point – but she was afraid of what his point might be. 'Because Trauma is a very demanding place to work – very demanding. I know you probably think you've seen quite a lot, in the days you've been here.' Four weeks, thought Gemma. 'And you have. You've probably learned more, and faster, than you ever will again. But it's the day-to-day strain of it that begins to take its toll.' Where exactly are you going with this? wondered Gemma. 'I wouldn't feel I was doing my duty if I didn't find out how you were likely to cope with this.'

'I think I've been doing alright,' said Gemma. 'I haven't –'

'No, no,' said Sir Reginald, 'I didn't mean just a few weeks. I mean over the months and, I hope, years to come. How will you be able to cope' – he paused – 'philosophically?'

Giving her no time to answer, he continued with what she had already realized was a set speech – a set speech with a set culmination. And perhaps, she thought, she had already guessed where they were going.

'Most people who work in medicine need to decide, sooner or later, exactly what it is they think they're doing.'

Sir Reginald continued in this vein for a while longer, and as he hadn't yet begun to approach his climax, Gemma was able to take a couple of sips of cooling black coffee and let her eyes casually scan the room.

At first she thought the others were still just as they had been before. Then she realized only two figures remained seated at the table by the till.

One of them was definitely Steele; she would have known his broad shoulders and noble head anywhere. But the other woman was sitting opposite him, her face and body obscured by his.

Previously, Patricia had been in that place, and at first glance Gemma assumed it must still be her. Another glance, however, coincided with laughter at that table – and Sarah's hilarious face swung into view.

Though brief, the moment was long enough for them to make eye-contact. Gemma was dismayed to catch a look, a smile, from Sarah that seemed unmistakably like triumph. What, Gemma wondered, are they talking about? Is he flirting with her? Is that what had made her laugh?

But Sir Reginald's rising tone and his hardening intensity made Gemma realize she needed to pay closer attention to the conversation on her own table.

'What I mean to say, without beating about the bush any longer, is, do you have any religious faith to sustain you? More bluntly still, do you believe in God?'

*

Helen Mugabe had finally persuaded Nikki Froth to stay, for the moment.

Nurse Ginger Bland, the ward nurse, had found her a clean towel and a hospital gown to wear.

Nikki wouldn't let them take her clothes away – insisted on taking them with her into the shower room.

As the hot water pressed into her face, Nikki wasn't sure if she was crying or not; she had allowed herself a moment to think about ordinary pleasures – about pleasures, not highs or blasts or buzzes: being warm, being safe, having some money to spend, having nice clothes. Perhaps it was possible, for her. Probably not. Something or someone would come along to fuck it up. Or she would fuck it up herself.

Helen had promised to get her some methadone, if that was what she wanted. But if she took it, she wouldn't be allowed to stay on this ward – and if she couldn't stay here, they might not have anywhere else to put her. So, she had a choice.

They had given her the time, while she showered, to think it over.

Nikki wanted to know what Spanner and Case were up to. Were they rampaging round the hospital looking for her?

She dried herself off.

Very exactly, she knew how long it would be before she started feeling like shit.

It was so simple to feel good, and so impossible.

She tied the gown on – she had worn one before, before the abortion, before the second abortion.

Helen Mugabe was waiting for her outside the door.

'Okay,' Nikki said. 'I'll try.'

'Good girl,' said Helen, and offered a hug. Nikki took it.

*

Spanner had brought black bin-bags, one each – in his optimistic state, he thought these would be inconspicuous, and they'd be able to walk out of the building unchallenged. First, however, he wanted to enjoy being in Heaven.

Whilst Case began to search single-mindedly for heavy tranquillizers, Spanner took a stroll along the aisles – his connoisseur's eye caressing the white boxes with their sexily informative writing. He admired the neatness with which they had been stacked, flush to the edges of the shelves: the pharmacists obviously put love into the keeping of their white domain, and for perhaps the first time it was fully appreciated by someone not one of them. Even the most obscure drugs, their packets yellowing slightly with age, were free from dust.

Spanner felt like applauding: he so rarely spent time in places where the floor was not sticky or crunchy, the walls were uncovered with graffiti, nicotine, soot, blood.

What it most reminded him of was a supermarket – a very puritanical supermarket. But as Spanner had been banned from just about every shop within walking distance of his house, these memories didn't come without another distance, that of nostalgia: the pharmacy to him was as the supermarket to a child, to *him* as a child.

'Got mazzies here,' said Case, almost breaking the reverie.

'Very good, very good,' said Spanner, in an aristocratically foppish way. Right now he was lord of the only manor he'd ever cared about. So many siren-voices – Placidyl, Xanax, Dilaudid, Stadol, Ritalin, Rohypnol – and he had *droit de seigneur* over all of them.

Which should he sample first?

*

Cropper was out of breath when he tottered into the security offices, still struggling to button up his uniform.

'Where?' he asked.

Pollard had the boy up on the main screen.

'Moving or not moving?'

'Heading down,' said Pollard.

'Right,' said Cropper. 'I'm going to get him. Are there any police around?'

'I saw a couple –'

'Get them down to A&E, asap.'

'Yes, sir,' said Pollard.

'And let me know if anything develops.'

Cropper was already halfway out the door when Pollard asked, 'Can I? You know . . .'

'No,' said Cropper. 'You stay here all the time. Understand? You do not move. We need someone to keep an eye on everything.'

'You're doing really well,' James said, for about the hundredth time. The miracle of birth, wish it didn't take quite so bloody long to be miraculous . . . Wish it wasn't quite so hard – labour was labour, hard labour . . . Why had no-one said? Why had they said the wrong thing? It coming, said midwife Honey Hopeful, it coming – the head is coming. It starting to crown. Will everyone shout push? Oh God Oh God. With the next contraction, I want you give me the biggest push you can. You hear me, dear? I don't want any of your old excuses. You got to get this baby out in the world. Nobody else around can help you. *You* have to do it. No messin'. I want to tell her to fuck off. It's a bit harsh being spoken to like that; should I say anything? This baby will be born in the next five minutes. Yes, it's . . . Right, push. PUSH!

I see the little head – I see the little top of its head. Give me your hand, give it here. Feel that. That the head of your baby. You feel that right there? Is it? How terribly shocking. She's lying. It can't be. It's probably my uterus coming out – but it's got hair. Lots of hair. Daddy, you alright? You ready for this? As ready as I'll ever be. You better be. You can't back out now, ha ha. Why did I say that? Why couldn't I think of something better to say? As I'll ever be. What am I going to say to him when he's born? Hey, baby! Hi! Right, lady, this here the big one. No excuses. This time you push like you serious. Like I didn't before? Like I haven't for the last hour? You bitch, oh fuck . . . Here we go! Go on! Push! PUSH! Gnnnn! Uh uh uh uh! The head's out – the head's out. Feel it. Just one more push. Tell her she did really well. Give her some encouragement – she really needs it. You've done this thousands of times, she hasn't. Don't forget that. Why do I never say these things? Almost there. I can't – I can't. It hurts, it really hurts. I just need a break – just five minutes. I can't even breathe. I don't want another contraction. If I could just skip one. Push, lady! Push! It's happening – it's on its way. I'm almost a father. That's his head. I can see the face – I can see his eye, his whole head. I'm all gone – there's nothing left.

'I believe in Something,' Gemma said, when she had managed to gather herself together a little. 'But I wouldn't call it God. It's not a Him, it's more like a sense that things don't just happen for no reason.'

'Oh,' said Sir Reginald, trying to hide his disappointment. 'I see. Do tell me more.'

'You can't *really* be interested,' said Gemma, relaxing more by the second. This was helped by the fact there hadn't been any more happy laughter from Steele and Sarah.

Leaning over the table towards her, Sir Reginald insisted, 'I am, indeed I very much am. You see I'm very glad to hear you say that. Keep going.'

'Like I said –' Gemma tried to elaborate, but really wasn't sure it went any further. 'I've never felt the presence of God, like people say they do – Christians, Muslims, whatever. But I don't feel like nothing's there, either. It's all got to mean something, hasn't it?'

'Oh, it has – definitely it has,' said Sir Reginald, and then added, seemingly as an addendum to a finished topic, 'But what about evil – the other side of things? Do you believe such a thing exists in the universe?'

'I'm sure it does,' said Gemma, blithely.

'And that it's a very powerful force which deeply changes everything it comes into contact with?'

'Oh yes,' said Gemma.

'In fact, that as an explanation of what happens on this planet, and particularly what we see of it in here' – he motioned around the canteen, but Gemma knew he wanted her to see Trauma – 'as an explanation of all these horrors, it is actually a lot more fitting than good?'

'I don't think the universe is an evil place,' Gemma replied, feeling as if she hadn't expressed an opinion on this, even to herself, for so long that she'd become a bit theologically rusty.

'But there *is* evil in it, you think?' Sir Reginald was leaning even closer now, and she could smell his breath, and it wasn't, truth be told, the most pleasant detail of her day so far.

'Yes,' Gemma said, hoping that firm agreement would bring this conversation to a close.

Sir Reginald, however, seemed to feel that they were only just now getting going. He began – quite elaborately – to explain just how entirely in agreement with Gemma he was, and how such a belief in the essential duality of creation helped him cope (spiritually) with the terrible illnesses and injuries they saw every day.

Gemma looked across again at Steele and Sarah, worried now that them chatting quietly was a worse sign than them laughing loudly. They might, she thought, be talking about something *important.* Then she tried to reason herself back into sense: if they were already a secret couple, they of course had plenty to talk about, but probably wouldn't do any of the personal stuff in the middle of the staff canteen – even when, like now, it was nearly empty.

'I've always had this sense,' Sir Reginald continued expanding, 'that the forces of good and evil in the universe are very evenly balanced. It's the only explanation for how things are. But this balance and equality is only maintained by a constant striving upon either side. And that if one or the other were to slacken, even for an instant, then –'

He was interrupted – thank God, thought Gemma (inconsistently) – by a sharp beeping. It came from two places at once: his trouser pocket and the bleep stuck on her lapel.

'Oh dear,' Sir Reginald said, not even bothering to check his. He stood up, stretched, and began to make his way to the door, quickly but without haste. 'The devil makes work for idle etcetera etcetera,' he said.

'It's two gunshot wounds,' said Gemma, who was trotting to catch up with him. Steele and Sarah were, she saw, a dozen paces ahead of them – but when they got into the lift, they stood and held the doors open for Sir Reginald. Luckily, one of the six had been there already, as if awaiting them.

As they travelled up to the 24th floor, Gemma stole a glance at Steele. He was staring impatiently up at the gradually increasing numbers above the lift door. So eager was he, if he could have ridden up to Trauma on a rocket . . .

The lift ride was long enough for Gemma to sense that the atmosphere between Steele and Sarah wasn't quite as relaxed as it had seemed in the cafeteria. Half her mind was on this and half on the patients who awaited them upstairs. Their concerns were far from romance and jealousy, though romance and jealousy might have been what brought them here – such emotions often had fatal results.

The first baby was born, the wee little girl, the baby girl, but something was wrong, not *seriously* wrong, not yet, but they had to take her away, just as a precaution, really, just to make sure her condition didn't worsen.

No! Not so soon!

It was Henderson MacVanish speaking – speaking to both of them, sombrely, with his mouth which contained tongue and teeth. He was a white-haired man in his late fifties, his eyes held in place by slack hammocks of flesh.

'No,' said Mary. 'I want her here.'

'But we need to take her to the Neo-Natal Unit.'

Mary was too destroyed to argue any more.

'You're sure you have to do this?' James asked, pointlessly.

'Absolutely,' said Henderson MacVanish.

'Come on, lady,' said the midwife Honey Hopeful. 'We still have plenty work here.'

'Peter?' said a voice, WPC Angel's.

'Yes,' he said, phlegmy.

'We've had a call. Security say they need us down in A&E – something to do with a boy. I'm sorry to disturb you.'

'I'll be out in a minute.'

To distract himself, PC Dixon looked around the graffiti in the cubicle. There was the usual: 'Cock fun. Every day. Here. 10pm.' Then, up in the top left-hand corner beside the door, a single word, ALL-BURNING, in black marker pen. What was that meant to mean? Some new band he hadn't heard of?

At the sinks, he washed his face. He was a little red-eyed but not too bad.

When he got out into the corridor, WPC Angel asked him if he was okay.

'Let's go,' he said, and they started off.

When they got in the lift, WPC Angel, not able to restrain herself any longer, said, 'She's a total bitch. You're well rid of her.'

'It's not that,' PC Dixon said. 'I'll tell you later.'

'I hope so,' said WPC Angel. She put her hand on his arm, briefly.

A woman wearing very bright prints got into the lift when it stopped on the 20th floor.

'Hello, Peter,' she said, chuckling.

It was Helen Mugabe.

'I'm sorry,' he said. 'I didn't recognize you.'

They had met on any number of previous occasions; Peter had handed youngsters over to her and she had handed them over to him.

He introduced WPC Melanie Angel.

'And what have you been doing?'

'Oh,' she said, 'the usual. Unfortunately.'

'Very young?' asked PC Dixon.

'They all seem young, these days.'

'Can you tell me?' WPC Angel asked.

'Girl wanting to escape from her pimp. Faked an overdose – not very well.'

This was just what PC Dixon didn't need to hear.

'Good luck,' he said.

And WPC Angel couldn't help but notice the bitterness in his voice.

'In fact,' said Helen, 'I might need one of you a little later, if she wants to make a formal statement. I'm just going to make some calls. Futile calls.'

'We'll be around,' said WPC Angel.

'Yes,' said PC Dixon, dreading it.

Othniel pushed his wheelchair into the lift and pressed for the minus 3rd floor.

The very bad feeling in his stomach had just been getting worse. Tonight was not a good night – it felt wrong.

There hadn't been any signs, not even the encounter with Pollard; that kind of thing happened all the time, meant nothing.

No, it was pure instinct that told him the ceremony shouldn't go ahead.

Othniel felt himself to be tuned into Hospital's vibe – and, right now, it was the weirdest vibe. Stir crazy. Worse. Cat in a tumble-dryer. Claws.

Two grizzled old porters got in on the 3rd floor, Luckson StJust and Fritzgerald Auxilaire. They had been working in Hospital for longer than just about anyone.

Othniel checked their faces for signs of anxiety – saw none, saw nothing but age.

'*Salut*,' they all said, then stood in silence. There was no awkwardness in this, just weariness. Energy would be needed soon. It was not to be wasted in weather-talk.

The next floor the boy came to was Neo-Natal.

Although he wanted to be out of the building as soon as possible, it was hard to resist a look-see.

Babies were lined up in neat rows, in trolleys – each of which had a kind of Perspex tray on top. An Asian nurse seated in a chair over by the wall was bottlefeeding a really small newborn.

As the boy watched, a man with white hair came in carrying a blood-covered object which, when he shifted position, turned out to be another baby.

The man took the baby to a side table and began to clean it up, using disposable wipes. It was amazing how many he had to use, how much blood came off. When he was satisfied, he took a soft clean white blanket off a nearby pile and swaddled the baby quite tightly.

Another nurse came over and offered to help, but the white-haired man shook his head and took the bundle back out into the corridor.

His curiosity satisfied, the boy carried on downwards.

Almost immediately, he heard a muttering – and at the next turn of the stairs, he saw an old man, squatting by the window, looking out: Johannes Fast.

'It's still there, daddy-o, the world, but it won't be for long – the world isn't long for this world, brother. I've seen what will happen, and it's not a pretty sight for sore eyes, believe you me. And these eyes of mine have bled from seeing, yessir. All sorts of madness coming, fast. The whole kit and caboodle up in flames – roots to canopy. But it's axiomatic: no-one listens to a prophet. Not in his own country, and not in foreign countries either. I've been abroad to check, and no-one listened to me in Paris, Limoges or Monte Carlo. Perhaps I should have learned the lingo. *La monde*, isn't it? It's *la fin de la monde*, like the newspaper. *La mode* is something else – fashion. See, I know some French from somewhere. *Au secours!* That's help. Help me! But there isn't any help. The game's up and under and left and right and over and done and dusted and gone to blazes. All of that's pretty standard, daddy cool – the usual apocalypso beat. Fire and flood, like for insurance. Acts of God. What I can't get my aching head round is the cows. Why are there cows everywhere? Reckon me that.'

The boy thought he might be expected to answer, but the man continued drawling on without looking round.

'If they won't listen, perhaps they'll read. All that's left for me to do are the johns on the sub-basement levels, and they're a devil to get to. I don't suppose that many influential people frequent them, but I have to do them all. Every single one. It's my mission. Then, maybe, the place will be protected.'

If he was quick, the boy was sure he could be round the man before he had a chance to stand up. Down these stairs, someone that old would never catch him.

'It's a wonderful thing, the black marker pen,' said Johannes Fast. 'But will it save the world? I can hardly hold out such hope for my humble little scribblings. It's nice handwriting, though – I'm sure it gives people pleasure to look at.'

The boy set off.

As he went past the old man's back, the droning continued: 'They won't heed. I could scream it from the rooftopsy-turvy. No-one listens to a prophet. Still, I better get moving – work to do.'

But the boy was already halfway to the next floor.

WPC Angel had known better than to force PC Dixon to talk. His bleary pink eyes told her most of what she needed to know; his weary trudge told her the rest. He was a good, kind and gentle man. She wouldn't let him suffer too much longer – she would treat him well. He needed her, and not as a colleague. They would have to find other beat-partners.

In silence, they proceeded to the ground floor.

'What can we do for you?' WPC Angel asked Sister Agnes Day.

'Not me,' she said. 'It's Security. They're on their way now. If you wouldn't mind staying for a short while.'

'Our pleasure,' said PC Dixon, managing to sound normal.

'Any real trouble, so far?' asked WPC Angel.

'I thought we might be having some,' Sister Agnes Day said. 'But I managed to pour oil.'

'I'll go and stand by the doors,' said PC Dixon. 'You stay here.'

WPC Angel nodded efficiently. She knew Peter needed a few quiet moments to himself, as if that were possible during The Flood.

As they strode into Trauma, they saw two young men on the examination tables – one Afro-Caribbean, one Asian, Marcus Sprint and Yogi Patel. It was hard not to think you knew their story already, but Gemma was prepared to give them both the benefit. Perhaps they had just been innocent bystanders. The black boy died after a couple of minutes' struggle. There was nothing more that could have been done (his mother could be told): he'd arrested twice on the way in – which was why they had only been bleeped so late. Hit three times by semi-automatic fire – once in the shoulder, once in the chest, once in the groin. One of his lungs had collapsed and there was severe pelvic bleeding. Although the chest bullet missed his heart, the groin one had punctured his bladder, flooding his system with toxins. In the slang of the team, he was well air-conditioned. Steele called the death at eleven forty.

On the other table, Sir Reginald – displaying his usual brilliance – was saving Yogi Patel's life. The young Asian man was unconscious, and a ventilator was breathing for him. Although he had taken five bullets, they'd hit far less important parts of the body – the vital organs had been bypassed. On his left hand, he had lost all the fingers except the index; his right knee was irreparably shattered and one shot had passed clean through his cheek. This, Gemma knew, was a very lucky young man.

But what was this happening during the examination? Although engrossed, as much as she could be, weren't those Steele's eggshell-blue eyes occasionally upon her? Didn't their hands, once or twice, brush against each other – albeit through latex gloves coated in slick-and-becoming-stickier blood? Hadn't half an hour passed during which Gemma thought of nothing but helping to save a young man's life but always also of helping Steele to save it? She was deeply grateful that she encountered nothing as controversial as the tension pneumothorax earlier.

She hated the idea of being put once again on the spot. Then her thoughts turned to the unconscious man with the photograph of the girl. Was he still alive?

The boy kept descending, getting closer and closer to the exit.

The 3rd floor was Antenatal, Gynaecology and Obstetrics. It was dark and completely deserted.

Closer and closer.

2nd floor was the urinogenital clinic. A waiting room with posters about sex.

1st floor was the pharmacy. Miles of shelves of bottles and packets.

And finally he reached G for Ground.

There was excitement in the small sub-basement locker-room in which they always met, there was always some excitement; but Othniel knew for certain that he was the only one of the men to be feeling *dread*.

Pierre Estime had warmly greeted Luckson StJust and Fritzgerald Auxilaire when they arrived; Othniel, too, had been embraced; Cyrille Delira shook hands with the old men, but to Othniel he merely said hello, in English.

The drummers tapped out tentative rhythms on their cardboard boxes. They had to be careful: if the music got too loud, it might be overheard by one of the pathologists working on the floor below.

Othniel finished at the sink, and dried his hands and face off with a towel held out to him by Excellent Excellent.

Excellent borrowed these from Maternity, returned

them direct to the laundry. He was expert at it; had never been caught.

With nothing more to do but wait, Othniel went and stood with his back against the lockers, arms crossed; terrified.

He watched Cyrille Delira laughing with Pierre Estime. Why did the man not see?

There was a quiet clucking sound coming from somewhere behind his feet.

The boy walked along the corridor towards the A&E waiting room, and beyond that the exit.

He was hyperalert. Every detail, every possible danger, appeared to him as if seen underwater in a swimming-pool; magnified, slower, boomy.

As he passed a security camera, it moved.

The servos which controlled its movements gave a little skirr; the lens watched him.

There was another camera in the next section of corridor, too, and it also watched him.

He doubled back, just to make sure: and the lens was on him all the way.

No!

How long did he have?

At a quarter to twelve, Sir Reginald's bleep went off. He had been sitting at a desk, writing up his notes on the gunshot wounds. He checked the whiteboard – quickly, this time. 'Well,' he said, 'that's me for the next hour or so. Everyone, I'm sure, can cope without me.'

'What is it?' asked Steele, the only one of them with sufficient seniority to inquire.

'Oh, I'm wanted underground,' replied Sir

Reginald, to all appearances quite calm. He pointed through the floor, and everyone knew he meant the Pathology department down in the sub-basement. Quite often he was called upon to confirm which wounds a deceased person had come in with, and which had been inflicted in the attempt to save their life. The young black man, Marcus Sprint, had already been sent down, to be kept on ice.

'Have fun,' said Nurse Fist, one of the younger nurses.

'Patricia,' added Sir Reginald, apparently as an afterthought, 'can you come with me? I'd quite like someone to back me up on this one.'

Patricia stepped away from the trolley she'd been re-stocking. 'I obey you in everything, oh lord and master,' she joked.

Together, they walked not-hurriedly off, and no-one in the Trauma team thought anything of it.

No-one, that is, apart from Steele. It was, he felt, very late for postmortems still to be going on. Perhaps Pathology had had a lousy day and were only just now catching up with themselves. Some of the ghouls down there liked working late. It hadn't seemed to him as though there had been a larger than usual number of deaths.

For several weeks, Steele had felt there was something vaguely suspicious between Sir Reginald and Patricia. If it had merely been an affair, he would have dismissed it as none of his business. Steele wasn't one to go looking for gossip – he had suffered enough from it himself. No, this was something altogether odder. A couple of times, he had interrupted them deep in conversation (they often retired to the storeroom). This wasn't the first time he had heard

Patricia call Sir Reginald 'master'. She hadn't sounded as if she were entirely joking – her tone hadn't clonged that way. And on one occasion, he had entered Sir Reginald's office immediately after knocking only to find the great man hurriedly stuffing a shiny black cloth into his desk-drawer.

Although he hadn't been able to put it down to anything definite, he'd sensed an increasing excitement between the two. Whatever their secret was, tonight he had a chance to learn. But if he wanted to follow them, he didn't have a second to lose.

Steele strolled into the lift lobby – just in time to see which of the six they'd got into. He watched the numbers above the door as they counted down. Of course, his only chance of knowing where they got out was if no-one got in the lift with them. 20–19–18–17–16. It hadn't stopped; it was still just them inside. 15–14–13. It stopped there. The 13th was an administrative floor, almost empty at this time. The only other things there were a suite of physical therapy rooms, the Chapel, a cultish coffee machine and some toilets. The lift paused for a few moments, then continued down to the ground floor. Here it stopped for about half a minute. Its next trip was up. 6–7–8. Perhaps they had forgotten something and were coming back. 12–13–14. They weren't stopping at the cafeteria. 19–20. He would wait there to see if they came back. 21–22–23 and the lift stopped. That suggested someone going from the ground floor to the Burns Unit; member of staff – it was too late for visitors. Which meant that the lift hadn't gone down far enough to take Patricia and Sir Reginald to Pathology. So, they had either got out on the 13th or the ground floor.

His decision made even before he realized it, Steele pressed the call button.

All of which had not passed unnoticed. A most devoted pair of eyes, those belonging to Gemma Swallow, had followed Steele to the lifts. Her footsteps, truth to tell, tended in that direction, as well. She was in little doubt as to *what* he was doing but *why* he was doing it she put down to quite the wrong reason. Her heart told her that he was watching Sir Reginald and Patricia so closely and suspiciously out of jealousy. Perhaps Steele had all along been in love with Patricia, and not Sarah as she'd thought before. Gemma was about to turn away for fear of being caught snooping when –

Some sixth sense told Steele he was being watched. He glanced round, and saw Gemma staring in his direction. At this moment, she looked quite adorable to him – exactly what he would choose in a life-partner: neat, pretty, understated, modest, ladylike and a little in awe of him. Hidden depths, too – passion and the like. But, right now, he couldn't allow himself to be distracted by desires of the flesh or even of the heart. He looked back at the floor numbers.

Gemma had now come over to him. 'What are you doing?' she bravely asked. He didn't exactly know how to reply.

'Something's going on,' he said. 'I don't know what it is but I don't like it.'

'Are you seeing where Sir Reginald went with Patricia?'

'No,' he replied, 'I think I know. I'm following them.'

'Didn't they go to Pathology?'

'Not that I saw.'

With that, the lift he'd called arrived.

'Be careful,' said Gemma. She hadn't been able to stop herself blurting it out, stupid and superstitious as it was.

'See you when I'm back,' said Steele, then stepped into the lift and was cut off by the closing doors.

The boy decided to get out as soon as he could – forget trying to blend in.

He started to run down the corridor.

A right turn brought him into A&E – and almost straight into the legs of a policewoman.

The boy did a quick sidestep, learned from football, and began to sprint: the exit was about twenty metres away.

'Stop!' shouted a high voice, WPC Angel's.

'Come back here,' said a woman's voice, Sister Agnes Day's.

With the shout, people in the waiting area became aware of what was going on; they stared at him as he ran past, hostile to his attempt.

'Stop him!' shouted Sister Day.

There was a Security Guard standing right in front of the exit – a familiar figure.

Light footsteps were running after him.

He jumped over some sticking-out feet and looked for a way through.

A man stood up, perhaps to try and grab him, so the boy turned to his left and made to jump over the backs of the chairs.

His foot caught, and he half stumbled into the next row – the same row the policeman was in.

There was nowhere for him to go; no way through: nothing but opposition – stopped.

Behind him, WPC Angel clambered over the chairs.

He was trapped between the two dark-blue uniforms, male and female.

Without hope he jumped back over the chairs and started to dash towards the exit.

Just then, someone came through in the other direction, pushing past Cropper – and, for a second, the guard was distracted by looking round.

The boy sped up, aiming for the gap he could see, the gap of a chance of escape.

He was past the blue uniform, with a hand grabbing for the door to pull himself through. The air of outside was all down his front; chilly.

But Cropper's arm came round his neck.

Elbows and kicks he aimed backwards; reverse headbutts, and all the time evasively wriggling. All he could do, he did, in the matter of violence.

No one tried to help.

The arm choked him, pulled him away from the door. His feet were lifted from the ground – and caught in the hands of Cropper.

It was over, for this time.

It wasn't the drugs *themselves* that had been their downfall – it was the large bottle of still mineral water left standing beside the dispensary window. If only *that* hadn't been there, they wouldn't have been able to swallow *quite* so many of the little capsules as they had. And if they hadn't swallowed all the shiny little red, white and blues, their neurotransmitters wouldn't have gone into slow-motion. Superadded to all of this was a large bottle of nitrous oxide from which less and less frequent hits had been taken.

The result?

Total incapacity.

Spanner and Case lay with their backs to the wall,

nearly motionless, completely fucked. Both of them *did* breathe – shallow, excited breaths. They were no longer functional human beings, however; they had become pharmaceutical cocktails perhaps unprecedented in the history of sedation, stimulation, narcosis and analgesis.

If someone had walked in, the two of them wouldn't have been able to run, stand, hide or do anything other than giggle in a way that left foam at the corners of their mouths and drool down their chins.

Spanner wasn't worried, though. He knew he was invisible. And when he held with great effort his hand up in front of his eyes, he was sure it belonged to someone else who he controlled through strange mind-powers.

It wasn't entirely clear to him either that the eyes through which he looked at the hand didn't also belong to someone else.

One person stuck two fingers up at another person and a third person chuckled in such a funny way that the first two started to chuckle as well.

Heaven was a good place to be.

Mimicking Steele's recent behaviour, though very nervous about being caught, Gemma stood in front of the lift looking up at the floor numbers. The lift descended without stopping to the 13th floor, paused, then rose to the 17th and then descended to the ground floor. Which meant the 13th must be where Sir Reginald and Patricia had gone – and where brave Steele had followed them.

Gemma returned to Trauma, deep in anxious thought. Unbeknown to her, her little trip to the lift had itself been noted – by Sarah Felt.

Although not close enough to see which floor Steele's lift stopped at, Sarah had got the general idea: the attractive young nurse was keeping an unusually close eye on Mr Steele. Now why might that be? She didn't need to wonder very long, however; she'd noticed enough other signs, recently. So, little Gemma Swallow had the hots for Steele? Well, let her have him, if that was what she wanted. Sarah herself was far more concerned with what Patricia was up to with Sir Reginald. Sarah had been meaning to warn Gemma about Patricia as soon as she joined the team, but somehow the opportunity had never arisen. Sarah only had a very slight suspicion that Gemma was jealous of her. The thought that *she* might be interested in Steele was so ludicrous to her. Men had never been her thing – ever since the age of twelve, she'd known. What she hadn't known was that it would be total bitches like Patricia who really buttered her muffin. Nurse Patricia was just so *bad*, so truly *evil.* Sarah saw this as a kind of vulnerable appeal. Just as some of her straight friends were fatally attracted to bad boys and felt it was their job to save the poor dear lambs, so she knew if she could *only* get to the tender side of Patricia, the whole thing would be exquisite. If anything had stopped Sarah warning Gemma about Patricia, it had been jealousy: the two of them seemed to get on so well, right from day one. Patricia had buddied up to the new girl straight away. Part of Sarah hoped this was a ruse, deliberately intended to pique her own jealousy and arouse yet further her ardour.

Even before Gemma arrived, Trauma had been a seething pit of jealous and betrayed lovers. Nurse Swallow's demure appeal, her slightly prim sexiness, had only added to this; fresh meat. The fact that she was unaware of what was going on increased yet further her allure. Sarah had not been the only person to recognize the startling resemblance between Gemma and a younger version of Sir Reginald's deceased wife. The only thing that surprised Sarah was just how long it had taken the older man to drag Gemma off for that intimate cup of coffee she had seen them having half an hour ago.

Gemma, for her part, had stopped thinking about the 13th floor and whatever was going on there and, instead, had returned to worrying about Steele and the Rubber Nurse. She had a break coming up in another couple of hours, and was intending to use it to get at least a look at this mysterious creature. Although from what trusty old Patricia said, she might be a very tricky customer to track down.

Although The Flood was in full spate down in A&E, Trauma had entered one of those short and inexplicable periods of calm which even the most frantic hospital departments sometimes experience. The helicopter had just left the helipad for the first time since the two gunshot wounds were brought in. Nurse Fist and Nurse Fanny Wall busied themselves with returning Trauma to as pristine a state as possible. They knew that it would take only *one* foot to slip off *one* brake-pedal for them to be dealing with a whole coachload of the dying and nearly dead, the seriously injured and the only savable by a miracle. It had happened before, many times.

Accidentally, Sarah made eye-contact with Gemma. Both women were embarrassed, but both smiled in a friendly manner before they looked away.

*

'Which ward are you from?' Sister Agnes Day asked him again. 'Was it Paediatrics?'

The boy refused to speak. He was trying to hide his disappointment at having got so close to escape – trying not to cry. The pain in his stomach was worse than ever.

After dragging him all the way up to Reception, Cropper had handed him over and swiftly departed.

'Can't hang around,' he'd said. 'Important things to do.'

The boy was glad Cropper had gone. He felt safer.

Sister Day said, 'We'll find out sooner or later, so you may as well tell us now.'

In reply, the boy said nothing.

'You'll have to put him somewhere,' said PC Dixon, with kindness in his voice.

'I know just the place,' said Sister Day, and picked up the phone.

Whoever it was at the other end, the situation didn't take much explaining. 'Yes, we'll sort all that out tomorrow,' Sister Day said; 'we just need to be sure he doesn't escape again tonight.' She listened to the receiver with an odd smile on her face. 'Lovely,' she said. 'He'll be up in a minute.'

PC Dixon noticed that WPC Angel was looking very curiously at the boy's face, as if he were in some way familiar.

'Paediatrics he's going to,' said Sister Day. 'Which is probably where he started in the first place, isn't it?'

The boy did not respond.

'Take him up to Nurse Bland, 20th floor, Pink Elephant ward, please.'

'Righto,' said PC Dixon.

'Pink not Blue. He'll be in with the girls tonight.'

'I'll stay here,' said WPC Angel, still looking at the boy. 'One of us should.'

PC Dixon glanced down at the boy. 'Come on, then, come with me.'

'I've *got* it,' said WPC Angel to herself.

'What?' WPC Dixon asked.

'Who he looks like,' she said, indicating the boy.

'And who is it?'

'The girl in the photograph. They could be brother and sister.'

'Do you have a sister?' PC Dixon asked the boy.

'No,' he replied, though he wasn't sure either way. What was this photograph they were talking about?

'We'll have to look into this later,' said WPC Angel. 'There might be a connection.'

'Alright,' said PC Dixon. 'If we've got time.' He really didn't care.

The sad policeman made the boy walk two paces in front of him.

There was no escape.

Down on the 13th floor, Steele was searching through the administration offices. The rooms, full of computers set aside in square little podules, were dark – lights off, part of a recent attempt to improve Hospital's energy efficiency and put less strain on the generators in the basement.

Now and again Steele had been called upon to attend meetings here during the day. The layout of the floor was familiar to him, but the place felt completely different now. He saw grey shapes, moving – himself reflected in floor-to-ceiling walls of glass. What little illumination there was came halogen orange from the carpark lamp-posts.

One side of the building looked out over the glistening city, the other towards a parallel wing of Hospital. But Steele was not interested in these familiar views.

He moved stealthily down the corridors. There was a loud clunk from further along and, for a second, he thought he'd been tricked into a trap. What if it were a Security Guard? That would be awkward – there was no real reason why he should be creeping about on an unoccupied floor of the building halfway through his shift. He hoped they would be busy coshing lairy pissheads down in A&E.

After he had explored the north-west and south-west corridors, he went deliberately towards the Chapel. He had suspected all along that this was where Sir Reginald and Patricia had been heading. For some reason, Steele remembered a rather strange conversation he'd had with Sir Reginald about a month after starting at Hospital. The great man had taken him for coffee in the canteen, rather as he'd done just this evening with pretty little Gemma, and begun to ask him some very penetrating questions about his religious beliefs. The one that had stuck most vividly in Steele's mind was, 'Do you believe in such a thing as pure, naked evil?' Steele found it hard to think what he might possibly have said in reply, apart from no.

Just as he was about to walk through the lift lobby, he heard a sharp ping as a lift arrived.

Stepping back into the shadows, Steele watched a fat Security Guard hurry out the door and turn in the direction of the Chapel. He couldn't be sure but he thought it was probably Cropper.

Just then an impulse hit him – stop; turn around;

go back to Trauma; forget the whole thing. But Steele overcame it, kept moving. Whatever was going on, he needed to know.

The thought of Trauma had reminded him of a danger: he pulled out his bleep and, breaking one of the most sacrosanct terms of his contract, turned it off. He couldn't risk it sounding and giving him away.

Steele took a deep breath, then set off to get a closer look.

Almost immediately, though, he had to pull back out of sight – *someone* had just stepped out through the Chapel door and, from what Steele had glimpsed, it was one of the guards; probably Cropper, again.

Kneeling down, Steele tried to calm his ragged breathing. This was when he heard the first sounds from the Chapel. It sounded like, but he couldn't at all be sure – it sounded like a service was in progress! There was the single voice, that of the priest, and there, louder but more mumbled, was the response of the congregation. Steele checked his watch: it was five minutes to twelve. Midnight mass? Possibly. Highly unlikely. Sir Reginald wasn't Catholic. Patricia he didn't know about for definite, she might be the sort.

Just then another less expected noise came down the corridor – it was a wail. Human or animal? Steele felt his stomach lurch. It came again, and Steele was able to identify it more exactly: it was the whimper of a baby – a hungry, discomforted or scared baby.

The second delivery wasn't any easier than the first – harder perhaps.

James was completely distracted by thoughts of his daughter: Where was she? What were they doing to her? Would she be alright?

Mary was in another place altogether: Planet Birth, one of their friends had called it; completely in another universe: tranced there.

'Come on,' said midwife Zandra Pandit. She had taken over when midwife Honey Hopeful had gone off shift, about half an hour ago. 'Be strong.'

Part of James couldn't help but be bored; bored even with the panic. This might go on for hours more. No-one had been able to prepare him for the time between one baby's birth and the next – the books had had nothing to say about it.

'I think it's starting to come,' said Zandra Pandit, removing her gloved hand from between Mary's legs. 'You have to be ready for this next one.'

Mary tried to force herself to breathe in.

Steele poked his head round the corner, low down, almost at floor level, and confirmed that Cropper was still in position – not quite the same position, though: he had turned around and opened the doors of the Chapel so that its gentle, flickering light illuminated him, head to toe.

Just as Steele was wondering how he could possibly get any closer without giving himself away, he saw Cropper nod as if in response to someone inside the Chapel. The Security Guard looked up and down the corridor, then stepped with a definite air of ceremony through the double doors and closed them behind him. Steele heard quite distinctly a key turn in a lock.

Wasting no more time, the brave surgeon scampered quickly along until he was crouching just outside the wooden doors.

At first he thought the priest was speaking gobbledegook, then he listened more closely. There was clearly some sense here, but of an odd sort. It took him a couple of minutes to realize – the gobbledegook was actually normal words said backwards, but normal words in a foreign language: Latin. He knew quite a bit of Latin from his medical training. What was even more disturbing than backwards Latin and all that might suggest was that Steele knew the voice: Sir Reginald Saint-Hellier was taking the service.

Slowly, being very careful not to make a noise, Steele stood up. Light was still coming out of the Chapel and into the corridor, through the stained-glass windows – one in each of the Chapel doors. They were just above head height, but Steele, quite tall, was able on tiptoe to peer in. The glass, depicting on one side the Lamb of God and on the other the dove descending, was of several different colours – red, yellow, green, blue. It just happened that Steele looked first of all through a red section – and so it was that the extraordinary scene revealed to him was suffused with a bloody crimson light.

Pierre Estime's brown eyes rolled back to reveal the whites, festooned with red veins, his tongue came out, half curled back on itself. To the whirling but subdued-in-case-anyone-should-hear-them rhythms, he wildly gyrated his body. The drumming was supplied by Jean-Paul, who, alternate weekends, played in a salsa band.

With uncanny accuracy, Pierre straightened his back until it resembled Mr Kissa's ramrod spine. His four fingers mimicked the ballpoint pens sticking from the pocket of Kissa's white short-sleeve shirt, crisply laundered every day. Bending down in rhythm with the cardboard-box drums, Pierre indicated a glare from the toes of each bare foot, shielding his eyes – these were Kissa's impeccably shined black leather uppers, enough to make a Royal Guardsman jealous on the eve of Trooping the Colour.

Those gathered in a tight hot quiet-clapping circle around Pierre understood and appreciated each detail. They had all of them tried, in voodoo and in general obedience, to placate Kissa. Now it was time to attack him – which was what this regular meeting of the Haitian Hospital Porters Local Religion and Healthworkers Union Representative Council had met to enact. It was for this that the blood of the terrified free-range chicken (raised in Luckson StJust's backyard, so not all *that* free) would very soon spatter upon the white sheet laid out to catch it. A copy of the *Daily Mail* had been spread out beneath this, upon the concrete floor, to prevent there being any difficult-to-explain bloodstains (though, in Hospital, bloodstains were almost never questioned).

Pierre juddered in the centre of the circle, performing a grotesque sequence of miscoordinated dance moves. The porters all recognized this as being a parody of the slightly tipsy Mr Kissa they had witnessed 'letting his hair down' to a disco megamix at the Christmas party. Pierre indicated with his four fingers that the pens were still in place, as indeed they had been on that famous night.

A doll was produced, resembling Kissa even more closely, sewn in a rough but practical way (during teabreaks). Pierre approached it with a rolling, arrogant walk that was indistinguishable from the one which brought Kissa through the locker-room door every morning with his clipboard clutched in his hand. The doll was held out towards him, a flopping, lifeless thing of cotton. Pierre grabbed it

– and at that moment, as the drumming reached a new height in muffled intensity, the doll seemed to take on the very spirit of Kissa which Pierre had called forth. Instantly the doll became more charismatic, more ridiculous and more terrifying. In Pierre's hands, it disco-danced, it rolled-strolled arrogantly, it checked its miniature clipboard and made sure that the following month's shift patterns caused the greatest inconvenience to the greatest number.

Pierre himself had reverted to his own fluid but slightly angular movements; he was just over six foot three, handsome, with several gaps where teeth should have been.

A skull-embroidered cushion went around the circle, and from this each of the men drew out a sharp hatpin.

About thirty people were in the Chapel. At the far end, on the dais in front of the altar, loomed a darkly hooded figure that Steele could only assume was Sir Reginald. Alongside him stood Patricia, who wasn't dressed in anything at all. My, but she had fine breasts! Steele was momentarily distracted by these and by her big hairy muff of a growler. But when he looked again, he could see Patricia wasn't *completely* naked: her ankles and wrists were bound in decorative brass clasps, and on top of her wiry Afro sat a small and very pointy silver crown.

Behind these two sinister figures, on the wall of the Chapel, Steele could see that the plaster crucifix had been inverted and six black candles were burning, three on either side.

The hospital chaplain, a man with whom Steele had had a few fleeting dealings, was standing to the left, apparently helping to officiate. He wore his usual garments, but back to front.

Part of Steele's view was blocked by the solid, wide, thick-necked back of Cropper. The central aisle was short. The place was designed and intended more for private devotion than for large services – it could contain eighty people at most. From the uniforms he could see, Steele was able to identify types – white-coated doctors, blue-dressed nurses, a couple more Security Guards, even a patient or two. With their backs turned, he had no way of telling who they individually were.

Steele had one last moment of normality, delusive, during which he allowed himself to think what he was seeing might just be a christening – a very weird and unusually timed christening but a christening all the same.

There was another wail from the baby, and Steele was able to catch sight of its tiny head – sticking out of a pile of black fabric on the altar. And there was another head, too – larger, adult, female. At first glance, he thought this was a head without a body, a decapitation, but then he saw that she, too, whoever she was, had been draped in ebon silk or satin.

Instantly, Steele realized the full terror of what he beheld: this was a Black Mass, and it was moments away from reaching its dreadful sacrificial climax! He saw Patricia pick something up off the altar: a long, ornate dagger. The baby was in terrible danger!

'So this is the young reprobate, is it?'

Nurse Ginger Bland was the thinnest person the boy had ever seen, even dying ones on television.

'Almost made it out the door,' said PC Dixon. 'Almost, but not quite.'

Nurse Bland looked at him for an unfocused moment. 'I see what you mean,' she said. 'Well, he won't be doing that again. I have a very nice bed for him, right here – next to the nurses' station, right under my nose.'

The boy hated the way adults spoke when they were self-consciously being adult. Nurse Bland was a particularly bad example of this – everything she said sounded insincere.

All around him, the walls and curtains and blankets and sheets were soft pink.

Even the noticeboard behind PC Dixon's head was that girl-colour. Only a single poster was pinned to it: Little Bleeders. Haemophiliac Children & Parent Support Group.

'You can do without brushing your teeth for one night,' said Nurse Bland. 'Hop in, unless you need to be escorted to the little girls' room?'

Although it seemed a concession to communication, the boy shook his head. His stomach was full of new levels of pain; it was all he could do not to whimper.

'Get to sleep, then – and don't forget, I'll be watching you every single second.'

'Can I go now?' asked PC Dixon, as if he needed permission.

The sheets felt very clean around the boy's feet. They smelled of cleanness, too – the cleanness of hospitals, not homes.

Turning so his back was towards Nurse Bland, the boy closed his eyes and tried to mind-control the stabbing sensation in his tummy.

*

In the ICU, Angela continued to look after the comatose man. What she did was mostly routine, so it left her plenty of time to think.

She had now recovered – just about – from her ex-husband's visit.

Already she was wishing that she hadn't been such a bitch. It was just that she had loved Peter so much, and trusted him so completely, and he had let her down so badly.

So badly that, ever since, she had found it impossible to believe anything that men said. Not just possible boyfriends – anyone male: politicians, pop stars, the Pope. The only ones she allowed herself to become attached to, or care for, were her patients. They might break your heart by dying but they never broke it by leaving you for a fucking whore.

Angela sobbed, then put her hand on the man's forehead. He felt cool, and his temperature was likely to decrease from now on.

If the girl in the photograph was his daughter . . . Angela thought for a moment. She had witnessed many visits by relatives. They were much more harrowing than the deaths of patients. She might have to meet the daughter – lead her the long and terrible walk from the lifts to the bedside.

Angela closed her eyes and took another deep breath. At home, she had meditation tapes, to help her deal with her life. Quickly, she tried to let go of painful things. She couldn't take back the scene with Peter and the policewoman. She couldn't do anything in advance about the daughter. Then she focused on the present moment.

I will look after him, she thought. I will look after this man as well as I possibly can. It is my job. It is my life.

*

Up on the 24th floor, the Trauma phone rang and Sarah Felt picked it up.

'Yes, I am,' she said, then listened. 'Yes,' she said, 'we're ready.' She listened some more. By now, the ears of most of the team – alert to the tiniest nuances in one another's voices – were pricked up. 'We can take ten initially,' she said, then put the receiver down. She didn't need to ask for quiet.

'A major incident has just taken place. Patients are already on their way in – ten of them, like I said – and there will be many more to follow. We are to expect severe burns, smoke inhalation, blast wounds and all the rest. The helicopter with the first couple has an ETA of five minutes. Ambulances will be coming, too. I'm sorry to say, this is a very bad one.'

Without Sir Reginald or Steele on the floor, Sarah Felt was the most senior member of staff. She pressed a button on one of the walls – which immediately put out an urgent 222 call for the other team members to return to their posts. She was annoyed with Sir Reginald and of course Patricia, but even more so with Steele for being away at a time like this.

As the others assembled from nearer by, she began to worry that it would be left to her alone to deal with this huge challenge to the team. She felt confident in her clinical and organizational skills but nervous of being forced to exercise them with so little time for mental preparation.

'Where are they?' she asked, turning to the nurse beside her. It was only after she'd asked the question that she realized she had addressed it to that touchy little thing, Nurse Swallow.

The young woman hesitated for a moment, then

said quietly to Sarah, 'Could I speak to you in private?'

Sarah was about to say, 'It better be important.' But a glance into Gemma's eyes told her this definitely *was* serious.

They stepped off into a corner, behind where the ECG machine stood, and Gemma explained tremblingly what she had seen: Steele following Sir Reginald and Patricia down to the 13th floor.

'They've turned them off – their bleeps. All three,' said Sarah. 'I've never known any of them do that.'

'We should get someone to go and find them,' Gemma said. Her sixth sense was telling her, very powerfully, that something was not right. Steele might even be in danger.

'Security,' they said, at one and the same time.

'You call them,' Sarah said. 'I have to go and get ready to receive these patients.' She looked up at the big circle of the clock on the wall. Four minutes to midnight.

As Sir Reginald held the sacrificial babe above his hooded head, Patricia – or the High Priestess, as she seemed to be – stood beside him clutching the curved dagger to her naked breast.

A few seconds ago, Sir Reginald had pulled the black silk veil off the young woman on the altar – and revealed her to be naked, brunette and tied down with thick black ropes.

Resting upon her flat stomach was a kidney-shaped stainless-steel bowl, of the sort Steele had very often himself used in operations. It was where they put excised organs, fat and other offcuts.

Sir Reginald began to intone, no less solemnly but this time in English:

'Lord, we beseech Thee, grant us, upon *this* earth, the eternal life promised us by Thy great enemy, in the other world, which we hope never to see – the Great Deceiver! The terrible Restricter of Appetite! The Hater of Lust and Despiser of the Body and All Things Energetic! Give us immortal life, Great Satan! Give us life everlasting, you huge Apocalyptic Beast! Give us life at any price. We care nothing for the world. We care nothing for our souls.'

It was quite clear to Steele that he had but a few short moments left to save the baby – which looked very small and newborn indeed. Where could they have stolen it from? Dismiss that question for now.

Steele's eggshell-blue eyes scanned the rest of the Chapel, feverishly trying to devise a plan.

Sir Reginald's invocations continued to rise, approaching hysteria. Although that voice had become very familiar to Steele over several years, he had never heard it with this high, shrill tone of blood-lust and mania. There was no longer any doubt that this satanic pantomime was in deadly earnest.

Steele crouched down to consider his options. He checked his Timex watch – three minutes to midnight. It seemed most likely that the unholy sacrifice would take place on the stroke of midnight. That gave Steele no time at all in which to fetch assistance. He was on his own.

Gemma got straight through to Security. She explained that she urgently needed them to search the 13th floor, find the three staff members and alert them to what was happening.

'Can't you see them on your screens?' Gemma asked.

The Security Guard (Pollard) was even more hostile than usual.

'We don't have cameras in every part of the building,' he said. 'Much as we'd like to – gynaecology, for instance.'

'Can you send someone?' Gemma asked.

'I'll go and look into it myself,' Pollard replied.

'This is urgent,' Gemma repeated. 'It's a matter of life and death!'

'Isn't everything here?' Pollard said, and hung up.

The security offices were on the 12th floor. Gemma feared that it would take at least ten minutes before Sir Reginald and the others were found and brought back to them. At this, she felt panic.

'They're going to do it,' she informed Sarah.

The emergency room was being readied for the arrival of the burns cases.

Meanwhile, Security Guard Pollard radioed to his boss, Cropper, who was standing in the Chapel. As they spoke, he watched the satanic service on his main monitor. So engrossed was he that he failed to notice the figure outside the Chapel doors on one of his smaller screens.

Steele knew what was about to happen. Sir Reginald's true character had been revealed to him. There was no way he wasn't going to slaughter this poor innocent mewling held-head-high babe, in tribute to his true master, Satan, Lord of Darkness. There was a strange glint in Sir Reginald's eyes, something which Steele had never seen before, but unmistakably it was bloodlust.

Steele had no time left for plans: he had to act, and *now*.

From inside the Chapel, he heard the crunch-chatter of the Security Guard's radio – only one word came through clearly, but that was enough to tell him what was going on: the word was *hurry.*

Steele rechecked his watch: two minutes to midnight. Even if help was on its way, it wouldn't get there in time.

As quietly as he could, Steele tried the aluminium door-handle of the Chapel – a gentle shove with his hip confirmed what he'd feared: the doors were firmly locked.

Steele took a couple of steps back. The doors to the House of God hadn't been constructed in order to keep people out. There was a chance . . .

Just then, inside the Chapel, Cropper, alerted by Pollard, was putting a key into the lock.

He would have to stand in the corridor and keep lookout, though this would mean him missing the climax of the ceremony, the reason he'd been talked into doing this in the first place, the cure for all his ills and the promise of eternal life for evermore afterwards!

When PC Dixon got back down to A&E, WPC Angel was nowhere to be seen.

He had to wait a couple of minutes before Sister Agnes Day came free – she was dealing with a young woman (Amy Waters) who had slashed her eye with a diamond ring whilst trying to take out a contact lens, pissed.

'Oh,' said Sister Day. 'That social worker, Helen Mugabe, came and took her away – said she needed her to take a statement from someone.'

'Where did she go?

'Pink Elephant ward.'

'But that's where I've just been.'

'Oh,' said Sister Day, completely uninterested, 'you must have crossed in the lifts.' Another couple of cases were already demanding her attention; bloody. 'She said she'd be back as soon as she could. You can stick around a while, can't you?'

'Of course,' said PC Dixon, and strolled across to stand beside the exit doors. From here, he was able to keep an eye on most of A&E – and lots of the people there, even the ones in pain, kept their eye on him.

It didn't bother PC Dixon; this was part of his job: being visible, being a target. He was, however, relieved to have been spared having to listen to the young woman's tale – it would have reminded him too much of Nikki.

The pain was too much – the boy said, 'Ow.'

'Are you crying?' asked Nurse Bland. 'It's no use crying and not saying anything. I'm sorry you weren't able to walk the streets at night, prey to anyone who might come along, but I'm afraid we're not allowed to discharge minors.'

With hardly touching hands, the boy felt his stomach – there was a knobby protruberance where his belly-button used to be.

Pink Elephant ward was dim. The only real light-source was the anglepoise lamp on Nurse Bland's desk. In the office behind her, visible through the blindless window, Helen Mugabe and WPC Melanie Angel were talking quietly to Nikki Froth.

When she walked in just now, the policewoman had taken another good look at the boy – as if mentally photographing his face; it made him very uneasy.

The boy pushed the blanket down so it covered only up to his knees and then tried to pull the sheet over his head.

It only came up to his nose.

'I'm still watching,' said Nurse Bland.

The boy shuffled down in the bed until he was completely covered, then he waited.

When he was sure the nasty nurse wasn't suddenly going to pull the sheets back, he undid the buttons on his pyjama top.

His abdomen was now bare, but it was too dark to see anything: what he felt was horrifying enough.

He would have to turn round the other way.

The Kissa doll made the rounds, receiving from each of the porters a (hopefully) deep wound.

The majority of the hatpins were slotted in to his cotton groin area – Kissa must no longer be cock of the walk.

It wasn't difficult to ascend into the porters' voodoo pantheon; all one had to do was be possessed of power. (There was even a place among their depicted and beseeched spirit-gods for the electricity generator which provided back-up for Hospital.) A few of the angrier men stuck their pins in Mr Kissa's face, aiming for his eyes, which had been made out of black buttons – sewn on by Pierre's daughter. (Voodoo was nothing if not a family-oriented religion.)

The oldest porters, Fritzgerald Auxilaire and Ludger Myrthil, saved their pins for the head – they knew that it was in the intelligence of Kissa's stupidity or perhaps the stupidity of his intelligence that his true power lay.

After the Kissa doll had circulated a few more times, Pierre felt the possessed little cotton thing having a fit of some sort – a good sign.

He placed the fetish of Kissa upon the white sheet

where, in the eyes of many present, it continued to twitch even though no longer touched by human hand.

Cynics might speculate that sewn up inside the doll was the small electric motor cannibalized from a hand-fan. They might recall a moment when Pierre appeared to fiddle for a switch. But whatever the sorcery or trickery (and in voodoo who will separate the two?), the pincushion doll twitched as *if* possessed with the agonized *spirit* of Kissa himself.

It was now, with practised rapidity, that the chicken was brought out of one of the lockers – the one with nine holes drilled in the side. From another place came a long ceremonial knife, as sharp as a scalpel.

Pierre held the bird up by its ankles whilst it tried to peck at his hands. Another man, Cyrille Delira, Pierre's assistant, boomalay-boomalay-boomalay-boom, grabbed the chicken by the head. Together they moved until they were holding it directly above the doll of Kissa.

It was a minute to midnight, and as he had been planning all along, Sir Reginald was holding the newborn baby just above the kidney-shaped tray.

The healthy little thing, born only a few hours ago, and fed only with milk tainted with the blood of all the congregation – collected over the previous weeks in sly moments by Patricia, in cubicles, when no-one was looking – the baby was kicking out in a slightly floppy way, as if it knew it was in imminent peril. Its blood-traced cheeks and conehead reminded Sir Reginald of his own two children just after they were born – as much as anything, he was doing this for them.

'Life eternal!' he cried, and raised the knife far up above his head. (Surreptitiously, just before this, he had checked his watch and seen all was right on schedule.) But just as he was uttering his valedictory invocation, Cropper unlocked the Chapel doors and a white figure crashed through.

'Accept this sacrifice, from us, your loyal servants,' shouted Sir Reginald, determined to continue.

The guard had been severely chinned by the doors and was out for the count. But Steele, coming through, had lost some momentum – though it was clear enough where he was heading. It made no difference: Sir Reginald doubted the Devil would mind if they missed midnight by a few seconds one way or the other. The blood of the freshest souls was what He was after. Steele, too, might have to provide some sacrifice.

The valiant surgeon ran down the aisle towards the unholy altar.

'Seize him!' shouted Patricia, and two figures stepped into his path.

Steele recognized both of them: one was Henderson MacVanish, Chief Obstetrical Consultant, the other, Molesworth, worked down in Pathology.

In only a second, Steele worked out how they had got hold of the baby and how they were intending to dispose of it, afterwards.

Steele tried to sidestep them, but they already had him by the arms – nor did they lack for reinforcements: four more men stepped forward to pin him back. Struggle as he might, the congregation was too strong for him.

'Stop!' he cried, desperate. 'You can't do this!'

*

It was what he'd thought it was: a shoot.

To touch it was to feel agony, but the boy traced its outline with the tips of his fingers.

A little arrow of leaves, pointing straight forward, away from him; two inches, perhaps.

The appletreeseed really *had* been growing, ever since he swallowed it.

He felt so sorry for himself. The only thing that kept him from crying was the thought that it would give Nurse Bland some satisfaction.

He was powerless – would never get home. It was certain he would die without seeing his mother, saying sorry.

His breathing low and feathery, he did the pyjama top back up. Perhaps Nurse Bland would be called away – an emergency, an asthma attack, a properly dying girl. There was always a chance something would happen to help him escape.

Then he remembered earlier – how wishing had seemed to work in saving him when the Security Guard Cropper was almost upon him.

Perhaps if he wished again. Perhaps if he used the wishes he'd saved up from blowing out the candles on his last three birthday cakes.

He'd wished so hard not to be caught that wish one was probably gone. That left him two.

But what could he wish for?

As the crescendo finally peaked, but mildly, Pierre neatly slit the chicken's throat so as to release the maximum amount of blood in the minimum amount of time. The bird would have made more noise had its body not been stretched out tight between him and Cyrille.

A triumph of the homemade, the doll soaked up each gout of chicken blood that fell upon it.

After allowing it to twitch a few more times as if in death throes, Pierre picked up the bloody doll and thrust it into a bag held out by Cyrille. (Whether or not he at the same time found and flicked off the switch to the hand-fan was a matter of personal conscience.)

The drumming, still not all that loud, sped up.

Wasting no time, Pierre began working himself into a yet deeper trance.

The first part of the ceremony was over, the negativity, as they called it. What followed was something even more important, the climax: an invocation of all the gods they had summoned, and also all those their powers were too feeble and their offerings too humble to summon.

Together, collectively, through the voice of Cyrille Delira, they would ask not for the things they wanted to happen to other people (bad things, mainly) but for the things they wanted for themselves: money, good health, increased potency, irresistible attractiveness to women, a sedan car with four doors, a better job, permanent British citizenship, good exam results for their sons, an end to political violence in their homeland – but most of all they asked for good health so that they could continue working and continue earning money to impress their girlfriends and satisfy their wives and feed their children and send to their parents and grandparents. Without the health, there would be no money; in the end, health was preferable to all but a very huge amount of money – more than they could imagine. Most of them had a few lottery tickets tucked into their pockets, in hopes that some of the good luck being sprinkled around would land upon them.

This time, however, during the call for prolonged life, Cyrille made some dangerous alterations to the usual requests. He asked the spirits not for *good* but for *perfect* health, not for *long* but for *eternal* life. Those to his left and right heard his mistakes, or that at least was what they assumed they were. Othniel, however, knew exactly what Cyrille was doing – the books he had read out of chagrin and humiliation had taught him there were things even more important than authenticity – such as sincerity, such as respect. He, out of all the men in that cramped, sweaty room, knew that spirits capable of making zombi . . . were easily capable of giving more than a strong, reliable erection – welcome and necessary as that might be.

Pierre Estime, Head Voodoo Man, was more animated than usual. In Haiti, he would have turned into lizards and horses and four-wheel-drive off-road vehicles and the sea; here, he was – one after the other – a hospital trolley, a centrifuge, the lights over an operating table, the back-up electricity generator. Whatever gave power and was worthy of worship. His eyes rolled back into his head and his body began violently to judder. Quickly, Excellent Excellent pulled off his belt and inserted it between Pierre's gnashing white teeth.

As if this had been the cue for something even more dramatic, Pierre fell to the floor and went into what any doctor would have diagnosed as an epileptic seizure. He felt as if he were weightless, flying, with the hospital flying around him in exactly the same direction at exactly the same speed. Then he was expanding, the building expanding with him

– exploding until he and it filled every part of the universe; Hospital was outside him but also he felt it inside himself. And then the universe was contracting and he and Hospital grew smaller and smaller until they were infinitely tinier than they had been to begin with.

Up in Trauma, Sarah, Gemma and the others stood waiting for the incoming patients. The helicopter had radioed to say it was only a couple of minutes off. One of the men it was carrying had already died, the other was critical.

'Where can they be?' said Nurse Fist to Nurse Digby Rutter. 'This isn't like Sir Reginald at all.'

'It must be something important,' Digby Rutter replied.

'Nothing's important enough to make him and Patricia and Steele all turn off their bleeps and go incommunicado at the same time.'

'It would take the end of the world to make Sir Reginald do that, surely,' Digby said.

'Let's get ready,' said Sarah, who knew that with the long downtime beforehand everybody was more than ready.

She checked her watch, expecting the helicopter to land in about thirty seconds – just on midnight.

'No! No!' a new voice screamed. It was the naked woman roped to the altar, the black veil now slipped from her shaking face. She was looking up at a mad-eyed Sir Reginald, whose surgically masterful hands were holding the sacrificial dagger at the blubbing infant's throat. Patricia stood there, evil and buxom, ready to catch every last drop of infant blood in the cup usually reserved for communion wine.

It was the cruellest parody of Sir Reginald's life, the truth of the man whom, until a quarter of an hour ago, Steele had respected above all others. Those hands which he had so often seen reach inside a patient and quite literally give them life, working the muscles of their heart for them – those hands with the gift of healing, of saving life, of saving beauty – those hands which now were tensed to kill.

Behind Steele, a second Security Guard rushed into the Chapel. It was Pollard. Steele felt a pulse of hope. Rescue! But 'Hurry up,' the guard said, 'they're missing you upstairs.'

The knife in those healing, satanic hands made a swift movement in and back.

'No!' repeated Steele, struggling to break free from the hands of the congregation.

The movement which he'd seen as preparatory was actually the *coup de grâce*, the death slice. The little baby's throat was neatly cut and a fine red mist of blood began to rise around Sir Reginald's fingers.

Steele was more distressed than ever in his life before. This was the collapse of his moral universe. 'You fuckers!' he screamed. 'You evil fucking fuckers!'

Patricia's eyes as she held out the pyx were alive now with the same evil glint he had seen in Sir Reginald's.

In Delivery Room Five, midwife Zandra Pandit told Mary to push and Mary pushed.

Pierre had never experienced anything like this – usually all he got was a mildly uncanny feeling of transportation. He often sensed that he had been overtaken by the spirits they had collectively conjured. But he had always felt distantly in control of himself, and of the ceremony. *This* was quite different: in an instant, the universe could be created anew or destroyed completely, and it was all down to him. It was too much to ask, too much responsibility – an elder from Haiti, his father or better still his father's father – that's who was needed. A man who wouldn't lose his head, go mad; too much responsibility, too much to ask.

Cut off my head! Cut it off before I go mad!

And then Pierre had a revelation, a huge, annihilating sense of understanding; there was logic, there was balance: too much was being asked of him because too much had been asked of the spirits. Treacherous Cyrille Delira had been greedy, or more than greedy.

Pierre felt his eyes being closed, as surely as if the fingers of a god had pressed the lids down.

He was dying – he was going to die!

A cosmic power surge was taking place, the spiritual circuitboard was becoming overloaded, a mortal fuse was about to blow. Power. Too much power!

Apart from Othniel, those in the clapping circle hadn't noticed anything out of the ordinary. Pierre was just putting on a particularly fine performance, this evening – tick – this morning – for at that moment, midnight went past.

Pierre tried to open his eyes, but when he did they were no longer mortal eyes, and what they saw was a world he had never known before.

The boy's eyes were screwed tight, with pain and hope and frustration. He was very aware that being selfish was what had caused him to be in this situation.

'I wish that everybody was completely well again,'

he muttered, so quiet that Nurse Bland would never hear.

He paused, not wanting to phrase his second wish badly.

And throughout Hospital, on floors for the most part below him, other wishes were formulated, other prayers were said and thought and said-denied and redrafted even when halfway through. Some, embarrassed by the possibility of God, didn't get further than thinking about thinking about saying them out loud, as long as no-one was near enough to hear. Others were happy to wail in abandon until told to shut up. And, overall, it was as if a mutter arose, which was the sound of quiet screaming: *Oh God or Someone Out There, stop this pain – stop it so I can gather my strength to face it again in the morning* and *Please, please, stop him making that clicking sound, just for half an hour, so I can get some sleep* and *Would someone just send a nurse to increase her dose, she's suffering so much?* and *Make me better, please*, and *I'll never be bad or cheeky again or even mind if Chemo calls me a mong*. But all these wishes, prayers and non-prayers did not simply rise in straight lines towards their intended recipient – although many were aimed confidently upwards, because that was the direction in which prayers *should* go. Instead, they formed what could be imagined as a thorny undergrowth of wish, a tangle, an Afro. Wishes went down and sideways, wishes twirled and twizzled, swirled and fizzled. Only a few flew off directly into the elsewhere, like matter from an explosion – and even these, after a certain distance, would lose momentum and, pulled by some unknown gravity, begin to curl back in towards the centre: Hospital. Seen from an imagined outside, with the building dissolved, prayer and wish, ask and beg, would appear as a gigantic hairball: this one boomeranging back to its sender, this one sozzling into the ground like a shot Spitfire, this one zigzagging kinky to no great end, this one not even getting launched.

Among all this, the boy felt the responsibility of his third wish. It was important; it would work.

The head was out – the second baby was seconds from being born.

Just one more push.

MIDNIGHT

On the stroke of midnight, every single light in Hospital went out, then flick-flickered into a dimmer life as the back-up generator took over. Throughout the vast building, there was sudden and startling silence, all the more startling for following on from what had been reasonable quiet – troubled only by the beeping of equipment, the rolling of rubber wheels, the thudding of doors. But the heating and air-conditioning systems which had been gently growling away for years were now dead. The atmosphere of corridors immediately seemed stiller, although their acoustics were more clattery. Then, as monitors restarted and computers rebooted, the wards and offices became a soundjungle of whirrs, jingles, beeps and hushbooms. These were the only non-human sounds. All noise from outside had, upon the very stroke of twelve, ceased utterly: no sirens approached, no helicopter rotorblades were to be heard. The cars on the nearby road had either all, as one, stopped and turned their engines off, or had disappeared entirely.

In the candle-lit Chapel, no-one noticed any change, and the sacrificial procedure continued, horribly uninterrupted. Sir Reginald, with all the slickness of a surgeon, completed the severing. The baby's body convulsed as he held it upside-down above the communion cup, the poor unknowing little lamb. He placed the head in the kidney-shaped dish. His hands as he did this were veiled in a delicate and tragic mist of red.

Steele saw it all. Sir Reginald, it was clear, was in no way dismayed by the tiny, inverted headless body he held dangling by the ankles – like a butcher exhibiting a prize chicken. It was cruel, not the way a parent, too afraid of dropping, would ever hold their child.

The last of the blood pulsed from the arteries and Patricia ran the cup around the neck to collect any remaining moisture.

'Eternal life,' she said, holding the cup up above her head, then brought it down for Sir Reginald to do something with.

Steele watched, appalled, as Sir Reginald poured in communion wine from a bottle and what must be holy water from a glass. This he swilled ceremonially around.

'Eternal life,' he said, 'for all who taste. And all who are here *will* and *must* taste.'

Steele struggled, but the grip upon his arms held firm.

Sir Reginald himself was first to drink. Then came Patricia, lipping the cup with flutteringly closed eyelids and an expression of expectant ecstasy upon her face – was this the elixir of youth she so craved? How she hoped it was! That was what she needed, a cure-all, a panacea, to save her from the trials of death she witnessed every day – that she had witnessed too many times and of which she had become mortally terrified.

The rest of the Satanists lined up in an orderly fashion, just as they would have done at a conventional Eucharist.

Patricia, now an immortal, perhaps, handed the cup back to the possibly everlasting Sir Reginald.

As each anti-communicant came up to kneel down

and drink, he held the cup out to them and tipped it slightly up – so they would not be too greedy with this precious and unholy admixture.

Greedy! They were all of them avaricious for everything they could get – so despicably attached to this shoddy life that they would risk their immortal souls to keep hold of it.

One by one they drank – the men taking turns to hold Steele by the arms.

After they had taken the diabolic sacrament, many of the anti-communicants turned and smiled at him with evil red teeth showing between lips stained dark purple. They had nothing to fear now, or so they thought.

Only one of them resisted – the brunette who was strapped to the altar. She seemed to be in a kind of trance of terror but tried to keep her mouth shut when Sir Reginald approached with the cup. It took two of the congregation, Patricia and midwife Honey Hopeful, to prise her lips apart. Sir Reginald poured in a drop or two and, with her nose pinched, the young woman couldn't help but swallow. After this, she fainted quite away.

'He too shall taste of life eternal,' said Sir Reginald. 'He too must join us.'

Steele struggled manfully but now what seemed like the whole devilish congregation came together to force him up the aisle. There was one chance and one chance only – their numbers would count against them.

Vaguely, even in his panic, he heard a voice behind him saying, 'I don't *feel* any different, do you?'

In their time, all the porters had seen more than enough dead bodies to know what one looked like –

and Pierre Estime was unmistakably dead. His shiny skin had yet to change colour, but its tone was completely different: cold, dull, giving nothing out.

'*Oui, il est mort!*'

Briefly, there was hope of a miraculous resurrection – that Pierre would come back to them from the grave, telling stories of the spirit world and the forces which had decided to spare him a little longer.

'*Non, il est mort.*'

Once they realized that Pierre wasn't shamming, that he really *had* died, there was an approach to pandemonium. Some embraced, others started tear-blind fistfights with whoever happened to be in front of them. Bodies were slammed back into lockers.

In that instant there seemed to be twice as many men in the room – and all of them were strangers, enemies, any one of them could have caused this to happen. Pierre was the only man there who they could be certain they knew, and Pierre, the only man they knew, was no longer there.

The flickering of the lights and the quietening of the ward had put the boy off making his third and final wish.

He was thinking of wishing himself home – that would be the simplest thing. But maybe that wasn't specific enough. Maybe if he wished that, he would be punished in some way. That was how fairytales seemed to work: get it wrong and it all went to the bad.

When he lifted his head above the sheets, Nurse Bland hadn't moved. The big-windowed office behind her was empty, though – a policewoman walking quickly out; a large black woman escorting a skinny young woman past the end of the boy's bed.

'Go to sleep,' Nurse Bland said, then seemed to relent. 'Don't worry. It happens all the time. Very fluky power in this place. But we've got a back-up generator, and that'll see us through until we get the mains up again. So you needn't worry, I'm not going anywhere.'

The boy fell back on the pillow and tried to work out if he felt any better in his stomach.

A quick, painful touch informed him the shoot hadn't magically, wishfully disappeared.

No, and it had continued to grow.

He needed to get home – more urgently than ever.

No-one could understand it at all. Something must have happened to the helicopter – it simply hadn't arrived.

Sarah Felt tried and tried again to raise the pilot on the radio; Digby Rutter attempted to call the paramedic on his cellphone. Neither worked – all Sarah heard was the empty crackle of static, Digby heard nothing, not even a dial-tone.

'It can't have crashed, can it?' asked Gemma.

'No way,' said Sarah, 'It was so close to Hospital – probably within sight. We would have heard.'

'Then where is it?' asked Nurse Fist.

To get her and her incipient panic out of the room, Sarah said to her, 'Go up to the roof and see what you can find out.' The young woman hesitated – this wasn't part of her job.

'Go!' shouted Sarah, and Gemma admired for a moment her leadership qualities.

As soon as the nervy nurse had gone, Sarah dialled the number of the helicopter station on the roof. The others stood around, listening to the one end of the conversation they could hear.

'Hello,' said Sarah, and explained who she was. 'So, you haven't seen the chopper? No? You can't see what? Let me get this clear: you're not expecting the helicopter to arrive now? You think it has crashed? Well, what do you mean, "just disappeared"? No! I don't understand.'

'What is he saying?' Gemma asked impatiently.

'He says,' Sarah replied quickly, her hand over the receiver, '"Everything has disappeared." I think some kind of freak fog has come down. Go and have a look.'

Taking these words to be directed at her, Gemma set off at a run towards the nearest outside window she could think of.

Case opened his eyes just after the lights went dim – then tried to open them a second time, even though he hadn't closed them again.

He looked to his left, where Spanner seemed to be asleep. He was grunting like a bulldog shagging someone's leg.

With each passing moment, Case's head seemed to be clearing a little more – which was a disappointment to him.

He leaned across and plucked up his large drug bag. From this, with rustling sounds, he extracted some blister packs. But in this artificial twilight, he couldn't tell one standard-sized sheet from another – the writing on the silver foil was just the wrong side of legible.

Case wanted to take some uppers, get himself straight.

Pushing himself up by means of Spanner's sinking shoulder, Case rose to almost his full height: the drugs in his system kept him semi-ape.

The walk across to the doorway took a very long time as the space in front of him expanded with every step he took. And when he finally got there, it wasn't worth the epic journey because no lights came on when he flicked the switches. Nor when he banged the switches with his fist.

He tried to open the door out into the corridor; it didn't move, was snugly locked.

The punch he aimed at it didn't connect, and he lost balance, stumbled, fell and smashed his head against the corner of some shelves.

This had a not dissimilar effect to the drugs, only now bleeding was involved.

As Steele stood pinioned in front of her, Patricia looked down gloatingly upon him. She was quite unabashed by her nakedness, seemed almost to be displaying herself to him – in hopes of who knows what savage rites of lust.

'Bring him,' intoned Sir Reginald.

Steele managed to get his left foot up on the edge of the altar. The cup was held out in front of Sir Reginald's chest.

'Drink,' he commanded.

Steele kicked as hard and as high as he could with his right foot – the only part of his body left free to move. He made good contact with the bottom of the cup, knocking it back over his and the congregation's heads. Spots of misty moisture fell upon them. Patricia's look changed from seductive to wrathful.

'Oh Lord, he rejects your offered life,' shouted

Sir Reginald, improvising, as if Steele's attempt to disrupt the ceremony had merely been part of it. 'And so he chooses death instead!'

It was almost with relief that Steele saw Sir Reginald, who had been knighted by the Queen of England, who had knelt before her and felt her sword upon his shoulderblades – reach again for the sacrificial dagger, fresh blood glistening all along its razor-sharp edge.

Just a few centimetres in front of him, the baby's dead body and dead head lay beside the naked woman's body. Her breasts heaved up and down. Steele felt nauseous in a way he had never before, not even as a young medical student taking part in his first facial dissection. He found himself thinking of Gemma Swallow – very glad she hadn't come with him to be part of this madness. Hopefully, when he didn't return, she would tell other people about his mysterious trip down to the 13th floor. There should be enough forensic evidence in this room to send the whole diabolic congregation to prison for a very long time. 'Wait!' shouted a voice behind him. It was one of the Security Guards – Cropper.

'Look,' he said, coming closer. 'There's still a drop or two left in the bottom.'

'It is a miracle,' said Patricia.

'O Satan, great Satan,' chanted Henderson MacVanish.

'Let me see,' said Sir Reginald.

The cup was passed to him and he looked into its bowl, as if reading Steele's tea-leaves. 'His life is saved,' he said. 'His death is postponed, perhaps infinitely. Now, hold him very still.'

Steele could feel that this time every single part of his body was fixed by strong medical hands. He tried to kick to headbutt to punch but found himself only gently wriggling about – the fly in the tightest part of the spider's web. It was no longer even clear to him if his feet were still touching the ground.

Sir Reginald reached out and put his fingers on either side of Steele's nose – nostrils – then pinched hard. This time there was to be no disruption, no kicking.

For the most part, Hospital was still in ignorance of the changes outside. Many floors were following their normal night-time routine. Panic was certainly present, and spreading, and accelerating, but only very slowly. At such an early hour, all the patients were meant to be asleep. Insomniacs of various sorts were looking towards outside, thinking fast thoughts about places elsewhere, doing accounts, worrying over children left with feckless fathers or dodgy uncles, yearning towards the world of health – but they couldn't see enough of the sky or the ground to know what was going on: gaps above curtains, slits through blinds. The ward nurses, for their part, were too busy to waste time looking through windows. Most of them noticed the brownout at midnight, when the emergency generators took over, but this was only one of a thousand mini-crises they had to deal with every hour. The business of reinserting drips which had been knocked out by violent sleepers, or inserted by incompetent junior doctors, kept them fully occupied.

However, Sister Agnes Day on the front desk in Reception had noticed that, very strangely, no-one had come in for over ten minutes. (This she had done despite a vicious itching behind her glass eye – and a feeling of increasing pressure.) As a result, A&E

was unusually quiet, and once they had cleared their whiteboard of cases, a junior doctor or two wandered curiously outside for a cigarette and to see what the hell was going on. They did not come back – neither one of them. Sister Agnes was just remarking on this to PC Dixon when WPC Angel walked in. 'What was that?' she asked.

'It's just a power-cut,' said Sister Agnes. 'Happens all the time. They should have it sorted pretty soon.'

'Well, I thought I'd better come down,' said WPC Angel.

'There hasn't been any trouble,' said PC Dixon.

WPC Angel couldn't bear how sad he looked; *really* like he might cry.

'I suppose I could go back up and finish.'

'Yes,' he said. Then couldn't prevent himself asking, 'How's it going?'

'Oh, you know,' said WPC Angel. 'She's scared, confused – wanting something to take away the pain.'

PC Dixon could see her, had seen her a thousand times before: shivering in an overheated room; lank hair, dull skin; making the furniture around her seem outsize and brutal.

'It's pretty quiet down here,' he said. 'The whole place seems dead.'

A silent pause confirmed this.

'I'm sure that boy is somehow related to the man in the coma,' said WPC Angel.

'The one you caught a while ago?' asked Sister Day.

'Yes.'

'Does he look like him, do you think?' asked PC Dixon.

'I'm not sure,' said WPC Angel. 'I'd need to see the man again. He certainly looks like the daughter.'

'We don't know it's his daughter,' PC Dixon said.

'Who else would she be?'

They were close to having an argument. Something WPC Angel definitely didn't want; not right now. 'Looks like there's a bit of a fog outside,' she said.

'Oh, yes,' said Sister Day.

'I hadn't noticed that,' replied PC Dixon, glancing round. 'God, that's thick.'

'You're still thinking about earlier, aren't you?' said WPC Angel, quiet enough so only PC Dixon could hear.

It took Dixon a moment to realize Melanie was talking about his ex-wife.

He didn't want to lie, though.

'No,' he said. 'I'd completely forgotten her. It's –'

Melanie didn't press it any further. 'I'll be back as soon as I can,' she said. 'If it's quiet, we can go and get a coffee.'

'Sure,' said PC Dixon, unconvincingly.

So sad.

Gemma's route towards a window took her out into the corridor and through a couple of offices – she barged their doors, not worrying whether or not they were occupied. This little journey gave her enough time to think of Steele, with anxiety and love. Where was he? Surely he should have been back by now? It was several minutes after midnight, a quick check of her watch told her.

The window when she reached it was a widescreen of blank. She looked up into the fog, vainly hoping to see the lights from the bottom of the helicopter; she looked down, and saw no difference in quality or intensity of light – up and down didn't seem to matter, outside, any more. The sight horrified her beyond explanation. She expected, at least, to be able to see the glow of the carpark. But it was just as the helicopter engineer had said, and as Sarah Felt had uncomprehendingly relayed: everything had disappeared into a cloud of featureless, grubby yellow.

To reassure herself that the outside world *was* still actually there, she opened one of the windows. Being so high up, and this being a hospital with its fair quota of suicidal people, patients and staff, the window only opened a crack, at the top.

Gemma pulled over a chair and got up on it, but even with her ear poised under the widest part, she could hear nothing from outside. The exterior acoustic had a dullness, a deadness, as if the fog were actively absorbing sounds. Gemma strained to hear something, anything, over her heartbeat's banging – the laugh of some smokers down in the ambulance bay, the beep of an angry car horn, the shimmer of a distant and approaching helicopter. But the world, if it was still out there at all, had gone completely silent.

A new thought struck Gemma: perhaps the fog was not fog at all, but chemical gas, either escaped from a nearby factory (she couldn't think of any, but she didn't know the area that well) or part of a terrorist attack. By allowing a gap, she would be letting whatever it was into the building – although she hadn't smelled anything chemical or noxious. She shut the window, fast, then ran back towards the Emergency Room – never perhaps so aptly named.

One of the porters had fetched a gurney and together, with gentle respect, they now laid their friend out upon it.

They couldn't simply take Pierre's corpse down to Pathology – he had been one of that department's most regular visitors; Dexter von Sinistre, Molesworth or one of the others would recognize him straight away: ask awkward questions.

All the porters knew that their actions throughout Hospital were recorded by security cameras (not in *this* room; they were sure of that – had checked). Their main difficulty would be finding some way of getting Pierre's body unsuspiciously into the incinerator, guarded by their great subterranean friend Fergus Moore. It wouldn't be possible just to heave a body-bag in through the burning-bright door. They would have to cut him into pieces and put those pieces where they would inevitably end up being destroyed. With bored expressions on their faces, the porters would have to take him down, dump him.

A household saw was produced: Excellent Excellent had been intending to visit his grandfather the following morning to help him make some bookshelves. A machete also appeared, without explanation. Yellow bags marked with warnings about medical waste were brought out of other lockers. They stole vast numbers of them to use for storing things at home.

With the body there, and the tools in place, the fact that *someone* would have to do the cutting could no longer be avoided.

All eyes, pupils dilated, turned to Cyrille Delira – now, with Pierre dead, he was temporary Head Voodoo Man.

'Othniel Calixte must do it,' he said, desperately improvising.

There was no logical reason why Othniel should

be chosen – and if he had been challenged, Cyrille would have been answerless. But no-one said a word.

Luckson StJust held out the saw for Othniel to take.

When Gemma got back, Sarah was addressing the whole team in her best keep-calm voice.

'. . . all return to normal,' she said, but then looked expectantly at Gemma.

The others, too, turned in her direction.

'The outside has disappeared,' Gemma said, with some bravery. 'You can't see it or hear it. It's covered up by what looks like a thick fog. But I'm not really sure it is still there at all. I think something very strange is happening.'

The reaction from the others in the team was just as Sarah had expected: they laughed and relaxed. It wasn't possible that the world outside the window, the world in general, had ceased to exist. Individually, internally, there may have been panic, but between them – socially – there were jokes.

Gemma felt ridiculed. 'Send someone else,' she said, 'if you don't believe me.'

'Oh, we do, we do,' chuckled Digby Rutter.

Quietly, though, one or two of them snuck off to nearby phones – tried to make calls out of the hospital, and found they were unable to: there was no dialling tone, no sound at all.

'That moment when the power cut out,' said Nurse Wall.

'I think we went onto the emergency generator,' Sarah replied.

'It was midnight, whoooo!' added Digby, spookily.

Sarah took herself into Sir Reginald's office and,

against Trauma policy (because they interfered with essential monitoring equipment), turned on her cellphone.

There was no signal. She held it above her head, squinting up into the screen – still no signal.

When she re-emerged into the emergency room it was clear that most of the others had made checks of their own – and not one of them had succeeded in contacting anyone outside Hospital.

And Nurse Fist had not yet returned from checking out the helipad (she was never to return – after she saw what she saw, or rather didn't see what she didn't see).

As a group, the team set off to follow the route Gemma had taken a few minutes earlier – and Gemma, wanting to be validated, went with them.

The first cut, head from neck, was the most difficult – after that a kind of trance-of-hacking took over; it stopped being dismemberment (plain and simple) and turned into labour. Also, it was hard physical labour: soon, the sweat of it was all Othniel knew.

To murder someone with a single gunshot to the temple feels like a terrible exertion of sin, though it involves nothing more than the squeezing of a trigger; but to dig their grave through heavy clay is always going to feel like the humiliating daily grind of an unvalued slave.

Othniel was used to working hard: sometimes, after he finished a night-shift at Hospital, he went straight to his cousins' yard and headed out for a painting and decorating job.

Now, he felt in his own bones the teeth of the saw heading into Pierre's; sometimes he found it hard to get the serrated metal into the sinews, to cut between the joints; he shouted to his assistants, Luckson and Fritzgerald – wanting them to twist the arm round until the white wet line became visible, cutting through the red blood layer. Pierre's life-warmth was waning, but he had not yet retreated to objecthood: the motor of his spirit was still radiating some energy out into the world.

Othniel, in a way, found this heat preferable to the chilly bodies, stiff, he often transported from upstairs to Pathology, Pathology to ambulance – funeral parlour, next, for laying out and burying, with tears; not like this. They were in body-bags, the dead, but, as a curious young new porter, he had unzipped and touched them; like the skin of a joint of pork, straight from the fridge.

This job of disposal was merely another in the endless series of initiations. Until there were more men junior to him than senior, Othniel would still be a focus – albeit diminishing – of regular humiliation. The rule of Cyrille was unlikely to be any more just than that of Pierre; the biggest victims of the old oppression were likely to prove the keenest supporters of the new.

Several times Othniel stopped and staggered away, eyes aflow with tears. It wasn't that he was doing this to his friend and old master, it was that someone might some day do this to him. The work seemed to get harder as Othniel went on. This, he supposed, was because rigor mortis was beginning to change the muscle structure – a texture of overdone roast chicken steaks. Othniel kept his mouth tightly closed.

They reached the wide window and their little atmosphere of joking immediately decompressed.

'I'm scared,' said Nurse Fanny Wall. 'Yes, I'm definitely scared. I don't understand it. I just don't understand what I'm seeing.'

Sarah went across and put her arm round her. 'I'm sure we'll be fine,' she said. 'Nothing's happened to us yet, has it?'

'That doesn't mean nothing will,' said Nurse Digby Rutter. 'If that's a poison-gas leak . . .'

'I think we'd know that by now,' said Gemma, deciding to back Sarah up.

'Then what is it?' asked Nurse Wall.

'I'm sure we'll find out soon enough,' said Sarah, every inch the health professional.

'Where's Sir Reginald?' asked Nurse Rutter, his voice ragged with suppressed panic.

Gemma had a moment's indecision, then spoke. She explained what she had seen: Sir Reginald and Patricia going off together, saying they were heading for Pathology; Steele's watching their lift down to the 13th floor and then his following them. She omitted nothing, nothing but Steele's final, sacred, intimate words to her: 'See you when I'm back.'

'What's on the 13th floor?' asked Nurse Wall, who was annoying everyone with her lost-it-ness.

'I don't know,' said Gemma.

'It's just offices, isn't it?' Nurse Rutter said.

'I've never been there,' said Nurse Wall. 'I've never had a reason to go.'

'Well, as we don't have any patients,' said Sarah, in charge, 'we might as well try and find a few of our staff. Gemma, I'd like you to come with me. Everyone else, go back to the emergency room and stay there. We'll bring Sir Reginald as soon as we can. Now, clear out of this room. It's not going to do anyone good, staring into a yellow cloud of nothingness.' She hadn't meant to put it quite so vividly.

There was a moment during which resistance to her rule might have begun, had Nurse Rutter spoken up or Nurse Wall broken down, but it passed.

The team turned as one and walked quietly back, in obedience to Sarah's orders.

Gemma was beginning to admire Sarah, for her coolness under extreme pressure. But as soon as the others were out of earshot, Sarah began to have what looked very like an asthma attack. 'Oh God oh God,' she said. 'Inhaler – need my inhaler.'

'Where is it?' asked Gemma.

'In my locker. Number eight. The key – here's the key,' Sarah managed to hiss, between deep rasping gasps for breath.

Spanner, when he next regained some sort of consciousness, looked around for Case – but the fucking cunt was gone.

The fucking cunt had probably run off home to watch television (after, that is, trading some of the drugs in for a television, since his last television had recently been traded in for drugs).

After achieving standing position, Spanner stuffed a few more packets into his bin-bag and began to float swayingly towards the door.

'Hello, feet,' he said, in an attempt to regain contact, but they ignored him; busy.

Next thing he knew, they had scuffed into something on the floor. Annoyed, he kicked it a couple of times, and the combination of give (copious) and resistance (minimal) encountered by his toes told him, with great certainty, that the object was Case, Case's gut. But this realization did not cause him to cause his feet to stop – that the obstacle was Case made him even more angry.

'Get out!' he screamed.

Instantly, a hand grabbed his left ankle and another hand cupped itself around the sole of his left foot; together, solidly anchored, the hands twisted through 180 degrees.

Spanner went down – falling face first into some shelves holding suppositories. His hands still holding the bag, what took the impact was his chin. The next time he opened his mouth, there would be more teeth in it: several would have split down the middle. He could feel this, even as his cheekbone impacted on the second, lower shelf: rehydration packs. I don't want to be ugly, he thought, as he continued down. I don't want – But this thought was interrupted by the bottom shelf, laxatives, and then irreparably shattered by the floor.

Case had moved fast, was now standing over him. 'I am your friend,' he said, then kicked Spanner, hard, in the balls. 'Don't kick me.'

Spanner pronounced the oh of *okay* before he was kicked again.

'Friends don't kick friends,' said Case, not without kindness in his tone. 'I'm just paying you back.'

This wasn't true: Case's kicks were much better than Spanner's.

'I'm just teaching you a fucking lesson, you fucking cunt.'

If the light hadn't been so bad, they would both have been able to see the pink frothing out of Spanner's mouth.

'Do you understand?'

The smell of Case's anger was in Spanner's nose, which was sensitized by having been broken.

He pulled his hands up to cover his eyes, to prevent any further damage to his beauty, but Case had already stopped.

'Do you understand, cunt?'

Spanner only now remembered that Case was meant to be his bodyguard. What kind of idiot attacked his own bodyguard?

This time he got to the end of *okay.*

'The door's locked,' said Case, sitting down on the floor beside his damaged friend.

Spanner's hand was already rootling among the bag full of drugs: painkillers, he needed good pain-killers; the best.

When he had finished, the saw was taken from Othniel's hand; tenderly, with added respect.

Someone he didn't recognize, although he knew them all, led him towards the corner of the room and told him that he was a brave and worthy man, and that he must strip and wash himself clean.

Othniel began to pluck at the buttons on his jacket. His fingers felt frostbitten. Behind him, they were already getting impatient. 'What does it matter?' one man, Janvier Baptiste, said.

Othniel succeeded in undoing the top button and moved down to the next. Just then, he felt his arms being held. A sideways glance showed him the flash of the machete – and then he felt one edge of it slicing down his back.

For several seconds, he didn't know whether he had been cut or not; if so, why not just stab him in the heart?

This thought was followed by another: if they killed him for dismembering Pierre's body, then someone would have to dismember him, and so on and so on, until only two men were left to fight for which of them survived.

The knife halted briefly at his buttocks, then he felt the waistband of his trousers loosen. It *was* his clothes they were cutting, not him; and carefully.

When Othniel was naked they took him to the sink, removed the bucket and mop, and made him squat under the tap.

The water was cold, Othniel knew this intellectually but didn't actually feel it on his skin; hands of others washed Pierre's blood from his hands.

His attention was drawn to the dark streaks chasing one another into the vortex of the plughole. There were toothpaste stripes in the water – a fact that seemed important, should be communicated.

Othniel realized that he could still hear – he knew there were voices around him and that some of them were using his name, presumably to address him; Othniel could hear but he couldn't listen.

He felt his nakedness more than his coldness, not that the other men had never seen him naked before. Their warm hands gripped him under the arms and lifted him clear. They dried him with rough paper as his eyes watched Luckson and Fritzgerald cleaning the large deep porcelain sink – they both had beautiful technique; it would be very clean.

He remembered again, there had been red stripes in the cold water which he had not felt washing Pierre's blood off his body.

A new set of blue overalls was brought in. His white Wellingtons were placed back on his feet, wet inside.

Gemma took Sarah's locker key and ran. She immediately wished she'd asked where *exactly* in the locker the inhaler was.

When she saw the backs of the Trauma team, just entering the emergency room, she slowed down. It wouldn't do for them to see her in a panic.

The lockers were located along a short stretch of corridor, a few doors away from Trauma. As the others sat or stood around and Digby Rutter lay down on the examination table, against all regulations, Gemma glided past. Luckily, no-one took any notice of her.

The lockers – the lockers. Gemma had the key ready in her hand, and did not fumble opening Sarah's.

Inside, it was very tidy. Gemma went straight for Sarah's handbag – what an opportunity to see if there was any evidence of an involvement with Steele!

She flipped through the fragrant compartments – the bag was leather, black, shiny, smelled of recently-boughtness. No inhaler. She went back through them a second time to check. There was a Tupperware dish. Nothing in it but an apple and a banana. The only other thing was Sarah's coat, and it was here deep in a side pocket, beneath a clean handkerchief, that Gemma found Sarah's inhaler.

Despite her hurry, Gemma made sure to leave the locker locked – she wasn't certain exactly why this was important.

As she strode purposefully back through Trauma, she thought about what she'd seen in Sarah's handbag – no photograph of Steele, no address book.

As far as she could tell, the others hadn't moved in the minute or two since she'd passed by. There was a definite increase in tension, though – this time they watched her, all eyes following.

She was glad to see Sarah was still upright, wasn't

lying gasping dying on the floor. 'Here you are,' Gemma said, handing over the inhaler.

Sarah mustn't have been too bad because she managed to wheeze out *thank you* before taking three very deep sucks on the greeny-grey plastic lifesaver.

'You'll be better in a minute,' said Gemma. 'Just take it easy.' She felt odd, comforting her deadly rival in love.

'Everything okay?' asked Digby Rutter loudly, from the doorway.

'Yes,' said Sarah and Gemma, at the same time.

'Go back,' added Sarah, with the inhaler concealed in her fist.

He did.

Sarah took another hit. 'Thanks,' she said, then looked out the window at the fog again. 'That's my ultimate-worst fear,' she said. 'Suffocation . . .'

Gemma was more than a little surprised. Although she had been working at Hospital for a month, she had had no idea Sarah was asthmatic. What would have happened if she'd had an attack whilst a patient was under her hand? Why didn't she carry her inhaler with her all the time? Surely she had been negligently putting lives at risk? But she was a wonderful anaesthetist. It would have been a travesty if she had been prevented from fulfilling her vocation.

Sarah continued to look out into the fog, as if it were the heavy contents of her lungs. She shivered, shook as many of the bad thoughts out of her head as she could, then turned to Gemma – who, for almost the first time, was feeling genuinely sympathetic towards her rival. 'Shall we go and find Steele, then?' Sarah asked, her breath now back but her face pinker than usual.

Unable to speak for the flood of jealous passion

that washed through her, Gemma merely nodded. Don't ever mention him again, she thought. Don't use his name. Don't even think his name. Sarah could have said, let's go and look for Sir Reginald. Why hadn't she?

They set off towards the lift, in silence. Sarah tried to break it, once, by thanking Gemma again for saving her.

'It's nothing,' said Gemma, but felt a small glow of power at what she'd done, and at her rival's revealed weakness.

Nurse Rutter was back on the exam table, to all appearances asleep. The others stood in a couple of groups of three – they were talking about what they thought would happen next; some sort of announcement over the hospital tannoy.

One of them had tried turning on a radio, only to encounter nothing but static from one end of the dial to the other.

Gemma and Sarah had reached the lifts.

'They might not be working,' said Sarah. 'I'm not sure if the back-up generator gives out enough power to keep them going as well as the life-support machines, the lights and everything. We might have to walk.' But when she pressed the call button, the red lightbulb behind it came on.

And when they looked up, they saw that the numbers above the door, from minus six to twenty-five, were changing.

Nurse Ginger Bland was no longer at her desk.

Further down the ward, quite a lot further, a young woman had started to have hysterics. From what the boy heard, she had been trying to attack one of the girls.

'She hit me!' came a very high screech, not from the woman.

Other high voices tried to join in but were immediately shushed by Nurse Bland.

It was the boy's chance.

He crawled to the end of the bed and looked in the direction of the noise.

Nurse Bland stood in the middle of the aisle, holding the very thin young woman by the left arm.

'Stop that,' she said.

'Tell them to fucking shut up!' the skinny woman shouted. 'They're all whispering about me.'

Another burst of struggle ensued, with Nurse Bland losing her grip.

The boy jumped down off the bed and ran for the door.

'Stop!' Nurse Bland shouted.

The boy could tell it was for him.

'I can see you,' she said, firmly. 'Get back in bed.'

He glanced round and saw that all the children in the ward were now looking at him – and the hysterical woman.

Just then another nurse came into the ward.

'Grab him,' shouted Nurse Bland. 'Grab that one beside you.'

The boy tried to flinch away, but the adult hand caught him. It had a strange texture, not like flesh.

'Oh, hello,' said the Rubber Nurse. 'It's you.'

'Just put him back in bed,' called Nurse Bland, 'while I deal with Nikki, here.'

'With pleasure,' the Rubber Nurse replied.

Humiliatingly, she swung the boy up into her arms and carried him, cradled, as if he were a little baby, back to his hateful bed.

'So naughty,' she cooed. 'Such a bad boy. Bed is always the best place for bad boys.'

She laid him on the sheets and then passed her squeaky hand across his forehead.

'You haven't got a temperature, so I don't need to take it. What's wrong with you?'

The boy was horrified by the idea of showing this bizarre woman his bizarre shoot.

'Nothing,' he said. 'I shouldn't be here. It's a mistake.'

'We'll look after you very well,' the Rubber Nurse said, pulling the covers over him and patting them down. 'We know how to take care of naughty boys who don't think they are ill. The treatment might hurt a little, or perhaps even a lot, but it's good for them in the end.'

'You can see I'm not ill,' said the boy. 'I want to go home.'

'Perhaps you can go home tomorrow,' the Rubber Nurse said. 'But, right now, you need to do exactly what I tell you to do – which is lie back and relax. Think nice thoughts. Don't think about anything bad or worry about anything worrying.'

As she spoke, she adjusted the tops of her shiny stockings. The boy had never seen a woman with such long legs – except on posters or in cartoons.

Then, with a squeak, she sat down on the chair for visitors.

'Don't worry,' he said, 'I won't try to escape again.'

'I'm sure you will,' she said. 'It takes a long time for naughty boys to learn their lesson.'

'Thank you,' said Nurse Bland, coming into sight. 'I think I've got everything under control, now.'

'This is a very naughty boy,' said the Rubber Nurse.

'He certainly is,' said Nurse Bland.

*

Fergus Moore would have the incinerator up and running now. Hospital policy was to do the bulk of its incineration at night, when the smoke could not be seen.

It had been decided, during a particularly antagonistic board meeting, that the cost of night-work was well worth it – otherwise, patients, seeing the chimney chugging as they arrived, were likely to think they would be leaving as smoke.

'We're not running a crematorium,' Sir Reginald had said.

'Nor a charity,' the Chief Executive, Duncan Bowis, had replied.

Among the porters, an argument had begun as to who should dispose of the body. Cyrille said that Othniel might as well finish the job; others – particularly Fritzgerald and Luckson – strongly disagreed. Eventually, as it often does, age won out over anger.

One by one, the porters set off towards the incinerator, carrying Pierre's body in doubled-up medical-waste bags; yellow, sloshy. They left at five-minute intervals, so as to be as inconspicuous as possible.

The porters were certain the locker-room contained no cameras – that was one of the reasons, apart from its isolated location (and proximity to the incinerator), they had chosen it for rituals. But the corridor immediately outside was under twenty-four-hour surveillance.

When they left, the porters wore baseball caps low down over their eyes – so it was impossible to tell which of them was which. Some went to places other than the incinerator; all had agreed to meet up back there in an hour.

Othniel was allowed to remain behind, to rest.

Alone, he felt disgusted with what he had done;

felt the motions of sawing still in his muscles. He looked at his hands and realized they were somehow familiar, but they belonged to someone else now, a person he would have to learn to become.

The lift came for Gemma and Sarah. Waiting for it that little while, each had been caught up in her own thoughts. Sarah was wondering how best to keep the department together, should they fail to find Sir Reginald. Gemma was completely lost in anxiety on Steele's behalf.

A Geriatrics nurse, Martha Castle, got in on the 22nd floor and pressed the button for the Ground. She was unpanicked, still in the world of routine – gave them a quick, tired smile as she got in but did not speak. Neither of them knew her.

On the 20th, the lift stopped again. When the doors opened, Gemma was amazed by what her lowered gaze saw: legs, legs going up, up, up from the floor – legs slim and shapely and tightly covered in a brightly shiny material.

The tall, bottle-blond woman strode slinkily into the lift, and the brighter light there made her glisten all over. Gemma's eyes met those of Sarah who, to disguise her real horror, gave a look of mock horror: for she had had a liaison of her own with the Rubber Nurse. And it was as if the words *Rubber Nurse* had flown from Sarah's mind directly into Gemma's. Of course, Gemma thought, *that's* who she is. As soon as she realized this, she could smell her – a sweet, catchy, well-lubricated smell. But the lift doors had closed, and now they were moving down.

Gemma wanted to speak, to warn this huge, bizarre creature off Steele.

The Rubber Nurse stood straight and tall. There

was no slope to her broad shoulders, her spine still stayed pertly curved – displaying her supernaturally pneumatic bust to its considerable best advantage. Without thinking – it didn't look to Gemma as if the Rubber Nurse *thought* very much – she gave a small, sexy sigh of impatience. Then she breathed in super-deeply (all three women were aware of her every last shift and squeak) – and then, disconcertingly, her arched white nostrils began to twitch. She lifted her bright blond head and sniffed the air – sniffing in the direction of each of them in turn.

'Ah,' she said, finally. 'Hello, Sarah Felt, Trauma. It's been such a *long* time since we *met*. You've been avoiding me, haven't you? But I never forget a . . . pheromone.'

Her voice was soft, husky and seemed lubricated by fluids most other throats did not contain.

The shiny creature gave Gemma a very thorough once-over with her eyes, and then, eyes closed, with her nose. It was worse than walking past a 1970s building site or a pavement café in Milan – Gemma felt as if she'd not only been assessed but *touched*, her labia parted, her clitoris twiddled and then measured for blood-flow and capacity. This was the kind of initial visual examination which the Rubber Nurse always performed. Gemma need not have worried, though. The Rubber Nurse's diagnosis was always the same: naughtiness – and all naughtiness deserved to be punished, severely but pleasurably.

'I'm surprised you remember me,' said Sarah.

'Oh,' said the Rubber Nurse, and the *Oh* went on for about half a floor. 'I remember all my patients – each and every one. But you, you naughty thing, you haven't introduced me to your beautiful little friend.'

Gemma was petrified. The Nurse towered over

her in her heeled boots, and seemed so brightly smiling as to be a kind of X-rated toothpaste advertisement.

'This is Nurse Gemma Swallow,' Sarah said, and Gemma felt afresh the school-room embarrassment of her name.

'Is it?' said the Rubber Nurse. 'Is it, really?'

The lift was a couple of floors above the 13th. The Rubber Nurse seemed fully in control. 'Well, I'm on my way to a very urgent case – not as urgent as you brave people deal with in Trauma.' The lift stopped with a lurch that Gemma hardly noticed for the constant lurching within her heart. 'But I'll see you three girls later.' She stepped out into the lobby, and turning away from them said, 'Especially *you*, Gemma Swallow, Trauma.'

The doors closed on a tightly wrapped powder-blue behind sashaying off towards some lucky or unlucky Oncology/Haematology patient.

Gemma looked at Sarah with what was meant to be sympathy. 'It was the end of a very long shift,' Sarah said defensively. 'No-one had warned me about her. She seemed a little mad but wasn't unfriendly. I thought we were just going to have a drink in her room.'

Gemma started to say, 'But I didn't –'

'Boy,' continued Sarah, 'you should see her room.'

'I have no intention of seeing her room.' As she said this, Gemma realized that, in fact, she had been intending to find her way there just as soon as she possibly could.

'Oh, you will,' said Sarah. 'You will. Everybody seems to end up in there, sooner or later.

'No,' said Gemma. 'I won't.'

But they were at their floor.

*

Sir Reginald was satisfied.

Everything had been organized meticulously; everything – despite the reluctance of the Virgin and Steele's best efforts – had gone to plan. (The mess could be cleaned up later, with the help of Fergus Moore, the disposal man.) No, tonight was the glorious culmination of many months of planning and many years of scheming. Sir Reginald had slowly built up his contacts, finding useful links in departments all through Hospital. (Often this began, as earlier this evening, with a quiet chat in the canteen. He liked to think of this as his Omega Course.)

The chaplain had at first said he didn't mind the Chapel being used for Devil worship, just so long as they cleaned up afterwards – he was ecumenically interdenominational by upbringing and inclination, and really just liked to see the place being used. Then he'd confessed his bum-curiosity and become an enthusiastic devotee; in return for a good hard seeing-to, Sir Reginald got unrestricted access not only to the Chapel but also to the communion wine and wafers.

Last to come on board had been Henderson MacVanish, who had resisted all encouragements, however young and firm-bodied. But then he was diagnosed with testicular cancer, and the offer of eternal life had become a lot more enticing (never mind that Sir Reginald had arranged with a couple of the oncological consultants to have the test results faked, just to up the pressure).

MacVanish it was who – in collaboration with Honey Hopeful – had been able to supply them with the newborn, unweaned baby.

The wee whelp's mother, the gynaecologist said, had been brought in to be delivered of twins. So, the parents would be able to keep one of them – which was very decent, Sir Reginald thought. Very decent, indeed.

As for the ceremony itself, the results – if any – would only gradually become apparent.

Right now, Sir Reginald was feeling marvellously invigorated – invigorated in all the right areas.

And it just so happened that there was a young virgin available to begin to satisfy his lusts.

Carrying Pierre Estime's head in a bag, the first porter, Excellent Excellent, was astonished to find the incinerator unmanned – working but abandoned; Fergus Moore nowhere to be seen.

Excellent did what he'd been planning: dumped the head as quickly as possible in one of the huge wheelie-bins: there, safe, it would be just another slushy load to be thrown to the flames.

Of course, Fergus might squint in afterwards and see the skull but, even then, it was very unlikely he'd do something about it; certainly not hook it out and cause a ruckus. Fergus could make anything you wanted disappear. And he never asked questions; mainly because he hardly ever spoke, except to swear. He had seen everything it was possible to see, and then he had burned it.

Usually, he was to be found sitting here with his chessboard, his indistinguishably grubby pieces and his book of the hundred greatest games – playing through them one by one for the hundredth time.

Some of the chess-playing porters had offered him a game, during their breaks, but he wasn't interested in that. He swore at them until they went away; he swore very eloquently. It was clear that he was an admirer of greatness not a self-satisfied patzer.

Another thing that had always been certain about Fergus was that, from sunset to sunrise, he would be right here, tending the incinerator. No-one had ever known him to be absent from his post, his corner, his three-legged wooden stool – none of the porters, anyway.

Excellent was so bemused that he was almost tempted to go and have a look inside the incinerator; that was the only place he could think of that Fergus might have gone. The idea of him outside the building, or even elsewhere within the building, was impossible to frame.

Just then, the second porter – Ludger Myrthil – arrived.

'*Fergus n'est pas là,*' said Excellent.

Ludger looked around, disbelieving.

'*Où est-il?*'

'*Je ne sais pas.*'

Bolder than Excellent, Ludger strode up to the incinerator, opened the door and – two-handed – swung his heavy bag, containing the torso, into the huge heat.

Excellent thought for a moment, then retrieved his bag from the wheelie-bin.

Looking guiltily around, he rushed over and threw it as far as he could into the brightness.

The two men shook hands.

'*Dans une heure,*' said Ludger.

'*Oui, oui,*' said Excellent.

He was going outside to get some fresh air and have a smoke.

They stood anxiously at the lift doors. At least the Rubber Nurse had made them temporarily forget about the fog outside – in that, she had fulfilled her usual and boasted function: an escape from one's worries.

The corridor looked different to the ones Gemma was familiar with. Because it was exclusively administrative, the floors were carpeted. No blood, faecal matter, urine or vomit was likely to be spilled here – and so the hospital bureaucrats had decided to make the place more welcoming with a thin but durable pile of orange-green.

'I think the Chapel is along here,' said Sarah.

'Have you been there before?'

'A couple of times – they have memorial services there, although it's not very big.'

Gemma trustingly followed Sarah. The carpet seemed sticky with something – and when she looked on the white rubber soles of her shoes, she saw a muddy red stain.

'It's blood,' confirmed Sarah. 'Come on.'

They hurried towards a pair of wide-open wooden doors inset at the top with stained glass.

But before they got there, a noise stopped them dead: grunting – sexual grunting.

'Shh,' said Sarah, but Gemma hadn't been saying anything.

They crept forwards and, as they did so, the sounds got louder, off to the right, definitely in one of the rooms there.

When they reached the next door, a fairly shocking vision was there to greet them: two Security Guards, Pollard and Shears, naked, the former buggering the latter.

The most striking detail of the scene were the two Security Guards' hats, one being worn by Pollard at a rakish angle, the other hanging in the far top corner of the room, covering a CCTV camera.

'. . . and all that blood,' said Pollard. 'And all that fucking blood gushing and gushing . . .'

Shears was the grunter, his volume increasing.

'Baby,' he said, 'baby.'

There was little danger they'd be spotted, but the two women snuck past as delicately as they could.

Once out of earshot, they hurried on.

'All finished,' said WPC Melanie Angel, on returning to A&E.

'Good,' said PC Dixon.

'Anything happening here?'

'No,' said PC Dixon. 'I've never known it this quiet. Neither has the good Sister Agnes. Half the A&E doctors have disappeared. She thinks they might be having a secret party somewhere. Either that or they got lost in the fog.'

'My radio's dead,' said WPC Angel.

PC Dixon checked his. 'Mine, too.'

There was a moment during which either one of them could have made a big issue of this; they didn't. The radios were fluky at the best of times – they'd come back on of their own accord.

'Well,' she said, 'while it's quiet, shall we go and have that coffee?'

'Alright,' said Dixon. 'There's a machine round the corner.'

'Doesn't this place have a canteen?'

'Of course,' he said. Then realized this was female code for wanting a proper chat.

They strolled up to the reception desk.

'Give us a shout if you need us,' said WPC Angel.

'Oh, sure,' said Sister Day, feet up, nothing to do, glass eye itching like mad.

'We'll be in the canteen,' said PC Dixon – just to

make sure any call reached them. He glanced round at the almost deserted room.

Approaching the lifts, WPC Angel couldn't think of anything to say. Then, in desperation: 'Funny name she had, that girl.'

'What? The one upstairs?'

'Froth. Now, what kind of name is that?'

PC Dixon knew *exactly* what kind.

But before he could speak, the lift doors opened and a crowd of overexcited people pushed past. They were talking loudly, showing off to one another – singing high notes and beating their chests. Some looked quite old, were wearing pyjamas. Perhaps it was some kind of party.

'Nikki Froth,' said WPC Angel, as if he hadn't heard first time – as if his life hadn't just changed.

The Chapel, when they reached it, was unoccupied apart from two very different figures lying on the table at the altar end. Sarah ran towards them, trying not to shriek, but Gemma strode forward steadily, her hand taking support from the backs of the pews. It was Steele – it was Steele, wasn't it? After all her tender hopes, all her delightful fantasies, it had come to this! Carnage!

His body was laid out across the table, but there was something terribly wrong with it: the head had been cut off, the head had been shrunk.

As she came closer, Gemma could see a beautifully neat neck wound – hardly any tearing of the flesh at all. Even in her extreme distress, she was able to form a theory as to which highly skilled pair of hands had done the cutting. But the head! How had that been accomplished?

Closer still, and she saw that it wasn't Steele's head

but that of a tiny baby. Gemma could tell it was a newborn because the top of the cranium was still coneshaped from the birth.

Then, behind Steele's body, feet going in the opposite direction, she saw the little infant's torso – and just as Steele had the baby's head, so the baby, with grotesque symmetry, had his. The wound on the baby's neck was equally neat.

Sarah stood over the bodies, hand covering her mouth. At first Gemma thought she was smelling something, but then it became clear she was drawing heavily on her inhaler to prevent another asthma attack – asthma and panic combined, perhaps.

Gemma, devastated inside but still somehow in control, went to stand beside Sarah. She put her arm around the anaesthetist's shoulders and looked down at the destruction of all her love: Steele's beautiful body, stripped of its clothes, with a large pentangle described in blood on his chest; the baby's body, laid out unnaturally flat, with the number 666 written on the tiny space of its forehead. It was a little girl.

'Who?' gasped Sarah. 'Who could –?' She turned away and frankly vomited.

Gemma kept her hands on Sarah's shoulders until she felt them stop contracting.

The puke, a little splosh of which had gone on her white shoes, was thin and coffee-coloured. Almost empty stomach. Gemma remembered Sarah's uneaten snack in her locker upstairs.

'We should get them down to the morgue,' Gemma said, 'before anyone sees them. People will be coming here, I'm sure.'

'Okay,' said Sarah, conceding. 'I'll go and get a trolley. Will you be alright here, on your own?'

Gemma was far from sure but said she would be.

'I won't be long,' said Sarah, then ran off down the aisle, giving a wild backward look just before she closed the Chapel doors.

At the conclusion of the Black Mass, High Priest Sir Reginald had led his congregation of diabolic celebrants down to the security offices on the 12th floor – leaving only Pollard and Shears behind to guard the bodies.

Here, the Satanists were disporting themselves all around the monitoring booth.

In front of the screens, the room was a pinky-gray mass of bodies – bodies interlocking and detaching, bending and arching. The floor, particularly, was all aslither – diagonals of flesh, stripes where arms embraced torsos and triangles where legs stood apart; few straight lines but plenty of bulges – overhanging paunches, breasts sliding around on chests like fried eggs in a pan; chicken-neck testicles and flaccid dicks; stretch-marks like traces of commuting slugs, to and from work in the bumcrack; broken veins mapping interstellar space – a gorgonzola of veins: blue-cheese universe; crispy-crunchy heels; peelable-chewable cuticles on calcium-deficient toenails; toenails of a troll (Cropper); fingernails turned red and brown by turns; the air stinking of scalp and locker-room, perfume and bum-juice; over here, thrust and wobble, over there fake moan and genuine grunt – squeals, too, squeals of what should be pleasure but which was ruined by demonstration; pleasure not inward but pornographic. Even as some voyeuristic ones moved around, touching themselves and avoiding being drawn into licks or kisses, they said, 'I'm sorry' and 'Excuse me' and 'You go first' and there being parody, too, 'After you, old chap – what what.'

The hospital chaplain was being forcefully buggered – it was a dirty job, the chaplain being sixty-two and not entirely continent, but someone had to do it. This time the task of shafting had fallen to Andy "Randy" Randall, a health service manager. The chaplain adored anal sex; it was something he'd been curious about ever since his rural childhood in Somerset where, one long-lost summer evening, he had happened upon three of the farmhands.

Henderson MacVanish had brought his speculum along and was opening midwife Honey Hopeful up as far as she could go – there were places he could touch that even *she* didn't know the names for. Neither did she know whether the experience was painful or pleasurable, but she was definitely enjoying it. The gynaecologist felt better than he ever had, since his orchidectomy – he had lost the right one; the left still did the business. The nausea was gone, and he'd cadged a Viagra from Cropper. After he'd finished spreading midwife Honey Hopeful for all she was worth, he intended to give her a decent seeing-to through the back door.

Patricia Parish, standing with her legs spread and resting her hands on the control desk, was being taken from behind by someone or other whilst simultaneously getting a major voyeuristic kick from spying on people throughout the hospital. Pandemonium might have been summoned up during Black Mass, but a milder form of confusion was spreading virally throughout the building. Several of the floors, she saw, her head jogging back and forth, her eyes sometimes closing in pleasure, sometimes opening in curiosity, were perfectly normal – nurses sat at their stations, patients slept or didn't sleep.

In other wards, even on the same floor just in an opposite wing, everyone was up, running delightedly from place to place, asking confused questions, trying to use the telephones. So intent was she on her search for sex elsewhere that she completely overlooked the view from the cameras in the Chapel, which showed from a high angle Gemma loyally waiting beside the dead body of Steele. Eventually she found what she had been looking for: a doctor and a nurse in a closed cubicle, fucking like there was no tomorrow. She knew both of them to say hello to, and this turned her on even more. Golly.

At the centre of it all stood the High Priest. He was less kempt than before – his naked torso delicately bloodsplattered, his double chin dappled with gore from Steele's neck. Right now, this was eagerly being licked off by Nurse Linda Loos – one of Sir Reginald's keenest disciples. Like many of the Satanists, she had been recruited by Patricia Parish. A passing interest in tarot cards had been scaled up into a full-blown crush on Satan, Lord of Evil, and a desire, as soon as possible, to become the Whore of Babylon and bring about the Apocalypse.

Sweet as they were, the High Priest was not satisfied with Linda's experienced caresses. And so, with a goat-like grunt, he turned the attention of his massive erection upon Nurse Hobsbawm, the brunette who had been their altar, the necessary-but-hard-to-obtain virgin. Blood always made him feel virile – and the blood-Viagra combination just couldn't be beaten. Tonight, however, he felt supernaturally splendid.

'Your time has come,' he said to the Virgin.

*

Despite being so distraught, Gemma was grateful for this brief time alone with what was left of Steele – though she kept a nervous eye and a scaredy ear out for the Security Guards. All her romantic dreams of their future together, an illusory future as it had turned out, never to be lived – all her unexpressed love came back to her. In one sense her love was thwarted: she could never now tell him of it – he had either known or he hadn't, had returned it or hadn't. Their little (so it turned out) parting scene in the lift lobby suggested to her that there would have been greater intimacies ahead. But the two of them had had no idea of the nature of the place in which they were working – a place where this unholy sort of slaughter was possible.

Ridiculously, Gemma felt a moment's hope: she put her hand to Steele's wrist, thinking she might feel for a pulse. There was none there but her own, so powerful it rendered her all a-tremble.

No, not even heartbeats, sobs – and it was only now she realized how hard she had been crying. Steele, in her blurry eyes, was breaking up into flesh-coloured stars of light.

Protected in some way by her distress, she went round to the left-hand end of the altar. Tenderly, she took the baby's small head in both her hands, though it would have fitted quite snugly in a single palm. She moved it nearer to the body from which it had been severed.

Next, and with still greater care, she took up Steele's head – the weight of it did not surprise her, she knew the waterlogged heft of the dead. She placed it back where it should be, on her never-to-be lover's shoulders, then looked around for something with which to cover their faces.

In a low cupboard beside the altar, she found a couple of altar cloths – purple trimmed with fake-gold thread.

As each second passed, Gemma became more and more certain that the Chapel would very soon be hosting the most terrified and repentant congregation it had ever witnessed. Once people became aware that the world had disappeared in a yellow fog, many of them would head straight here. At times, she thought she could already hear hundreds of feet rumbling down the corridor towards her. What would they think if they discovered her here, presiding over this scene of extreme desecration? They would probably lynch her, too. That was a risk she was prepared to take; she wasn't leaving Steele.

One of her hands had found its way under the altar cloth and was touching Steele's dark curls. This had been unconscious, though she was aware it had given her some little comfort. When she withdrew her hand, shocked and disgusted, there was blood on the fingertips. Instinctively, she wiped this off on the front of her uniform – that was what it was for. (Steele's wasn't the only blood there this evening.)

How long would it take Sarah to return? Perhaps she'd hit trouble – been attacked, caught by the guards?

Gemma stood lovingly beside the body of the man with whom she had hoped to share her life, sharing instead his death.

Strangely, she was very conscious, just then, of her tongue, burned by the coffee she'd had with Sir Reginald. It felt as if nothing had happened to it at all – it felt, but surely not, healed.

*

Spanner's pain was gone but he was starting to suspect it hadn't been chemically killed.

In the middle of his face, his nose felt – there was no other way to put it – *mended*; inside his mouth, the sharp lines he had been feeling down the middle of his teeth had sealed up; his gut no longer ached and his chin felt beautiful.

With great love, his hands – now definitely *his* hands – moved over and over his face, touching flesh that felt smoother than it had this morning.

Spanner hardly dared check the abscess on his left thigh (Sister Agnes had been right), but when he touched where it had been he found only the tickle of hairs and the unbroken surface of skin.

And he wasn't alone: throughout Hospital, the healing had begun – quietly, often unnoticed even by those to whom it was happening.

Wounds became less juicy, less like smoked salmon and cream cheese bagels (puss), less like bacon-burgers with ketchup (blood).

Joined bone-ends knitted themselves up, acceleratedly – a week of work taking place within an hour.

Bruises paled, scars shrank, lesions desiccated, ulcers ceased to weep, fingers and toes pushed out new cuticles, hair thickened upon scalps and pudenda. Re-epithelialization was everywhere.

Arthritic fingers began to untwist, their inveterate ache fading to a consciousness that the ache had now gone.

In emphysemic lungs, the air-blood exchange happened more blithely.

Necrotic tissue pinkened, nerves were re-galvanized, urea was efficiently absorbed by softer kidneys, trapped wind was expelled; prostates put on muscle, irritable bowels chilled out, hernias tucked themselves up, cancers started to dissolve.

On every ward, agony was replaced by lull, pain by tingle, discomfort by comfort, illness by health.

In A&E, Sister Agnes Day's glass eye finally popped out and shattered on the floor. For the first time in years, she saw in 3-D.

It's a dream, Spanner thought, disappointed. He had corrupted a Hospital porter, waltzed into the pharmacy, achieved every druggie's greatest ambition – and, like a crappy film, it was all a wish-fulfilment dream.

Still, he felt good about regaining his looks. Although he hadn't had an erection in two years, there was always the chance some limber miniskirted nurse would find her way into the pharmacy – a bottle blonde, with shiny, high-heeled boots on; rubber boots; white.

'I feel better,' he said.

'I know what you mean,' replied Case, who had been more preoccupied with trying to stay stoned. The water from the bottle was all long gone, but he had managed to swallow about a dozen more pills. Unfortunately, they didn't have the same effect as the ones before midnight – he felt a mental clarity that was as pristine as it was unwelcome. And there was something else: his cravings were gone. His body seemed content, tingly, bathed in a kind of self-directed goodwill. Could this be health?

'I feel like I could –'

'Fuck,' said Case, lustily.

'Yes. I fucking could. I could fuck.'

'Fuck, yeah.'

'I could fucking fuck . . .' He was thinking of his imaginary nurse.

'Go on,' encouraged Case.

'I could fuck for England.'

'Please don't,' Nurse Hobsbawm said, weakly.

In her fantasies of losing it, the taker had never looked like Sir Reginald (the member, though, had borne some resemblance to this one – large, craggy, club-like and thickly veined). She had imagined love and perhaps a beach outside and gently waving curtains and candles (not black ones with knobbled shafts, a bit like Sir Reginald's penis) – what she had never thought possible-or-likely was a crowd of lustful witnesses. The Virgin looked around her in terror and disgust – at her eye-level, she saw genitals: camel-hoof crotches and hairy dangling giblet cock'n'balls, spread-wide pink-orange-red lesion-like porncunts, pubic triangles of greying furze. Her legs felt itchy with terror, a raging rising.

Somehow, such was the High Priest's charisma, those in all parts of the room, whatever they had been doing or having done to them, stopped – and began to gather round in a circle. Touching continued, exploratory strokes of the buttocks of potential partners, but everyone's attention was fixed upon the Bride of Satan. She sat back with her buttocks perched on the CCTV control panel. Sir Reginald moved forwards until he was fully between her legs. Her cunt was dry; this he sorted out with spit. And then, he was gently sliding the very end of his knob inside her. Around him arose a wail, part banshee hoedown, part rugby terrace.

Sir Reginald briefly wished he were a true aristocrat, and that his congregation were made up entirely of gentlemen. But this was distracting him from his imminent pleasure.

Nurse Hobsbawm felt as if she were swallowing marbles with every breath. She looked up, past Sir Reginald's brown-spotted shoulder, at the square speckled white ceiling tiles and screamed.

Sarah sighed impatiently – the lift was taking what seemed like an age to arrive.

When it did come, there were two patients standing guiltily in the corners. One, Lou Champion, was big-fat and attached to an oxygen tank on wheels; the other, Titch Lopez, was so tall he almost touched the ceiling. Smokers.

As soon as the doors opened, they stopped what had clearly been an argument. Sarah heard only the word *healthy*. They were breathing heavily.

Sarah pressed the button for the floor she wanted, then turned to face them. 'It's a bit late for you to be walking around, isn't it?' she asked.

'We were just . . .' said Lou Champion.

'He wasn't feeling well,' said Titch Lopez.

Sarah almost said, *This is a hospital, you're not meant to feel well.* They had gone down a floor by now, she guessed. The men took the look she gave them as disapproving, disbelieving.

'There's something funny going on,' said Lou.

'Outside,' said Titch. 'We're just going to have a –' Ping, and the lift had arrived.

As the doors began to open, Sarah said, 'I should tell you to go back to bed, but . . .' And then they were on her, pushing her back, almost knocking her over, fighting desperately to get into the lift. There were five or six of them, all patients. They shoved her back, pressed the button for the ground floor, pressed it and kept pressing. All of them seemed to be speaking at once – they were a group of old women – but what they said was just a repetition of what they'd heard said: 'It was outside.' – 'I saw it.' – 'I saw it first.' – 'They can't contact anyone.' – 'Because it's outside.' – 'She saw it.' – 'No, I saw it.'

The lift continued down; in a very short time it would be on the ground floor; and then who knew whether she'd be able to catch it back up, with all these people wanting to get out.

Sarah squeezed through the mini-mob, closer and closer to the buttons. She reached out and blindly pressed.

After a very strange, slow lift-ride, PC Dixon and WPC Angel arrived on the 15th floor.

They had stopped on the 2nd, 4th, 7th, 9th, 11th floors – numbers of people wanting to get in, but all to go down; and none of them wanted to get in with two uniformed police officers.

Again, the people were very happy-seeming; in other circumstances, PC Dixon might have suspected them of being drunk or stoned.

'Something's up,' said WPC Angel. 'Far too much good cheer for a hospital.'

PC Dixon was unable to stop himself thinking of the Pink Elephant ward, of Nikki, of how close to him she was.

'You're not in much of a mood, are you?' WPC Angel said.

'Sorry,' he replied and, making his mind up right then, said, 'I'll explain when we've sat down.'

They served themselves from the machines, dutifully left a couple of coins in the honesty box and chose one of the many empty tables.

'I haven't been divorced,' said WPC Angel, 'so I have no idea what it's like, but if it's any comfort –'

'I know her,' said PC Dixon. 'I know Nikki Froth. She's the one. I mean, she's the one Angela was mocking me about. This isn't coming out very clearly.' He told himself to take a deep breath and managed half of one. 'Look, Nikki Froth is the girl I tried to save.'

'The prostitute,' said WPC Angel, but not unkindly, just to make sure she was up to speed.

'She started sleeping with men very young,' said PC Dixon. 'She got a really vicious pimp – one of the worst.' And then he told Melanie the story of his involvement with Nikki; most of it.

She listened so carefully and understandingly that he knew she would be a wonderful person to be loved by, and that, either because or in spite of this, he could never love her.

The satyrical circle looked on with lust. After Sir Reginald was finished, this fresh flesh would be multiply ravished. He was merely, as you might have it, opening the flood-gates – doing a little sluicing on Juicy Lucy. They knew one another's bodies a little too well, by now, the excesses of their monthly orgies (every full moon) having become routine.

For a moment, what with the High Priest's shaggy grey chest hair, Nurse Hobsbawm had the impression she was about to be mounted not by a man but by a horny old billy goat.

The tears forming on the surface of her eyes turned the world to a plateful of shining diamonds on a sky full of blazing stars.

Sir Reginald jerked his hairy buttocks forward with a cry that he no doubt intended to be feral and blood-curdling but which came out as a cross between yabba-dabba-doo and Tarzan's jungle holler.

Something wasn't happening as it should. Sir Reginald thrust and thrust again, his engorged member smashing like a battering ram against the barricaded doors of a castle. He began to sweat, and the encouraging cries of those around him, his beloved co-celebrants of the rites of Beelzebub, became necessary rather than just jocular. This had never happened before – this, as more than one of the young women around him knew to their cost, or benefit, was completely unprecedented. Virginal defloration was a long-term specialism of his. But it was not that Sir Reginald's manhood stood forth any less proudly, although the extreme tip was becoming a little sore and resembled, if he had withdrawn it fully, a scoop of raspberry-ripple ice-cream. There was no fault with the workman's tool. The High Priest refused to be defeated – this hymen, like all the others before it, would fall. He banged away, sweating, changing angle, withdrawing almost fully and then following up with his full and not inconsiderable body-weight. It was becoming painful for him as well as for the Virgin – and the congregation, though disciplined, was becoming restive. None of the men doubted his virility, but he could sense they all felt that, given the chance, they would have succeeded where he so far had signally failed. He gave the hardest-fastest thrust he could manage, and felt his bell-end hit the superstrong hymen and twist round and down to one side: there was no way through. Not this way. The pain made him slightly flaccid, so he pumped a couple of times more to get himself back up to speed, then withdrew. Turning round to the Chief Obstetrical Consultant, he requested the use of the speculum. With alacrity, Henderson MacVanish handed it over. Expertly, though this was not one of his declared specializations, Sir Reginald opened the deeper secrets of Nurse Hobsbawm's cunt to general view. With his fingers, he probed the partially exposed hymen, trying initially to test its strength and then, when this strength proved considerable (even under his powerful digits), trying to weaken it.

'Just a moment,' said Sir Reginald, changing in manner from the High Priest to the Head of Trauma. 'Don't worry – we'll have this fixed in a trice.'

His penis, as the whole congregation noticed, was visibly shrinking.

'Priestess,' he said to Patricia, 'please bring me the sacrificial dagger.'

Nurse Hobsbawm felt true fear. She had had an image of Sir Reginald, standing above her, as an outsized goblin. His unusual hairiness did nothing to reassure her. In fact, he seemed to be growing hairier: he was unusually shiningly bald, but, from where she lay, she saw that his pate was now covering itself with a fine grey pelt. Nurse Hobsbawm began to struggle for her life. She knew that the Devil-worshippers had a rule: any virgin who couldn't be successfully deflowered had instead to be sacrificed.

'Hold her down,' said Sir Reginald. 'Hold her very still.'

The speculum was now really beginning to hurt. Nurse Hobsbawm felt as if she were being torn apart, ruined – she would be too slack to grip any man, after this. She could feel the blade touching her, up inside. Her wince away was controlled by the crowd with all its hands upon her; she had never been touched by so many people at once, and she hated it. She tried to scream but a hand that had a moment before been on her forehead moved down to cover her mouth. This was a human web: sweat formed between her and their palms, where they touched.

Sir Reginald was concentrating upon his work. With the sharp, pointed tip of the crescent-moon-shaped blade he intended to make one small cross-shaped incision. After that, he would complete the work of de-hymenization with his newly erect penis.

'Don't stand in my light,' he said, and Cropper, not able to get through the crowd to help hold the Virgin down, took this as an order, showed some initiative. From a nearby shelf, he collected a torch. 'Let me through,' he said, and once they realized what he was about, his path was cleared.

'Point it *there*,' said Sir Reginald, gesturing unnecessarily into the glistening forced-apart pinkness.

The great practitioner of emergency medicine, with no further impediments or irritations, placed the tip of the blade against the membrane of the young girl's hymen and gently pushed.

When the lift stopped on the 10th floor, yet more people crowded in – and it was already over capacity. However, despite the crush, Sarah managed to manoeuvre herself until she was right beside the door.

On the 9th floor, as soon as the doors were wide enough, she began pushing through. She threw her whole weight out – and fell flat on the floor of a completely empty lobby.

News of whatever-was-happening obviously hadn't reached this floor, or, if it had, the patients and staff were being much more stoic about it.

Although anxious to get back to Gemma as soon as possible, Sarah still wanted to find out the truth of what was going on. She checked one ward – the patients were all asleep, the nurses seated at their station. It looked on the surface an idyllically quiet night. In the second ward, she saw a spare trolley pushed back against the wall. The two nurses on duty were engrossed in a discussion of the window-boxes of their flats. Sarah bent down and, with her hand, released the foot-brake. She gave the trolley a little push, hoping very hard that this wouldn't be one of the ones which squeaked. It wasn't – and she made it back to the lift without being intercepted. No-one now was going to challenge a nurse wheeling a gurney. She could even find an excuse in being a member of the team, wandering around on this distant and irrelevant (to them) floor. She called the lift and waited. The lights above the door counted down to Ground; then up again – to three, to five, to six, but then back again to Ground. Many patients must be trying to escape.

Sarah remembered Steele telling her off not so long ago for using the high-speed emergency lift. She felt stupid for not having thought of it before. The door was just round the corridor (it needed a security code to get in).

When she pressed the button, the lift arrived within seconds – some discipline was holding in Hospital, at least among the staff. Sarah anticipated no more difficulties in getting back to the 13th floor.

It was with great delight that Sir Reginald felt the knife slide in. He pulled the blade out, twisted it through 90 degrees and pushed it in again.

Those with their hands on Nurse Hobsbawm's body felt her temperature rise – a sort of electricity ran from her to them, of terror and of awe. After this, the orgy would surely be the best ever; this improvised operation was an astonishing aphrodisiac.

Sir Reginald completed the second incision and carefully extracted the sacrificial dagger. He could not believe his eyes: the first cut had disappeared and the second was sealing up like a spoonmark in runny custard, like water in slow motion. Two seconds later, the hymen looked as if it had never been touched.

'Did anyone see that?' he asked, used to the supernatural just as much as the scientific, but still deeply unnerved. 'Watch this!'

He made another incision, wider this time, just to be certain. Even before he had fully withdrawn the blade, the wound had begun to heal.

There were gasps of disbelief. Whoever had been holding their hand over Nurse Hobsbawm's mouth let go enough for her to gulp and then attempt a scream.

'Do it again,' Patricia said.

Sir Reginald did, making the most definite incision yet.

The crowd felt the Virgin's body shuddering.

As the blade was removed, Sir Reginald and most of the others watched the hymen repair itself.

Frustrated both sexually and professionally, Sir Reginald stabbed the blade in a good couple of centimetres, wiggled it about, widening the hole – a hole this time, not a slit.

The wound closed over with a quiet but easily audible pop.

He stuck the knife in again and again, and every time Nurse Hobsbawm's body healed itself.

*

Gemma was starting to wonder whether Sarah was ever going to come back. She had no guarantee – Sarah had been traumatized by the sight of Steele. (Strangely, Gemma did not for a moment think that it might have been the baby which Sarah had found most upsetting.) There was a real danger, Gemma feared, that she would be caught here. As far as she could see, there were two CCTV cameras in the Chapel – where were the Security Guards? Surely they had seen what was lying on the altar? And shouldn't they have footage of whatever went on here? And what about those two down the corridor – were they still hard at it?

Gemma was distracted from these thoughts by something that seemed to have entered the room – something, not someone. We're doomed, she thought, as she looked through the thickening air.

It's the fog – that's what she thought in the first couple of instants – *it's the fog from outside. It's got into the building.*

The room seemed to be slowly filling with *something* pale and floating. But it wasn't like any fog Gemma had ever seen before. Tiny pinpricks of white hung in the air, now in denser constellations, now as single points. They did not move, to flow or be blown about, but just stayed frozen in the air, exactly where they had appeared.

Gemma walked towards them, and felt a slight tingling across her chest.

Looking behind her, she saw that she had walked into – or through – a smaller cluster of the specks.

She headed towards a larger clump of them, immediately to the left of the door. With a tentative hand, she tried to touch them. On the skin, they felt like sunburn. But they passed through her fingers – *through*, not between: there was no touching them. She watched the white shapes emerge from the top of her palm. The sensation as they did so wasn't entirely unpleasant – a little like pins and needles; tiny, tiny pains that weren't sufficient enough, even when superadded, to cause pain.

Gemma stood there with her hands on her hips, back to the doors; this definitely wasn't the fog. Next thing she knew she'd been bashed on the back of the head and was falling forwards onto the last row of chairs. She looked round, fully expecting to see the Security Guards. But it was only Sarah, backing through the doors with the trolley behind her.

'Was that you?' Sarah asked. 'I'm sorry.'

Gemma picked herself up. 'You got one. Well done.'

'I used the emergency lift,' Sarah said. There was a moment of irony between them. 'I'd call this an emergency,' Sarah added.

'Why were you standing by the door?'

'These things,' Gemma said.

'I know,' Sarah replied. 'They've just started to appear in the corridor.'

'They hurt,' Gemma said; 'they sting.'

'It's not a gas, is it?' Sarah asked, then answered her own question. 'When I walked down the corridor, they seemed to go straight through me. There are a lot more out there.'

Gemma pushed open the other Chapel door and had a look. Sarah was right: a thicker mist down the middle of the corridor – and it was at its densest about ten centimetres above floor level. 'Well,' she said, coming back inside, 'we can't do anything about that.' But Sarah had already wheeled the trolley up to the altar and was waiting there for her to come and help.

Together, they managed to heave Steele's once-powerful body onto the trolley. Sarah quickly moved his head across. Gemma felt a sharp stab of jealousy but the act was explained when Sarah said, 'You do it – I can't.' She meant moving the baby.

As she had already touched the head, Gemma felt less squeamish. With as much care as she could, she picked up the tiny body and put it between Steele's legs on the trolley – there wasn't room elsewhere. This felt worse than moving Steele: the floppy body reminded her of the few newborns she had been privileged to hold. You didn't expect their little shapes to be cold, though, and that was deeply upsetting.

After this, she tenderly moved the baby's head. The altar was bloodstained. Only two specks of light hung above it, one in the air, one down roundabout where Steele's heart had been. They covered over Steele and the baby as best they could with the altar cloths. This would attract attention but they should be able to get where they were going without encountering too many nosy parkers. Wordlessly, the two young women wheeled the two bodies out of the Chapel, feeling the sting of the mist around their ankles and across their chests.

'Don't worry about those Security Guards,' said Sarah. 'They've gone somewhere.'

Pushing down the corridor was a little like walking through a nettle-patch. Their feet and lower legs passed through dozens of lights. Both Gemma and Sarah wondered if they were some sort of radioactive particle.

The emergency lift, when they reached it, was travelling up to the roof. But it came down to them in obedience to their call.

Once inside, Sarah pressed for the minus 4th floor: Pathology.

Turning to the nearest holding arm, Sir Reginald made a swiping motion with the dagger – and left behind a smart little cut.

'Ow,' said Patricia, but Sir Reginald had grabbed her by the wrist. This wound, too, closed over.

Patricia watched, aghast. 'Do it again,' she said.

Sir Reginald made a more generous slash; a little blood came out this time, then retreated, but the final result was the same.

'Do me,' said paramedic Bill "Zapper" Billson.

'And me,' said midwife Honey Hopeful.

'And me,' said disposal man Fergus Moore.

Just then Pollard and Shears snuck in from upstairs, hoping to rejoin the congregation with as little fuss as possible.

Sir Reginald began to distribute small wounds among his congregation. He did this fairly, evenly, just as earlier he had made sure everyone drank of the anti-communion wine. There were gasps of pain followed almost immediately by cries of delight and disbelief.

'Yes!' said Patricia. '*Yes!*'

'It's worked,' said Sir Reginald.

'Look at mine!' said all the other cut and healed ones, each thinking their disappeared wound the most amazing of all. 'It's gone – it's really gone.'

In their joy, Nurse Hobsbawm was forgotten. She drew herself up foetally onto the CCTV control desk. The speculum still held her vagina gapingly open. She was sobbing, unable to take in that Sir Reginald could no longer harm her, physically at least.

'Cut me!' shouted Cropper, who had again missed out. 'Cut me here!' He indicated the veins in his tattooed forearm.

'No! shouted the chaplain. 'Cut my throat!'

'It's worked!' shouted Sir Reginald in diabolic triumph. 'We are immortal! We are gods! We can no longer die!'

To celebrate, he turned the dagger around in his hand and dragged the blade all across his belly. The wound, through inches of fat, gaped as wide as the jaws of Hell. But that wasn't enough for the High Priest. A second, deeper slice took Sir Reginald through to his own intestines. Faecal matter spurted out onto the diabolists' feet, but they took no notice because already Sir Reginald's body was zipping itself up like a magic purse. The shit was evaporating back to where it had come from, too; just as had the blood from all their wounds.

After this amazing demonstration, there was no restraining the diabolists. Cropper made a successful grab for the dagger, and he was not so chary of using it as Sir Reginald. Side to side he slashed, distributing ugly gashes on all who could get close enough. 'Blind me! Blind me!' Nurse Loos begged. After such an outrageous request, the guard made a favourite of her and punctured the orb of each eyeball. But the first had begun to mend itself even before the second was wounded.

It was only as Gemma and Sarah were wheeling Steele out of the Chapel that their movement on the screen caught anyone's eye.

'Fuck!!' said Cropper, who had glanced over out of habit. 'Look!'

Sir Reginald was not easily distracted, still pondering the problem of the unbreakable hymen.

'They've stolen the fucking bodies!'

'Who?'

'Them!'

Cropper pulled Gemma and Sarah, now approaching the 13th-floor lifts, up on the biggest screen. The congregation stopped to watch.

'Where are Pollard and Shears?' asked Sir Reginald. He was stepping forward to look at the screen.

'Here,' said Pollard. Shears shuffled into view beside him.

'Idiots,' said Sir Reginald, then returned his attention to Sarah and Gemma. 'Well-de-well-well. It seems as if someone has decided to do our tidying up for us.'

'Where are they going?' Cropper asked.

'It hardly matters now,' said Sir Reginald. 'Pollard, Shears, keep an eye on them. They'll not get far.'

What no-one had noticed, whilst all this other exciting malarkey was taking place, was that something less spectacular but equally strange was happening on the screens. What looked like bands of fuzz were whiting out the picture-images; some places, those in operating theatres and Geriatrics, were blanked out almost completely.

Nurse Bland was very distressed – the smoke or whatever it was had taken over much of Pink Elephant ward.

She was thinking about evacuating the girls, and boy, and the young heroin addict. If this was from a fire on a lower floor, she would have to lead them down one of the staircases: all in a line, holding hands, orderly, without panic.

When she tried to waft the smoke with her hand, it didn't move. Instead, she felt prickles on her skin and, although this was impossible, inside her fingers.

The only thing she could think of was that it was some kind of acidic gas. But that too would smell, surely.

She put her nose close to the cloud and inhaled as deeply as she dared.

No – no scent at all, just the hygienic smell of any ward, a smell she had lived in unthinkingly for most of her working life.

The girls, too, were fascinated by the stuff. She would have told them to get back in bed, but that was where the white was thickest – right where their bodies lay, their flat little chests.

'It's horrible,' said Celia Iden, appendectomy, to Holly Gonne, gastroenteritis.

'I like it,' said Sukie Lu, jaundice.

'Stay calm,' said Nurse Bland.

'We are calm,' said Sukie Lu.

'I'm not,' said Celia Iden. 'I'm very very scared.'

'Shh,' said Nurse Bland. 'It's nothing to be scared of.'

'What is it?' asked Holly Gonne.

'Make it go away,' said Celia.

Voices – high enough to begin with – were rising all along the ward. From years of experience, Nurse Bland could sense that control was about to be lost.

'Girls,' she said, then remembered the one boy. 'And –'

She turned to glance at him, but he was no longer there.

'And that's why I have to see her,' said PC Dixon, drawing to the best conclusion he could manage.

WPC Angel gave herself a few moments. 'I understand,' she said, 'I understand exactly. But right now,' she said carefully, 'that might not be the best idea.

'How is she?' PC Dixon asked, very simply.

Melanie was beginning to understand the reasons for his sadness. 'Like I said before, scared.'

It was all Dixon could do not to rush straight for the lifts. He took a sip of black coffee.

'She's safe now,' said Melanie, remembering the cosy atmosphere of Pink Elephant ward. 'That social worker is a good person to have on your side.'

'Please tell me how she was,' Dixon said.

'I think there's hope,' said Melanie. 'She's come looking for help – that's a good sign, isn't it?'

'So, she faked an overdose –'

'To get away from her friends. They were waiting for her in A&E.'

Dixon tried to remember seeing them; couldn't.

'I want to see her,' he said. 'I want to see she's okay.'

Melanie knew it wasn't worth trying to stop him; better to go along and try to keep things calm.

'Then let's go,' she said.

This time they had to wait a long while for a lift that was going up; all the ones stopping on this floor were full of more bizarrely happy people. Of course, as soon as they saw the police uniform they went quiet.

The lift they finally caught stopped at every floor between the 15th and the 20th. Even the lift lobbies seemed to have turned into full-on party zones. But what was even odder were the millions of speckles of light in the air, the tingles when they passed through them. PC Dixon, however, seemed hardly to notice them.

'Are you sure you want to do this?' Melanie asked.

'Never more certain of anything,' said PC Dixon.

The boy kept moving, fast.

He had got away from Nurse Bland, that was something achieved – she had enjoyed holding him prisoner, he could tell.

When he looked up at the cameras along the corridors, they did not seem to be following him any more. The white stuff in the air didn't bother him at all – it was just another dose of weirdness.

His best plan seemed to be, take one of the lifts down to a floor just above ground level and then approach with extreme caution.

The lift lobby, when he reached it, was empty; but the lift, which took ages to arrive, was sardine-packed.

A stooped, gray-haired figure lurched out, groaning, drooling, then another, another and another. Unconcealed by their white gowns, their arms and legs were scrawny-sinewy and covered with moles, veins, warts and liver spots. Hands grabbed him and foul-smelling breath came closer – truly foul-smelling, like cat-shit mixed with dog-puke. An unshaven chin scraped roughly against the boy's forehead. He saw behind one of the gowns: cock and balls dangling white-hairy and turkey-bits-like.

For a moment, with their wet mouths so close and open, the boy thought they were going to eat him. Their groans became louder and more insistent – and he realized they were trying to say something.

At first he thought it was the letter *D*, then the letter *T*, but then he realized it was a whole word, *tea*.

'I don't have any.'

They looked at one another, with bewilderment.

'Tea,' they insisted.

'If I had some I'd give you it.'

Their grip on his upper arms was surprisingly powerful; the boy felt his fingers starting to tingle as the blood supply was cut off.

Behind the first few, a crowd of others stood blocking the doors to the lift – which banged repeatedly into their shoulders. They gave no sign of even being aware of this.

A streak of drool, warm and stringy, traced itself down his arm.

The groaning became almost a howling.

'Tea!'

'Down there,' said the boy, improvising. 'Round the corner. There's lots of tea. There's a tea-room. Tea and cake.'

The leader, at least the one with the tightest grip, brought his face right up close. Although the boy did not know it, this was Billy Stickers, the former film star from Harold's ward.

'Urn?' Billy asked. 'Tea urn?'

'Chocolate cake?' asked a foetid voice behind his right ear; Marsh Blunt.

'Yes,' the boy lied. 'Big tea urn – just round the corner. Very close.'

If they had decided to hold him captive until they sent someone to check, he would have been doomed. But luckily their craving for tea was all-overwhelming.

Issuing a series of almost sexual groans and grunts, Billy Stickers shuffled off around the corridor – closely followed by the rest of the tea-zombies.

The boy watched them go, and by the time he turned back the lift doors had shut.

*

The emergency lift, before they started moving, was thick with light particles, or whatever they were. Most of them, Gemma noticed, were about the height of Steele's body on the trolley. But as the lift began to sink down, all the lights as one seemed to rise and keep rising. They splashed past Gemma's face like a tingling freezing sea wave. Sarah gave a scream, but the light-mist had already risen over their heads.

'Thank God,' she said. Her respite was short – another wave of mist rose through the lift, sweeping past them, then another and, faster still as they sped up, another. It was like memories of childhood showers – standing in front of a hyperactive lawn sprinkler on a very cold morning. They seemed to be falling through a stripy stratosphere. On each floor, the density of the cloud was different – but they were going far too fast, and were far too unnerved, to be able to take these graduations in.

They looked at one another, horrified, just as another layer of white swept from their feet to their bellies up to their chins and over their heads. Even at this speed, the mist prickled and minorly pained them, going past fast.

No-one stopped the lift, and they dropped the seventeen floors to the minus 4th in less than a minute.

For the last few underground floors, it seemed as if the mist had dissipated completely – or had never been there to begin with.

'What is it?' Sarah asked, as they came to a stop.

'Your guess . . .' replied Gemma, then said, 'Do you know your way around, down here?'

'Unfortunately,' said Sarah, 'I do – very well.'

At Pathology, the doors of the lift sprang open. Sarah half expected a crowd of frantic patients to crowd in, zombie-like. They didn't.

*

The Satanists were experimenting, in a spirit of scientific inquiry, with amputations. If you cut something off completely, would it grow back alive again? It seemed so. Fergus Moore offered up his whole ring finger, although the blinded-and-unblinded Linda Loos (a nutter) would have been more than happy for them to dismember her immediately and completely. Fergus Moore placed his gnarled digit on the edge of the console, and the dagger – held by a surgeon – did its work. The same reconstitution happened again; this time, with more molecules to watch and eyes more alert for them, the diabolic congregation saw what was going on: the substance of his finger, held several feet away from Fergus's gently bleeding hand, turned into what looked almost like a snake made of red smoke. The person holding the finger, even if they'd been asked, couldn't have described the sensation of it dematerializing in their hands. The substance of it didn't become hotter or colder, just less of it was there, though in the same shape, and then less still, and then none.

'Cut off my penis!' the chaplain declared. 'Please. I want you to do it – cut it off, and my balls as well.'

He plonked them out on the console and after only a moment's hesitation Sir Reginald went to work.

Afterwards, the chaplain wouldn't let anyone else touch them – he held them triumphantly, high above his head, balls in one hand, penis in the other, and watched as they reassembled in his curly gray-haired crotch. 'It is a miracle!' he said. 'It is a greater miracle than Christ ever performed.'

'What about Lazarus?' asked Bill "Zapper" Billson, who knew his scripture surprisingly well for a satanic paramedic.

Patricia stepped up to the surgeon. 'Kill me,' she said.

For a few seconds, the same thought had been in the heads of everyone present: this was the ultimate and necessary test. The High Priestess was the bravest of them – and it was most fitting she be the one to offer herself.

Acting quickly, Sir Reginald grabbed Patricia by the hair and pulled her naked flesh towards him. With his left hand he covered her eyes and put her head at an angle, with his right he held the dagger to her neck. Giving her no chance to change her mind (his curiosity was such), he dragged the blade straight through her carotid artery, her windpipe, her oesophagus. The sharp edge of the metal slid neatly between two of her vertebrae (Sir Reginald always kept his instruments meticulously sharp). Those in front of him were squirted, not for the first time that night, with gouts of blood. But hardly had the first spray landed on them than the red began to return to Patricia's body. Her eyes had turned to white, her tongue lolled, long. The surgeon checked her pulse, which was weaker but still going.

'Look,' Cropper said. The neckslash wound was knitting itself back up, as neatly and completely as the Virgin's hymen.

(One of the male nurses had relieved the Virgin of the agony of the speculum. He was not doing this out of kindness – it would get in the way of him buggering her, which he fully intended, if she couldn't be had up the front.)

With a gurgling sound as the artery closed up, Patricia was self-mended. Her voice, when it came out, was annoyed. 'I didn't die. That wasn't quick enough. Stab me through the heart.'

She stood back from Sir Reginald who, again without hesitation, put the dagger through her – so it came out her back. It went in almost up to the hilt. He could feel the swish of her myocardial blood against the blade. Putting both hands on the handle, he twisted the blade round and round – it pushed her ribs apart and widened the spurting hole in her chest. Blood sprayed out rhythmically, as if from a lawn-sprinkler – the surgeon kept the blade as far in as it would go. The flesh began to seal up around its sharp edges. Patricia remained on her feet. She was impatient – her hands were on her hips.

'Does it hurt?' someone asked her.

'Yesss,' she hissed, but it was hard to tell whether the ssss was coming from her mouth or her chest cavity. When it felt like the dagger was about to be grasped by her healing flesh, the surgeon pulled it out – and stood watching as the gash above her breasts disappeared.

'We can't be killed,' said Sir Reginald. 'We can do anything we like!'

'Someone needs their head cutting off,' said Patricia. 'Then we'd know for certain.'

One of the nurses, Nina Spinks, ran out through the door, finally terrified.

'Is it just us, do you think?' asked Zapper. He was posing the question which was on all their minds. 'I mean, having eternal life.'

Naked as they all were, they turned towards the door and began to run out through it. There was only one way to find out if they, exclusively, and through the power and might of Satan, had been granted immortality: kill someone or fail to kill them.

The Virgin remained behind, abandoned even by her violators. She crawled beneath the console, into a corner littered with triangular corners of crisp packets and tabs from the tops of chewing-gum packs – went foetal, sobbing, and waited for them to come back and torment her again.

Like most places, the Pink Elephant ward was full of ghost-mist – but, unlike elsewhere, it was also full of dust and polyester fluff and supersonic squeals.

Once it had become clear that Nurse Bland had lost control, a pillow-fight started up: either Celia Iden had hit Holly Gonne or Holly Gonne had hit Celia Iden – no-one could agree which, and the disagreement had been the cause of more and more hitting.

By the time the two PCs arrived, most of the pillows had been destroyed, and the girls were all running towards Blue Elephant ward – more supplies were needed.

PC Dixon saw Nikki as she sprinted past, giggling, but he said nothing; he was unable to move; she looked so well.

'I think we may be needed here,' said WPC Angel, waving her hand in front of her face; dust swirled. 'Shall we go and try to establish some order?'

In Blue Elephant ward, it was Girls *v.* Boys and the Boys were losing badly.

Why? Because Nikki Froth *ruled*! – shouting out orders, organizing their defences.

WPC Angel waded in to try to calm things down.

PC Dixon just stood there and watched Nikki. None of his recovery fantasies, not even the most sentimental, had approached the slow-motion cuteness of this.

There she was, fluff in her hair – her bright, shiny, unlank hair; fluff on her skin – her soft, glowing, ungray skin. Just as beautiful as she should be; just as young as she was.

PC Dixon cried for the second time that night; tears of shame, tears of joy.

He had always known she was innocent.

First thing Spanner and Case knew of the changes going on outside was the door-handle moving.

It twisted one way, then the other. Then it turned violently as far as it could go, several times. Then it shook with a kind of metallic rage.

'Let's hide,' said Spanner.

The room – as they already knew – contained no cupboards or hidey-holes, so they retreated behind a couple of shelves; over the packets, they could see vague shapes moving behind the frosted door-pane.

After a couple of minutes' wait, a loud crash sounded, then another. Someone was breaking in.

When the next lift came, it was full of another load of zombies (the boy kept well back out of their reach) – and the one after that, too.

The second lot was led by Wim van der Vries, a victim of alcoholic poisoning from the same ward as Harold. Their cry was different.

'Beer,' they moaned, before the doors shut.

The boy decided to try the stairs instead – less chance of being seen there, anyway.

He would get back to what he knew, take roughly the same route down through the building: north-west wing.

A few minutes' walk brought him to the familiar fire doors. But behind them was something else entirely: white bandages formed into the shape of a person, a man.

He seemed to be fighting quite violently with himself, trying with one arm to rip the other arm off.

As he did so, he made a savage grunting, which came loudly through the glass.

The boy watched him for a few moments more, not worried about being seen – the man only had a thin slit to see through and wasn't thinking about looking.

Then the boy understood: this was one of the burns victims from a floor or two above; perhaps one of the ones he'd met already – and he was trying to rip his bandages off.

'Hold on,' said the boy, pushing open the door. 'Stop.'

The white figure did so immediately.

'I'll help you.'

'I know your voice,' said the man. 'You were the angel. You brought me water.'

It was Bob Packard, the fireman.

'Stay still,' said the boy.

The bandages were held in place by what, before Bob's struggles, must have been a neat alignment of safety-pins with baby-blue ends.

The boy began to undo them one by one.

'I don't know what I'd have done if you hadn't come along. The others refused to help – they're just lying there. I told them that my skin was better.'

Certainly the first piece to be revealed seemed a lot less frazzled than the boy was expecting; it wasn't red, glistening, raw, stringy. Instead, it looked like normal skin, though hairless.

The easiest thing, it became clear, was for Bob to turn in circles whilst the boy rolled the removed bandages up into balls.

First his torso was revealed, then his head. He had

a friendly face, freckled and younger than his voice suggested; about twenty-five years old.

'I think I'll keep these,' he said of the bandages on his lower half. 'I'm pretty sure I haven't got anything on underneath.'

Then he stood up straight and reached his hand out. The boy thought for a moment he was trying to grab him, but then he saw a handshake was being offered. Before, adults had only done this to him ironically, to mock; this was sincere, he could tell.

'Thank you, again,' said the young fireman. But he was distracted almost immediately by the sight of his own chest. 'Someone must have been listening,' he said. 'I thought I'd be a crispy critter for the rest of my life. They didn't believe me, upstairs. I told them I felt different.'

'Was it very bad?' the boy asked, thinking of the pain he'd been feeling recently.

'Being burned?' Bob said. 'It was as bad as you can imagine, and then worse.'

'You're better now,' said the boy.

'I'll have to go and show them,' said Bob. 'Is there anything I can do for you?'

The boy thought about asking him for a map of Hospital, but it wasn't worth it – he'd never have one.

'Just don't tell anyone you saw me,' he said.

'Are you still going home?'

'I was caught – I was almost out.'

'Better luck this time.'

Bob set off back up the stairs.

The morgue was always one of the quietest areas in Hospital – just as you might expect. Pathology was often crowded but rarely overcrowded; sometimes busy, but never busy-busy.

The arrival of the emergency lift drew the immediate attention of the Head Pathologist, Mr Dexter von Sinistre. It was almost unknown for its doors to open on this floor – as far as the dead were concerned, there were never any real emergencies.

Sarah Felt wanted to get out of there and back up to the security of Trauma as soon as possible. She gave a shiver which was not entirely due to the lower room-temperature. Whatever troubles there were among the Trauma team, they were better than having to deal with the ghastly freaks down in the basement – of whom von Sinistre was by far the worst. He was only interested in fascinomas, freakish or medically unprecedented presentations. He was famous for his out-of-tens. Whenever a body was handed over to him, he immediately gave it an interest-level rating. This depended, in his words, on how 'sexy' it was as a 'po-mo' (postmortem). Zero was reserved for old ladies dead from pneumonia or hypothermia. Sarah was pretty sure that what they were pushing towards him now would merit top marks – a bang-on ten; and an eight and a half was the highest rating he'd ever been known to give before.

'Well, well, well,' he said, bringing his latexed hands together with a cold sharp slap, 'what have we here?'

'It's Steele,' said Gemma, half wanting to take the body away from this place.

Von Sinistre did not immediately hear anything but an amputated noun or a verb: steel, steal.

He was a very tall man – the tallest person working in any department of Hospital. There was not a hair on his greyly shining head, and his glasses were round and so thick as to be surely no use at all in seeing. His nose was large, long and shaped at the end like the inverted glans of a penis – so much so that, when he moved, it was surprising not to see it dangle. Sinistre's strong preference was for the night-shift, when only one or at most two of his colleagues were around – (none tonight, Molesworth had disappeared earlier, saying he had 'business' upstairs) – to receive those lucky ones who, more often than not, had died in their sleep. All the popular, clichéd expectations of a morgue attendant, von Sinistre fulfilled and overfulfilled them. If he wasn't a practising necrophile, it wasn't hard to imagine him as one. Easier still was to imagine him *as* a corpse – easier and far more reassuring.

Sarah and Gemma pulled the altar cloths off Steele and the baby – probably, Sarah thought, the last thing either of them would do for him. After this, if the world outside returned to normal, there would be a postmortem, an inquest, a funeral, a memorial service.

'Oh yes,' said von Sinistre, his fingers touching his lips – a mannerism of his, unnerving and disgusting. 'He didn't come here often – usually sent one of you lot to deliver the meat. But I do remember having met him before. Who cut his head off?'

The question was devastatingly matter of fact.

'We don't know,' said Gemma.

'Look,' said Sarah, becoming assertive, 'all you need to do is put him somewhere safe for the next few hours. The police will be coming to look at him.'

These words made Gemma want to cover Steele over. She wished he were buried or better still cremated already – better that than this, than von Sinistre.

'I can do that,' said the tall pale pathologist. 'Definitely I can do that.'

He came closer and caught sight of the baby's body, previously hidden between Steele's legs. 'That's terrible,' he said, flatly. 'How could anyone do that to a tiny little baby? Look at it – it's hardly been born.' To Sarah's great surprise, this seemed really to have got to von Sinistre: he was on the point of tears – no, he had begun to cry. 'Oh, the poor little thing,' he said. 'Who could do that?' He put his hands over his eyes, and Sarah very much feared she would have to give him some comfort – put her arm around his shoulders or, as she couldn't reach that high, his lower back. At the same time, she didn't know whether or not to take him seriously. Perhaps he was just parodying a normal grief and in a second his long grinning face would burst out from behind the screen of hands.

Gemma, who didn't know von Sinistre as well, had taken his reaction from the first for genuine, and was finding it hard not to sob herself. She was very afraid of starting, for once she did she had no idea whether she'd be able to stop.

'I'm sorry,' said von Sinistre, emerging more humanly than ever before, his gunmetal-gray eyes shining twice as bright. 'The little ones always get me.'

Sarah was almost obscenely relieved she wouldn't be called upon to touch him.

'Don't worry,' he said, 'I'll take care of everything.'

Sarah still felt there was an air of perversity to von Sinistre – a foul, grave-smelling, cavity-opening air. Perhaps his newly discovered sentimentality was merely the usually hidden underside of this.

'Is something funny going on upstairs?' von

Sinistre asked. 'No-one seems to be answering their phone.'

Sarah looked around – there were almost no specks of mist down here. How could he know?

'We've been cut off by a very thick fog,' Sarah said. 'Some of it has got inside.'

'The emergency generator started on the stroke of twelve,' von Sinistre said. 'Is that anything to do with it?'

Gemma, for the first time, got a sense of Dexter von Sinistre's extreme loneliness, down among the dead.

Before they ran off, Cropper had had the foresight to check the screens – he knew where the nearest live person was: three floors up in Oncology/Haematology.

'Follow me,' he said. Sir Reginald gave him the nod.

Pollard and Shears had tracked Gemma and Sarah down to the morgue.

'We'll deal with them later,' said Sir Reginald. 'This is more important.'

He led them, fleshy and high-spirited, carnivalesque, along the corridor to the staircase. Some self-harmed in minor ways as they went – breaking their hands against walls, smashing them through glass doors. Of course, they met no-one on their way. If they had, they would have fallen upon them very much like a pack of ravening wolves.

'Left,' said Cropper, signalling the direction as he'd seen actors do in countless movies. His mind was almost nothing but cinematic references: British gangster flicks and American shoot-'em-ups.

As they went, members of the congregation remarked upon how they felt, which was miraculously better than before. All minor aches, pains, twinges, niggles and nags seemed to have vacated their bodies. Henderson MacVanish held out great hopes that his cancer had been cured. Nurse Linda Loos felt as if she'd been gifted with a completely new spine. 'I had a cold,' Pollard said, trying to join in. 'I had a bad cold and now I feel completely fine.' All in all, they thought themselves not only immortal but close to perfected. Sir Reginald's hair continued to grow back – he looked generally more youthful; they all did.

Emerging onto the 15th floor, the Satanists were startled by the thickness of the mist. The corridors surrounding the Chapel had always been administrative; hardly anyone had died there. But now they were in a ward which, since the 1970s, had been occupied by the very old. A thick white cloud of specks ran down the middle of the corridor and climbed up the walls to chest height on either side. This was where the fatal strokes and heart attacks, the final collapses and letting-gos had taken place: those walking down the corridor, dead in an instant, those swaying to support themselves against the walls as the world went loop-the-loop, traced an ampersand, tied itself into a bow, disappeared through a hole in itself. Where their hearts had been when they died, there a small white smudge of pain appeared: ghost-mist.

Now they were near live souls, Sir Reginald took charge again – with Linda Loos' assistance. There were eight beds in this ward, all occupied, all lost in mist. With some vestige of compassion, Sir Reginald cast his clinician's eye over the bed-chart of each sleeping patient.

When he came to an old woman noted down as

'dementia' and 'confused' with runners along the side of her bed to stop her falling out, he said, 'This one will do.'

'No, said Nurse Linda Loos, 'this one – please.' She meant Janet Dammers, her bitter *bête noire.*

'No,' said Sir Reginald. 'This one.' He did not give his reasons.

Her name was Betty Steppingford, eighty-two and mother of three, grandmother of six, waitress and then carer for her elderly mother and disabled brother. Betty had been dreaming of softness or rather, the softness that was her had been experiencing a dreamlike state in which warm alternated with cool and wet with dry. This was how Betty experienced incontinence.

She was covered almost completely by the white of the mist. To gain vision of her, they had to move her bed a few feet to the left – where there was a clearer spot, a gap between clouds.

An old man at the end of the ward was woken up by the sound of so many bare, shuffling feet. The sight that greeted him when he opened his gummy eyes – of naked men and women surrounded by clouds of smoke – convinced him he must be having a nightmare; a particularly vivid and erotic one.

Two of the satanic nurses drew the curtain around the demented old lady's bed and, dagger in hand, Sir Reginald looked around the eyes of the Devil's devotees. 'Now for the moment of truth,' he said.

Since midnight, there had been remarkably little pain from the shoot, encouraging hopes that his wish had worked (for him – he was sure it had worked for others); now, however, the boy sat down on the fire stairs of the 18th floor, winded, gutted.

Eventually, the pain reduced itself to a bearable level; the boy unscrewed his eyes and tried to examine himself – what was growing out of him.

There wasn't much light to see by. He glanced out of the window, but could see nothing.

Curious – a very thick yellow fog seemed to have taken over; not at all like the white mist elsewhere.

When he'd regathered his strength, he continued the downwards journey.

Perhaps, the boy started to think, it might be worth trying the lifts again. But the memory of the hands tight on his arms and the breath vommy-max in his face stopped him, dead.

This route, though laborious, was safer; fewer security cameras, fewer people.

But just then, he heard footsteps in the stairwell, several floors above him. They slapped regularly, rapidly. Coming down or going up?

Louder and closer – coming down.

The boy made it to the next set of fire doors, 17th floor, and got through them before whoever it was caught him.

PC Peter Dixon had never been so happy; look! look!

It took him several minutes to work up the courage, but then he'd gone over to where Nikki Froth was standing on one of the beds, squealing just for the joy of squealing.

She was wearing a backless hospital gown, and when she jumped up and down he could see all the way up her legs – he could see above her legs, too.

But it was an innocent seeing; delighted and proud. That was a healthy, girlish stomach she had; with a little belly on it, to finish it off.

PC Dixon touched Nikki's smooth knee, and at

first she didn't notice him. Then she gave an even louder squeal and jumped down into his arms.

'Pete the Pet! Pete the Pet!'

That's what she was squealing, now: it had been her nickname for him; delightfully embarrassing.

'It is!' he said, struggling to rise to her level of ecstasy; this was hard, given the uniform and his age. 'It's me!'

'What are you doing here?'

She was still jumping, or rather dancing; he still held her. PC Dixon imagined this was what it was like trying to have a conversation in the middle of a rave.

'I heard you were here. I came to see you.'

Unseen, a girl, Holly Gonne, came up behind PC Dixon and knocked his helmet off with one soft bash of her pillow.

He caught it and turned round, not angry.

'Sorry,' she said, and ran away.

Dixon could see Melanie, still trying to calm things down at the far end.

'I feel so *good*,' shouted Nikki. 'I've got so much energy.'

They were dancing and there wasn't any music.

'What's happened to you?' asked Dixon.

'I don't know. But it's fucking great, whatever it is! Better than drugs. A lot better than sex.'

Dixon had never liked to hear her swear; even when she was doing much worse, he'd always tried to get her to speak properly.

'You look fantastic,' he said.

'Thank you, Pete the Pet,' Nikki said. 'You were always so nice to me. And I didn't deserve it.'

'You did.'

'I didn't.'

'You did!'

'Didn't.'

'Did.'

And suddenly PC Dixon remembered what being a boy had been like; how this was the way he'd argued, without disagreeing, without really arguing.

'Come here,' said Nikki, and grabbing his ears she gave him a beautifully clumsy kiss on the lips, still bouncing.

The moment would have been perfect – if PC Dixon hadn't opened his eyes and seen WPC Angel, staring, horrified.

The hinges of the pharmacy door had resisted for quarter of an hour, but now – with a ping – they finally gave way.

Spanner and Case had almost got bored with waiting. If they had been able to let the attackers in, they might even have done so – just to get over the suspense of finding out who they were.

With so little light, it was hard to make out any details of the first figures through the door.

But some things were certain: there were lots of them, and they moved fast, and – as soon as they were inside – they headed for the nearest shelves.

Spanner could hear the rattling of blister packs in boxes, and the light smack as boxes hit the floor.

'Do you think they'll have cocaine?' asked a voice belonging, so it happened, to a rejuvenated Billy Stickers. 'It's been such a very long time since I've had a toot.'

'It's every man for himself, I think,' replied Andy Woods, former burns victim.

Someone came to the end of the aisle Spanner and Case were hiding in, but took no notice of them.

A minute more, and they could pass for intruders like everyone else.

'Where's all the fucking methadone?' said another voice, Welsh: Owyn Parry.

'Let's go,' said Spanner.

'There's about one pack here. The rest of the shelf's cleared out.'

They began to stroll towards the door, acutely aware of how loudly their drug-stuffed bags were rustling.

'Someone's had it away already.'

Spanner was almost there.

'Which is the fucker here that's got my methadone?'

The eyes attached to the voice were looking at Case, who looked back, guilty.

'Give me the bag,' said Parry.

'Run,' said Spanner.

Dexter von Sinistre had now finished crying over the decapitated baby, and was weighing its tiny corpse in a pair of scales: 5lb 1oz.

Gemma and Sarah, although assured there was nothing more they could do, felt a deep reluctance to abandon Steele – even a dead and beyond-real-injury Steele. They didn't want to leave his precious body alone with von Sinistre.

For want of anything better to do Gemma looked around the room. She wasn't completely unfamiliar with the place: on her induction day, they had been brought down here. One wall was made up entirely of the doors of storage compartments, where the dead were laid down on sliding metal trays. They were stacked three high. As part of the tour, Dexter von Sinistre had been delighted to open one of these up and show them a fascinoma (eight points) – a man with another man inside his head; vestigial twin, fetus in fetu.

'Shall we?' said Sarah.

Gemma could only nod.

They were about to leave when von Sinistre spoke. 'The baby is getting warmer,' he said.

Gemma and Sarah looked at one another – this was exactly the sort of prank they expected from mortuary staff.

'It is,' von Sinistre said, opening a well-organized drawer and producing a thermometer.

As he was turning the body over, in order to insert the thermometer up its rectum – 'Jesus,' he said, 'its heart's beating.'

He laid the should-be-dead body on the metal counter; the head was still in the scales.

'Come and feel,' he said. 'This is extraordinary. It can't be happening.'

Gemma was the braver or more gullible of the two. She went across, stood at von Sinistre's side and placed two fingers on the little infant's chest.

With a swift movement, Sir Reginald began to slice open Betty Steppingford's neck.

The energy of Sir Reginald's first cut was partly lost in the looseness of Betty's skin, and so he followed it quickly with a second and a third. Apart from a small glugging gurgle, the old woman made no sound. Blood pumped-jumped from her neck, but her weak old heart could not force it to fly in their faces as had the hard, panicked life-muscle of Steele.

Soon, Sir Reginald's raking passes had cut through to the spine. He found a joint – a meeting point of two vertebrae – severed the spinal cord.

There was little scientific point in continuing to full decapitation – what he had already done was more than enough to kill the old woman, were she indeed going to die. However, Sir Reginald was determined there should be no doubt. He did not fear arrest for murder. What sentence could they give him? Life? He finished the job by running the dagger through the stringy trapezius muscles at the back of Betty's head – then it was off, completely.

He gave a grunt of satisfaction; the blade was becoming slightly blunt with all this use, and the beheading had been harder work than he'd expected.

Inside, Sir Reginald was celebrating a triumph he should have been anticipating (death to all but devotees) – but as he tried to remove the knife, pull it up and out, it became stuck on something. For a second he thought this was a troublesome vein he had missed first time through, that in the gore had managed to slip round the side of his hands. But, no, there was no mistake – it was skin, skin of the old woman's foreneck, and it was regrowing.

The surgeon in Sir Reginald wanted to see what was going on, so he cut at the skin – just in time to see the spinal cord rejoin itself like a line drawn by an ECG machine, smooth and continuous. The vertebrae grated like horses' teeth as muscles, reassuming their accustomed positions, pulled them together. Sir Reginald could see the major arteries moving their severed mouths together in healing kisses – blood inflowing.

He stepped back and began to wail, though he didn't quite know why. The emotions he felt were those of a four-year-old who not only want-want-wants a toy but wants the rest of the world, and especially their best friend, not to have it. Especially people like Betty, whose purpose it was to die and clear the bed for the long line of Bettys waiting to die in it. The neck finished healing itself – and the doolally old woman, completely unknowing, slept on immortally.

WPC Angel had run off, away from Blue Elephant ward – away from the sight of PC Dixon kissing that young girl.

And he had gone after her.

'Wait,' Dixon cried out. 'Melanie! You don't understand.'

She whipped round to face him. They were in a corridor up and down which children ran wildly.

'No,' she said, 'I think I do understand – I understand only too well.'

'She's back from the dead,' Dixon said. 'I'm just so pleased to see her. We were kissing for joy, that's all. For the joy of being alive.'

'It didn't look like that to me.'

He gave her his honest look, with just a hint of puppy; Melanie felt a little nauseated.

'It was,' Dixon said. 'If you had seen how she was the last time.'

'I saw her less than an hour ago,' she said. 'Remember?'

Dixon had, in truth, forgotten.

'But she's better,' he said. 'I've never seen her looking so well.'

Melanie felt a fresh stab of jealousy.

'We are still on shift,' she said. 'We can't just hang around here all night.'

'But something's happened,' said Dixon. 'Can't you feel it? Something miraculous.'

'Even if that's the case,' said Melanie, 'I think we

need to investigate. You wanted to see her and you've seen her. You know she's alright.'

'This is so important to me,' Dixon said.

'You look ridiculous together,' said Melanie. 'It will never last.'

'I don't expect it to. Did you think I did?'

Melanie had no answer.

'I gave up on me and Nikki a long time ago.'

'But you said everything had changed.'

'It has, and I'm pleased for her. But she hurt me too much. I can't go back to that.'

Melanie said the words she didn't want to say: 'What about me?'

'I like you,' said Dixon.

'You *like* me?'

'I don't mean to be cruel.'

'Well, you're not doing a very good job.'

Dixon had made Melanie cry, and he was ashamed.

'I'm sorry,' he said. 'I wish it were different. You're such a good person.'

'That's so feeble,' said Melanie, though it made her feel a little pointlessly proud.

'I mean it,' Dixon said.

'We still have jobs to do,' said Melanie. 'Are you coming with me?'

'No,' said Dixon.

Celia Iden ran up to them and blew just the biggest raspberry.

Buh-boom-buh-boom – von Sinistre wasn't joking. And now, as Gemma watched, standing very close, a trail of what looked like pinky red began to snake out of the newborn's neck. It reminded von Sinistre of the spray that comes off bodies as the Stryker saw glides down through their flesh – before the serrated edge meets the grind of bones and dusty motes fly up. Another snake of smoke was coming from the scales – of the same girth and colour. There *was* something smoky about their movements as well as snaky; they were made up of exactly half of each, smokesnake, snakesmoke. But the snake was made out of blood, and the smoke was, too.

The two heads, although they had no wedge-shapes or eyes – the two head-ends met. If you had just seen the shape of them, their silhouette, you would have sworn that they were shaking hands. Then they joined and strengthened, each continuing their air-slither towards the detached and lost otherpart. The snake did not become twice as thick, it was still the width of the baby's neck, but it was darker now, almost opaque.

With the blunt handle end of a scalpel, von Sinistre tried to make a pass through the thing. However, the substance was more solid now. The surface resisted being broken; instead it was pressed down by the metal but flowed both ways uninterrupted.

'Have you ever seen anything like this?' asked von Sinistre. 'I'm going to get it on film.'

From his locker he fetched a camera. The other two tried hard not to think about what it was 'normally' used to record.

Once the flesh snake met the body part it had been searching out (all this took only a couple of minutes), the rope between them – the join-thing between them began to resemble proper outside-body flesh. What it looked like right now was a very grotesquely long neck. The tray in the scales began to tip: the baby, there could be no mistaking, was reclaiming its severed head.

Instinctively, Gemma put her hand out to stop the soft dragged skull falling on the hard metal worktop. The neck of flesh was strong enough, though – it carried the head over Gemma's hand, only gradually bringing it down to its own lying level.

As they watched this supersupernatural event, they all heard and ignored a sound from behind them which might or might not have been a groan.

The baby's head was gently dragged towards the body (the eyelids flickered, the eyes opened, a bubble formed on the lips, a tongue stuck out; it hiccuped) – a rope joined them, then a swan's neck, then a normal baby's neck.

The baby girl's body had miraculously reassembled itself. Being a newborn, it wasn't doing all that much, moving its limbs randomly, but it was definitely and healthily alive.

Gemma thought the little thing looked like she was going to start crying, so bravely she picked her up.

The baby's body felt like a normal newborn's body, squishy and tender, although it couldn't possibly be.

There was a cough and another groan.

As one, they turned around to see Steele trying to lift his head up from the trolley.

Von Sinistre, who was weeping with bizarre and conflicted joy (partly at having caught a little of the resurrection on camera), didn't want to break the moment for his anticipated several billion viewers. He held the viewfinder in place and looked over – he kept the lens in the same direction but looked over with his eyes.

Steele looked over towards Gemma and saw her holding a naked baby in her arms, looking wonderfully motherly.

'I'm – ' said Steele. 'Am I – ?'

*

When they came into sight, the boy – squinting through the reinforced glass of the door – recognized them, although they had changed since last he saw them.

It was three men from Harold's ward, the Spaceman, Sukhveer Blenkinsop and Yi Qu; but they were in better shape than a couple of hours ago: younger.

The Spaceman was chatting happily, Sukhveer Blenkinsop was less scrawny, and Yi Qu was laughing at something or other, perhaps just because he could laugh without having to spend five minutes desperately catching his breath.

'Like I said, but of course no-one believed me,' said the Spaceman. 'When we get there, I'll receive orders what to do. There'll probably be a couple of EVA missions. Don't worry, I can talk you through anything technical.'

'How can you tell?' asked Sukhveer.

'That it's a hydrogen cloud?' The Spaceman turned and gazed out of the window. 'Well, just look at it. Have you ever seen anything like it before?'

Sukhveer shook his head, and Yi Qu did likewise, although he was just copying – out of politeness and a sense of fun.

'Well, I have seen it, plenty of times. That opaque quality, that uniform distribution of light – we're at the outer edge of a nebula, probably a horsehead. We're deep in the space dust. This is what's left of a supernova going supernova. It's an exciting business, although we can't see very much from where we are.'

'I still think we should have waited for Harold.'

'He'll be fine. He was getting better with every minute that passed. Harold can join us later, if he likes. But, for us, there's no time to waste. Let's go. The signals are very clear.'

They continued talking as they went out of earshot, despite the boy re-entering the stairwell and leaning over the banister to try and catch what was being said.

The corridor outside the pharmacy was crowded with people trying to get in.

Spanner and Case made it about ten metres before the Welshman Parry caught them.

'I think you've got something of mine,' he said.

He was armed with a machete, so Spanner gave him the bag he was carrying.

'Nicely,' Parry said. 'Very nicely.'

Case told him to fuck off – he was keeping his.

The first slash missed, the second cut his chest, the third took off half an ear.

'Fucking hell,' said Spanner, who had no idea it would regrow. 'Give him the bag.'

Case threw it at the Welshman's face, then followed in with a kick to the balls.

It missed, unlike Parry's machete, which plunged into Case's forehead just above his left eye.

Spanner gagged.

Case dropped.

There was more light in the corridor than in the pharmacy.

Parry tipped all the drugs out onto the floor: a mistake – as one, the waiting crowd pounced.

Two minutes later, there was nothing left, not even the bin-bags.

His hands full of capsules, Parry told Spanner to pull the machete out.

'I want it back,' he said. 'It might come in handy.'

Case was still rolling around, not dead.

'I can't,' wailed Spanner. 'You've only fucking killed him.'

'Here, hold these,' said Parry, and put the drugs in Spanner's hands.

He knelt down on Case's agonized chest and, with both hands, grabbed the handle of the machete.

The blade came out with a sucking sound.

Parry was surprised by Spanner's reaction. 'Oh,' he said, 'it's nothing – he'll be fine in a couple of minutes. No hard feelings, eh?'

'Fine?' said Spanner, dropping everything he held.

Down by Case's side, he grabbed his hand and got ready to say some final words: *mate* and *love* were two of them.

The sight of the wound closing up blew them completely from his mind.

'See?' said Parry, and went off in search of needles.

PC Peter Dixon went back into Blue Elephant ward. He felt very guilty about Melanie. Surely he was making a mistake. If he went after her now, maybe she would still take him back.

Take him back? She'd never had him in the first place. But it was pretty clear that, given a bit more time, Melanie would have done – would have loved him. Now all that was messed up. He seemed to mess everything up.

Nikki was still there, though – still looking radiantly innocent as she joshed around with the other girls and boys. They were all so young. She'd already been through so much more than they ever would. Under normal circumstances.

Peter tried to join them, join in their games. They were playing a version of Tag.

When he became It, they ran away from him with something close to fear.

He tried and tried but couldn't catch any of them. Under and over beds they went – far quicker than he was.

Soon they got bored, and another game spontaneously started up. This was Hide-and-Seek.

Peter found a good place to hide, in a cupboard in the nurses' station. No-one came to look for him, however. He waited for minutes, hardly breathing, then crept out to see what was going on.

Another game of Tag had begun.

Again, he tried to join in.

Holly Gonne had tagged Nikki. She was It.

He pretended to stumble, letting her get close enough to touch his arm. But instead she just stopped and stared at him. The whole room came to a standstill. Finally, she said, 'Go away. You're ruining it. No-one wants you to be here. You're not one of us.'

Peter knew it was true. Although he felt younger than he'd done in years, he was still a middle-aged policeman ridiculously pretending to be a child.

He felt the eyes of the ward upon him.

'Yeah,' said Celia Iden. 'Go away.'

A chant started up: *Go away! Go away!*

Emotionally, he was transported straight back to school, to the playground – alone, without a friend, in the middle of a hostile crowd of kids.

'I just want to play,' he said, as he had said then.

'No!' shouted Nikki. 'You can't!'

Nothing had hurt him so much in years.

'Let me!' he pleaded.

'No!' said Nikki. He couldn't hear the word for the chanting, but he lip-read it easily enough.

PC Peter Dixon turned and walked slowly out

of the ward, to the accompaniment of high-pitched cheers.

Steele coughed for a minute. Gemma hardly dared approach him. Her disbelief at the anonymous baby's coming back to life was doubled and redoubled in his lovely case.

They knew better than to give him any water to drink – that would just make him choke. 'Take your time,' said Gemma, feeling extraordinarily odd to be using one of her day-to-day nursing phrases on Steele, her heart's desire, her one-and-only, her resurrected lover.

He tried to sit up, and Sarah helped him. He perhaps needed to get his neck vertical.

A few more coughs and he brought up a couple of dark bloodclots – these he spat into his palm, where, unnoticed, they thinly snaked away up his nostrils and back into his bloodstream.

'What happened?' Steele asked. 'Did you come and rescue me?'

Gemma, from extreme emotion, found herself unable to speak. Von Sinistre kept his camera focused on the whole scene, drawing back to get a wide shot of them all.

'A few moments ago, viewers,' he whispered, 'this man was lying dead and decapitated, just like that baby. There are three witnesses – reliable medical experts. This is a ten out of ten – an eleven.'

'We didn't rescue you,' said Sarah, stepping in. 'We found you in the Chapel.'

'I remember,' Steele said, still a little fuzzy. 'They were going to kill me.'

'I think they succeeded,' Sarah said. 'For a while, at least.'

'Is that a baby?' he asked.

'Yes,' Gemma managed to say.

'I remember a baby,' Steele said, then shook his dark curls at the image. 'They killed it.'

'The baby was dead, too,' von Sinistre said. 'It just came back to life. Hold it up to the camera.'

Gemma let him get a few seconds of footage. She was finding it hard to keep herself under control. All her tenderly loving emotions were coming back to her, sweeping over her like the seventh wave of the sea. Then she could no longer restrain her passion. She rushed across to Steele and threw one of her arms around him, still holding the baby in the other, and almost crushed all three of them in a powerful embrace.

Steele didn't understand all the words she was saying, hot and teary, into his right ear, 'Oh, I thought I'd lost you. I can't believe it. I thought you were gone for ever and that I'd never ever see you again – that I was going to have to mourn you for the rest of my life, because you were the one. You are the one.' But he caught the final three words, which were beautifully predictable: *I love you.* He had put his powerful arms around her, and now they enfolded her more intimately still.

Gemma was aware that she was where she had always (or, at least, since she'd met Steele in the carpark) wanted to be. She felt completely overwhelmed by his masculinity and his self-control.

At the same time, she was waiting for him to reply to her declaration.

Was this, a hug, a very sweet and meaningful and tender hug – was this all she was going to get from him?

*

After losing their drugs, Spanner and Case walked the one floor back down to A&E to see if Nikki had returned.

They could hardly get through the door; the waiting room was rammed with people trying to get out.

'We'll never find her here,' said Case, worried.

'She's alright,' said Spanner. 'She'll find her own fucking way home, later.'

People continued to push past them; Spanner held up his fist and bared his teeth. 'Care-*ful*,' he said threateningly, to no-one in particular.

'So, what do we do now?' asked Case.

'You come with me,' said a female voice – sort of a female voice; it had a slightly parodic, robotic edge to it.

Spanner looked straight at his fantasy, tall and shiny – astonishing: the Rubber Nurse.

She was standing there, looking down at them from the heights of her six-inch heels.

'Okay,' he said, 'we go with you.'

They followed her to a lift marked EMERGENCY, giving one another looks behind her back.

'Keep up,' she called back to them.

Spanner bit his knuckle and rolled his eyes; Case puffed his cheeks and shook his head.

Once inside the lift, the Rubber Nurse gave them her speech: 'I am taking you to my room. This means you have been very naughty, and I am going to have to punish you, severely. There is a great deal of equipment in my room, all specially designed for punishment. I have already decided what I am going to do to you and, I warn you, it will be *very* painful. You will scream and beg me to stop. But I will not stop. I will keep going, because you are naughty and need to be thoroughly punished. No-one will come to your rescue. My room is soundproofed and, once we are inside, I will lock the door to make sure we are not interrupted. Whilst I am dealing with one of you, the other one will have to be stripped, gagged, blindfolded and caged.'

'Sounds good to me,' said Spanner.

'Do you think it's the whole hospital,' Patricia asked, 'or just this floor?'

'How do I know?' Sir Reginald replied tetchily. He was furious with Satan and all his trickeries. Betty Steppingford had made no sacrifices upon his altar. Why should she benefit from the hard work and risks of the Devil's most devoted servants?

Sir Reginald had always been possessed of a terrible temper, but had managed, because it suited his purposes, to keep it strictly under control whilst at work. He needed people to like and trust him – it was a necessary stage before they were taught to fear and worship him. Now, as a confirmed immortal, there was no longer any reason to restrain himself. Raising the knife high, he looked down on Betty's soft sleeping form. He loathed her. She was all the lives he'd ever fought to save whilst knowing they couldn't possibly be *worth* saving. She was the men and women turned into vegetables they would never have wanted to be. She was beauty disfigured, athleticism hobbled, intelligence blurred, youth aged. And the dagger came down through her skull, then again through her fractured skull, then through her chest, her chest, her abdomen. Sir Reginald wasn't aware of the cry that came out of his mouth, and how terrifying it was to those that surrounded him – far more terrifying than his violence, which meant nothing.

Betty's head, when he finally left it alone, began reassembling itself – mush and splinters becoming brain and eggshell skull. Sir Reginald sounded, as was right, inhuman; it would have to be something else – something post-human, non-mortal, not-yet-a-god.

After four or five minutes of screaming gore, gore that only succeeded in waking and traumatizing the entire ward, Sir Reginald desisted.

A minute or two later, slumbering Betty was whole again, as if never touched – even the blood had retreated into its arteries and veins.

As he walked out from behind the curtain, disgusted, the eyes of the seven wide-awake patients were upon him.

'It's a fancy-dress party,' said Linda Loos, in explanation. 'Just go back to sleep.'

'Is Betty alright?' asked Janet Dammers, who was sure these bizarre young people had come to murder her in her bed.

'She's fine,' said Patricia, and drew back the curtain to reveal a peacefully sleeping form. Mrs Dammers accepted Betty did indeed look fine. She could hear her snoring – a characteristic fluty whistle coming out of the one nostril. (She could also hear the clicking of Mr Froth's jaw.) But how then to account for those terrible noises, the crackings and slurpings and smashings of crazed butchery? These were doctors and nurses – Mrs Dammers believed that, even though they wore no uniforms, wore no clothes. 'I'm glad she's alright,' she said. She wanted to ask for someone to bring her a glass of water but, wisely, she didn't.

'What shall we do now?' asked the chaplain, after turning to Sir Reginald. The High Priest was properly taking in the ghost-mist for the first time. What was it?

'Do what thou wilt shall be the whole of the law,' he said, then gave an ironic laugh. 'It really shall.'

Cropper, who had read his Aleister Crowley, smiled but was unsatisfied. He wanted to be told what he wanted. Some of the others, though, needed no further hint. The mood of their intimate little orgy had been smashed, along with Betty's skull, and a new mood had replaced it, more lustful, more energized, but still orgiastic.

It had taken a while, but WPC Melanie Angel was now back in control of herself.

The scene in the Elephant wards had seemed chaotic. Compared to elsewhere, however, it was just a slightly out-of-hand sleepover party.

Melanie had done what she could to calm people down; only infrequently had she dealt with such genuine high spirits. Several men had tried to kiss her; they had not succeeded.

With her radio spewing static, and PC Dixon off with the fairies, Melanie had to decide for herself what to do next. A&E was the obvious place for her to go – the chaos there was always greatest. But what was the point of trying to maintain law and order in a world gone majorly loopy? No-one would pay any attention. Personally, though, she was still curious about the comatose man; she wanted another look at him, and at his photograph.

After a few minutes spent waiting for a lift that was never going to come, Melanie decided to take the stairs – and although they were far from empty, she was able to make her way up to the ICU.

The thought of facing PC Dixon's ex-wife again

didn't fill her with joy. But she had to admit that Angela's angry words had been proven right: Dixon *had* let her down. He'd dumped *both* of them for Nikki Froth.

When Melanie walked through the fire doors and into the ICU ward, she found a different place from before. The only thing that seemed to remain the same was the comatose man. He hadn't moved or been moved. Angela Dixon was there at his side, holding his hand, looking exhausted. All the other beds were empty.

'What happened?' Melanie asked.

Angela shrugged vaguely. How could she ever explain? It had been wonderful, but also in a way frustrating, to watch as each comatose figure started to twitch, to groan, to flex and unflex. It had been stunning to see their eyes open and slowly take in where they were. It had been dreamlike to remove their catheters, lines, pads and restraints. And it had been a great wrench to watch as they tottered out on atrophied but gradually bulking legs.

There was something different about the unknown man, however; he had shown no sign of waking – in fact, his condition had continued gently to decline. Under normal circumstances, Angela (taking the hopeless prognosis of his stats) would have expected him to last out another day or two. He might arrest a couple of times more, before his organs all gave up on him. There was brain function, quite a lot, a surprising amount, but large areas of the cortex had already shut down and, as he continued to die, others would follow.

'They all got better,' said Angela, finally. 'All except him.'

'It's happening on other floors, too,' Melanie replied. She had seen enough to have worked that out; giddy laughter on the stairs.

'I'm staying here,' Angela said.

Melanie remembered her reason for returning. She spoke calmly: 'I'd like another look at that photograph, if possible.'

'Oh, yes,' said Angela, still vague.

The two women walked down the empty ward. Sounds came to them from floors above and below – ecstatic and terrifying sounds.

'I'm sorry about earlier,' Angela said.

'That's okay,' Melanie replied.

'Peter hurt me very deeply.'

Melanie thought for a moment. Did she want to tell this woman about Dixon's second betrayal?

Angela interrupted Melanie's thoughts by handing her the baggie containing the photograph.

'Do you think it's his daughter?' Melanie asked. 'The man's.'

'Yes, I do,' Angela said, after a quick check. 'She looks just like him.'

'There's a boy, too,' said Melanie, and told Angela briefly what she knew.

'How strange,' said Angela. 'But, then, it's not your average night, is it?'

'I don't know if it even matters any more.'

'We have to go on doing our jobs,' said Angela. 'That's what I think.'

'Yes,' said Melanie.

'So, go and arrest someone.'

Melanie looked at Angela sharply, but it had been a well-meant joke.

'Disturbing the peace,' Melanie said.

The two women laughed.

'See you later,' said Melanie, when they were again at the bedside.

'Maybe,' said Angela, who had her doubts.

Melanie went out through the fire doors and started down the stairs.

A&E – she *should* go to A&E – at least, if she were doing her job, she should. But the boy was also her job. Perhaps she could find him. Not by wandering randomly round, though; by going to the security offices and using the CCTV cameras. She'd never been there before, but she knew where they were: 12th floor.

Suddenly, it seemed, the stairwell was echoing – below and above – with many more footsteps and excited voices.

The boy was in between the 16th, Cardiology, and the 15th, Oncology/Haematology.

A rush of people came out onto the next landing, many of them naked, all of them ecstatic; some cried, some let out high yells, some giggled.

'No bad pain, no bad pain,' he heard a woman loudly sing. It was Omifunke Osunkunle, formerly pancreatic cancer. 'I got no bad pain, and I'm right as rain!'

There were other exclamations, joyous and joyously obscene: 'It's a fucking miracle. Thank fucking Christ.' – 'He's going home, he's going home, he's going, Trevor's going home!' – 'Praise Jah, the Almighty, and Praise his Imperial Majesty, the Emperor Haile Selassie, I!' – 'I said I'd beat you, you little bastard, and I did, I fucking nailed you, you cunt, you fucking bastard cunt.' Quite a few were in languages the boy had never heard.

He stood waiting for the flow to stop, but after five minutes it showed no sign of doing so; and it had been joined by those rushing down from floors above.

There could be little doubt where they were all heading: home, and as fast as they could.

The boy joined in for a couple of flights.

People around him were being joyously reckless, newly cured; and because they knew that any minor injuries would heal as well, they near threw themselves down the stairs. Ankles were twisted, and shins fractured, but those going down were stepped over or, increasingly, stepped on.

On the 14th floor, he decided it was getting too dangerous. He might spend hours there, trying to get up from the trampled floor. If he'd been a bit bigger, heavier, stronger, he might have continued. As it was, he needed to find some other way down.

'I was dead,' Steele said. 'They killed me, and I was dead, and somehow I'm alive again.'

Gemma wanted to stay on the subject of love but knew this miraculous resurrection was something that had to be interrogated.

'Who?' she asked, simply.

'The Devil-worshippers,' he said. 'All of them, but it was Sir Reginald who cut my head off.'

'Sir Reginald did that?' asked Gemma, shocked.

Steele started to choke again. His hand went to his neck. For one horrible instant, Gemma feared that the killing wound would open up again – that Steele's reprieve had been only temporary, and that his head was about to slide off his neck and fall down between them onto her lap. Steele's chokes turned to sobs, deep sobs.

‘You’re alright, though,’ Gemma felt confident enough to say. ‘You came back from the dead.’ She held him in his moment of horror.

‘Sir Reginald was one of the “Devil-worshippers”?’ asked Sarah, reluctant to interfere with their little scene.

When Steele pulled his head away from her shoulder to speak, Gemma felt a pang of the most awful jealousy.

‘It was a Black Mass,’ Steele said, and laughed ironically-disbelievingly. ‘Sir Reginald was High Priest and Patricia was assisting him.’

‘So that’s why they didn’t come back to Trauma,’ Sarah said. She seemed to accept their Satanism quite unblinkingly. Her feelings towards Patricia she was determined to keep secret.

Dexter von Sinistre drew close, too. ‘What did they do to you?’

‘They were trying to kill that baby,’ Steele said, indicating the tiny figure in Gemma’s arms. ‘I burst in upon them. There was no-one else around. No Security. I had to try and save it.’

‘Of course you did,’ Gemma replied, pushing flat his dark curls. ‘You were very brave.’ She knew she was talking to him like a child, but couldn’t help herself.

‘And then . . .’ Steele told them what had happened in a very few, remarkably calm words. He was over the worst, emotionally.

Gemma held the baby more tightly as he came to the part where its throat was cut, and did the same for him when his moment came.

‘Sir Reginald,’ said von Sinistre. ‘He visits us down here quite often.’

‘I’ll bet he does,’ Sarah said. ‘I always thought

there was something odd going on between him and Patricia, but I never suspected this.'

'Can you remember anything else?' Gemma wanted to know. 'Anything from after you died?'

'I'm not sure,' said Steele. 'It's all a bit confused. Until recently, I never thought Sir Reginald was anything other than a brilliant, kind emergency-medicine specialist. But then . . .' Steele found himself unable to explain quite how his suspicions had begun. The confirmation of them, so ludicrously, had erased all memory of their origin.

Gemma realized her physical hold on him was, in some ways, emotionally superfluous – if she kept him that close for too much longer, it would become truly ridiculous. And so, with grace but great tearing of her heart, she tried to release him from her embrace. But he wouldn't let her go.

'I heard what you said.' The words, she could hardly believe it, were coming from his mouth straight into her ear. 'I don't think now is quite the time, but . . .'

For a moment, Gemma felt as if all her silly dreams were about to come true. His lips would crush down onto hers, parting them with irresistible force. 'I heard what you said,' he repeated, in a whisper. 'I understand.'

This, she thought was bad; *understand* was a let-down word. He drew her even closer. He didn't want to say it in front of the others, but . . .

'We'll talk about it later,' he whispered, his voice gruff with emotion. However, when she drew back from him, she saw only his inscrutable eggshell-blue eyes and his infuriatingly kissable mouth. 'I –' he began to say, but his sentence, whatever it was going to be, was interrupted by a shrill scream.

*

Do what thou wilt . . .

Cropper and Pollard headed quickly back towards their locker-room on the 16th floor – they were going to get tooled up: Pollard had an air-pistol, Cropper a couple of flick-knives. The opportunity of a killing spree without consequences was too much for them. They also felt awkward being naked.

One young nurse, Suzi Lerph, went off to find a sharps bin – she had always secretly been a self-cutter. Her greatest fantasy had been severing herself completely from her labia. It disappointed her that the slashes of the scalpel would no longer leave their lovely long silvery traces; scarification was part of the secret charisma of the blade in the bathroom. As she left the room, she wondered if she would be able to cut her nipples off fast enough so they were both gone at the same time.

Another of the nurses, Audrey Keith, for her own reasons, decided to go home. 'I resign,' she said. 'I'm never ever going to see this bloody place again.' No-one tried to stop her – why should they? She headed off towards the lift, her locker and her home clothes.

Sir Reginald's congregation, its purpose fantastically fulfilled, was breaking up. But Patricia, along with Linda Loos, midwife Honey Hopeful and quite a few others, intended to remain loyally by his side. Among them was Bill "Zapper" Billson, who had never known what to do with himself. He was devoted to Sir Reginald. It had been he who had driven the ambulance which killed Sir Reginald's wife – not an accident, oh no.

'Go away,' Sir Reginald said. 'I want to be able to think about this. I want to be able to think this whole thing through.'

'Shall we go back to the Chapel?' Patricia asked.

'My dear,' he said, 'you can all go to hell as far as I'm concerned.'

Still clutching the sacrificial dagger, he pushed out of their circle and headed for the emergency lift. The patients, too, watched him.

'She did this,' said Zapper, pointing at Betty. 'She made him leave us.'

'She did nothing,' said Janet Dammers, enraged. 'I'm going to report all this in the morning. It's highly irregular.'

'Shut your trap,' said Zapper.

The boy stumbled out of the shaft of the 14th-floor stairwell, now thick with panicking, escaping people.

Patients, and some staff also, were pushing and fighting one another in the attempt to descend.

Within the last few moments, the boy had seen several slip and break hips juddering down the hard stairs. Those who fell stood no chance of rising again; their bones cracked under heavy-falling bare feet.

He was lucky that the 14th, being administrative, was devoid of people – no-one to attack him, he hoped.

By now, the boy surmised, all the lifts must be completely jammed. They might be worth a quick try, though – and after that, the staircase at the opposite end of the building.

He started off down a long dim corridor. Light came through from the fog outside, and the few floating white specks gave another, ghostlier kind of illumination – making it easy to see where the dark walls were.

Here was almost totally silent, especially when he

left behind him the whoops and screeches of the fire stairs. The heating system gave an ambient buzz, but apart from that the only sounds were the ones he made.

Paradoxically, this gave him a stronger sense than the berserk staircase that a sudden hand was about to land on his shoulder, grabbing him again, pulling him back upstairs.

The shoot was now sticking out about six inches from his belly and, as he approached the lift lobby, he could feel the roots brushing against his back.

The first scream was followed, almost without gap, by a second, louder scream. A pulse or two later, angry banging started up.

Gemma, Sarah, Steele and von Sinistre looked around the apparently empty room.

A particularly loud bang came from one of the steel doors, behind which lay what they had up until this moment assumed was a safely dead body.

Von Sinistre stepped bravely over, moving jerkily hyperfast, like a stop-motion figurine, and opened the door.

A pair of bright white feet gave another kick but, meeting no resistance, their momentum tugged the body a few inches out into the light. There was more screaming now, some of which was comprehensible.

'I'm alive! I'm alive!' – 'Don't bury me! Let me out!' – 'Listen, I'm not bloody dead!'

There were some simple obscenities.

The thumping made it seem as if the whole metal wall were about to explode, a raging force of water behind it.

The man, who was naked, covered his eyes and screamed.

'Oh, bugger!' said von Sinistre. 'They're all sealed up in plastic bags. Quick!'

Sarah and Steele immediately joined him in opening the metal doors. Gemma took a moment to place the baby girl carefully back in the scales.

Behind Gemma's first door was a young black man with a closely shaved head (Marcus Sprint, gunshot wounds) trying to claw his way out of a transparent plastic body-bag. Gemma tried tearing the writhing plastic, but it was too thick and her fingernails could get no purchase. 'I need something to cut it with!' she shouted, looking down in panic into the young man's terrified face.

'Over there!' shouted von Sinistre, and Gemma saw he was pointing to what looked like a metal baking tray.

When she got over to it, she saw that it was full of sharps ready to be disinfected. She wished she was wearing protective gloves, but there was no time for that. Tentatively, she took the uppermost scalpel. Then she hurried back to the bag containing Marcus Sprint. He was thrashing around so much that it was difficult to see where to make the incision – the wrong place and Gemma could easily slice through his ear or straight into an artery. And there was no way of talking to him, calming him; Gemma was pretty sure the young man had no idea what was going on outside the asphyxiating bag – that someone was trying to rescue him. The young man pushed upwards with both his hands, doing his best to split whatever held him in. Gemma gambled that he would hold this pose for a few seconds, and jabbed the scalpel into the triangle of taut plastic. The young man's cries for help came louder, but he kept pushing and pushing up. Gemma reinserted the scalpel into the hole and slashed downwards as far as she dared, without risking cutting into the man's flesh.

With this one saved, Gemma moved onto the next. It was a young white woman, Jill Name, and she was kicking and punching very violently.

Gemma waited her moment, then punctured the plastic – did it again and again; each time, she was glad to see, without wounding her.

Jill Name realized quite quickly that fresh air was coming into the bag, and felt her way to the holes. She would do the rest of the work of opening them.

Next was an old man, Eugene Uno, who was lying completely still. He seemed to have resigned himself to death, or to the fact that death was like being perpetually suffocated in plastic. Gemma pulled his bag away from his chest and put two long slits in it.

Steele, Sarah and von Sinistre were working faster than she was, and had saved five or six each.

The next tray, when Gemma pulled it open, contained a blond boy of about eleven. He immediately succeeded, by a series of frantic kicks, in flipping himself onto the floor. It was hard, marble, and though he landed on his back he also hit his head. The sound it made was like the tock of a coconut shell. He went motionless immediately. Gemma cut a neat hole above his face, then checked to see if he was still breathing. Luckily, he was.

'Is that it?' Sarah shouted.

Sounds of gasping and retching filled the air. A couple of naked figures staggered around, coughing and slipping on the floor, toe-tags tied to their big toes.

Von Sinistre stood back and looked over the wall of doors, every one now open. Then with annoyance he remembered. 'We have another twenty, back there. Older bodies,' he said. 'Come on.'

*

'Come and have a look at this,' said Zapper.

Playing with the blue curtains at the end of the ward, he had seen the blankness outside. He pulled the curtains apart as Linda and the others slowly approached.

'Do you think it's the same as this stuff?' Patricia asked, gesturing towards the ghost-mist.

They were still on the 15th floor. The windows in Hospital did not open fully, only tipped inwards slightly on their metal hinges. Very rarely, though, had that ever been done. The patients liked it as warm as toast.

The fog gave Patricia an idea. She picked up a vase full of tulips and threw it, without warning, at the windowpane.

'Hey,' said Janet Dammers, to whom it had belonged.

Only the inner layer of double-glazing shattered, but Patricia immediately plucked up another vase. Not minding that her bare feet were treading on sharp slivers of glass, she stood close up to the window and smashed her way through.

Whilst she was making the hole big enough, the rest of the congregation was led by Nurse Linda Loos to Mrs Dammers' beside.

'On three,' said Henderson MacVanish. 'One, two,' and with 'three' they picked her up.

'What are you doing? What in hell's name do you think you're doing?' Mrs Dammers asked, as she was carried shoulder high to the hole in the window.

'On my count again,' said the High Priestess.

In three seconds, Mrs Dammers and her unspoken words had been swung out into the mist.

Another old woman, opposite, Myrtle Plymouth, protested, screamed.

'Shh!' they all said. She kept quiet. They listened, but heard no landing thud. Mr Froth's jaw clicked.

The next thing to do was obvious – clear the ward.

The boy had been waiting five minutes for a lift, but none had stopped on his floor, the 14th.

He watched the above-door numbers to work out what was happening – and observed, with annoyance, that they were changing only very slowly, increasing and decreasing by one.

Most were stuck around the ground floor, struggling to ascend further than the 7th or 8th; two of them, it seemed, were not moving at all – at least they didn't whilst he was watching; both frozen, maybe broken, on the floor.

And then he heard it: a high scream, getting louder, coming closer – echoey.

The boy looked around him to check he wasn't going to be attacked, and realized as he did so that the terrifying sound was coming from *inside* one of the lift shafts; it had a metallic zing to it, rebounding off the walls and wires.

He watched the falling figure, in imagination, as it wailed past the 14th floor – arms outstretched, hair blown back, unable to catch hold of anything, doomed; the siren of a police car, a police car gone off a cliff.

Stilling his breath, the boy listened for the quietest of thuds or crunches.

He thought he heard *something*.

A few steps took him across to the lift shaft the man or woman had fallen down – it had sounded more like a man; he put his ear against the metal door, expecting maybe to hear whimpering, death-rattling.

Maybe.

For a couple of minutes more, the boy kept his eye on the numbers: 22 and 22 did not change, the others still seemed unable to reach double figures.

He was left no choice but to keep going until he came to one of the staircases at the east of the building. North-east or south-east wing, didn't seem to make much difference, but he chose north – as the part he'd spent most time in.

There was almost no ghost-mist on this floor: very few people had died here, although the boy didn't know this was the reason.

Dexter von Sinistre led them into a second long and narrow room, backing onto the first.

Systematically, they worked their way along the row. By the end, they were tiring and also, slowly, coming to a realization. But it was only when Gemma had cut through to the final Lazarus that they were able to talk.

From start to finish it had taken them about ten minutes to free all the suffocating people. The last few had no longer been kicking and struggling. Instead, they were oddly calm.

It was von Sinistre who finally said it. 'This lot weren't dying. I think we could have left them there for a week, and they'd still have been alive.'

Gemma nodded, unable to speak – she was still catching her breath.

Von Sinistre gave them a significant look, then went over to a large basket on wheels.

'These are all the clothes I've got down here,' he said. 'It's what they were wearing when they were brought in – bagged up and ready to go.'

He rolled the basket along the line of choking,

coughing, crying figures. To each, he gave what he could.

One woman, Marit Person, suicide by hanging, had been brought straight in from home, and after she protested loudly, he returned to her a little black dress and some high-heeled shoes. Her best underwear seemed mysteriously to have gone missing. Most, not so lucky, were given backless hospital gowns.

The resurrected folk were in a wide range of different moods: some sobbed in ecstasy – several had fallen down on their knees to pray; quite a few went straight into shock and lay foetally, shivering.

'Can you raise the temperature in here?' asked Sarah.

Von Sinistre went off to adjust the thermostat.

'I suppose we should stay and look after these,' said Gemma.

But before they could do anything, von Sinistre had re-entered. 'You've got to see this,' he said.

Gemma noticed a very strange look in his dull gray eyes – as if during his few seconds in the other room, he'd been brainwashed.

'It's the museum,' he said. 'It's . . .' But he couldn't manage any more.

They fought, the old ones, fought for their lives – kicking and wriggling and gummily biting and screeching for help – fought and still died. If they had co-operated with one another, they might, one or two of them, have saved themselves. Instead, they went individually – were posted out the window – sobbing with terror. The Satanists dealt with them one by one, taking the ward anticlockwise, just as they would have done on rounds. As there were fewer and fewer to scream, the congregation listened closely for the sound of the bodies hitting the ground. No thumps or crackings were heard.

'Perhaps they just floated off.'

'No, if that were the case I'm sure we'd have heard them complaining,' said Linda Loos. '"This fog isn't thick enough – it should be much thicker than this. It used to be much thicker, in my day." Fuck off!' she screamed out of the hole, the sound going null. 'Fuck off, get cancer and die, Mrs Dammers!'

Midwife Honey Hopeful laughed in sympathy – oh, those pregnant whiners! Suffer!

Wanting to scream some more, Linda went right up to the window and leaned out. But when she put her head into the fog, it silently disappeared – and when her skinny body slumped down onto the floor, it was severed at the neck.

The diminished congregation stood round in a horrified circle, horrified but still fully expecting her head to grow back.

When it didn't, the horror overtook them completely.

'I thought we were immortal.'

'I don't want to die!'

'What happened? That shouldn't happen.'

'Oh my god oh my god.'

Henderson MacVanish remained calm. He noted with interest that no lifeblood was gushing, as it should have done, from the several arteries in the ward sister's neck.

Kneeling down for a closer inspection, he saw that what looked like a skin was rapidly forming over the stump. At first, it resembled the skin on boiling milk – then it gained the colour and texture of real skin. Finally, and even he was astonished to see this, hairs grew upon it – hairs short and dry and kinky, like armpit or pubic hairs, not at all like head hairs.

He reached for Linda's arm, grabbed her thin wrist; she was warm, as he had expected, and her pulse was strong, as he had feared.

'She's alive,' he informed the others. 'She's probably still immortal – she's just lost her head.'

He didn't mean it as a joke, and at first none of them laughed. But Patricia began to snigger, gasping a little for breath; she had seen a lot of disgusting things, but nothing ever as disgusting as the pubic-hair neck. 'Come on,' said Henderson MacVanish, who had a plan. 'Let's pick her up.'

'We're not . . .'

'What?'

'We're not throwing her out the window, too, are we?'

'I just want to see if what I surmise is correct,' said MacVanish, with authority. 'Turn her round.'

With the living but headless body of the ward sister in their arms, they shuffled out in a tight circle.

'Now,' said the gynaecologist, 'I want you to be very careful. Let's take a wee step forwards and put her feet out the window. Be very careful not to let any part of your own body go outside. Not,' he added, 'unless you *want* to lose it, that is.'

Obeying their temporary leader, the diabolists glided the ward sister's feet towards and then out through the window. MacVanish kept his head as close as he could, but always pressed up against the protecting glass.

'Keep coming,' he said.

They reached a point where Linda's calf had a faint horizontal white scar running across it (from her early days of self-harm). Just before this distinguishing feature passed into the fog, MacVanish said, 'Stop! Alrighty, now pull her back.'

The bulk of the body, which had remained inside the hospital, was, of course, still intact; the ankles and feet, however, had disappeared.

Henderson MacVanish inspected what remained with great interest as the skin grew – not this time hairy, but hard, shiny. The cut-off point was exactly where he had predicted – everything beyond the scar had gone.

Quickly, he went and picked up a pillow from the nearest bed. This, too, he thrust out into the fog.

When he drew it back, fluff fell to the floor. A guillotine could never have sliced half as neatly.

Casually, he chucked the rest of the pillow through the hole.

'Well,' he said, looking round the expectant faces of Sir Reginald's followers. 'We know where to come if we ever want to end it all.'

'This means . . .' said Patricia, but stopped.

'We can't go outside?' asked Zapper.

'I don't think there *is* an outside,' replied Henderson MacVanish.

All the way down the fire staircase, Melanie had been telling people to stop running. Her uniform still commanded some obedience – enough to keep her, and perhaps a few others, from being crushed.

In comparison, the 12th floor was very calm.

Melanie found the security offices without too much difficulty. But the door wouldn't open.

'Hello,' she said. 'Hello, this is the police. We need to speak to you.'

No-one replied – although Melanie was sure the room wouldn't just have been abandoned.

'We are looking for a boy. We think he's still somewhere in the building. You can help.'

Melanie waited, and heard a movement inside.

'Are you really the police?' asked a female voice.

'Yes,' said Melanie, who couldn't remember any female security officers working here.

The door opened. A young woman, who appeared to be naked, peered out through the gap.

'I was raped,' she said. 'Or they tried to rape me, but couldn't. They stabbed me, as well, but I healed up, so there's no evidence.'

'Who did?'

'He did,' said the Virgin, and stepped back from the door. She was pointing to the largest of the screens, where Sir Reginald was approaching his office.

'That's a very serious accusation,' said Melanie. 'Who is he?'

The Virgin tried to explain.

'Can I come in?' asked Melanie.

She wasn't really able to take in what this young woman was saying, although she didn't really doubt it. Her attention was fixed upon the screens, and all the crimes being committed. If she were to start writing them all down, it would have filled her notebook in about one minute flat.

'My god,' she said.

'I know,' said the Virgin.

The boy had been walking along the corridor for quite a while now; ages.

He sensed he had already gone further than the distance from the opposite staircase to the lifts. But he had no way of checking this, or finding out for certain.

Split down the narrow middle, Hospital was symmetrical; the legs of the H on one side were of equal length to those on the other. It wasn't logical, this extension of walking-forwards-into-space, of taking-unnecessary-time.

In front of him, the corridor went as far as he could see, which was a very long distance: there was no ghost-mist, but a dim light helped vision.

The boy felt, in a way he couldn't explain, that it was a failure of imagination that was causing him to be stuck where he was. If he could have seen a bit further, he could have pictured what it would be like to be there – and that would have taken him there. Instead, he felt like a cartoon character, running again and again past the same cactus, the same five tumbledown buildings.

Just to make sure that it wasn't the same wooden office door every time, the boy began to keep track of the names: Dr Green, Dr Warwick, Dr Sickman, Dr Watson, Dr Hardy, Dr Cunningham, Dr Kilgore, Dr Benway, Dr Knonk, Dr Mitchell, Dr De'ath, Dr Jekyll, Dr Bywaters, Dr Wilson, Dr Octa, Dr Doom, Dr Graham, Dr Grover, Dr Beat, Dr No, Dr Vaughan, Dr Curry, Dr Weller, Dr Who, Dr Patel, Dr Smith.

After about fifty, there was still no repetition.

The boy kept going at an even pace.

In a kind of trance of anticipation of terror, they followed von Sinistre through the door at the far end of the room – into the museum.

Whatever they had been expecting was nothing in comparison to the thing itself, to the things, the many, many things. The shelves of the room, and it was mostly shelves, were full of glass jars of various usual sizes and shapes which, in turn, were full of human specimens – some contained only a single body part, others an entire little embryo, foetus or homunculus. This was where Hospital stored its necessary nightmare educational oddities – though right now even von Sinistre would have been quite unable to explain exactly what that necessity had been.

Each jar, whatever its exhibit, pale through years of darkness and formaldehyde – each jar now had one thing in common with all the others: it contained movement.

A long row of smaller vessels on a high shelf near the door exemplified congenital heart defects: these dense, veiny, meaty muscles were clutching and unclutching like a heavyweight boxer's fists. In those immediately below, carcinogenic lungs bobbed up and down in their choppy jars like seals in rough seas (of their own making).

The room was filled with the sound of tinkling and drumming, as glass shivered against glass and tapdanced on metal.

It was the babies who most of all attracted the attention of Gemma and Sarah. Near by, in a long row, were fifteen or more jars of gradually increasing size, every one of which was intended to illustrate normal *in utero* development. And even the smallest of these samples, hardly bigger than a fingernail, gave signs of vibrating life. The largest few in this series were making elegant-eloquent movements – the eight months one week was frantically sucking its thumb, whilst the full-term had its hands cupped over its ears as if it could hear the tinkling-tinking getting louder, the banging becoming more violent – which they were. Gemma stepped forward, instinctively intent on saving the babies, but von Sinistre put his hand out to grab her.

'They're not drowning,' he said. 'Don't worry –'

'But . . .' said Gemma, who a couple of hours ago could never have imagined finding herself in such a grotesque situation.

'I can't believe it,' said Sarah. 'What should we do?'

'In fact, they seem quite comfortable where they are,' von Sinistre continued, his gray eyes newly bright but his voice calm.

Then, he remembered the camera in his coat pocket and began filming methodically along each shelf, starting at the near end and working his way towards the back wall.

Unnerved as they were, Gemma and Sarah couldn't help but follow him deeper into the strange distance of the room. Here were more hearts all a-pulse, more lungs beating like fat wings; here were noses and ears twitching, kidneys quivering as if being fried.

Round the next corner, and a row of severed heads looked at them – *really* looked at them, with at least some understanding of the pickle they were in.

Unlike the embryos and foetuses, the heads were definitely not comfortable. Many of them were scrunch-eyed, mouths wide as they could go, screaming without lungs into air that wasn't air but methanol and other, older preserving fluids. Even so, Gemma expected to see bubbles rising from the mouths – of course there were none; oxygen had been to them an unfamiliar element for many years: dead, they had had no familiarity with anything.

One was the face of a young girl, her scalp shaved of all hair. Distressingly, she alone did not seem distressed by her situation, but looked out at them with smiling curiosity, as if they were shapes hard to discern – which perhaps they were, through the distortions of the curving glass. But the fact she was *seeing* at all, surely that must have freaked her out?

Gemma, unable to resist, put her own face as close up to the silvery jar as she dared. The girl's eyes, which a moment before had been bleached almost colourless, slowly, as Gemma watched, regained an eggshell blue.

Banging had now almost completely effaced tinkling. The museum seemed earthquake-struck, though the concrete floor beneath their feet felt absolutely stable – about the only thing that was.

Gemma stepped back from her inspection and bumped into Sarah, who put her hand out to steady herself – and in doing so knocked over a small vitrine containing a body part neither of them could immediately identify.

The glass shattered, the cloudy liquid poured nauseatingly out and the shapeless black splodge lay there on the steel shelf surrounded by shards.

Sarah turned her head sideways and read the ink-running label. 'It's a kind of advanced Kaposi's sarcoma,' she said.

Although this was the first sound of smashing in the museum room, it seemed to call forth a quick series of others – as if the specimens had merely been waiting to be shown how to escape.

A very tall jar with a high centre of gravity containing the muscular arm of what must have been a boxer or weightlifter – this swayed, swayed and began to spin on its circular base; the elbow bent, the fist grabbed and the formalin span up into a waterspout. Finally, after what seemed an age but must have only been instants, the base struck the slightly raised edge of the shelf and overbalanced. When it fell it was in slow motion.

The two young women watched as the glass column exploded on the floor. They had to step back to stop the gushwave of preserving fluid reaching their shoes.

For a moment, the arm seemed stunned by the fall, but then it began to feel around in the shards, touching real objects for the first time since death, and in the process cutting its softened fingertips to shreds.

PC Peter Dixon had lost it.

He had been wandering around, looking at things – things which were probably people but which he found hard to connect to anything he could recognize as human. Many of them were naked, many were running, many were copulating; some he took for vampires, some for pigs.

He wanted to do something, make a difference. Once or twice, half-heartedly, he tried to arrest one of the things.

'Stop,' he shouted.

But no-one listened.

'Stop, police!'

They laughed.

A female thing tried to steal his gun, and almost succeeded.

'Get off,' said PC Dixon.

The thing giggled as she went. He saw flesh and hair.

'I don't recognize you,' said PC Dixon, his voice breaking. 'I don't recognize myself. What's happening?'

He was offered sex.

'That's not an answer,' he said. 'I broke her heart. She broke my heart.' He sobbed.

This must be what LSD was like, when it went wrong: woozy, terrifying. He looked at the ceiling – at least it wasn't dripping dolphins.

'I need answers!' he shouted.

A kindly hand took his arm, a kindly perfume filled his nose. Both belonged to Nurse Martha Castle. 'Try asking the Lord,' she said, in a gentle voice. 'I always find it works for me.'

'Really?' PC Dixon asked, as if the thought had never occurred to him.

'Every time.'

'I'm lost,' said Peter. 'I've ruined everything.'

'Why don't you go to the Chapel?' Nurse Castle suggested. 'It's on the 13th floor.'

'I could go to the Chapel,' said Peter, hoarsely. Perhaps he would have grasped at anything, perhaps he would have listened to anyone, but anything and anyone hadn't come along; Nurse Castle had, and she smelled trustworthy. 'I could go and pray.'

'I think you should,' Nurse Castle said.

'Will God listen?'

'Of course He will,' she said. 'He's God.'

Perhaps, the boy thought, this corridor really *was* infinite. He felt not exactly tired but weighed down in his soul by boredom and repetition and effort and lack of reward; trudging on; keeping trudging on – and on.

If the walls had changed colour, or the floor been any other pattern than crossways black and white stripes, everything would have improved – he would have been travelling.

Right now, all he had to prove that was the series of a hundred-plus non-repeating names. There had been a couple of Dr Patels and Dr Smiths, which had given him a fright, but on closer inspection they'd had different initials to the ones earlier in the corridor. At least, he thought so. But despite the risk of misremembering, there was no way he was going back to check.

The boy began to jog. He knew that if the corridor went on for ever this would make no difference. It was necessary for him to do *something*, though – to show belief, to himself, that one day he would be out of this situation.

Part of him was sure that if only he could believe strongly enough that he would soon arrive at the end of the corridor, he would immediately arrive at the end of the corridor.

He made an effort, clenching his fists (as if that might help); he visualized the safety-glass door – the greenish tint of it; the grid of wire within it.

The corridor continued, exactly the same.

Melanie had taken a brief statement from the Virgin.

'I'll make it a priority,' she said, then looked back at the screens. How, with all that going on, could she prioritize anything? 'You should really do a rape kit.'

'But he never managed to . . .'

'All the same,' said Melanie. 'Do you mind if I look for the boy?'

'No,' replied the Virgin. 'Just as long as I can keep an eye on *him*.'

Sir Reginald was nearing his office.

'Of course,' said Melanie, then sat down to make a survey of the whole building. There were a couple of hundred cameras, covering most of the main corridors and public areas. She started to flick through them, looking for the boy's small, vulnerable figure.

The Virgin stood by her side, trying her best to help. Time passed, until –

'That's horrible,' said Melanie. She had just caught sight of Mary Walker.

'I know,' said the Virgin. 'She's one of the worst things.'

The Rubber Nurse was finished with Spanner and Case.

They had been sufficiently punished for all earlier naughtiness, and so she kicked them (literally) out of her room – although Spanner begged to be let back in. It had all been too brief.

'No,' the Rubber Nurse said, wagging her shiny finger. 'I have work to do *elsewhere*.'

'We're looking for a friend,' said Case. 'Perhaps you could help.'

'As if she's fucking going to know,' said Spanner.

'You'd be surprised,' the Rubber Nurse said. 'I know almost everything about Hospital. Try me.'

Case gave a brief description of Nikki, her admission, her appearance.

'They took her up to Pink Elephant ward, 20th floor,' said the Rubber Nurse. 'I saw her there very recently.'

'You see,' said Case.

'Fuck you,' replied Spanner.

'How do we get there?'

'I shouldn't do this,' said the Rubber Nurse. 'But as you're going to be such good boys from now on . . . Follow me.'

She led them to the emergency lift, opened the door with her key and pressed the button they needed.

'Be good,' she said.

'Oh, we will,' said Spanner.

*

Von Sinistre came round the corner, attracted by the sounds of destruction.

A glance at Gemma's and Sarah's horrified faces told him they hadn't deliberately released this incomplete monster-person. If they had been intending that, they would have started with the babies – that, he thought, is what women are like.

Gemma and Sarah covered their hands with their mouths. The smell coming up from the wet floor scoured their nostrils and made their lungs prickle. Von Sinistre, who was quite used to it, smiled and went back to filming.

Another jar crashed down in the next alley along, then another, and soon there were fewer silent gaps between than loud smashes.

The floor was covered in glass, formalin, bases, lids, labels and, most of all, in twitching body parts. Just as with the arm, these did not remain still once they hit the floor. They flopped around like haddock and cod in the hold of a trawler. The banging was backed by an undertone of slapping as flaccid flesh tried to make something of itself – and began, gradually, to succeed. The lone arm which had started the whole thing, which had been the most determined escapologist of all, was pinking up and, as the two of them watched, extending its deltoid muscle until it met the diagonal gelatinous shape of a clavicle.

Both the women stepped closer, risking cuts from the glass: this couldn't help but be fascinating to them – it was an anatomy lesson in reverse, only with the advantage that the subject was, more or less, less becoming more, alive.

The subclavian muscle stretched across towards the first of the ribs. A body was being built, of that there could be no doubt. The muscles looked like the thick, hanky hair of a tough old black-haired woman, once gone grey, now dyed pink. The supraclavicular nerve traced itself over the slippery surface, just out-running the incoming wave of adipose fat which, in turn, was followed by recognizable skin – with hair, moles, age, character.

The arm unexpectedly flexed, and flipped itself until it was the other way up. A couple of pieces of glass had stuck themselves into the flesh just above the scapula; perhaps the arm had moved in pain or irritation – though how could it feel these things without a cerebral cortex? The arm-thing, however, was working on that: vertebrae were climbing up into the nothing of implication that had been there before. With another shake, the stuck shards fell out of the skin – which closed over the holes as quickly as double cream.

Sarah gave a gasp at this. Gemma, for reasons she could never have explained, had begun to weep. 'It's beautiful,' was all she could think to say. But her feelings would just as well have been expressed by, 'It's horrible.'

Ribs were traversing out from the sternal bone – itself defiantly fist-shaped. Between them they glimpsed the spongy grey of lungs, forming like clouds on a just-rained-on hillside.

(All around the arm, other refugees of the specimen jar were making themselves whole. Von Sinistre continued to film, giving occasional whoops of anatomical joy.)

Skin closed over the ribs, a cover drawn over a budgie's cage, and a male nipple blossomed out upon it, with etchings of wet hairs all around.

(Gemma couldn't help but worry about what Steele was getting up to in the other room. No sounds were coming through, over the flip-flap of expanding tissue.)

Crimson arteries and purplish veins climbed out of the trunk of the neck, ascending into a mini-floret that was the medulla oblongata. Around this, the brain grew: it was a tinned oyster, then a foetus, then an alien with an extraordinarily large head, then a cauliflower, then lots of bums – bums that climbed all over one another without ever becoming a body; bums that at the same time were worms and intestines and cerebral foldings.

The pink turned white as the skull, motorbike visor, swept across the frontal lobes; this, in turn, was soon colonized by skin and, out of the skin, stringy brown hair. The lower vertebrae had ended in a comical tail, branching out into hipbones.

But Gemma and Sarah were full of expectation for the face. It grew first of all as a scowl in the empty air, then somehow seemed to fit flesh to its expression. Perhaps this was agony: when the lungs could take their first breath, they would know.

Muscles shot angularly down from the hipbones, meeting the knot of the knee. There was grace in the shape of the skinless calf. And then the man-thing had spokelike tendons, piano-keylike bones. Then he had feet. Then he was finished. He did not speak. His scowl remained. He was shivering. Naked, with pubic hair and formalin dripping from his thighs, he picked himself gingerly up. The glass wounds on his abdomen healed themselves. He stood to a full, unsteady height, complete as he hadn't been since lying on a dissection table – perhaps not even in Hospital.

For the first time, he met their gaze. Then he looked down to his left, where a diseased liver had managed to work itself up into an abdominal cavity and was rapidly branching out into a lymphatic system.

Each body part, now they had a chance to notice, reconstructed itself in quite a different way. The diseased hearts achieved the greatest beauty, building themselves first a whole filigree of venous and arterial tissues; they were trace-people, hardly there, red and blue lines in the air. Gemma was desperate to touch one of them – she was sure they would feel like hot seaweed.

They waited for the arm-man to say something, far from sure that he would. There was suspense, more suspense, and then it was broken by the loudest scream either had ever heard. But of joy.

Hide-and-seek was okay for a while, and so was Tag, especially when it turned into Kiss-chase. But it didn't take all that long before Nikki lost interest.

Some of the kids around her, very well brought up, were overjoyed by the simple thought of staying up so much past bedtime. If they could, they'd probably have wee'd themselves. In this delight, Nikki couldn't share: her bedtime was usually around daybreak, and she slept on a settee or the floor more often than a bed.

Celia Iden and Holly Gonne had decided they wanted to get away from the boys. They kept nagging her to go with them back to Pink Elephant ward and do hair-plaiting or Sindy-play.

'Come *on*, Nikki,' they said. 'It'll be such *fun*!'

'Oh yes, oh yes,' said a voice Nikki recognized with horror. 'Let's play with our lickle dollies.'

She turned round.

Spanner was standing in the middle of the ward,

a big smirk on his face; Case hung back behind him.

All the other children, sensing trouble, immediately stopped what they were doing.

'Did you get the drugs?' Nikki asked.

'What drugs?' Celia Iden asked.

'Yes,' said Spanner.

'No,' said Case.

'Would you just fucking shut up?' said Spanner.

'You said *fucking*,' said Holly Gonne.

'Oh did I?' mimicked Spanner. 'Oh dear. Oh how fucking terribly fucking naughty.'

'You said it again,' said Holly Gonne. 'Twice.'

'Come on,' said Spanner. 'Enough of this – you're coming with us.'

'No, I'm not,' said Nikki.

'Yes, you *are*.'

He took an aggressive step towards Nikki. Case followed.

'I wouldn't try it if I were you,' said Nikki.

Spanner kept coming.

'Oh yeah. And who's going to stop me?'

'Get them!' ordered Nikki.

Ten figures now stood along the alley, re-formed from larger specimens. At least another twenty or thirty seemed set to join them within the next couple of minutes. And then there was all the rest of the museum.

'How many are there?' Gemma shouted across to von Sinistre.

'Oh,' he said, 'hundreds.'

Sarah followed Gemma's logic. 'Exactly,' she asked, 'how many exactly?'

'Maybe a thousand,' von Sinistre said.

'We have to get out of here,' Gemma said. 'There isn't enough space.'

Already the floor was a sea of knee-high flesh, a rising tide of bodies.

'Get out,' Sarah shouted to the joy-screaming arm-man. 'Go through the next room and up the stairs. Someone there will help you.'

'Yes, Nurse,' said the man, A. I. Dunk, who had died in 1916. Then he hesitated, looking down. 'But I amnt wearing any clothes.'

'Someone will give you clothes. Now, go!'

Gemma led him to the door. Steele, she saw, was standing amid those earlier resurrectees. He was trying to calm some of them down, explaining as best he could what had happened.

'Steele!' Gemma shouted. 'They all need to head towards the stairs – we have a crowd of people to get out of here. And it's growing.'

For a moment it looked as if he was going to come towards her. There was admiration in his eyes. She wanted so much to tell him she loved him – tell him again.

'Go!' she shouted.

A couple of men stumbled past her.

'Follow him,' she ordered. 'Follow that man.'

Steele nodded and began to herd the naked, shambling mob out of the room. 'It's very dangerous here,' he said, in a masterful voice. 'We have to go upstairs, now.' Then he turned back to Gemma. 'I'll meet you back in Trauma – whenever I can.'

Othniel sat on his own, brooding – what Cyrille had done during the ceremony, it was unforgivable; no matter that Pierre Estime had died, no matter that very weird things had been happening ever since:

wounds healing, people getting younger. (Some of the other porters had snuck back to the locker-room, unable to stay away. They had brought wild news of what was happening in the rest of Hospital. When Othniel disbelieved, they cut themselves.) No, the greatest insult of all was to voodun itself. Cyrille had been so foolish as to ask the powers for eternal life – and maybe, just maybe, they had granted it. But at what cost? He must not be allowed to get away with this; he must be forced to give up his power.

Upstairs, too, many floors in the air, in the whatever-it-was fog, Sir Reginald was broodingly preoccupied with the way events had turned out.

How was it possible that the reward for an offering made by his followers should be given to all the dying scum of Hospital?

He felt that the Devil had *personally* betrayed him – felt, and it almost made him laugh, that to do *this* the Devil really must be evil.

Reward had come twinned with punishment; it was justly unjust, unjustly just.

But, given this abhorrent situation, what was there to be done?

Sir Reginald had a drink from his secret stash, then another. The alcohol seemed to have less effect than usual, and he finished the first bottle without difficulty.

Never mind, there was plenty more.

He sat there, looking at some pine cones in a bowl on his desk; something was happening to them – tiny green shoots seemed to be emerging.

Spanner and Case had been trashed by the kids of Blue and Pink Elephant wards.

When Nikki finally called a halt, their faces were scratched to pieces and they ached all over. A pile of about ten lay on top of each of them.

'Leave me alone,' said Nikki. 'I'm safe now – you're never going to be able to get near me.'

'Okay, okay,' said Spanner.

'I just want to look after you,' said Case.

Nikki frowned. 'If you want to look after me,' she said, 'keep *him* away from me.'

The kids reluctantly let the bad men go free.

'See you,' said Spanner, as he walked out of the ward.

'You won't,' said Nikki.

As soon as they were gone, she started to head in the opposite direction.

'Where are you going?' asked Celia.

'I don't know,' said Nikki, 'but I'm not staying here. They'll come back. I'm sure they will.'

'But we'll protect you,' said Holly.

Nikki shook her head and left the Blue Elephant ward via the fire stairs.

Her decision to go up rather than down was not completely random: the crowd, thinner here than on lower floors, was heading in that direction. Nikki had never followed the crowd.

What she didn't see was Celia and Holly, following her.

'I can't see him anywhere,' said Melanie, meaning the boy.

They had gone through all the cameras a couple of times. Ghost-mist obscured much of their view. What a few screens showed was completely nonsensical – one, for example, appeared to show a corridor so long that the end of it disappeared into the vanishing point. The scenes from the blood bank were hardly less incredible: a surging river of plasma, cascading down the stairs of south-east wing and turning, as it did so, into a dense crowd of panicked people.

The search seemed hopeless. 'Perhaps he's already left,' said Melanie. 'He almost escaped last time.'

She could see A&E, the outflowing crowds.

'Perhaps,' said the Virgin.

Melanie took a deep breath. 'I'm going to have to go now,' she said. 'I have to do my job. Will you be alright here?'

'Yes,' said the Virgin.

'You'll be quite safe. If I can, I'll come back. Don't worry,' she said, 'Sir Reginald won't get away with it.'

Melanie stepped out into the corridor. Behind her, the Virgin locked the door.

Gemma had finally been able to overcome her squeamishness and touch one of the still-growing ones; out of necessity, not curiosity. It was a head with only half the upper body. Grabbing the man under the armpits, she dragged him through the door – feeling even as she did his body-mass increase; matter created *ex nihilo*.

As she returned to the fray, she saw Sarah trying to give orders to a bewildered fat woman. 'Forget them,' Gemma shouted. 'Go for the small ones – the ones you can carry, or throw! We've got to save as many –'

Sarah gave a nod which shut Gemma up. Point taken.

But even in the moments they had paused, the flesh-tide had risen still further.

Dexter von Sinistre, for the first time, took his eye away from the viewfinder and looked at the general situation around him. He was now only head and shoulders above the specimen-folk, and they were densely packed and thrashing all around him. Within the bodies, he felt strong hearts beating. He realized, as he hadn't before, the consequences of this.

Glancing across, Gemma saw him climb onto one of the shelf units.

They worked, Gemma and Sarah, pulling as many clear as possible.

Pretty soon they had to change tactics yet again – the regrown ones were now too big and too many. It was best just to try and order them out the door, the ones that were within earshot – and had ears. 'Go now,' Gemma calmly shouted. 'Follow the others.'

Five went, then ten, and they were beginning to get a flow – some following even without hearing. But it was clear it was never going to be fast enough.

Despite having been running for quite some time, the boy didn't feel puffed.

He sped up, gradually.

Doors kept going past him; he no longer checked the names upon them – he was pushing on regardless; forget it.

Something would have to change for him to reach the staircase. Belief.

Now almost at a sprint, he began to overstride and lose balance; toppling forwards, he kept running as fast and as far as he could – eyes to the floor – hoping that he would catch up with himself, regain his upright stance, not fall.

Just as he went down, the boy had a pulse of fear: what if he finally arrived at the glass door? What if he fell into it and banged his head really hard and blanked out?

And that was exactly what happened.

Bonk!

Crunk.

The comatose man's condition had been rapidly worsening for the past quarter of an hour – a long decline of small sign after small sign – and now it went critical.

His heart stopped.

Resus was routine, for Angela Dixon; everyday, nightly. But, usually, the flatline beeeeeeeep would have brought other members of the ICU team running to the bedside. There would have been a collective engagement, although calm, with the procedures.

Now, however, with the room empty, everything depended upon her. Although the man's life was in many ways over, she wasn't going to let him down. Angela would do her best.

Without panic, she began CPR.

She was aware of people on the staircase, peering at her suspiciously as she gave mouth-to-mouth. A few pressed their faces against the glass.

The last thing she wanted was for some of them to come in for a closer look, or to offer useless help.

Beneath her hands, the man felt dead.

Von Sinistre, holding his camera high, teetered along the shelf; growing arms flailed into his shins, threatening to knock his feet out from under him.

Once, he almost lost his balance, but managed to regain it by grabbing at a light fitting. He was still only halfway to the door.

The sea of bodies had reached a point where they did not fit, side to side – the alleys were too narrow.

Sarah pulled another man out through the door but realized she wasn't going to be able to force her way back in. Gemma was still there, three or four metres into the crowd. And as those around her continued to grow, her head disappeared from sight.

Frantically, Sarah began grabbing whoever she could reach and yanking them hard in her direction. They were slippery with sweat and preserving fluid, which helped them squeeze through. But with each passing moment they bulked, and it was harder to get them through the gap of the door.

She jumped up and down on the spot, trying to catch a glimpse, and saw von Sinistre crowdsurfing his way across the room – but he was heading in the wrong direction.

Jumping again, she saw him reach above his head and punch out one of the ceiling tiles, but then he fell back down into the seething, screaming mass.

Five bodies now crushed together across the face of the door, and there seemed no way to pull any of them out. Gemma was surely about to die.

Sir Reginald was done with sulking. He had been watching the green shoots rise out of the pine cones and he had come to a slow decision, the most momentous decision of his life.

Hospital must be taken.

All of it.

Top to bottom.

There must be absolutely no resistance left – not the tiniest little bit.

With a sudden leap, he was out of his leather chair and across the room.

He would go back to the Chapel, via Oncology/ Haematology. He would rejoin his congregation. And then, he would rule unchallenged for ever.

Satisfied, he trotted towards the emergency lift.

With no external sign, the man's heart started beating again.

Angela was relieved that the wail of the ECG was finished – although she had little doubt that further resuscitation would be required, the next time he died.

Efficiently, she made a number of checks. Then, her own heart starting to settle, she sat back down beside him. It could go on like this for days: calm then crisis, calm then crisis.

First there was nausea, then there was head-pain, then there was a head to feel the pain, and then, after a while longer, there was a boy to own the head.

He pushed himself up off the floor; in front of him, through the glass, he could see the legs of people trying to descend. They were a dense crowd – lifted knees touching straightened thighs, toes splaying by mistake around ankles.

The boy's arms wobbled, and he thought they might collapse, but new strength entered them from somewhere; enough to turn him round, so that he was slumped against the fire door – able to look back along the infinite corridor.

The boy's sense of the thing became vertiginous: he felt as if the glass touching his shoulderblades were the ceiling, and the corridor an immeasurably long drop – a bottomless lift shaft.

If he wasn't careful, he might start believing this, and it might become so; there did seem to be some relationship between his wishes, conscious or not, and the way Hospital was.

The nausea had gone back to wherever it came from, and the boy's head wasn't hurting so much.

He stood up, without dizziness.

Looking down, he saw that the shoot – like a tiny tent-pole – was holding the pyjamas away from his tummy. It was about eight inches long.

Just when Sarah had given Gemma up for dead, an arm shot out from between the five trapped figures' legs. Sarah recognized the colour of the uniform, and rushed to try tugging. But there was no budging her.

Sarah sprinted across to where a rack of tools hung on the wall. Arming herself with a large saw, she turned back to the doorway.

Once there, she set to work on the legs of the blocking man – expertly hacking through at knee level, severing ligaments and avoiding going through bone.

Gemma's hand waved frantically.

Sarah sawed through two legs, then three – enough to make a gap for Gemma to crawl through.

But to Sarah's horror, almost as soon as she'd finished detaching them, a snake of flesh began to reach out from the torso and find its way to the severed limb. The bodies were quickly re-membering themselves.

Just then Sarah heard a loud crash behind her. Glancing around, she saw Dexter von Sinistre dropping down onto one of the dissecting tables, a hole in the roof above him.

'Gemma's trapped!' she shouted. 'You've got to help.'

Von Sinistre made his way over, but saw at a

glance that they couldn't succeed in digging Gemma out this way.

Gemma's hand grabbed at Sarah's wrist and wouldn't let go.

Von Sinistre crossed the room until he came to the Stryker electric saw. He brought it over to the door and plugged it in to a nearby socket. 'Stand back,' he said.

Cropper, now in the 16th-floor locker-room, was putting his uniform back on.

Pollard hadn't bothered with this – he'd just grabbed his gun and gone.

Standing in front of his door-gallery of busty and gagging-for-it blondes, Cropper yanked at his midnight-blue tie.

Although he'd enjoyed the orgy well enough, it was violence, and not sex, that was his real turn-on: the violence of bone-breaking and disfigurement as well as the violence of authority and control. Violent sex was his hobby (hence marriage); sexualized violence his vocation (hence Security).

He looked in the small mirror – pink flesh, blue cloth, steel buttons – and thought himself an almost unbearably beautiful thing; worth a wank then and there.

Like many others, Cropper had discovered that, under the new biophysics, his ejaculate, like blood, like all other bodily fluids, re-entered his body in a snakelike form. Once back inside, it was ready to go again – no sense of soreness or fatigue. You could even spill it all over cloth, and the cloth would be good-as-new in a matter of minutes.

So, thought Cropper, looking himself in the eye, why not?

*

The boy decided to continue down these stairs – north-east – there was no better way.

He pushed against the door, and a brief gap in the crowd allowed him through to join the descent.

The crowd seemed excited by this break to their routine; delighted by their regained health.

The boy joined the flow of people. It wasn't quite as bad here as on the other side of the building; a rush but not yet a panic.

The five stuck in the doorway began screaming when they realized what von Sinistre was intending. To end this caterwaul, he cut their heads off. Then he began to bisect the central blocking figure down the middle, from throat to anus. As he was doing this, the severed five necks turned into snakes of fleshsmoke which slowly retrieved the heads – which then began screaming again, louder, though.

Sarah, who a moment before had been spattered in the face with bone fragments and blood, felt herself grow clean again – though an aftersense of having been touched by such matter remained.

Von Sinistre realized he wasn't going to be able to cut fast enough this way. Instead, he tried a different tactic – squatting down, he severed the legs of the five through the knee joints.

He gathered up four lower legs and ran to the other room, the smoke of reconnection trailing behind him. He locked the amputated limbs in one of the hermetically sealed body-storage drawers.

As he had hoped, the legs regrew more slowly than the heads. He cut off another four, feeling the tendons resist then snap.

'Take these!' he shouted at Sarah. 'You're going to have to help!'

Sarah let go of Gemma's hand and did what von Sinistre told her. They were one layer of legs away from Gemma.

Von Sinistre knelt down and blithely sawed through the remaining barrier. Five more legs came off, and these he passed to Sarah.

They were in a cave whose roof was made of patellas, raw like knuckles of beef in a butcher's window. The first-cut layer were regrowing downwards, but slowly. Hopefully slowly enough.

Von Sinistre grabbed Gemma's hand. With all his strength, he managed to budge her a centimetre or two closer to the door.

Sarah returned, put her arms reluctantly around von Sinistre's waist and joined him in the pull-pulling. 'On three,' he shouted. 'One . . . two . . .' and on three they all heaved.

Gemma budged a little more this time, her hips having come through some obstruction. But von Sinistre felt himself about to be trapped and crushed. He slid out of the cave and immediately grabbed the electric saw. Gemma wiped her eyes and now could see Sarah's face for the first time; progress had been made, agonizingly slowly. 'We'll have you out soon,' Sarah promised.

This time, von Sinistre went straight through the middle of the doorblockers' thighs. Each time he reached a thick femur, it held him up and made the saw scream as if it too was agonized. But the blade went buttery through biceps – blood spurting out; unserious.

Finished, von Sinistre put the saw aside and grabbed Gemma's left hand, Sarah got her other one and, with immense effort, they managed to haul her completely out of the museum.

*

Cropper – on the 13th floor – was descending the last flight, almost at the security offices.

It was time for him to take over Hospital. He would be able to direct operations from the command centre, watching events unfold on the screens. If necessary, he could dash out and intervene. His uniform would ensure he was obeyed – people would get out of his way when they saw him coming, just like always.

He felt sick to his stomach, but that would probably pass. Maybe something to do with those burgers he'd had on the way in – all three of them.

As he looked ahead of him down the staircase, he thought he saw a figure he recognized – a slight, small figure in stripy blue and white pyjamas.

All of them were breathing very hard, and so they sat for a few minutes with their backs against a dissecting table and watched the thighs and legs snake back into wholeness.

'Thanks,' Gemma gasped, surprised to find herself feeling such gratitude towards von Sinistre.

'You cut my head off,' said one of the doorway screamers, Geoff Vowles, abdominal aortic aneurysm, 1974. 'Twice. And my legs.'

'And I'll do it again,' said von Sinistre, 'if you don't shut up.'

The screamer Geoff thought about continuing the verbal attack, but then looked at the electric saw. Boy, had decapitation been painful.

Sarah avoided looking into the eyes of the other faces, traumatized by what had been done to them – even though it hadn't proved permanent.

Gemma felt her face and hair drying as the blood

which had covered her went back to its proper place – other, thinner fluids joined it.

The room they were in was now completely empty of people. All the rest of the back-to-lifers had headed upstairs at Steele's command.

'I'm going to stay here and get as many out as possible,' said von Sinistre. 'At least, until this and all the spare saws burn out.'

'You don't need our help?' Gemma asked.

'Me!' shouted the screamer, Geoff Vowles, mind changed. 'Do me!'

'Shut up,' von Sinistre said, and hacked off the head. 'No,' he said to Gemma, 'I'll be fine.'

Gemma looked at Sarah, who seemed to be thinking the same thing: could von Sinistre actually be enjoying this? Perhaps it was better than just another boring day down among the dead men.

'How are you?' Sarah asked.

Gemma was surprised at her rival's concern, but even more surprised at how well she felt; with the return of her breath, her health had also come back. The agony of broken ribs was over. All the lacerations on her hands, knees and belly were healed. She wasn't even all that tired any more. But she did feel nauseous – hardly surprising, given the circumstances. Her stomach felt over-agile.

'I'm okay,' said Gemma. 'What shall we do?'

Sarah was about to reply, but just then they heard a high, tense crying – the baby!

'Oi!' shouted a horribly familiar voice, louder than the hubbub around him. 'Oi, you!'

The boy didn't even bother to look round – it was the Security Guard from earlier, the fat one.

There were only a few more steps to go before the landing of the 12th floor.

Using his youthful speed and diminutive stature, the boy slipped in between descending people.

He made it to the fire door, but that opened inwards: with the bodies all around him, there was no way he could get it open.

He glanced up.

The Security Guard was only a few metres away, pushing through as fast as he could.

People bumped the boy roughly as they turned the corner. There were sounds of coughing and retching.

The boy pulled hard on the door and someone saw him doing this – kindly Herbert Hoof from Geriatrics.

Sticking his arms out to his side, a green-faced Herbert held the crowd back just long enough for the boy to get through the fire door; incidentally, he also held Cropper off for a vital couple of seconds.

The porters had all now returned to the underground locker-room. As they came in, one by one, they had greeted Othniel familiarly, but he was very aware that – after what he had done – they were for ever distanced from him. He knew that this distance could be turned vertically, into power; he didn't want that power.

Cyrille was speaking. He was suggesting what they should do. First, he had mentioned the camera outside the room they were in. Of course, he said, it would have recorded Pierre entering the room but there would never be any footage of him coming out again. To deal with this, he suggested, they would have to keep his death a secret as long as possible;

until the tapes were wiped, two weeks later. 'We will say he is ill,' he announced. 'Kissa must be told lies. We must all say the same lies.' He looked around the room. 'Does anyone disagree?' His eyes fell finally upon Othniel.

'No,' Othniel said, and the others followed him.

But then the conversation broke down – all of them had seen weird things happening around Hospital, and many put them down to the earlier ceremony.

'People are cured,' said Ludger.

'The arthritis in my toes has gone,' confirmed Fritzgerald.

'And in my hands,' said Luckson.

'My erection is hyper-powerful,' said Excellent, smugly.

'I agree,' said Cyrille. 'The magic was powerful. It was a success, but still we must think of the future. Pierre sacrificed himself. He knew what he was doing.'

That is a lie, said Othniel, to himself. That is not true.

'We must find someone to replace him,' Cyrille said. 'I suggest myself as the obvious candidate.'

Othniel felt horribly queasy. Something wasn't right inside him. But, still, he was glad he hadn't murdered anyone. That would have made him sick in a different way – sick to his soul. What preoccupied him now, however, wasn't his body and its trivial sensations, it was Cyrille, Cyrille's arrogance, Cyrille's guilt. He must be stopped.

A&E, when Steele finally reached it, was madly crowded. The patients knew *something* weird was going on but not exactly what; staff were hardly any better informed – freaked out by the phones not working, the mist inside and the fog out.

Sister Agnes Day was standing on her desk, shouting: 'Calm down! Please, calm down!' But the fact she was a nurse, standing on a desk, shouting, served only to make people panic.

A very ugly Hispanic man, Zeke Bogart, *luxatio erecta*, was stamping on the already flattened remains of his cellphone. 'You motherfucker!' he shouted. 'You fucking motherfucker!'

Two Japanese girls with bandages around their wrists had somehow arranged themselves into a position where they could cry on one another's shoulders; Ai Ooki and Io Aoki.

Nearby, two fat young English girls with Croydon facelifts were trying to do the same, unsuccessfully – their burly bodies just didn't seem to fit the same way; Tanya Cropper and Charmayne White.

Ogden Chomsky-ffountayne, tympanic membrane rupture, naked from the waist down, stopped in front of Steele, bent forwards and pulled his bumcheeks apart, 'I want it,' he said, 'I want it! I want it!'

Steele told the man to pull himself together, and Ogden Chomsky-ffountayne ran away to offer himself to someone-anyone else.

Another man, J. Guthrie Down, completely naked, and with a belly that made him appear pregnant, shuffled around in small circles repeating, 'It was twenty-four or twenty-five. It was twenty-four or twenty-five. I think it was twenty-four. But it could have been twenty-five. If it wasn't twenty-four it was definitely twenty-five. I'd say it was twenty-four, probably. Either that or maybe twenty-five.'

Just at that moment, Steele began to feel very

nauseous – and a strange motion began inside his stomach. He was going to vomit.

As soon as he was into the new corridor, the boy began – once again – to sprint as fast as he could.

Cropper emerged behind him, but something had gone from his pursuit: momentum, conviction.

The unpleasantly fat Security Guard gagged, but nothing came out; dry heaves. His stomach was bulging even more than usual, bulging and sloshing in a very freaky way – as if someone were inside prodding him; someone or something.

Even as he ran away, the boy could hear these sounds behind him.

A glance over his shoulder showed him the Security Guard, stopped, bent double.

Cropper felt a kick in his stomach. And then, with no more warning than this, he exploded. Red bits, either of him or more likely not of him, flew onto the walls of the corridor.

The boy had turned to watch, still backing away.

The Security Guard lay flat, examining his ribs – which were spread out like a cricketer's fingers about to catch a ball.

'Fuck me,' he said, or rather hissed, there being no lungs to bring air into his mouth.

The boy started running again. He hadn't wished for this to happen to the Security Guard, but it was to his advantage: he should get away before anyone else came along.

Gemma turned aside and was sick onto the concrete floor: orange-brown slush.

Sarah was fine, without nausea; she hadn't eaten anything all day.

Von Sinistre, they didn't know about – he had gone off to some fardistant storeroom, in quest of cutting equipment.

'I don't understand,' said Gemma, looking down at carrots and chickpeas reconstituting into recognizable shapes.

'Forget it,' said Sarah. 'This is more important.'

The baby girl was looking much healthier than when she had first shown signs of life. Sarah held her with great tenderness. Perhaps it was an illusion, but the little thing's arms and legs seemed slightly more substantial – as if the return of blood to the tissues had bulked them up. A few wisps of red were still to be seen disappearing into the soft dark hairless ovals of the baby's nostrils. They seemed to be seeping out of the lift shaft, from upstairs.

'What are we going to do with you, eh? What are we going to do with you?' It was Sarah, cooing.

'Shall we take her back to Maternity?' said Gemma. 'She's only newborn – we should be able to find out who she belongs to.'

'She'll need feeding pretty soon,' Sarah said. 'I think we should try Neo-Natal first.'

'But we're looking for the mother. She's more likely to be in Maternity.'

'Neo-Natal is on our way. And, besides, if I was going to steal a baby, that's where I'd steal it from.'

Gemma said nothing more. Sarah seemed determined.

From above, they could hear loud sounds of collapse – as if a huge bomb were being set off. But they ignored them, concentrating on the matter in hand. Together, they wound the altar cloth around the randomly moving limbs.

'You're so beautiful,' said Sarah. 'I'm sure your mummy is missing you ever so much.'

The baby opened its eyes and, for a moment, they appeared to focus on Gemma's face. 'Oh, I feel very strange,' she said. But it was Sarah who started to weep.

A minute passed.

'Come on,' said Gemma. 'Let's go.'

They made their way into the emergency lift. The doors closed behind them.

'She's sleeping,' Sarah said, as they began to rise. 'Let's hope this doesn't wake her up again.'

'Poor little thing,' said Gemma, leaning in for a closer look; she loved babies. 'Not much of a welcome to the world, is it?'

The explosions or whatever within the building were much louder now – shaking the lift compartment from side to side.

'I know quite a few of the midwives,' Sarah said. 'I'm sure they'll help us.'

'Let's hope so,' replied Gemma.

'She seems fine,' said Sarah. 'A bit of a weight, in fact.'

Although she didn't want to admit the possibility, it felt to her as if the baby had bulked up even as she was holding it.

He heard them before he saw them and he felt them before he heard them: a rumbling in the very structure of the building – as if something were hitting the frame with such force that it had begun to ring out.

Then the boy heard something he couldn't believe he was hearing – mooing which didn't sound like mooing but like some strange bovine war-whoop, as if some cows were pretending to be Red Indians. It came from many long, straining, moist throats at once; all in sympathy, all shit-scared with panic.

The first thing he caught sight of, over his shoulder, was a heavily swinging oblong, in black and white, which turned out to be the rear end of the front cow. When he focused on the beast's head, he saw that it was low down, in full-on charge mode.

Fast as he could, the boy ran.

In A&E, Steele had regurgitated a lamb. Around him, far worse was happening. The room was full of people with cows coming out of them: here a Sikh man, Trilochan Singh, being split by the rump, there a Muslim woman, Shatha Al-Nuaimi, ruptured by the head. The man over by the door with the incredibly red face and the fat ankles, Raymond Gill, was being outvaded by a fine Guernsey heifer. One unlucky chap, Dickie Bedford, had managed to regurgitate most of his steak and kidney pudding, but a particularly troublesome chunk had got caught in his throat – and he was soon choking as a cow's foot ran the length of his oesophagus and began kicking him in the stomach. Eventually, Dickie's spine snapped, as the top of the haunch was added to the thighbone. When the cow had fully formed, it stepped out of and away from Dickie's exploded body – leaving him to deal with the mental trauma.

Other animals appeared too, but less dramatically. A woman called Horatia Spugg-Warfield, rheumatoid arthritis, found, to her great displeasure, a fish swimming up her gullet – a cod, to be precise.

Those, including Sister Agnes Day, who had opted for the vegetarian option, were more than a little smug – several who mentioned the fact found themselves on the receiving end of prolonged beatings and repetitive murders.

Elsewhere in Hospital, pigs trotted through Immunobiology and chickens (previously nuggets) pecked at the floor of the children's wards. A rabbit made from a Security Guard's lucky-charm keyring padded its way placidly through Oncology. Beneath the tables of the staff canteen, pigs rooted for non-existent truffles. In the Secretary to the Executive Director of Operations' office, mice rode the Rolodex for fun. Slugs silvered the Conference Room flipchart. A hare, from who knows where, streaked past the delivery rooms in Maternity.

On the fire stairs, the crush became extreme: animals superadded to human bodies bulked the landings out, pretty soon bursting the floor-to-ceiling windows. And through these, into the fog, much of the remaining livestock was to be forced.

The kitchens, however, were the most chaotic place of all. What had happened in the pathology museum with the body parts – the medical specimens – now happened here also, but with even greater intensity.

A pile of struggling meat grew towards the ceiling, panicked cows with their legs in the air carried upwards on a wave-tide of pigs, chickens, rats, cats, dogs and (the chefs might or might not have been surprised to see) horses. Scraps fallen between work-surfaces re-formed in flattened, trapped attitudes. One of the cows had five legs, another staggered. There was even one slaughterhouseman, Jock McKnock, who had lost his index finger in the rendering process.

The freezer door slammed back under the

accumulated pressure of thousands and thousands of animal bodies.

Eventually, a huge bolus formed, weighing massively on the concrete floor. Hospital had never been designed to take this kind of internal pressure. The concrete sagged, then gave way completely.

Down through floor after floor smashed the huge fist of flesh – crushing all in its path. Below the 12th floor, that area of the building was almost completely destroyed. And the north-east wing beyond it became cut off at most levels.

Looking around the juddering chaos of A&E, Steele soon realized where he would be most needed: the 7th-floor Surgical Unit. The insane noise told him enough; the writhing and pleading were confirmation. It was part of what seemed to be the same process. First, all the patients had been cured; wounds healed, cancers evaporated. Then the dead (including himself) had come back to life. Now, it seemed, other organic matter was returning to its living form. And so there would be hundreds of patients (like these), agonized with drowning-terrified animals trapped inside them: pecking and scratching chickens, most of all.

He took off at a fast trot for the emergency lift. But when he got there, he found that someone was using it, ascending (as he watched) to the 4th floor. Who could it be? He pressed the button and waited, impatient.

Down in the basement, the porters had puked like everyone else (mainly chickens, which were easy to shoo out of the storeroom). However, they returned to the business in hand (Pierre's successor), remarkably undistracted; voodoo had long inured them to such transformations of human into animal. The only one of them not to join in with the discussion was Othniel. He waited, his anger growing yet greater: Cyrille could not be allowed to triumph from his stupidity and greed.

'Does anyone object?' asked Fritzgerald, speaking over huge rumblings from elsewhere. 'Cyrille will be official Head of the Union and also Head Voodoo Man.'

'If not, we will formally –' said Ludger.

'No,' said Othniel. 'This must not happen.'

'Why?' said Cyrille, glad the challenge had finally come.

'You are guilty,' said Othniel.

'Of what?'

'You are guilty of asking for too much.'

'You are lying.'

'Everyone heard.'

'Heard what?'

The room was frozen in a moment of tense anticipation.

'Othniel is right,' said Fritzgerald.

'I remember, too,' said Ludger.

The boy could smell the cows, now – hot, beefy (beefy like cooked beef, not living cowflesh).

Door after door after door he tried, all locked; the next, locked like the last.

He could hear the cows' panicked breathing.

Before now, he'd thought there was a small chance they would calm and slow down. But their panic was a boulder rolling down a mountainside; once it had started to move, momentum wasn't an issue. The cows were working out the differential calculus of their fear.

He looked for somewhere to climb, get above them, avoid the corridor-corrida, but there were no handholds.

A little further up, on the left-hand side, were the security offices. There would be guards here – they might let him in. But then they would capture him.

He tried a couple more doors; no luck – the cows were only fifteen metres or so away, now.

And the boy made the only choice he could, in the face of their moving, thundering, unstoppable, killing mass.

He ran down the corridor and made a lunge for the handle of the security offices. They, too, were locked.

'No!' he shouted.

With tight fists, he banged as hard as he could on the mahogany veneer of the door.

The cows were five metres away.

He banged louder.

The front cow's eyes were mostly yellow – *glaring* up at the ceiling, not at him. It had no intent. Its neck strained upwards, too, as if it were hoping to take flight; Jumbo Jet halfway down the runway, full of lead-weight passengers.

His fists continued to beat against the door, but more out of anger and frustration than hope.

The rumble of the floor, so close were the cows, was almost enough to take his feet from under him. Each cow, he noticed at the very last moment, had a star-shape of hair in the middle of its forehead.

The mood had altered, and not for the better. Angry white eyes and bright grimaces surrounded Cyrille. He *had* asked for too much and, as a result, Pierre was dead and everything was weirdus maximus.

Cyrille was about to start begging for his life (like a little girlie) when he noticed the fetish bag on the floor in the corner – the gris-gris: it was shaking, it was moving.

'Agh!' shrieked Cyrille, like a little girlie.

One or two of the others had already followed the glare of his wide-eyed stare to whatever it was they were witnessing: more supernature.

'*Sacré!*'

'*Merde!*'

'*Alors!*'

Cyrille seized his chance.

'Look!' he exclaimed, 'It is alive!'

As one, the porters stopped and turned; all of them looked at the gris-gris – just in time to see it give its biggest and most unmistakable shudder. '*Qu'est-ce que c'est?*'

'*C'est vif – il est vif!*'

'*Un monstre!*'

The circle drew closer; there was another shudder, and the gris-gris rolled a little; the circle retreated, terrified. This was the kind of bad-news voodoo they had always known might come down upon them; freaky stuff and Death with a capital D. Pierre Estime, the bravest and most experienced, had always been what had protected them from *les mals* – the demons and evil spirits – and Pierre was dead; Pierre was dead, unless he had turned into this thing-in-a-bag.

Cyrille reached down and picked the gris-gris up by the drawstring. The tiny fabric pouch continued to twitch in his hand – its movements shot up his arm like electricity, a galvanic force.

The porters were now pressed back against the walls and locker doors. Cyrille felt the power of the gris-gris enter him; unknown quality. 'Don't be afraid,' he said.

He began to undo the drawstring.

'*Non!*'

'*Tu es fou!*'

'*Je suis effrayé!*'

'*O Jésus – Jésus!*'

He pulled the mouth of the gris-gris open, like a stagy magician, and peered inside, with genuine ignorance. Stunned at what he saw, it was all he could do not to hurl the evil little bag from him (originally bought by Pierre's daughter for her Sindy doll's make-up, it bulged, fuller than it had ever been before – impossibly putting on matter and weighing more and more).

'*Qu'est-ce que c'est?*'

If he mishandled this moment, the other porters would definitely kill him.

Cyrille stepped forward and shook-shook the contents of the gris-gris out onto the floor: centipedes, moths, worms, slugs, maggots, and none of them dried dead ones (as had been there before, presumably) but wriggling, flittering, fluttering, oozing live ones – and, half buried beneath these insects, a lithe and very alert COBRA!

Sarah led Gemma into Neo-Natal. Behind them, the emergency lift was immediately called away.

The ward was very quiet – all the babies seemed to be contentedly asleep.

'They grow,' said a teenage Japanese nurse, Akiko Beep, stepping out sideways from behind a curtain. She was unbelievably cute, with a button nose, huge eyes and long slender limbs. The colour of her hair was fuchsia. 'I never seen something like this.' Her face was bright, as if illuminated from within – but there was something feverish about her excitement. 'They cannot really grow, not so fast.'

'What do you mean, growing?' asked Gemma.

'I weigh all of them, just to check,' Nurse Akiko Beep said. 'But there is no need. Their nappy sizes change, now. But I know it just by one looking – I know each of them very well.'

'Have you ever seen this baby before?' asked Sarah, and held the little girl so that the neo-natal nurse could see her face.

'No,' she said. 'What is she called?'

'We don't know,' said Sarah. 'We just found her.'

'She is lovely,' Nurse Beep said. 'I think I remember her, if we met.'

'How many babies have been admitted today?' asked Sarah.

'Four,' said Nurse Beep.

'And they're all here?' Gemma asked.

'They are all very well babies,' said Nurse Beep. 'At midnight hour, their lines fall out. I rush everywhere to put them back, but they fall out again. And also their feeding tubes come out. But they are good. I turn off their oxygen, and then make sure they keep warm. Then they start to grow. This is happening upstairs-downstairs? Some nurses say they go to Chapel and pray. Many people here go home scared. Me, too, I am very scared.'

'Please,' said Gemma. 'Try to calm down. We just need to be certain that you can't help us identify this baby.'

'I cannot,' Nurse Beep said, a little dismayed.

'Thank you,' said Sarah.

Some fairly lusty crying started up from a nearby child.

'I must – ' said Nurse Beep, and excused herself.

'Maternity,' said Gemma.

The emergency lift took a short while to return from the 7th floor. Gemma wondered who might be going to the Surgical Unit in such a hurry. Of course, her affections brought her only one answer; correct.

Then the security offices' door flew open, and the boy collapsed through it – but not soon enough to prevent the lead cow's horn from ripping the arm of his pyjamas.

He scrabbled backwards, away from the black and white wave-wall of the herd stampeding past. There was no need to close the door – their momentum meant they couldn't turn aside. As long as he stayed far enough back, he was as safe as if he had been watching it on a television screen.

Which, in fact, was what the Virgin had been doing for the past half-hour. Not that it had been cows she was looking at. Most of all, she wanted to know where Sir Reginald was. She feared that he might come back, armed with more equipment, and have another go at raping her.

The Virgin had made herself a promise: if Sir Reginald got within a floor of her, she would run to the fire staircase. She preferred to risk herself in the crush, which she could see on several of the functioning screens.

Even as the cows continued to boom past, she glanced towards the screen where Sir Reginald had a moment ago been displayed in all his evil glory – addressing those parts of his congregation who had loyally awaited his return.

But they had gone – the ward was empty!

The Virgin left it to the boy to watch the more tardy of the heifers trundle past, their huge udders sloshing between their hind legs.

Frantic, she looked from screen to screen, waiting for the picture to change and give her another view.

Then a different angle of the 15th floor appeared, and with great relief the Virgin saw that Sir Reginald and his followers had merely joined the crowds on the fire staircase.

But her relief lasted only a moment or two – for the Satanists were heading *downwards*, in her direction, only a couple of floors from where she sat! And with their forceful numbers, they were able to move quite fast. Were they coming back?

What sounded like the last of the cows went past, ululating loudly, as if to tell the others it would be along just as soon as it could. Its hoofs kept skidding out from under it, on the soiled floor. A brown snaky mist hung in the air, sucking the dung after the anuses from which it had splashed.

The boy risked putting his head out the door, and almost had it taken off by the horns of one more, even slower cow. This one couldn't even be bothered to trot.

After listening more carefully for hoofbeats, the boy peered again, up and down the corridor: there were gouges out of the walls; the optimistic artworks, still-life paintings and watercolour landscapes had been dashed to the floor.

'Come here,' said the Virgin, who the boy was embarrassed to notice wasn't wearing a skirt, trousers or any knickers.

Because of the position of his bed, right next to the fire staircase, and because of his continued critical status, the man had begun to attract a certain amount of attention.

As the queue to descend became thicker and its progress slower, people naturally spent more and more time staring through into ICU.

When it became clear they wouldn't lose too much time in doing so, one or two men and women forced their way through the door and asked what was going on? 'Why doesn't he get better, like everyone else? What's wrong with him?'

'I'm sorry,' Angela Dixon said, 'I have no idea. And I'm afraid I'm going to have to ask you to leave.'

Since the arrest, the man's condition had stabilized; visitors, however, were not what either of them needed.

'You'll be alright,' one woman, Nessa Long, diabetes, whispered in his ear. 'You must be very special, to be kept like this.'

These first visitors, unwitting pilgrims, returned to the stairwell with tales of what they had seen – which, in turn, travelled up and down the queue, losing accuracy, gaining fascination.

'He's still asleep, and no-one's still asleep.'

'I've heard he's still dying, and *no-one's* still dying.'

'That's impossible: no-one can die any more.'

'Well, this bloke's there for all the world to see, and he's making a fairly good go of it.'

Eventually, word of the man reached marker-pen prophet Johannes Fast, who experienced then and there a moment of perfect revelation: now he understood the cows (resurrection of the flesh), now he understood *everything* (Hello, Mr Messiah).

Quite a while ago, poor Johannes had been ousted from his customary perch by the window on the 5th-floor staircase – the descending crowds had forced him to stand up, back into a corner. And so used was he to fighting against the prevailing direction, that he had eventually decided – when they began to bump and bother him – that he would climb towards the top of the building: if most people thought down was the best direction, up must be right.

Progress, which had been slow to begin with, was now a matter of centimetres per minute; squeezing, shifting, he had reached the 19th floor.

But when he heard his first description of the ill (dying! ill! *dying!*) man, Johannes knew immediately that his vertical calling had been correct: he must keep ascending, he must go and worship Him.

At the sight of the cobra, Carl-Henry Bien-Aimé (a drummer – all drummers are cowards) bolted from the room and the others pressed even further back against the walls and locker doors.

Cyrille knew everything now depended upon him: he had released the snake from the bag, it was his job to get it back in there. If he didn't, he would never be Head Voodoo Man.

'*Tais-toi*,' he said, the commanding tone of his voice renewing his own confidence. Perhaps he really *was* capable of taking over from Pierre.

The snake slid free of the insect-pile, which was itself spreading out into a wider circle-of-twitch. Centipedes fought losing battles with millipedes; a death's-head moth flew into the flame of a candle – Pierre's gris-gris recipe was there on display, reanimated, for anyone who wanted to take note of it: no-one did.

Cyrille stepped forward, the emptied Sindy bag in his left hand. He was no longer sure if the snake – growing? – would fit inside it. With its neck hood fully inflated, it looked bigger and fiercer. He advanced towards it, and they began their ritual dance.

With no drummer to lead them, the remaining porters began to chant and clap; call and response followed; all this made them feel mysteriously safer: the deep African rhythm, the warm noise of voices – as if this were just another of the ceremonies they had performed a thousand times before.

Cyrille circled the cobra with feet-of-weight, trying not to become dizzy with the spin of the room and the prospect of the power he might, if he bagged the serpent, be about to seize; over Pierre's dead body, it was true – but Pierre would never have yielded whilst alive.

The cobra was enraged. Cyrille felt as if he could see the cold blood churning up and down its length; frappuccino snake, created.

The wingèd-fangèd head swayed from side to side, and Cyrille remembered just in time the bit about it hypnotizing its prey.

He leaped to one side – the cobra struck in the empty floor-space he'd left behind.

Cyrille saw his opportunity: the snake was now looking the wrong way, distracted by another member of the circle, Excellent Excellent.

With as much speed and bravery as he could, Cyrille crushed his foot down on the cobra's back. He felt the sickening crack of its ribs, four or five of them; and then, even more sickening, it turned its remorseless eyes upon him.

There was still more than enough length between where he had it pinned and the fangs in its mouth for the cobra to make another attack.

Which it did – Cyrille again just managing to dodge out of the way in time.

When the snake's fangs hit the floor, a little transparent venom spurted out. This was real, oh yes.

So splattered had Cropper been that it took him quite a while to reconstitute.

But once he did, he lay there, naked, his beautiful uniform in rags all around him, and began to cry hot tears of frustration.

The bastard little boy had unfairly eluded him a second time. Someone had let him go free – roaming around, doing whatever the hell he liked (never mind that everybody else was too).

Cropper thought for a moment about pursuing the boy, and the cows, down the corridor.

Maybe he could capture him a second time.

But, no – he wanted the comfort of putting his spare uniform on. He wanted the succour of being once more among his satanic mates. He wanted, most of all, for Sir Reginald to give him some orders to obey.

With a heave, he got to his feet.

One bitter glance in the boy's direction was all he allowed himself before he set off at a heavy jog towards the locker-room.

'I'll get you,' he muttered to himself.

The operating theatres were working as fast as they could, faster than they had ever worked before: cut-and-run taken to the nth.

But trainee surgeon Iqbal Fermier, in the midst of all this, was finding the experience exhilarating and dispiriting at one and the same time.

Finally, he was getting hands-on experience. In fact, he was able to practise a slangy battlezone surgery, ignoring most of the standard procedures he had been trying so hard to perfect (on unreal cadavers) –

he didn't need to scrub, or worry at all about keeping things antiseptic; there was no point trying to take the least invasive option or making incisions neat; peripheral damage to secondary organs didn't have to be avoided. As a result, he was able to work with obscene speed. However, this made it feel a little like hacking a computer game to give yourself infinite lives. All the tension and most of the skill had gone out of his vocation; he had already realized that if things stayed as they were, surgery as previously known would cease to exist. It might, perhaps, be necessary to remove small items that people had swallowed by mistake and could not excrete. But that would be a five-minute job; simple. Cancers, internal bleeding, tumours of all sorts, lesions, infarcts, transplants – the whole repertoire of necessary invasion would become obsolete. It seemed to him as if he had already performed his last truly meaningful operation, and this was supposed to be the beginning of his career.

With pain, usually, the first thing to do was ameliorate, palliate, then hopefully a diagnosis could tentatively begin to be made. Tonight, for the first time, he was conducting truly *exploratory* surgery. What he found, mostly, were scrabbling chickens covered in stomach acid. But when he went in, it was with only the vaguest of ideas where he was going – no prep, no X-rays, no scans, no pre-op. 'Where does it hurt?' That was it. The nurse lined them up; the anaesthetist knocked them out. Whilst Patient Z was going under Patient Y was under the knife and Patient X was self-healing or being pushed away on a trolley.

The other surgeons had a competition going – see how many procedures they could perform in an hour.

It was pointless; some of them seemed to believe they would one day be reading about this session *mirabilis* in the *Lancet.* They didn't realize that by rushing through these cases they were rapidly rendering themselves redundant. Cosmetic surgery, even, would be impossible – features would reset into their previous form.

The surgical unit had reached some sort of peak of busyness when John Steele arrived. None of the other surgeons wanted to stop, they were not tired, so Iqbal Fermier, as the most junior, was the obvious one to step aside.

'I'm sorry,' said Steele, after explaining the situation. 'But I think I can work faster than you.'

Iqbal's disappointment was obvious.

'You can assist,' said Steele.

'There's nothing for me to do,' Iqbal replied.

'Well,' said Steele, already beginning his first operation, 'why don't you go and find someone who needs special attention?'

Iqbal thought for a second. 'Okay,' he said. He had no wish to antagonize his hero.

There was a bang that was also a splat and a crunch, and it seemed to come from on top of the emergency lift.

Gemma and Sarah looked up, terrified – they had only just started moving.

Before they had the chance to ask one another *What was –?* a second bang and then a third made the whole lift compartment shudder. These close-up explosions had been preceded by a scream which got very loud very fast, and stopped immediately upon impact – for that's what it must have been.

The terrified baby woke up and started to cry.

Gemma could feel the lift swaying on its long wires as it continued to ascend.

Sarah whispered, 'Shh, shh, it's alright.'

Another bang, and Gemma said, 'It's people, isn't it? It's people jumping.'

As if to confirm this, a loud gurgling-groaning started up just above their heads. 'Nnn-o,' a voice seemed to say. It was abruptly silenced by another impact.

'Shall we get off?' Gemma asked, and moved to put her finger on the 5th-floor button.

'Let's just get there as soon as possible,' said Sarah.

One bang followed another, some softer, some louder – bodies landing on bodies or on the roof of the lift.

'How many is that?' asked Gemma.

'Eight or nine,' replied Sarah.

Two more followed, in quick succession.

Gemma's eyes checked the lift's capacity: MAX 10 PERSONS.

The voice saying *no* started up again.

Sarah said, 'It's alright,' to the baby, but Gemma took some comfort from the words, as well.

The 5th floor went past with three further bangs on the roof.

They were moving much more slowly now, and there was an eerie sense of mechanical strain – no dramatic noises from the cables, but the distant engine was labouring; too much mass to be lifted, almost.

Gemma pushed the 6th-floor button several times, although it was already lit up.

'We've got to get out,' she said.

*

After their comprehensive defeat by Nikki and the Pink-Blue kids, Spanner and Case wandered the building in search of a way down.

They tried the lifts, then one set of fire stairs, then another; both crowded out. Finally, with them still only on the 19th floor, Spanner suggested they go back up and try to abduct Nikki.

'That's not going to happen,' said Case.

'Don't you wanna see her again?'

'You're not going nowhere near her.'

Spanner stood up to Case, who smashed him in the teeth with a shatteringly hard right.

When Spanner had dentally recovered, they walked to the north-west fire stairs and joined the slow queue for down.

Every so often, Spanner looked at Case to see if he'd changed his mind. But that, too, wasn't going to happen.

Clapping, drumming, chanting – the circle around Cyrille was totally abandoned. *Merde alors!* Who cared if Dexter von Sinistre (one floor down) heard? What did anything else matter? Cyrille might be a clumsy amateur, but this snake-dance was the closest any of them had come to the real voodoo for years. A dried-out cobra in Sindy's old make-up bag was one thing, a twisting, whipping cobra out loose was quite another. Particularly an enraged and murderous cobra that was attacking someone else – someone they hated.

The snake was moving faster now, and the circle increased the slinky pace of its rhythm, too.

'Kill, kill, kill . . .' they chanted, and Cyrille knew that they didn't really mind whether he or the animal obeyed their command.

Again and again it struck at his bare feet, and again and again he managed by inches to elude it.

Suddenly, remembering his playground football skills, Cyrille tried to nutmeg the cobra. He dummied to the left, faked right, then went left.

Unfortunately, following him or following the original dummy, the snake was either too slow or too fast – whichever way, it went for him exactly where he stood, momentarily off balance. (He'd played goalkeeper most of the time – last to be picked.)

Cyrille felt the bone of its head rap against his kneecap. He expected to feel the fangs, razor-sharp, puncturing the skin; they didn't, he didn't.

He stepped to one side and the cobra came with him; although it hadn't got its long curved teeth into him, they'd gone through the fabric of his trousers: he could feel them, just below his knee, tickling at the very top of his shinbone.

This was his chance!

Before the deadly snake could free itself, Cyrille made a grab for it. Triumph! Glory! Power! Yes!

He was surprised how easily his fingers went around the scaly body – his fear had magnified the snake; it wasn't that big at all.

No, not that big but very very fast: retracting its teeth in an instant, the cobra turned and struck again.

Stupidly, Cyrille had only grabbed it halfway along; not near enough the head.

As the fangs went into his left arm, he realized with horror his mistake, and already knew it was fatal.

Despite the young woman's partial nudity, what was on screen was of even greater interest to the boy: the stampeding cows had, for reasons of their own, turned left when they reached the jink of the lift lobby.

The long corridor, diagonally opposite to the one from where they watched, was one of the four arms of the H, and a dead end – leading only to the fire door and, beyond that, a landing, and then a floor-to-ceiling pane of glass with a bar across the middle for infirm walkers.

The Virgin and the boy watched as the front cow tried to slow down but was pushed forwards by the massive blind trundling panic of those behind her.

'No,' said the Virgin, unable to prevent.

The cows hit the glass of the fire door one after the other, not breaking through straight away but with enough momentum between them to take the whole glass wall out in one.

The landing was full of people, but they couldn't stop the massive onwards force – and neither could the floor-to-ceiling window.

The lead cow, head to the side, neck broken, was first to exit, but the others swiftly followed – taking with them anyone unlucky enough to be in their path. They flowed across the grey screen and out into the yellow fog.

The boy stood beside the Virgin, both watching, speechless.

As the herd began to slow down and thin out, the two of them expected an exceptional cow to stop – shy away from the void and its obvious beckoning death: none did.

Without forethought, each trotted onwards – kept going, perhaps, by the sight of the rear end in front of it – as if each head took orders from the nearest tail.

The screen was silent, so did not convey that no

sounds came back out of the fog, either of exultation or dismay – dismoo.

'No,' said the Virgin, again.

The final, slowest cow rumbled trustingly along the corridor, paused for a moment to sniff at something (still in hopes of grass), then loyally followed all the others out the window.

Melanie Angel arrived in A&E – which wasn't as chaotic as she'd been expecting. Certainly it was a lot calmer than the fire staircase.

A steady column of people walked, despite the warnings of those standing to right and left, through the main exit and out into whatever did or didn't await them in the fog. They weren't suicidal so much as determinedly fatalistic in their desire to get out of the building. The logic of their departing was clear: we are cured so we do not need to be here. Many were distressed at finding themselves unable to speak to family members by phone, and were determined to make contact directly. Although the column was steady, those departing were in all the various human moods: some went sobbing as if into exile, some shipped out as if camping it up for television cameras. There were a few couples, arms around one another, but the majority went alone. Being England, a queue had formed and was almost universally adhered to.

Out they went, the electronic doors jerking a couple of inches in hopes of closing but then sensing that, no, yet another person-shaped thing did want to come through.

'You're stepping into the void. You'll never come back,' said the Spaceman, to all of them.

'I hope not,' came the usual reply. 'I never want to see another hospital so long as I live.'

The Spaceman was standing there with the very loyal Sukhveer Blenkinsop; Yi Qu, however, had spotted another Mandarin-speaker, and together they had decided to leave.

'But you'll never return,' said the Spaceman.

'*Xiexie ni*,' said Yi Qu, happily. '*Zaijian*.'

There were other front-door johnnies and hangers-on, groupies of disappearance, autograph-hunters of the void. They stood there, awaiting with religious hope the revelation of a return! Or something.

Melanie went and stood to one side. If trouble started, she would be there to deal with it.

The emergency lift was taking longer between floors than it usually did to go from top to bottom of the building. Its upward movements came in little jerks, almost spasmodic.

Gemma and Sarah could hear speech – those who had jumped were talking among themselves.

'I think there's enough room.'

'It's a bit tight.'

'What does that matter?'

'Go on.'

'Are you chicken?'

'Oh, very funny.'

'Okay. See you at the bottom.'

There was a light scratching against the outside of the lift compartment – fingernails?

A voice began to say *yes* then fell away, away, away.

'Me next,' someone said.

But another bang came, and then another.

There was more scratching.

'Can you hear a baby crying?' someone asked.

Another couple of voices fell away.

But bang, bang – they landed.

*

From the other screens, which the boy now took in, it was obvious that the cows were far from being the only animals come back from the dead.

'I never used to believe in the Devil,' said the Virgin, apropos of nothing in particular. 'But now I suppose I'm going to have to.'

The boy was still very conscious that her fanny, if he looked in the right direction, was available for viewing. Among the mayhem on the screens, he saw one female figure even more distracting although familiar.

'Who's that?' he asked, pointing just as the screen flicked to another view.

Luckily, the strange woman was visible from the succeeding angle. She was on the 20th floor.

'Her?' said the Virgin, distracted. 'I think they call her the Rubber Nurse. You'd be better off asking a man, if you know what I mean.'

The boy felt, very distantly, that he did, though it wasn't a knowledge he was yet able to explain himself.

'Can you see the Devil on these screens, then?' the boy asked, aware he was changing the subject, and feeling quite grown up for doing so. Yet he kept tracking the Rubber Nurse as she strolled through the wards – wards full of riot and celebration. Occasionally, she stopped to help people, usually men, usually naked.

'I can see the Devil everywhere, now,' said the Virgin. 'I can see him in what people do and what they want to do.'

This was the boy's first opportunity to take the measure of the whole building, and he did so with remarkable coolness. He could see his objective: the exit doors in A&E. The policewoman from earlier was there, but she wasn't stopping anyone. Perhaps fifty or sixty people flowed out every minute – the camera showed nothing of them once they entered the fog; and perhaps there was nothing to show: the screens upon which external views were meant to appear were broadcasting either static or a test signal. It was as if, the boy for the first time thought, the outside world had simply ceased to exist.

Elsewhere, a couple of surviving cameras looked out across the emptiness left behind by the animal-bolus; it was like a crater within the building. People crowded at its edges, staring downwards.

Amidst all this chaos, the sight of the single figure lying motionless in the ICU could have been easy to overlook – but the boy, for a moment or two at least, was fascinated. The man with the bandaged head was still there, a single orange-haired nurse at his side.

Cyrille felt the venom flowing coldly into his veins – it tingled like ice.

The chanting and clapping had, he was aware, died away.

He now, belatedly, made good on his mistake – grabbing the cobra just behind the base of its skull, he twisted it so its fangs slid free.

Then, in defeated triumph, he held the serpent up above his head.

The circle around him went wild; whatever they had wanted, he had given it to them: death or death.

With a clear determination that he would finish the job, even if it had already killed him, Cyrille looked around on the floor for the gris-gris bag he'd dropped a few moments before – when forty or fifty years of life were ahead of him, an improved life of power and fear and fun.

It was hard to find the bag. His vision was as if through a rainy windscreen: beady, dripping. He felt feverish and at the same time colder than he'd ever been. That loud drum-drumming – that must be his heart; the rhythm wasn't as regular as it should be – as regular as he would have wished.

Eventually, with no help from those around him, staggering Cyrille spotted the fat toad and the bag lying next to it.

His muscles no longer obeying him, he bent down and seized the gris-gris; its mouth hung open – he plunged the writhing cobra in.

With his teeth, he drew the drawstring until the bag was gently gripping his arm.

Fingers released the snake (his fingers?) – he tried to pull them free, but as he did so he felt another bite hit him; thumb.

Cyrille went down on his knees. His right hand was free and the gris-gris dangled from his left, the cobra's head sticking out like a baby's from swaddling clothes.

Cyrille's vision tunnelled down until all he could see was the cobra's forked tongue. Woozily, he put his thumb on the snake's shiny nose and pushed it all the way into the gris-gris.

Then darkness overtook him completely. He listened to his heartbeat until it was no longer there for him to listen to, and he was no longer there to listen to it.

Almost there! – the number above the lift doors had changed to 6, but their progress was now by the centimetre.

'Come on,' said Sarah.

Both of them were looking up, willing on.

A final couple of jerks and they felt the compartment stiffen slightly.

They weren't moving – they had stopped completely.

Then the doors opened.

Sarah rushed through, cradling the baby, and Gemma followed.

Instinctively, they moved away from the lift.

'Phew,' said Sarah.

Looking back, they saw the compartment judder as another couple of bodies hit.

Two more, and it sickeningly began to sink.

The doors tried to close but jammed after a quarter of the way.

From up in the lift shaft came the metallic sound of rending.

'Wait,' said Gemma.

Then, all of a sudden, there was a lurch – the lift fell a metre, and they saw the naked crowd on top of the compartment: some of them were standing up, others were hardly recognizable as human; offal, pulp.

An open-mouthed man looked out at them, just as the cables finally gave way.

They watched as his face dropped aghast into darkness; Mohammed Mohammed, self-immolator.

Gemma was about to step forwards to look down the shaft but Sarah held her back.

There was a whistling sound and a clanging, getting louder and louder.

And then a cable lashed out through the doors and tore a huge chunk from the floor.

In an instant, it was gone – pulled downwards by the falling lift.

Enough time for a single intake of breath.

The crash when it hit the bottom wasn't quite as loud as they'd expected.

'Think of the ones underneath,' said Sarah.

Gemma worked her away around the hole in the floor and tentatively gazed down the shaft. She couldn't see anything, but she could hear something – something unbearable.

Soon, the boy realized, he would have to form a plan – and religious philosophizing, however interesting, didn't get him a step nearer the exit. Still, this conversation wasn't finished, and it needed to be, otherwise this young woman (semi-naked) wouldn't pay enough attention to help him. 'Can you point to him?' he asked. 'The Devil.'

Without hesitation the Virgin put her finger onto the screen showing Sir Reginald on the 14th floor. 'That's him,' she said, 'if anyone is.' Then she spat at the screen – and because the spit landed a couple of inches above Sir Reginald, she put her finger in it and dragged it down until it was distorting his head. He looked, the boy thought, quite like a horned devil – and it was then that he realized that he'd seen those grey curls before: when he was trying to make his escape from Trauma.

'Do you want to get away from him?' the boy asked, in what he thought was another cunning change of subject.

'He tried to rape me,' the Virgin said. 'And he couldn't.' This was a conversation beyond embarrassment.

'That's good,' said the boy, who thought he knew what rape was. 'I suppose. It is good, isn't it?'

'He couldn't because he couldn't get it up inside

me – even by cutting. I kept healing, then others kept healing. Everyone heals now,' she said. 'You will, too.' But when the boy looked at the wound from the cow's horn, he saw it was just as it had been before – the blood had started to thicken, maybe, but no faster than usual. He was slightly glad: he wanted a scar to show his friends, so they believed in the adventure he'd had when everything in Hospital went weird. The boy was sure he had friends, although he couldn't remember anything about them.

'It means I'll always be a virgin,' the Virgin said. 'No-one will ever be able to make love to me, not even people I like.'

The boy was desperately anxious that her next sentence not be: 'I like you.' But she became distracted by drawing pentangles on top of the man she called the Devil, with what was left of the spit (the rest had snaked back into her mouth).

'I want to get out,' the boy said. 'I want to go home.' He thought for a moment that he might trust her – she seemed very believing, perhaps she would believe him about the appleseed and it not being his fault. But she seemed to believe the weirdest things, anything really, devils and such, so it didn't mean very much if she did believe him. He was too ashamed to show her the shoot, and she was too preoccupied to notice it. 'I am trying to get down to the ground floor. Do you know any secret ways?' He pointed to the screens on which the four fire staircases were shown – each was completely full of people, and they were hardly moving at all. If things stayed as they were, the boy would be stuck on this floor for hours. The Virgin continued to trace significant shapes on Sir Reginald's agitated face.

'He isn't really the Devil,' she said. 'He just put a telephone call through to the Devil and ordered a takeout.' This made her laugh.

The boy got the distinct idea that the young woman was about to go mad.

'And the lifts aren't working,' he said, and pointed to those trapped inside them.

'Well, there is another way out,' she said.

Behind them was the 6th-floor lift lobby; in front of them was a small flock of lambs.

A woman lay on the floor clutching her abdomen and sobbing violently. Her name was Minnie Raus, and her dinner of lamb tikka masala had just finished kicking its way out of her.

Gemma went over and spoke a few gentle words.

'Let's get her back to bed, shall we?' suggested Sarah.

'No,' said Minnie. 'I want to not move for a while. Let me be in this place.'

Gemma and Sarah made eye-contact and, in that eye-contact, made a decision: prioritize the baby, deal with others afterwards.

'This way,' said Sarah, leading Gemma left then right towards Maternity.

When they emerged through the door, there were no midwives behind the reception desk.

'You stay here,' said Gemma to Sarah, who still held the baby. 'I'll find someone.'

Gemma pulled back curtain after curtain, but most of the beds were empty. Although she didn't know it, quite a few of the mothers, after grabbing their babies, had decided to take their chances in the rush downstairs.

When Gemma did find a midwife, Zandra Pandit,

she was backed into a far corner of the ward by three cows; steak and kidney pie.

'We need your help,' said Gemma, then did her best to explain the situation.

Midwife Pandit was half listening, Gemma could tell, but the other half was intensely terrified. 'They came out of me,' she said. 'I think they want to go back.'

'Come here,' said Gemma.

When this didn't work, she pushed her way through to midwife Pandit and took her by the hand. 'We need to go and check your records,' Gemma said.

They left the cows still staring, for whatever reasons of their own, into the corner of the room.

The porters were now faced with another dead body: Cyrille. The room went silent, but not completely. There was a tap-tap-tapping sound – also a kind of whining. It was coming from the lockers.

'Whose locker is it?' asked Fritzgerald.

'It belonged to Cyrille,' said Othniel.

'What if it is another snake?' asked Ludger.

When no-one else moved, Othniel went across and pulled the door open.

At first they saw dark skin, then an arm, then a twisted head – it was only after another whine that they recognized the dark Brylcreemed hair, the brown staring eye: Kissa.

Just as the animals in the gris-gris had come back to life, so he must have been reborn out of the voodoo doll. It was known to have contained nail-clippings from his wastepaper basket, hairs from his comb.

Othniel was tempted to close the door, but he didn't.

Kissa's body was distorted in a far more radical way than any contortionist had ever achieved. His feet were behind his head, his spine at an acute angle. The light tapping had been fingertips only; nothing else was capable of movement.

The whining became louder.

'We will get you out,' said Othniel.

The porters pulled the locker away from the wall. It was made of gray sheet-metal. First, they bent the door back and broke it off. Next, they gripped either side and began to pull it apart.

They were surprised how easily the thing buckled. A diamond-shape was formed where the door had been. The hole was much larger, but Kissa seemed to expand to fill the space.

It would be easier to work with the locker horizontal, so they laid it on the floor.

Removing the shelf with a few well-aimed kicks allowed them to make the diamond-shape fatter in the middle.

Still Kissa grew and would not come out.

Finally, they overturned another locker and put it beneath the one they were pulling apart. By bending it down at top and bottom, Kissa was popped out, like a pea from a pod.

'You animals,' he said. 'Who put me in there? Did you drug me with narcotics?'

Just then they heard a grunting from the floor: Cyrille, too, was coming back to life.

'There's an external fire escape,' said the Virgin. 'It goes down the side of the building. It's near the fire staircase, but off to one side. You can't see it on this screen – it's through that door. The fire door itself will be alarmed.'

Several red lights were flashing on the control panel in front of her. In fact, almost all the lights that were red rather than amber or green were flashing. She pressed a couple of buttons, and on the screen people uncovered their ears with relieved expressions on their faces; alarm bells off. For the first time, the Virgin realized that, from where she was sitting, she could exercise a measure of control over the building.

'How do I get to it?' the boy asked.

She gave him directions, then added, 'Once you've opened the door, you should be able to climb straight down. At the bottom, you'll find yourself in the carpark.'

The boy felt a stab of pain from the shoot. If he didn't get to see his mother within the next few hours, he was going to be paralysed by it.

He looked throughout the building, to see if anyone else there had a tree growing out of their tummy. But what he saw was something else entirely.

Upstairs, in Sir Reginald's office, the pine cones in the bowl on his desk had continued to grow with alarming speed. By the time Sir Reginald had left to rejoin his followers, they were already a couple of feet long. With no ground in which to anchor themselves, the saplings had extended themselves higgledy-piggledy. Two or three, though, leaning teepee fashion against one another, had managed to heighten until their uppermost boughs were touching the ceiling. When this happened, the speckled tiles were easily pushed aside – but then they reached the concrete of the ceiling proper. With greater resistance here, the force of their extension had turned downwards through the desk. Added to the weight of the several tree trunks it was already supporting, this pressure had caused the legs to buckle and the desktop to capsize.

By the time the boy caught sight of them, the exactly vertical trees extended from floor to ceiling, and were still nowhere near their maximum size. Their upper branches were repeatedly shattering in the attempt to push upwards: ceiling and floor, for the moment equally strong, would neither of them give. But the force of the trees together was irresistible; their trunks would thicken and their intertwined boughs offer lateral support. The concrete of the building hadn't been designed to withstand this kind of localized internal force.

'I have to go now. I have to get out of here.'

The Virgin said nothing. She was still watching Sir Reginald with total fascination, as if he were her father but visible even though in the afterlife. He was making his way down the fire staircase – had almost reached the 13th floor.

And so, the boy left without saying goodbye.

'I'll watch over you,' the Virgin called out, as she saw him (on a screen) emerging onto the corridor a few feet behind her. 'I'll be your angel,' she said. 'If it looks like you're in danger, I'll try to set off an alarm somewhere near you. I don't know if there's much else I can do. So, if you hear an alarm start up at any time, watch out!' There was almost fun in her voice, and this was something to which the boy found it impossible not to respond. Turn it into a game, that was good; a life and death game, it was true, but even so a game. 'Close the door behind you!' she shouted, and obediently he did.

After infinite difficulties of in-breathing and physical negotiation, Johannes Fast reached the ICU.

His first sight of the comatose one, through the reinforced glass, was no disappointment: there was, in Johannes's eyes, a holy calm to the recumbent figure. The instruments around him, still functioning despite the power cut (those in Intensive Care were on a separate circuit and would be the last of all to go off) – his screens and lights, coming through the ghost-mist, surrounded him in a radiant multi-coloured halo.

'It is He, brother,' said Johannes Fast. Then turned to those on the staircase and commenced to preach. 'It is He! The new Messiah. The new, *improved* Jesus Christ. Praise him, daddy-oh. For He has come to us with a gospel which is silence, a covenant which is imperceptible and a blessing so powerful it does not even need to be offered to be received. But then, I hear you ask, if he *is* Jesus, why does He need all those machines to stay alive? What I say to you is, those machines aren't a mistake. No, sir. They aren't incidental details. Uh-oh. They are the very perfection of His incarnation. For they demonstrate that this new Son of God is truly one of *us*, and that without the power of our electricity and the science of our monitoring equipment, this immortal would die, brother, die. This is not coma, I say, it is the appearance of a man in direct and perpetual communion with the Divinity but, at the very same instant, completely and utterly dependent upon the circuits and switches of mankind. This is not coma, I say, but covenant. Amen! This is the new electric gospel. Amen! Without this man, there is no world, there is no Hospital, there is no us!'

The majority continued to shuffle slowly past. Johannes Fast was merely another one of the raving loons who had turned a decent hospital into a place that any sane person wanted out of asap. But one very young woman, who had come in from the fire staircase, seemed caught by his intensity. It was Nikki Froth, and she was listening to him harder than she'd listened to anyone ever before. Since leaving the Blue Elephant ward, she'd climbed to the top of Hospital, but found nothing there worth her time. This man, this wild man, he was different – he really *believed* what he said. Nikki hadn't met that many people like that.

Smiling angelically, decision made, Nikki passed sideways through the door into the ICU.

Johannes Fast had his first convert.

From having one unwanted dead body to dispose of, the porters now had two unwanted live ones.

'I will sack every last one of you,' threatened Kissa. 'You are the worst kind of scum.'

'We did not put you in the locker,' said Othniel, calmly. He was surprised how glad he was that Cyrille was still alive.

'Then kindly explain how it was that I got there.'

'You appeared.'

'That is not an adequate explanation!' Kissa shouted *adequate*.

'It's all you'll get, because it's the truth.'

'I will go straight to the board. I will demand compensation.'

Othniel was reluctant to do so, but the order was obvious: 'Gag him.'

Cyrille continued to flop around, in front of everyone.

'What have you done to him?' Kissa asked, before the T-shirt went into his mouth. 'Has he been drugged, too?'

'Is he alright?' asked Othniel of Cyrille.

Excellent went across and put his hand on the writhing figure's forehead.

'Cold,' he said, 'but sweaty.'

This wasn't much of a diagnosis, but Othniel took it positively.

'Look after him,' he said.

Fritzgerald and Ludger stepped forward and, grabbing Cyrille under the arms, dragged him off towards the far corner.

'We must decide what to do with Mr Kissa,' said Othniel.

He looked around the circle of eyes.

'Do your computers still work?' asked Sarah.

'This one does,' replied midwife Pandit in a floaty voice, then turned to Gemma. 'Thank you for rescuing me.'

'We need to see the babies born in the last twenty-four hours,' Gemma said. 'We're looking for the mother of this little one.'

Midwife Pandit seemed for the first time to come into focus: a baby, she dealt with those all the time; a *baby.*

'Do you recognize her?' Sarah asked. She held the bundle up so that the midwife, by the light of the screen, could see the tiny girl's wizened face.

'No,' said midwife Pandit. 'I don't think so. Where did you get her?'

'We can't really say,' Gemma replied, before Sarah could speak. 'Can you check the records?'

The midwife found them quickly enough. 'In the last twenty-four hours,' she said, 'there have been fifteen babies born.'

Gemma looked despairingly at Sarah.

'And how many have been discharged already?'

Midwife Pandit's fingers executed a swift series of keystrokes.

'Five,' she said.

'Of those ten,' Sarah asked, 'how many had one or other non-white parent?'

Gemma heard the quiet plastic QWERTY clatter.

'Again, five,' said midwife Pandit.

'And how many were girls?' Gemma asked, realizing this was the question they should have started with.

'Two,' came the answer.

'Show us their details,' said Sarah.

'This is the first,' said the midwife.

All three examined the screen –

Parents: Mrs Jenny Ebb.

'She's still here,' midwife Pandit said. 'I was just trying to calm her down.'

'Is her baby with her?' Gemma asked.

'Yes, she's holding it very tight.'

'Then show us the other one,' said Sarah.

Up came the details –

Parents: Mrs Mary Walker and Mr James Walker
Delivery Room: 4
Midwife: Honey Hopeful
Consultant: Henderson MacVanish
Twins, one male, one female.

'Where's Delivery Room Four?' asked Sarah.

'They're not there,' said midwife Pandit.

'Are you sure?'

'Yes, I'm sure.'

'How are you sure?'

She hesitated, then said, 'They were the reason I had to calm down Mrs Ebb. I've never seen anything like it.'

The boy followed the Devil's hooftracks of the cows down the dirty corridor.

Stepping round the splashes of cow-shit, he eventually came to some clean floor where they had stampeded left, and here he kept straight.

The corridor in front of him was long, dark and empty. He hadn't walked more than a couple of steps down it when the lights came on. The Virgin – she was making good on her promise to look after him.

He looked around for a camera, found it in a top corner, smiled a thankyou and gave the a-okay finger signal.

The camera nodded in response.

It took the boy another couple of minutes to reach the end of the corridor. Then he turned right into an office, just as the Virgin had directed: there it was – a glass door with a panic bolt across the middle.

Without hesitation, the boy tried pushing down on this. No movement. He tried again, but it was unbudgeable. There was a fire extinguisher attached to the wall near by. He went and, with some difficulty, lifted it off its supports. With this weight in his hands, he tried bashing down on the bar – but only succeeded in putting a big kink in its middle.

The boy thought for a moment about using the extinguisher to smash through the glass, but in bare feet he wouldn't be able to get out that way.

Despairingly, he looked up at the nearest camera. It went from side to side in response – the Virgin doing her best, robotically, electronically, to shake her head in sympathetic disappointment.

Partly for fun, and because he'd always wanted to, but also out of frustration, annoyance and not a little anger, the boy let the extinguisher off all over the fire-exit door. It was a foam-based one, so covered the glass with a satisfyingly thick white goo.

Another glance at the camera showed it rolling around in circles, which he interpreted as amusement rather than disapproval. Although he was mostly glad to be watched over by the Virgin, it also annoyed him slightly.

The boy walked back towards the staircase. He was stuck.

From the safety of the security offices, the Virgin was also keeping an eye on events in the Chapel; it was now occupied by what, as far as she could make out, was an ecumenical congregation led in rough, improvised worship by one of the patients. She wished she had sound, because he seemed to be giving a never-ending sermon to the crammed aisles. In all its history, the hospital Chapel had never been so full.

In fact, the speaker was Mr Proudfoot. After the healing, when his leg (including foot) had regrown, Mr Proudfoot had been seized with an overwhelming desire to testify, though he had never done so before – and where better than in the hospital Chapel? Very soon, he would come to be known as the Crap Preacher, but, right now, he was saying this:

'We want to be very careful what we do and say in the next few hours. The fires of Hell are awaiting us, down below us. Lower than the basement, lower than the earth beneath the basement, yes, oh yes.

Very low indeed, but not actually in the middle of the earth because we no longer believe in that, do we? Hell is a state of mind, a low-ish state of mind, not a particular place like Buckingham Palace or the Taj Mahal or Kentucky Fried Chicken on the high street or that farmers market on a Saturday where you can get very nice organic vegetables – or could get them, before the end of the world came. Because, brothers and sisters, what need have we now for the cucumber or the potato, for the organic carrot or the home-grown parsley? None, I tell you! Their day is dead and buried, and, in its place, the future we face is a time of great difficulty and danger. Therefore I ask you to *worry* about that – to be anxious and in serious fear of the terrible things that are waiting just around the corner, like thugs armed with clubs with nails stuck in them. For all God cares, they may as well be thugs armed with vegetables. He created He them – He created He all of them, and they shall know Him even, yea, though they walked in ignorance of Him from now until the middle of next week. Nothing shall appear all that different, or changed to the naked eye. But those who keep their eyes peeled, like unto onions, shall see Him face to face and shall cry, like as if they were peeling onions. Yea, you shall weep and wail-wail-wail, and there shall be gnashing of teeth and renting of garments. The one man won't know whose T-shirt the other man wears. For in this time which is the time after time has decided to run out, like a child in front of a bus – for in this time there shall be no certainty, none at all. Neither of root vegetables nor direct-debit payments nor horror films nor municipal buildings. It is the wise child that knows its own father, and you shall find a father in the Lord, and the Lord is my shepherd and He maketh me to lie down – in fact, we should probably all lie down. We should all expose our naughtiness to His mightiness. For we have been *very* naughty, or else this judgement would not have fallen so heavily upon us. Although, looking back, it was probably inevitable from the very moment of creation. When Eve gave Adam that first taste of fruit, a thing he had never known before – that was when the rot set in, and I don't mean tooth decay. For the serpent upon his belly laughed at them, yea, it sniggered, and while it may actually have been a pomegranate and not what we call an apple, what it stood for is what Adam's apple has always stood for: it is a lump in the throat of the universe. And thus, by this sign of an unholy vegetable He saith unto you, "Worship me and no other for of all gods I am the One true God – the other gods are just trying to have you on, and though they may look pretty convincing, I am the One who really sits on a comfortable throne in heaven. And verily, I will show you the path of My righteousness – which is all paths and, at the same time, in a spookily mystical way, is no paths. Beware of false prophets. Ye shall know them by the colour of their money, for they will ask you for cash in advance. I ask *nothing*, only that you come to Me on your knees pleading for mercy and begging for forgiveness and sincerely regretting your sins and knowing that you are a worm beneath My almighty boot-heel." Yea, I say, a worm within the apple which came from the tree which stood quite near the exit to the Garden of Eden – because otherwise when Adam and Eve committed the great evil of snacking, for which we have all until this hour been suffering in dire punishment, otherwise they would not have been able to make it out the door quite so quickly.

And God, who must have foreseen this, for He knows everything that happens or will ever happen, when God makethèd the garden, He put all apple trees in the places where all *should* be put, in the right Ph of soil and everything. Therefore I say unto you *all*: Repent while there is still time. You may even yet save yourselves from His anger and resentment, for we have made a bollocks of His world in a quite extraordinary way. We have made war upon one another for the sake of some meaningless trees and fields and business parks. There shall be no excuse for this, when we go to His office and stand before the desk in the New Improved Jerusalem having crossed over Jordan and left behind us the sins of Sodom and Gomorrah and Egypt and Babylon. There will be fire in the sky and water, also, but not like rain, more like sleet, really – all the elements shall become one and the dead shall squeak and gibber in the high street. Things fall apart; the shopping centre cannot hold you safe nor shall the purchases of thy labour and credit rating be unto you a succour in this time of mortal dread. Nay, they shall turn upon you like sticky serpents and you shall feel their sting upon your rotten thieving hands! And so I say unto you, I simply say this, I say I say I say, *I told you so*. And He told you so, too. He told you again and again and again that He was going to come back, and now He has. Did you listen? Did you turn the sound down for one minute and pay heedful attention? He promised that the evil would be judged, and mark my words, they will be. And ten out of ten is not the mark they'll be getting, oh no. But I was talking a little earlier about those necessary fruits of the earth, vegetables. Well, let me tell you something else about vegetables . . .'

'Crap,' said Dr Norman LeStrange, a very thin man now standing up in the middle of the congregation. 'I've never heard such a crap preacher. You are the crappest most nonsensical piece of crap I've ever heard.'

'The voice of the non-believer,' the Crap Preacher, Mr Proudfoot, said. 'He will try to tempt you wrongfully. He may be a vegetarian.'

'If this truly is the end-time,' said the naysayer LeStrange, 'then there is no such thing as temptation. What might a man tempt another man to do? He can't steal, property means nothing; he can't kill, we've all seen that he can't kill.'

'He can commit immorality,' said the Crap Preacher.

'What immorality? In order to be immoral, the act has to have consequences and in order for there to be consequences, time has to be running forwards. But, as far as I can tell, time as we once knew it has stopped. We are in limbo. God, as a courtesy, has allowed us the illusion of the dimension of time so that we can continue to exist as beings recognizable to ourselves.'

'No! To give us an opportunity,' the Crap Preacher said, seizing his, 'to give us one final chance.'

'Final is finished,' Dr Norman LeStrange definitively replied. 'We are living after the end. Our acts are now meaningless – they aren't even really acts. Those who are doing what you would call "sin", they are merely dramatizing their own damnation.'

'No,' said the Crap Preacher, 'every act you perform is still, *could* still, be crucial to the life-expectancy of your soul. There are many scenarios God hasn't vouchsafed us any insight into.'

'You're both wrong,' said another man, Billy

Stickers, former film star. 'I agree that time is over, and I agree we can no longer sin. But I believe that means that the decision is already made – the logic of what you said before dictates that. And that means that whether they are acts or not, whether they exist in time or not, we can behave as we wish now. Those going to heaven are already over halfway there, they just don't know it yet. They can spend the time – call it time, for the sake of argument – they can spend their time between now and then buggering and raping and all the other things we've seen going on. Or, they can sit in here with us, listening to crap, I agree about that, as well – listening to crap because the televisions no longer work and arguing over meaningless theology. We will find out the truth soon enough.'

'You will,' said the Crap Preacher.

'It seems to me,' said a third man, Dirk Trent, necrotizing fasciitis, 'that at this point in time, of after-time, the quality of our religion is irrelevant. We may be changing channels, but we're still watching television. I happen to be enjoying the Crap Preacher. He's like a stand-up comedian, only he doesn't know it. So I propose to sit back down and listen to him until I get bored, at which point I will go and find something else to do.'

'Thank you for your support, my brother,' said the preacher.

There was a hearty round of applause punctuated by slightly embarrassed and palefaced *Amens!*

'Hallelujah,' said PC Peter Dixon. He firmly believed every word the Crap Preacher said. The Chapel had turned out to be everything Martha Castle had promised, and more.

'Hey,' said Dr Norman LeStrange, defeated but

wishing to add something to his earlier testimony. 'I don't mind this being the Church of Crap,' he said. 'And I'm not going to argue with you over details.'

'It's what you did with him,' Lady Grace Jansen, Le Fort-Wagstaffe fracture, shouted loudly from the back.

'Let him finish,' said Vanessa Queen, MRSA.

'Yes,' said several, the loudest being PC Dixon.

'No,' said others, fewer.

'We all know one thing now,' said thin LeStrange. 'That Jesus Christ is Lord of all, and that He is coming soon to judge us, man, woman and –'

'Lies!' a powerful voice, slightly posh, shouted from the doorway of the Chapel. 'This resurrection of which you are so smugly proud is not the work of your bleating lamb of an idol, the illegitimate son of Joseph of Galilee – the carpenter's bastard boy. Upon this altar at the hour of midnight, I, as High Priest of the Church of Satan, made an unholy sacrifice to the true Lord of Power. For two thousand years, you have been praying to the Nazarene and He has ignored you. Eternal life was promised but was not received. *We* have delivered!'

'It is simple,' said Othniel. 'We must let him go.'

He had let the others make their suggestions as to the problem of Kissa; no-one had suggested killing him – not seriously.

During this time, Cyrille had revived enough to stand up. He looked green and was sweating what looked like jelly.

'No,' Cyrille said. 'We will keep him here. This is my decision.'

From the corner came the sound of Kissa's whimper.

Ludger, his hair darker than before, his back straighter, stepped forwards: 'Your decision is not our decision. Your will is not our will.'

Fritzgerald nodded his approval.

'We need a new Head Voodoo Man,' said Ludger. 'I believe it would not be wise to choose a fool. I believe it would be foolish to choose a greedy man.'

'It is Othniel,' said Fritzgerald. 'We know already it is Othniel. He is the best.'

A murmur went all round the room, of approval, of warmth.

Othniel bowed his head. 'I know too little,' he said. 'I do not wish for the power.'

'He knew too much,' said Ludger, jabbing a finger towards Cyrille's eyes. 'And he wanted too much. He is a danger.'

'It is not for you to accept,' said Fritzgerald. 'It is for us to give. What do we say?'

'Yes,' said all the porters – all but Cyrille.

'It should be you, my friends,' said Othniel to Ludger and Fritzgerald. 'You have the wisdom.'

'Othniel Calixte, you are Head Voodoo Man,' said Fritzgerald. 'What shall we do?'

'Let Kissa go,' said Othniel, feeling full of a new energy. 'We do not need to worry about losing our jobs.'

The health service manager was unbound and ungagged.

He stood defiantly in front of Othniel, recognizing his leadership: 'I don't know exactly what has been going on here, but I am determined to find out. There will be a wide-ranging inquiry, after which all necessary measures will be taken. The police will be involved at an early stage.'

'Go,' said Othniel, 'quickly.'

Kissa looked once more at the faces surrounding him, as if to memorize them.

'The chief executive will hear of this,' he said. 'And the prime minister, if necessary.'

All of them listened to his footsteps as they faded away; he was marching towards the lifts.

'And the queen!' he shouted.

'That was a bad mistake,' said Cyrille.

'Keep quiet,' said Excellent.

Cyrille was about to say something else, but Othniel interrupted him: 'Tell me about upstairs. You have seen other dead people come back to life?'

'Everyone,' said Fritzgerald.

'Without exception,' said Ludger.

After midwife Pandit had finished explaining, as much as she could, both Gemma and Sarah could quite understand Mrs Ebb's distress.

'So the second baby was still being born?' Gemma asked, just to confirm.

'Mr and Mrs Walker were hysterical,' said midwife Pandit. 'I tried to get them to stop.'

'And there was something wrong with the first baby, the girl?' asked Sarah.

'It says here that it was taken to Surgery. The consultant gynaecologist took it, Henderson MacVanish.'

'And you told Mr and Mrs Walker that.'

'I did,' midwife Pandit said. 'I thought he would hit me.'

'What else did you tell them?'

'Nothing,' she said. 'Just that it was one floor up.'

Both Gemma and Sarah knew where they had to go next. But first they had to feed the baby. They asked midwife Pandit to help.

'I would,' she said, then hesitated.

'What is it?' asked Sarah.

'It's weird,' said the midwife. 'I don't understand it.'

'Yes?'

'Ever since midnight, none of the babies have been able to keep anything down. I don't mean they've been sick like we have, with cows and fish. I mean they don't seem hungry – and if you try to force the milk into them, they just start choking.'

'Bottle and breast?' Sarah asked.

'Everything,' said midwife Pandit. 'They're just not interested.'

'We have to try,' said Gemma. 'Can you get us a bottle of milk?'

'Formula?'

'Yes,' said Sarah. 'As quick as you can.'

For quite some time, the boy had been wanting to examine the shoot. But, what with the cows and the Virgin, there had been little or no opportunity. Now, however, he decided that the time had come.

Positioning himself directly beneath one of the security cameras, and out of sight – as far as he could tell – of any others, he slowly undid the buttons on his pyjama top.

It had grown alarmingly; at least twice as much as he had feared. Altogether, from base to tip, it was about twelve inches long. Not long enough to be a real hindrance, but pretty difficult to keep hidden from anyone less distracted than the Virgin.

There was still a chance he might be able to get home, but not if he took the route of conventional panic. The only thing the boy could think of was going back to the fire exit and smashing through the door. He went over and picked up the foamy fire extinguisher again.

A dull thud sounded out, as if something had exploded on a distant floor.

The boy ignored it – too caught up in what he was doing.

Nearer by, he heard a squeaking: the CCTV camera in the top corner of the room was waving frantically from side to side. The Virgin was telling him no, but no to what?

He looked at it directly, and the lens shot upwards as if looking through the ceiling. Perhaps she thought he should go to a higher floor, where he wouldn't have to smash his way out?

Another thud, this time louder.

There was no point delaying.

An alarm went off, near by.

The boy swung the fire extinguisher back, and was just choosing the weakest spot on the glass when he felt the whole building shake.

A speckled tile fell spinning to the floor, then another – which split into two rough triangles.

The boy put down the extinguisher and went over to have a closer look.

'No! No! No!' said the CCTV camera, moving as fast as it could.

There was a tremendous crash, and the floor trampolined beneath him – he spun round, off balance, and saw that a huge artificial boulder of concrete had fallen behind him, just missing him.

Suddenly, a long line of ceiling tiles in the middle of the room all fell at once – stripping off like a sticking-plaster being unpeeled.

Dodging back, the boy avoided being clobbered on the head.

Above him, the huge noise got louder. It sounded

almost as if a giant were inside the building, trying to rip it apart.

Loudly, so as to be heard over the crashing, rending noises, Sir Reginald continued, 'Satan, Lord of All, has isolated us, and has granted us – but only within this Hospital – perfect health and immortality. We can make of this place either a false heaven or a true hell. I don't know if you have taken a wander through some of the wards, but I have a pretty clear sense of which way the building is going. Right now, you have a choice –'

'Shut up,' shouted Vanessa Queen. 'You're just making a fool of yourself, in your silly cape . . .'

'This is blasphemy,' said the Crap Preacher, having remembered the word at last.

'No, it's not. To blaspheme is to insult the truth of the true God; what I am doing is asserting it, insisting upon it.'

'No, you're not,' said Lady Grace Jansen. 'This is all a horrible nightmare – I'm having a nightmare and soon I'm going to wake up, safe in bed.'

'This is real,' said Sir Reginald, younger now by about ten years. 'This is the *only* reality. Myself and my followers, when we sacrificed the innocent child – the so-called innocent child –'

There was an uproar in the Chapel.

'You what?'

'Did he say –'

'Murderer!'

'We ended one pathetic and mediocre life to buy us all our immortality,' said Sir Reginald. 'Was it not a fair bargain?' He was surfing his authority over the rising tide of protest, perfectly audible. 'Look at it as organ donation, embryo research. And the experiment, as you have seen, was successful.'

'Repeat what you just said,' came a shout from Dr Norman LeStrange.

'The experiment was successful.'

'No, about the killing.'

'For our sacrifice we required the blood of one unweaned infant child –'

'There's no blood on the altar,' said Dirk Trent.

'We slaughtered it,' shouted Pollard standing by Sir Reginald's side. 'We drank its blood with holy water and communion wine.'

Dirk Trent picked the golden cup off the altar. 'It does have something in it,' he confirmed. A couple of sniffs within the rim. 'Smells like wine. But then, I wouldn't know the smell of baby blood.'

'Bastard! Bastard!' screamed Margaret Pfister, mastectomy.

'Whose was it? Whose baby did you kill?' came a ragged voice from even further back: Kitty Somerled, retired midwife, cataracts.

Sir Reginald watched as one person after another turned to confront him. 'That is unimportant. It was the firstborn whelp of some ignorant bitch. She had a second to make up for its loss – we were very compassionate, really.'

Margaret Pfister grabbed his arm and began ineffectually to jiggle it up and down. 'Don't you say that! Don't you!'

He felt a sly punch to his kidneys – everything was going to plan. Forget that it was a new plan, conceived whilst he had been speaking. If the only way to break up this crowd and bring the satanic energies back to the Chapel was to have the congregation attack him, then so be it. After all, what harm could they do? They couldn't kill him, and anything they did in anger would be a pleasure in the sight of his downward master, not theirs.

'We sacrificed it to bring you life eternal,' Sir Reginald crowed. 'If you want to have it that way, *you* are as much the beneficiaries of its extinction as *we* are.'

Any crowd, he knew, would resent such a polysyllabic attack. His collar was grabbed; he felt the fabric tighten round his throat.

The boy looked up; cracks appeared in the exposed concrete in the middle of the ceiling, and he moved over to the doorway.

Then chunks started to fall off, gray and lethal, and a thick dust joined what few specks of ghost-mist there were on this administrative floor.

Through this, almost above his head, a grid of rusty steel became visible – metal which had been encased in artificial stone for almost half a century.

The corridor was, at that moment, much too dangerous to repass: blocks of concrete which could easily pancake him crashed unpredictably to the floor, causing gashes to appear in the lino.

He put his pyjama sleeve over his mouth to avoid breathing in any of the dust. Perhaps, he reasoned, it was more cows causing more damage – just by being so heavy and so many of them. In the north-west wing of the building, he would have been right: the bolus of reconstituted meat had smashed its way down from the kitchen to the minus 6th floor. But the true cause soon became apparent.

It was with genuine horror that the boy first glimpsed the roots now poking through the buckled concrete grid – long, dangly, shaggy, grasping roots, with little hairs coming off them; larger versions of the roots growing out of his back.

Perhaps it was an illusion of sympathy, but he felt the appletree within him put on a heave of growth and suddenly become a little heavier.

The roots grew down very quickly, from ceiling to floor, almost as if they were the ropes of a hundred mountaineers being paid out for an abseil. They tried to coil when they hit the floor but weren't flexible enough.

Pierre Estime – where was he? What *exactly* had they done with him? Othniel needed to know. He might still be alive! If others had resurrected . . .

'I put my bag in the fire,' said Ludger.

'I, too,' said Excellent.

'We all did,' said Fritzgerald. 'Fergus Moore wasn't there.'

Othniel broke through the circle and dashed out of the door – and the others all ran after him, knowing where he was going.

The stairs weren't empty, as usual; naked people were ascending. They smelled of death and of formaldehyde.

On the minus 4th floor, Pathology, there were more of them; bewildered, asking the way out.

Othniel pushed past them. The next flight down, he took the stairs three at a time.

Still there were naked people, but this lot smelled of something even worse – a smell Othniel knew all too well: medical waste.

A long corridor lined with wheelie-bins, crammed with living bodies (not Pierre's); some people still stuck inside the bins, wailing – and when Othniel had finally fought his way to the end of it all, the incinerator.

He fell down on his knees and peered through the bright door.

There were shapes in there, moving; maybe they were human. Was that a skull?

'Hey,' said a rich voice Othniel had thought was gone for ever.

Othniel turned, hardly daring to, and saw Pierre Estime standing in the doorway to Fergus Moore's storeroom.

Despite the violent noises coming from above them, they carried on with the feeding.

And just as midwife Pandit had said, the baby either wasn't interested in the milk or wasn't capable of swallowing it.

When Sarah suggested it might just be this baby that had the problem, the midwife took them down the ward. Mrs Jenny Ebb was trying with much distress but without success to get her little girl to breastfeed.

'She'll suck,' the new mother said, 'but only for comfort. And I'm not sure if she's getting anything. Watch this.'

She gently took the round brown areola away from the baby's mouth and gave it a squeeze.

A thick, waxy substance of egg-custardy white was exuded from four or five holes in the nipple.

'Colostrum,' said midwife Pandit. 'Very good. Just as it should be.'

'Yes, but look,' said Mrs Ebb.

And as they all watched, the white squirt-ends were sucked back up into the woman's breasts.

'I won't be able to feed her,' Mrs Ebb said, with

a wail. 'She'll die. There's something wrong with me.'

'No, no, no,' said the midwife. 'In the morning you'll be able to see a specialist breastfeeding counsellor.'

'We'll leave you to deal with this,' said Sarah.

'Is it alright if we take the bottle?' Gemma asked.

'Sure,' said midwife Pandit, and turned back to Mrs Ebb.

For a while, all Sir Reginald saw were feet, fast and coming towards him; then, when his skull collapsed and his eyeballs were pulped, he concentrated – with the pleasure of success – on the rhythm of the thumps. He had asked so many patients to describe their pain so that he could categorize it: sharp or dull, localized or diffused, constant or intermittent? Sir Reginald's pain, if he had asked himself to describe it, was dull, diffused and intermittent.

The enraged worshippers were mostly barefoot, and their kicks were more like slaps. Some in the crowd must have recognized this, or stubbed their toes on him, for they started to stamp with their heels – one of them repeatedly crushed Sir Reginald's testicles, as if this might be the proper punishment for what he said he'd done.

Through it all, Sir Reginald smiled. He had brought down the church, desecrated the Chapel – a second time – and it had been so easy.

Up on the altar the Crap Preacher stood appealing for the crowd to stop the violence. 'We want peace and reconciliation, not this; we want love and understanding, not hate.'

Outside the Chapel, a few more of Sir Reginald's followers walked quietly away, sensible in their wish not to become objects of righteous Christian murderous wrath.

But, unseen by almost all, a lithe figure in a brightly coloured pastiche of a nurse's outfit crawled between the feet of the crowd – crawled on hands and knees towards the kicking feet.

When the Rubber Nurse, for, yes, it was she – when she reached Sir Reginald, she covered him with her impossibly long-limbed body. Those kicking the bloody pulp which had been their infuriator found they were hurting their toes – the surface they now struck against absorbed little energy but bounced it straight back.

Quite quickly, Sir Reginald's eyes re-formed themselves and he was able to see his rescuer.

The Rubber Nurse was far from unfamiliar to him – he had been one of her earliest conquests, though he could hardly have been called resistant. Why was she doing this? He had no idea – until he heard the grunts of her pleasure as the kicks came in. 'Come on,' he heard her whisper, 'more.'

A few of the men lifted the Rubber Nurse off him, her soft chemical scent going with her.

They picked Sir Reginald up, too, and carried him out the door of the church. Turning into the corridor, a rabble a crowd a mob became instantly a procession, and one with a definite aim.

It did not take long for Sir Reginald to understand what this was.

He panicked, looking wildly around for any of his followers – eyeballing the hate-filled faces with increasing desperation.

Above his head, the boy watched the roots coming through the metal grid. He stepped back as another section of ceiling collapsed – much more and the corridor would become impassable. Then he *really would* be trapped.

The dangling roots were both repulsive and attractive, he wanted to try swinging on them and he hated the idea of having to touch them.

The boy watched as, all along the corridor, right the way to the fire stairs, tiles came down; dust and concrete fell, roots pushed through.

But there was a temporary lull in the other direction.

The boy decided to take his chance – starting off at a sprint, he dodged between the roots. When they brushed against his hands they felt cold and humanly hairy.

Where he had just been, the ceiling came down with a huge bang – an impact that would surely have crushed him to an inch thick.

But he had no time to congratulate himself on having made the right decision, the roots were dangling down more and more densely.

If he didn't get clear of them, there was a good chance that he would be trapped here just as totally as beneath a pile of rubble.

He pushed past the roots still flexible enough to move; those that had stiffened he slid round. They grew beneath his hands; swelling.

Caught between two particularly fast growers, the boy could feel them beginning to squeeze him, like the rollers of a mangle. He breathed in, pivoted his hips and lifted himself through.

Sounds from behind him told of huge collapses, and the floor rippled every time an impact took place.

A few more roots pushed aside, thinner ones, but smelling strangely of alcohol (Sir Reginald's drinks cabinet had been crushed to pieces by the trunk of a pine tree) – a few final ropy danglers, and the boy was out into clear but dusty corridor.

He ran a few paces until he felt reasonably sure the roof wouldn't come down on him, then he turned to look back.

By now the impacts were so frequent that it was hard for him to keep his feet. It was a very strange sensation, but he could hear the metal substructure of the building twanging.

The roots continued to thicken, but as the metal grids finally gave way under the huge weights above, the trunks of the trees began to press through – like industrial hammers pounding out templates, like industrial hammers in a smelting works.

A forest was forming, violently descending, and now the boy could smell the spice of the bark and the freshness of the needles overhead.

He walked back until he was a few feet away from the nearest hole.

Someone touched his shoulder and he made a grab for their hand, intending to bite it before running away – but *where?*

They tried the lifts first, but all of them were broken – and descending screams came frequently from each of the shafts. There were other noises, too, huge rendings from overhead.

'Stairs,' said Gemma.

But when the two young women reached them, they found them to be absolutely crammed with people.

'We'll never get up here,' said Sarah.

'We have to try,' said Gemma. 'There's no other way up, is there?'

Sarah thought for a moment. 'You could crawl through a ventilation pipe, I suppose – like they do in movies. But not with a baby.'

'Then we have to go up the stairs.'

She turned and began to rap on the glass door.

Eventually enough room was made to let them through.

'We need to go up,' Gemma explained. 'We are nurses and we need to get this baby to Surgery. It is *very* urgent. I realize you don't have much room to move, but if you could just try to let us through.'

Sarah was impressed – not such a mouse after all, little Gemma.

People still respected the uniform. A narrow gap appeared, and Sarah began to follow Gemma through it, holding the baby tight to her chest.

Their progress was very slow. At almost every step, Gemma had to make another pleading speech. It was going to take them a very long time to climb just one floor.

The touch on the boy's shoulder had only been a tap, and the someone, he saw, as soon as he turned round, was the Virgin.

'I just came to see for myself,' she said. 'They're amazing, aren't they?'

'The fire door was stuck,' the boy said; 'there was nothing I could do to get it open.'

'I saw,' said the young woman. 'Didn't you see me waggling the camera about? I felt sick looking at it.

'They're growing so fast,' she shouted. 'They started out on the top floor. And the heavier they get, the easier it is for them to go down.'

There were three consecutive thud-shudders. 'That's it! Go on,' she said, encouragingly. It sounded almost as if the trees were the Virgin's football team.

'They grow very tall,' she added. 'I wouldn't be surprised if they ended up poking out through the helipad. Sir Reginald's office just doesn't exist any more.'

The trunks, descending before their eyes with stately judders, were a dark brown. Lower branches appeared, often broken and split. But as they watched, these too healed themselves, just like the Virgin's knifed hymen.

'It smells of . . .' the Virgin said, and inhaled as far back into her lungs as she could. 'It smells of outside,' she said. 'It smells of nature and everything which isn't white and sterilized and chemical.'

Just then, a particularly violent sag of the floor knocked them over, and as the boy hit the ground he felt the shoot snap against his belly.

The pain was so great he almost lost consciousness. He knew this hadn't happened only because he could still hear the Virgin's voice. She was cradling his head and stroking his hair.

'Let me tell you,' said Pierre Estime, 'I won't do it again, never – not to live. Not just to stay alive in this shitty life.'

And with that he finished.

Whilst Pierre had been speaking, the others had all sat around, motionless, completely silent; nauseous. Noises, however, came in from the corridor outside; they were in Fergus Moore's storeroom – Pierre enthroned upon the three-legged stool, the only seat.

'It is serious,' said Fritzgerald, tears down his cheeks. 'We are glad you have returned to us, through such pain.'

Ludger, who had been crying, too, started to say

something but then found himself unable to speak. Instead, he lurched across and took Pierre in his arms.

Cyrille whispered to Othniel, 'This means you are not Head Voodoo Man.'

'And I am *glad*,' said Othniel, loudly. 'For I would not do what you did to gain power. You have ruined many things.'

Cyrille stood up, and Othniel did so, too; eyeball to eyeball, the two of them.

Pierre caught sight of them over Ludger's shoulder.

'Step apart,' he said.

Othniel backed off; Cyrille remained where he was.

Ludger let go of his beloved young friend.

'You,' said Pierre, and at first it wasn't clear who he was addressing. 'You are a very stupid man.'

Cyrille looked smug, sure Pierre meant Othniel.

'Because of you, I died.'

Pierre approached Cyrille; got uncomfortably close.

'Because of you, I suffered.'

In an instant, Cyrille realized the weakness of his position; panicked.

'I didn't –'

'You died also, they tell me. But you have not suffered. I believe you should suffer.'

A flick of the eyes from Pierre was all it took: Cyrille was seized by the crowd.

'Bring him to the incinerator,' said the Head Voodoo Man. 'Before he starts making excuses.'

They carried Cyrille, pig-wriggling, up to the door and then, at a nod from Pierre, threw him in.

Othniel took no part, although he understood that it was a fitting punishment; then, unable to watch any longer, he walked away – hoping they would not leave Cyrille to burn for too long.

Unable to stop himself, the boy clutched his hands to his belly-button area. In doing so, he clumsily pressed down on the fractured stem – right in the worst possible place. The pain this time came as nausea – if his stomach had been full, he would have emptied it.

With the swift movements of a nurse used to seizing her moment in the middle of a writhe, the Virgin undid a couple of pyjama buttons and parted the two sides of the top.

'What have we got here then?' she asked. But when she actually saw what they'd got, she was dumbfounded.

Now that someone else knew, there seemed no point in the boy not allowing himself a proper inspection.

The shoot was bright green – apple-green. Though it had a moment ago been snapped almost completely off, it was again vertical (he was lying on his back) and pulsing with health, almost as if it were his blood and not its own sap that ran through it.

'What a little beauty,' said the Virgin.

Deciding to reveal all, the boy said, 'And there are these, too.'

He turned sideways, careful not to touch the shoot, and lifted up the stripy material.

'Oh dear,' the Virgin said, trying to take what she saw as normal, on this most unnormal of nights. 'Do they hurt?'

'Not like the one at the front. If you want, you can touch them.'

She stroked the roots, very gently at first, then,

when she saw it didn't hurt him, ran her fingers through them. For the boy, it was the strangest of sensations – a very distant twanging, as if he were a stringed instrument. The feeling wasn't localized; and overall it was delightfully pleasurable, like being tickled with powerful beams of light – although he only realized quite how much he was enjoying it when she took her hands away.

'We'll have to do something about that little lot,' the Virgin said. 'Do you want me to try clipping them off?'

'What do they look like?'

She moved her face in closer.

'White,' she said, 'white with a hint of green – and shaggy.'

'What happened was I swallowed an appleseed by mistake, you see,' the boy word-tumblingly confessed.

'An apple tree,' she said, ruminatively. 'That's a lot better than one of these brutes. I'm sure we can deal with an apple tree.'

'How?' the boy asked. He could tell she thought she was good at dealing with people, and the truth was she was.

'We'll have to cut it out. I could probably do it with a sharp enough pair of scissors.'

'No!' said the boy. 'It hurts too much.'

'You saw the kind of things that are going on. Once it was out, you'd be mended in two minutes flat – right as rain.'

'I couldn't stand it,' the boy said, hating to have to confess weakness to a woman. 'It's the most painful thing you've ever felt.'

'Well, if we don't do something about it, it'll just keep on growing – then you'll need a tree-surgeon.'

'Can't you give me a general anaesthetic?'

'If they caught me doing that, I'd be fired – you have to do years of training before they let you put people to sleep. Of course, if you're a nurse, you can kill them on your very first shift – no-one cares about that at all.'

Without warning, before the Virgin had finished her sentence, she grabbed the shoot and gave it a hard tug. The boy screamed and kicked her hard in the belly. She fell backwards onto the floor, winded, and for a couple of minutes they felt a not dissimilar pain, though in very different degrees.

They, the execution-procession, slowly approached the window. It was already smashed, floor to ceiling, and Sir Reginald thought he could feel a chill coming off the dull grey fog. 'On three,' said a voice he found half familiar. 'One . . .' They swung him forwards. 'Two . . .' His eight bearers swung him again. In a moment he would be out the window; in a moment, he would be obliterated. 'Three!'

Sir Reginald felt himself falling falling . . . but not sideways out into oblivion – straight down.

He hit the floor hard but, in his newly youthful body, without injury. Those men who had been carrying him were now standing with their backs to him. He looked at their feet and saw that they had formed themselves into a protective circle around him. Shouts came from the crowd. Above their bare feet, two of the men wore navy-blue trousers – the Security Guard uniform. 'Just keep back,' he heard Cropper say. His loyal servant, come back just when he needed him!

As he stood slowly up, Sir Reginald saw raised fists and a heck of a lot of furious eyeballing.

'Come on,' shouted the thin man called Norman LeStrange. 'We can push them all out!'

'But that's murder,' said Lady Grace Jansen.

'You were willing enough a moment ago,' said Billy Stickers.

The crowd turned upon itself, no longer a tidal wave, more a choppy sea. It was the opportunity the High Priest's protectors had been hoping for.

'Scrum down,' Cropper said. (They played rugby together at the weekends.) Immediately, five of them formed themselves into a flankerless pack – with Sir Reginald between the two at the front, in the position of hooker. Heads down, ready ready now! They drove into the confusion of the broken-up congregation of nice.

Faced with the rampaging scrum, the crowd began to part. The pack picked up speed. A brave and idealistic young man tried to stop it by throwing himself beneath its twelve feet – he was kicked, trampled and left with two broken ribs and a few less teeth, temporarily.

In a few seconds, the scrum had forced its way through to open corridor. With no opposing force, it split up – the hefty lads unbinding arms and rising from a crouch to a run, sweat-smelly.

'To the Chapel,' Sir Reginald said. 'We'll take the Chapel.'

The crowd behind them realized what was going on, and set off in belated pursuit.

Iqbal Fermier came into the theatre Steele had made his own.

'Sir,' he said, 'I think you need to come and see this.'

Quickly, he finished the now-routine operation,

then followed Fermier out into the corridor. It was thick with ghost-mist; soul-remnants of patients who had died just going into or coming out of surgery.

A man was standing there, waiting.

'I'm James Walker,' he said. 'My wife's down here.'

Steele bent down to see beneath the ghost-mist – and, of all the grotesque things he had witnessed, this was the most extreme. Unable, for some reason, to walk normally, foot in front of foot, the woman's back was arched and she went on all fours, like a person cheating at limbo dancing, supporting themselves with their hands, feet first. Her still-huge belly jutted up in the air, undulating with kicks, like the shell of a giant Galapagos tortoise. She was naked, veins Stiltoning her skin, and long hair swishing tail-like on the floor behind her. But most extreme of all, the part-born baby's head stuck forth between her legs – eyes open, looking straight ahead; driver in an armoured car. With her screeching and its stare, the infant seemed more like the head of this hybrid creature, and the mouth some kind of propulsive, flatulent anus. The baby's own mouth had cleared the vagina, and it clearly wanted to scream too but wasn't able to fill its lungs with enough air, so what came out was a wheezy, intermittent squeak; comic, in other circumstances.

'Where's my baby?' the woman wailed. 'Do you have my baby?'

Othniel's feet had taken him up the stairs and his ears had drawn him across into Pathology; now, his eyes had difficulty believing what they saw.

The bolus of animals from the kitchen had crashed down through the building – as far as it could go. In other words, until it hit the concrete of the foundations.

What he was looking at now was the edge of the middle of it, reaching up through the shattered ceiling.

More exactly, what he was looking at was Dexter von Sinistre using his circular saw to cut through the neck of a cow.

This was what Othniel had heard; this, and the cries of the animals.

Around his feet, chickens pecked among the steel tables where dissections usually took place.

Othniel was prepared to wait for a pause in the cow-cutting, but then the saw began to make a high, screeching sound; mechanical torture; metallic death.

Gray smoke came from beneath the plastic. The sound rose to a barely audible whine then a hiss then stopped.

Dexter von Sinistre dropped the saw and backed away from the wall of animals.

'Sorry,' he said. 'That's the last one. I could try with a manual saw, but I know it wouldn't work. You're stuck, and I'm going to leave.'

Othniel stepped forwards, and was able to see a hand waving down at floor level. A face was also there, behind the re-forming neck of the cow.

'What?' said von Sinistre, surprised to have been overheard. 'Oh, it's you.'

Without delay, Othniel grabbed the hand and braced his foot against the side of the cow.

'It's no use,' von Sinistre said. 'I've already tried.'

Othniel pulled, and felt the body attached to it shift a little.

'Come on,' he said.

Von Sinistre joined him, pulling at the wrist.

The head came out; and soon they were able to get their hands under the man's armpits: Jock McKnock, slaughterhouseman.

'Cheers, mate,' he said to each of them in turn.

'And now I'm finished,' said von Sinistre. 'And now I'm going home.'

He and Jock made their way to the stairs.

Othniel looked closely at the pile, but could see no more human body parts.

Then he, too, set off up the stairs; perhaps there would be something for him to do there, too.

'Sorry,' the Virgin said, 'I just wanted to see if it would come out easily.'

'If you'd asked, I could have told you. It's got roots – they're all through me, probably, not just sticking out the back. That's why I need to get home. My mother told me the story of the boy and the appleseed. My mother knows how to make it better.'

The shoot when he looked at it was about sixteen inches long – if anything, pain seemed to have stimulated a growth spurt in it.

Just then, one of the floor-to-floor jumpers dropped down between them yelling a yell that sounded silly with joy.

With a cracking of snapped ankles and shattered knees, the figure crumpled onto the floor. It was a man; they could easily tell that because he was naked and because, as naked, he clearly wasn't a woman. From the tone of his skin, baggy and crinkly but still with some elasticity, the Virgin estimated his age at around fifty-five. He rolled onto his back, screaming with an emotion which still sounded a bit like joy but was largely comprised of temporary pain. It was, perhaps, a joy like the very end of childbirth: extreme agony and achievement at one and the same moment.

When he rolled onto his back, the boy took a look at his face. The man's eyes were closed, and it was only when he opened them, moss-green, that the boy recognized: 'Harold!'

When they got to it, the Chapel door was locked.

The Satanists were about to form themselves into a battering ram when Sir Reginald held up an authoritative finger. Then he pointed at a young man, Holgate Washburn, bilateral orchidectomy, and beckoned him across.

When Holgate got close, the High Priest whispered in his ear. Holgate nodded and approached the door. He knocked lightly with his knuckles, then cleared his nervous throat.

'It's over,' he said. 'Can you let us in?'

Sir Reginald had chosen well. The young man's voice (even after the return of his testicles) was high and silvery-trumpetlike in tone. It didn't just inspire trust, it ensured it – the sound was so innocent, though Holgate had been among the keenest blood-drinkers.

'Really?'

'Really.'

The door gave a dull click and opened a crack. Sir Reginald's rugby team shoved their way through, battering aside the three young women who had been crouching – listening – there.

Sir Reginald looked the Chapel over – almost the whole congregation had gone to watch the defenestration. Those pacifists left behind were no danger to him and his group of rugby-playing Satanists. 'If you want to leave,' he said, 'you have ten seconds.'

Of the nine who had been there, soon only one remained. It was hard to tell if he, Asif Prakash, with his ginger hair and startled expression, was a willing addition or just too terrified to move.

'Close the door,' Sir Reginald threw out over his shoulder as he walked towards the altar. A new authority had descended upon him, ascended to him. 'Barricade it with some of the pews. Make it strong.' He strode round to the back of the Chapel, unhooked the crucifix from the wall and replaced it, inverted.

There were two painting hooks in the back of the wooden figure – one behind his shoulders, one in his feet. Sir Reginald had screwed in the second one several years ago, and no-one had ever noticed: which didn't surprise him. Jesus was only very infrequently dusted: Christians – so trusting.

The barricade was finished in doublequick time – long before the hubbub outside started up. Soon there was a rainstorm of angry fists thudding against the door – hailstorm, perhaps.

'Do you think they'll be able to break in?' Sir Reginald asked, less to question his latest triumph than to confirm it.

'Not unless they get something pretty heavy to hit it with,' said Cropper.

Sir Reginald spoke *ex cathedra*. 'I thank you for saving my life. Whoever organized it, well done.' He nodded towards Cropper. Another Security Guard, Cutmore, took some credit, too. 'But now we must do something even more important – we must destroy this place completely. Everything in this room must cease to exist. Especially Him.' He meant upside-down Jesus. 'We must set it on fire.'

There was no opposition to this – and no questioning of whether or not they would be able to put it out again afterwards. The understanding, almost immediately, was that they wouldn't.

In the space where the pews had lately been, the followers of Satan formed a large pyre of Bibles, hymnals and Books of Common Prayer. To make them burn better, they ripped the covers off and tore chunks out of the pages.

As his followers went about their diabolical work, Sir Reginald calmly used his duplicate key on the stores cupboard. From here he unloaded all the spare candles, white and black.

'Stand back,' he said, as he pushed them into the gaps in the bottom of the construction.

Then he went round gathering other pieces of ecclesiastical paraphernalia: the candlesticks from the altar, the sacramental wine and communion wafers. The wine and wafers he handed to the chaplain.

'Consecrate them,' he said.

Briefly, the chaplain obeyed.

'Now give them to me,' Sir Reginald said.

Once in possession, he crumbled the wafers onto the floor by the doors, so that the faithful would trample upon them when they entered; the wine, he merely drank and then passed on.

When everything that could be piled up was, the High Priest produced a cigarette lighter from his pocket – miraculously unbroken in the *mêlée* – and lit a black candle he had set aside especially.

He improvised a brief anti-sermon, in which he dedicated the desecration and destruction of this Chapel to the True and False Lord of All Things. Then he set off the wick of the candle, transferred the fire to some salient points on the pyre, and stood back to watch as the flames took hold of the books.

Nikki Froth had not long remained a lone disciple; first one, then five, then twenty entered the Intensive Care Unit and sat around gazing at the nothing-doing of the comatose man. Angela Dixon had tried to force them out, but had given up when she saw it was impossible. They weren't causing any trouble – far from it; Celia Iden and Holly Gonne sat, good as gold.

Johannes Fast had remained out in the stairwell, testifying. But among those who heard him, there were some who took on the holy fire without signing up to his particular doctrine. Other men – they were invariably men – had begun to preach rival gospels and to establish rival sects.

As no more than one voice could be heard in the echoey, muttery stairwell, Johannes Fast and the other speakers came to an agreement: they would all retire into the ICU and each would take turns (five minutes) in spreading the Gospel according to himself. They would preach to the converted but also, by ripping the door off its hinges, their voices would reach the unbelievers moving past.

One man argued that although this was, as Johannes Fast rightly said, the new Covenant, yet it was incomplete: the only way to reunite Him with His father would be to put Him out into the amorphous fog. In this way, too, they would reunite Hospital with the world, from which it had become so unfortunately separated.

Another pleaded that this was not *Jesus* lying before them but John the Baptist. The saviour could not come without first being announced. Many of this preacher's devotees argued with him that he was himself the announcer, *he* was John the Baptist. One became so convinced of this that he began to preach against his master. He, too, gained a few followers, but they were an unhappy little sect.

Another man tried to assert that, of course, and for all the reasons given by Johannes Fast, this must be not Jesus but the Antichrist. Technology was an abhorrence, and the true reborn Saviour would have nothing to do with it; certainly there would be no craven dependence upon it. He agreed that the best thing would be to put this anathema out the window.

Yet another argued that the miracle of this man was that he was simply a man. *Ecce homo!* In offering praise and prayers to him they were doing nothing more than honouring their previous selves, their mortal selves, now that they seemed irrevocably lost.

Others opposed the very idea that this was a new *Christian* messiah, was the Second Coming of Jesus. Why not Mohammed? Or the Buddha? Or Emperor Haile Selassie?

But whenever Johannes Fast got up to speak, he was listened to in deepest silence and with greatest respect. Only Nurse Angela Dixon dared move during these moments – performing the duties necessary to keep the comatose one comfortable, as he died.

'Please,' said Mary. 'I just want him to be alright.'

Steele didn't like conscious patients, and he hated having to talk to them in order to explain even the simplest procedures. He had watched Gemma Swallow do this with great admiration; she was so calm, so well informed. She seemed to know exactly what the patients needed to hear.

'Don't worry,' he said, 'we'll do our best.' The implication being that with such a best in the room, the woman should stop worrying immediately.

'We haven't got time to put a screen up,' said Iqbal Fermier, taking over customer care. 'So, if you don't want to see what's going on, I'd advise you to keep your eyes shut.'

James looked at them fairly calmly and said, 'Please just get on with it.'

Nurse Wilson wiped down Mary's bulging belly with a disinfectant swab which left behind it a yellowish stain, to show where it had been and cleaned.

Beneath the tight dome of the skin they could see knees, hips, elbows poking about.

Steele felt around until he was sure he knew where everything was. As he did this, the midwife – Zandra Pandit, newly arrived from Maternity – explained what she called 'the lay of the land', but Steele ignored her, preferring the evidence of his own observations and the preservation of his instincts. He asked Nurse Wilson for the sharpest scalpel they had left. She handed him a brand-new CutmeisterPro-9 and he gave her a chastising look. 'I was saving it,' the young woman said, with a wink.

'For a special occasion?' Steele asked back, then gave her a smile. 'Well, then let's hope this is.'

The husband, who didn't appreciate OT banter, tutted sharply.

Then, without hesitation, Steele made the first Caesarean incision: about twenty centimetres crossways. He opened the gap through which the baby's stuck head could pass.

Iqbal kept an eye on the husband; didn't want him keeling over, not in here – but he was wisely concentrating on words of comfort.

Steele could see the baby's feet, the body was further in. He passed the bloodied scalpel to the nurse and hooked both his index fingers under the baby's arms.

Mary chose this moment, of course, to take a look; the sight of her slashed midriff seemed to fascinate rather than upset her.

'Don't,' said the husband.

'I want to see – I want to see he's alright,' Mary replied.

Steele put his hands around the baby, gripping it textbook manner. As usual at this miraculous moment, he was aware that his were the first human hands to have touched this new flesh. Very few things in surgery any longer gave him a feeling of ever-expanding wonder, but this always did. There was a medical adjunct to this – the fear that the baby might be allergic to latex. He brought the head out, supporting it between thumb and forefinger – taking care, at the same time, not to block the child's airway. The youngest baby rose up into the world, dripping wombic fluid and trailing behind it a veiny rope of umbilical cord.

The mother's eyes went wide.

Steele lifted the baby higher still, to look it over.

'Yes, he's definitely a boy,' said midwife Pandit, but the interruption was welcome.

'It's the boy! It's the boy, isn't it?' Harold said. 'My God, did that hurt – but, God, did it feel good. If you wait a couple of minutes, I'll be mended. Then we can talk properly.'

Harold closed his eyes and seemed to be concentrating, making an effort to fix himself – as if he could speed the process up. Tears formed a web down the still craggy sides of his face – in the outward directions of a cat's whiskers. He breathed jaggedly.

In other – more normal – circumstances, the Virgin might have been worried by a man of his age presenting in such a condition. Instead, she pulled the boy aside and asked, 'You know him?'

'Yes,' he said, 'but he was different then – older, and not so optimistic.'

The ankles put themselves back into their normal downwards shapes, still pale and sparsely haired.

'That's the job,' Harold said, rubbing knobbly hands up and down his legs, 'I think I'm mended up now. What do you think's doing the trick? Something they put in the air?'

The Virgin looked at them both, then decided she had better not try and explain what – as far as she was concerned, anyway – had happened, and what her part in it had been. 'Probably,' she said. 'They can do marvellous things these days.'

'Look at me,' said Harold, standing up. 'It's all I ever wanted – I'm younger. Most of my aches and pains have gone. And nothing can hurt me any more. There was a man in my ward, the Spaceman his name was, at least that's what we called the chap – he showed me with his safety razor. Two cuts on his arm, and they disappeared just like that.' His fingers flew up, ending with a loud snap! 'Then I tried and, hey presto! It worked on me, too. So now I'm better, I'm getting out of here as soon as soon can be. What about you? Still on your way home?'

'Yes,' said the boy. He was very conscious of the wound he'd received from the cow, still unhealed, but as Harold hadn't mentioned it, he didn't see why he, the boy, should. But the older man's attention was elsewhere –

'Wowzers,' said Harold. 'That's a thing, isn't it? Boy-oh-boy. Apple leaf, if I'm not much mistaken. Used to grow these myself.'

Harold had accepted the bizarreness of it so easily that the boy began to wish he'd told him earlier. But back then, before midnight, yesterday, the other miracles hadn't started to happen – probably Harold wouldn't have believed him. All the same, he wished he'd given him the chance.

As if reading the boy's thoughts, Harold said, 'Well, I can help you now, even if I couldn't before.'

He stood proudly naked in the corridor. It was clear to the Virgin that he did this because he was so happy with his rapidly returning vigour, and so inured to the humiliations of long-term hospital life (Mr Upward, we'd just like to do a quick prostocopy, if you don't mind . . .). 'Shall we try to get you some clothes?' she asked.

'Oh,' said Harold. 'I suppose so – though I'm feeling so tip-top that I really don't mind people seeing me like this. You never know, I might get lucky.' He nudged the boy and looked towards the Virgin.

'Not *that* lucky,' she said, with bitter irony.

A quick search of a nearby office turned up a macintosh. It wasn't much but at least it was a start.

'What's the plan?' asked Harold.

'Would you like to cut the cord?' Iqbal Fermier asked the husband.

'No, thank you. You can do it.' James's manner was warmer already.

The nurse handed Iqbal the scissors as Steele held the baby boy still.

'We don't have a proper clip,' said Nurse Wilson. 'But I have this –' It was a clothes peg.

'I'll tie it,' said Steele. 'Like they used to. Leave a little bit longer than usual.'

Snip.

Steele held the baby where the mother could see it, then took it to a side table and knotted the umbilical as close to the tummy as he could. It was here that he first noticed something unusual. And by now he had enough experience of the new laws of medical physics to know what it most likely meant. The cleanly cut end of the umbilical cord seemed to be dissolving into a mist. He continued tying the knot, but a feeling of helpless horror started up inside him, like a rusty dishwasher. It probably wouldn't help but he had to try something; be heroic.

'The baby's fine,' he said.

'Can I hold him?' Mary asked weakly. 'I want to hold him.'

'I'm just going to take it into the other room for a few moments.'

Midwife Zandra Pandit held the door open for him; her face, puzzled – she knew this was far from usual.

'No!' screamed Mary. 'Not again! Not again!'

The husband said, 'You can't do that. We've already had one baby taken away.'

'Come with me, then,' Steele said to the husband.

'No,' he said. 'I'm staying here.'

Steele left.

Iqbal delivered the placenta; when he pulled it out, the efficient nurse already had a metal tray ready to receive it.

This was handed to the midwife, glad that her position was still being recognized. She looked in the tray and was surprised to see – as never before – a reddish smoke rising from the mother-end of the umbilical cord. As she continued to watch, it snaked upwards and turned towards the door through which Steele had just passed.

Mary was crying. 'What's going on?'

'He's alright,' the husband said. 'They just want to weigh him, probably.' But he could see the scales in the corner of the room. 'It's routine. Don't worry. All this is routine. We have a beautiful baby boy. Did you see him? He's beautiful.' James knew he was babbling; there would be a lot of that in the coming months, hopefully.

'Yes,' said Mary. 'He's beautiful, isn't he?'

'And everything's alright. They will bring him back in a few moments.'

He glanced at Iqbal, who didn't look so sure.

Othniel Calixte made it up to the ground floor.

He was just walking towards A&E when he felt somebody leap on him from behind. An arm went round his throat and a familiar elbow stuck out under his chin.

'Authority!' shrieked Mr Kissa. 'Authority!'

Othniel could feel the bones of the man's knees digging into his lower back.

He hesitated for a moment: Kissa was still his boss. He could be fired. Then he felt himself beginning to choke.

With both hands, Othniel grabbed Kissa's forearm. It was scrawny and without power, although younger than before.

Othniel put his head down and charged towards the nearest wall.

There was a gristly crunch as Kissa's head hit the framed poster – which just happened to be a smiling image of himself. The whole corridor was lined with similarly glowing portraits of hospital employees. When volunteers had been asked for, Kissa was first in line, pens in pocket.

Othniel let the limp body slide forwards, onto the floor. He might have broken Kissa's neck, but that didn't matter.

There were some seats opposite, and he sat down on them to wait for his boss to come round.

The first word Kissa said was the same as the last, 'Authority.'

Othniel wagged his finger gently. 'Don't try to attack me again.'

'There is no authority,' said Kissa, sitting up. 'Instead, there are chickens. I left my village to avoid chickens. I became a health service manager to avoid chickens. This is a hospital, not a farm. This is a clean place. For it to be a clean place, there must be authority. When there is authority, *then* we can form a plan to get rid of the chickens. I have asked everywhere – and people tell me crazy made-up facts about the Devil or about a man who is Jesus. They are mad.'

No, thought Othniel, you are mad.

'Go home,' he said. 'Go to sleep.'

'I *was* in bed. I *was* asleep. And then I wake up here, with my body all inside one of your lockers.'

'We did not put you there,' said Othniel.

Kissa looked at him with suspicion.

'We did nothing wrong,' said Othniel.

'I cannot go home. I need to make my report. None of the usual information feedback systems are in operation. There are important lessons to be learned for future practice –'

Othniel could see the man wasn't going to give up.

'Then why don't you find a quiet office, sit down and write a full statement of what happened?'

'With pen and paper?'

'Take as much time as you need, Mr Kissa.'

'From start to finish?'

'In triplicate,' said Othniel.

'Yes,' said Kissa. 'I will. That's exactly what I'll do. I will make valid suggestions, for local implementation, especially concerning a chicken-removal protocol.'

'Good,' said Othniel. 'And don't forget to mention me.'

But Kissa was already off, muttering to himself.

Shaking his head, Othniel stood up and continued to A&E.

'I think we should try the fire escape again,' said the boy.

'Quite right. And not the stairs,' Harold said. 'I've tried those – they're chokka.'

'He means the external one,' said the Virgin to Harold. 'It's at the end of this corridor.'

'But it's locked and I couldn't get it open,' the boy said. He explained about the glass, the fire extinguisher and the bare feet.

'We probably can't reach it, anyway,' said Harold. 'Not unless we clamber up then hike across then drop down again. This floor looks impassable, and the trees are pretty thick up there, too.'

A holding-hands couple fell past. This way down was rapidly becoming popular.

'We could try and find a way on a floor below,' said the boy. 'To another fire escape.'

'Or just see how far down these trees take us,' replied Harold.

'I'm not coming,' said the Virgin. 'I want to stay here, where I can see everything going on.'

Harold looked at her, puzzled, so she explained about the surveillance room.

'Like to have a gander at that,' he said.

'No,' said the boy. 'We can't waste any more time. I need to get home before this gets too big for me to carry.'

Harold looked at the green of the leaves. 'Well, I said I'd help you and I will,' he said.

'You should come,' the boy said to the Virgin. 'It might seem safe here but it's not. The whole building could collapse – I wouldn't be surprised if it did.'

'No,' she said, 'that's not what I'm scared of.'

The boy could see that the Virgin wanted very badly to get back to her screens – check up on the Devil. 'Will you watch us?' he asked.

'Of course I will.'

'Side to side for no, up and down for yes.'

'And round and round for laughing,' the Virgin said. She smiled but made no move to touch either of them. 'Goodbye,' she said, 'again.'

'You should come,' Harold said one final time. 'You never know – I might reach twenty-five. It remains to be seen what the prime of life really is.'

The Virgin walked away, without looking back – not tempted; not at all.

'Ready for action?' said Harold to the boy.

'Yes,' came the reply – but just then a jumper-down landed on Harold's back and tipped him over the edge for a further fall.

They went down at least two floors before the boy lost sight of them. A pig appeared, running from the direction the Virgin had just taken: Security Guard Cutmore's bacon sarnie.

The boy got among the branches and began to descend. He was good at tree-climbing.

Once Sir Reginald was satisfied the fire was unput-outable, he passed the candle to Cropper and told him to light the curtains.

The sprinkler system started up, showering, but not torrentially, into the Chapel.

Out in the corridor, the crowd was surprised by this sudden shower. A smell of smoke came from under the door, as if in explanation, as if to say *too late, too late.*

Sir Reginald looked up at the ceiling – was he to be thwarted? The water from the sprinklers looked like blown-inside-out umbrellas. Stupid not to cover the smoke alarms; stupid to risk a truly damp squib. He felt the droplets spattering his bald pate, his bare but hairy chest.

The Devil-worshippers watched the pyre being browbeaten. In an evil tone, it began to hiss – expressing its solidarity with Satan, perhaps. *Give me a chance; I can do great things – great damage.*

Throughout the 13th and the two adjacent floors, the sprinklers were activated. Water fell on computers and electrical equipment – computers, monitors, ventilators – some of these fused with loud cracks, sending off sparks which, in turn, were to be the cause of other, localized fires.

Many of the patients welcomed the sprinklers' moisture-from-above – they hadn't been outside for months or years, and this, to them, was rain.

It ran down the faces of the healed where their tears should have been – all were unable to cry, just as they were unable to urinate or defecate; spitting brought a water-snake back into the mouth.

The corridors became more treacherous – the cows' hooves skidded out from them even more often; the flopping fish moved with greater ease across the lino. Orgiastic bodies were dowsed then lubricated.

Outflow gushed down the holes in the floors around the pine trees, wetting the trunks and the people clinging to the branches.

But the tepid cloudburst had hardly begun before it started to thin, first to a drizzle and then to a few stutteringly annoying drops; do one thing or the other, why don't you?

Suddenly as it had started, the water cut off completely.

In the Chapel, thick black smoke rose vertically from the kindling pews and then billowed out sideways once it reached the ceiling; encountering the walls brought a downturn and a foldback. Then, all at once, tall flames began to spike up from the bright centre of the pyre.

Steele was walking swiftly down the corridor towards the X-ray room.

When he got there, he found it deserted, as expected. He took the baby boy inside the X-ray chamber and closed the door behind them.

This room, Steele knew, was meant to be completely airtight – yet a trail of red vapour snaked down towards the corner, where two of the walls met the floor. Clearly, someone hadn't done their job properly.

Steele looked around the room – the best thing would be some Vaseline; there was a pot of paint.

The baby was wriggling in his arms; he seemed healthy enough.

He put the tiny boy down on one of the shelves,

wrapped up in the pink-stained blanket: quite safe from rolling. Then he prised open the tin and poured some of the white (it turned out) paint over the hole.

There was no brush around, not so far as he could see.

The baby gave a gurgling whimper. Steele stepped over to him and quickly checked his airway – clear.

The flesh-smoke had, with the sealing of the hole, stopped snaking its way back to the mother; it wasn't ghostly, then; couldn't travel through solid walls – although, presumably, the molecules would be small enough.

So his theory was correct: if the baby was hermetically isolated from its mother, the two of them could be kept separate. Otherwise . . .

However, this room clearly wasn't suitable, long term. They would have to try somewhere else. The isolation units in Tropical Medicine on the 9th floor were a possibility, if only they could get down there. Better still . . .

He opened the door, picked up the baby boy and carried him back to his parents. Unless they saw for themselves, they would never believe.

It didn't take Othniel long to work out the situation in A&E: either he could join the queue for the exit or he could stand to one side and watch the queue for the exit. But Othniel didn't want to leave, not in an emergency like this. And he didn't want to stay where there was nothing to be done.

The fire staircase, coming out at the far end of the room, was where the crowd was at its thickest – and there was no reason to think that the other staircases wouldn't be exactly the same. And the lifts.

Othniel was sick of being underground, of feeling

trapped. He wanted to go somewhere he could get a good overall view of things.

The roof. The helipad.

Knowing Hospital as well as he did, he immediately thought of another way up; laborious but possible – a ventilation shaft that ran up the middle of north-west wing. It had a ladder in it, for maintenance access.

Othniel pushed his way through the crowd, which parted easily because he was heading away from the exit.

He quickly located the shaft entrance. The office door had been conveniently kicked in by someone or other – the room had been trashed.

With the screwdriver on his penknife, he undid the four screws and pulled off the gray-slatted cover.

Sticking his head through the rectangular hole, Othniel was able to look upwards a dizzying distance.

Time to climb.

The boy made fairly steady downward progress.

The first floor had gone past quickly enough, but there were some difficult manoeuvres to be made between the thicker but further apart branches lower down. And the pain every time he brushed the leaves sticking out through his pyjamas didn't help. Neither did the more abandoned of the fallers. They had a tendency to roll down through the branches, giggling. When the sprinklers started up, the boy just kept going.

Harold was waiting for him after two more floors, already mended. 'I've just heard the oddest thing,' he said. 'You know how everyone is getting better – healing faster than anyone has ever healed before.' The boy was getting impatient; he knew this already.

Harold might be getting younger, but he still – like lots of old people – repeated things that didn't need repeating. 'Well, that's all except one person: he's alive, but he's in the Intensive Care Unit. He's still unconscious. Everyone else is conscious, moving around. Brain damage seems to have been fixed along with cuts and bruises. But this chap seems to prefer kipping. He's completely out of it.'

'I saw him,' said the boy.

'This is a big hospital, by any rights it could have been someone else.'

'But I saw him, I tell you – on the screen.'

'Anyway, some people have gathered around him. They seem to think he's some kind of Jesus Christ, silly idiots. And they're sending out evangelists –'

'Shut up,' said Simon Bolland. 'You don't know what you're talking about.'

'I should give you a good hiding,' said Harold. 'You're the one who fell on me from a great height.'

'I've seen him – he sleeps for all of us. He's the only one left who's ill – that must mean *something*.'

'Exception that proves the rule,' said Harold, smartly.

'I'm going to tell people on the lower floors. They need to know – someone needs to tell them. He is here.'

'Well, you'd best get a move on then, hadn't you? Don't want someone else to get there first.'

'When he awakes the world will end,' the follower Simon Bolland said.

'I've no doubt that it shall,' said Harold, who could feel his strength return with every passing minute. 'Why don't I try to hurry things along a little?' he said, and gave the follower a mighty push in the chest.

The young man disappeared down the hole.

'He *was* a bit tiresome, wasn't he?' said Harold. 'I'm going to enjoy this, however long it lasts.'

The boy was impressed by the directness of Harold's approach.

Continuing downwards – Harold first, the boy coming after – they had to pass through an extremely thick cloud of ghost-mist. Though they didn't know it, this was a cardiovascular ward and a vast number of deaths had taken place here.

They went faster and faster, though Harold, obviously, given the choice, would have preferred to have been jumping down.

The diabolists were forced back by the intensifying heat.

With a sweeping gesture, the High Priest gathered them on the doorward side of their small holocaust. They were beginning to choke, and he did not want to risk any of them losing consciousness through asphyxiation: not out of concern for their health, but in the next few minutes, numbers might be crucial. He ordered them, with silent signs, to clear the doorway, tossing the removed pews on top of the roaring fire.

Those outside were still beating on the wood of the door but had stopped trying the handle – and so it wasn't until Sir Reginald threw it open, the flames of something that looked very like Hell blazing behind him, that the congregation realized *exactly* what was going on.

Two thick black horns of smoke puffed out of the doorway directly over Sir Reginald's head, emphasizing his horns of grey hair, just as if he'd willed it as a special effect.

'Burn them!' shouted the Crap Preacher. 'Force the heretics back inside!'

This time there was no lack of cohesion from the congregation. Three men stepped forward and shoved Sir Reginald back into the burning room. Another reached in for the door-handle and pulled it shut. This, he held on to, shouting – crying out for help. Some put their arms round his waist to anchor him; others grabbed his hands to keep them and the handle they whitely grasped from being twisted – for the devils inside were already doing their best to free themselves from the inferno of their own making.

A tug of war followed, in which the Satanists managed once or twice to get the doors open a crack but were unable to press (pull) home their advantage. Without a fire directly behind them, those outside could get more bodies onto the inward-opening door. The angelic forces' triumph seemed assured when they heard a metallic snap on the other side of the door, and felt the tugging on the handle cease.

Next thing they knew, though, there was a huge crash-crash-crash and the wood of the door shuddered.

The new parents, temporary parents, were overjoyed to be reunited with their child. After nine months of it (him) as an idea and then as a bump which kicked, they had their little boy to see and touch and smell and love.

Steele hesitated – should he explain or should he let them see for themselves; which would be least distressing?

'He's so beautiful,' said James.

There was a thickish smear in the air where the placenta was snaking back into Mary's womb.

Iqbal Fermier was working away at stitching up the Caesarean section – pointless effort. The midwife was standing back, clearly thinking her work was done.

'You can stop that,' said Steele to Fermier.

'Fine,' he replied – the hole had been opening up from the other end, a mouth swallowing vapour; cigarette blowback.

'I have some bad news,' said Steele. 'Your baby is perfectly healthy – there is nothing to be worried about there.' He began to explain, only to be met with disbelief, denial and then denunciations. 'I have explained what is happening.' He pointed once again to the dissolving umbilical cord; it had halved in length.

'But you said he was fine,' said Mary, the mother-in-reverse.

'He is,' Steele said, 'and he will continue to be fine when he is drawn back up inside you. We don't know how this happens, it's something new. From what I've worked out, if something was part of the body before, without independent life of its own, it can no longer be separated.'

Mary held the baby boy tighter to her breast – as if that would prevent them being divided by being profoundly reunited.

Steele gave up trying to convince the parents of the truth of what he was saying; events over the next few minutes would do this for him.

The surgeon in him wanted to go next door and perform some more emergency operations, but the doctor knew that his duty of care was with this family.

Mary screamed continually.

*

Spanner and Case continued to descend the north-west fire stairs.

'Makes you wonder, dunnit?' said Case.

'What?'

'What it all means, you know – why all this?'

'No.'

'You mean, you're not even curious? All these fucking animals and shit – everything coming down at the same time.'

'I'm not even paying attention, me. I *rise* above it.'

'But this could be the whole fucking point. This could be the reason we were put on earth to start with.'

'We weren't put on earth, you hippie bastard. Your dad fucked your mum and was disappointed when a fucker like you dribbled out nine months later – so he fucked off.'

'That's no explanation.'

'It's good enough for me,' said Spanner. 'Look, I know waxing a bit poetic helps with the bitches. But you're not trying to fuck me, are you? At least, I hope you're not trying to fuck me because it's a bit fucking crowded in here – know what I mean?'

'The universe has a reason.'

'It's got a fucking alibi, I'll give it that. The jammy bugger was always somewhere else at the time. Never at the scene of the crime.'

'Some people think this is the end of the world. I've heard them.'

'If they're still capable of fucking *thinking*, it's not the end of fucking anything.'

'No, they mean this is the build-up. The end will probably be tomorrow, or the day after.'

'Then they should be a bit more careful in fucking expressing themselves.'

'Armageddon.'

'No, that would feel different from this. This is just like queuing for a very big kebab van.'

'Maybe it's Hell, then.'

'So, Hell is a queue.'

'A queue where you never get to buy anything.'

'I never knew you was so profound.'

'I love her.'

'I know. Would you shut up about it?'

'I've lost her.'

'Yes, you have. Look, I preferred it when you was talking Armageddon, because that's a lot less depressing.'

'They're both the end of the world.'

'Listen. Here's one: my girlfriend dumped me last night, so I went out and had fifteen beers and the hottest curry I could find. Yesterday, the bottom fell out of my world. This morning, the world fell out of my bottom.'

Case did not reply.

They came to a point, Harold and the boy, where they could descend no further by the trees.

The branches had become thicker and thicker the further down the trunk they went, but the gaps between them had also increased. Finally, they ran out altogether, and all they were left with was a drop of three or four floors – into an unpredictable darkness speckled with traces of ghost-mist. Men and women but mostly men dropped past them into this abyss. From their cries at first of agony, it seemed they landed badly (perhaps on top of one another), and from their silence afterwards, it was likely they had got themselves into a difficult situation.

Harold tried to have shouted conversations with anyone in the hole but got no replies.

When the boy looked around, he saw the floor they were on had a particularly thick dusting of ghost-mist.

Harold gave up with the fallers, and they went to explore where they were – rapidly discovering a queue of people and at the end of it an operating theatre.

The boy's shoot had grown to about a foot and a half, and the possible presence of surgical instruments gave Harold the chance to broach a difficult subject. 'That little tree you've got growing there,' he said. 'It hurts when you touch it, doesn't it?'

'More than anything ever,' the boy replied.

'But you want to get rid of it, don't you?'

'Yes,' said the boy, already suspecting what Harold was going to suggest.

'And you know that when I fell down on that floor, I was all broken bones, and yet five minutes later I was up and about again, fit as a fiddle, right as rain. It stung for a while but not for very long. And pain is a lot more bearable when you know it's not going to last.' Harold thought of the chronic pains, now gone, which he had borne for over fifty years.

'It's still painful.'

'Oh yes – it's terrible. A fellow has to be very brave to go through it. And the thing is, young captain, I think you're a very brave fellow. What's more, I think that if we don't do something about that growth of yours pretty soon, it's going to start getting in the way of things.'

'I can still carry it. It's not getting too heavy for me.'

'Not yet – but eventually it will.'

The boy was worried about how much longer he had before the appletree unbalanced him completely.

It had been growing in surges, not steadily, but if anything was speeding up: twenty inches long, now.

'We could even try and find some painkillers,' Harold said.

The boy did not reply, and Harold took this as an indication of possible consent – which is what it was. More than anything, probably more than survival, the boy was determined not to seem a coward. He wanted to get home – he knew his mother could help him like no-one else. But even if all they could do was slow the growth of the tree, that would still be a help.

Sir Reginald had ordered his rapidly suffocating followers to pick the least burned pew off the fire and to use it as a battering ram upon the doors.

The blue curtains had burned all the way up to the ceiling and the flames of the pyre jabbed like accusing fingers into the speckled white tiles. It was so thick with smoke that they could hardly be sure if they were attacking the doors now and not a solid wall.

Smash went the bench; crunch went the impact-point.

'Faster!' Sir Reginald shouted, feeling the heat scald his back. 'Harder!'

Again, smash!

The wood split and light from the corridor sliced into the choking air of the Chapel.

Sir Reginald repositioned the battering ram – a couple more blows made another hole; still not big enough to get out of. At least a little air was getting in, and the gap gave his smoke-blind followers hope. He made them lift the ram onto their shoulders and joined them in their next series of charges.

All at once the top hinge of the left-hand door gave way – the thing pivoted diagonally, leaving a triangle of space through which Sir Reginald was first to step. His long cape was smoking and the gag-stench of singed hair came off his head.

Those on the side of the angels stood back, unable to stop themselves feeling shock and dismay; evil was unconfined.

The other Satanists stumbled out with a less masterful demeanour – clutching their throats and coughing, patting their scorched but mending legs.

'Your Church is fallen,' said Sir Reginald. 'You have seen the victory of the truest God of all. I will accept any who want to follow me in following Him.'

One man stepped resolutely forward, convinced by what he'd seen and heard: PC Peter Dixon. A few more followed him, moving across to the side of evil. But the majority of the congregation were in retreat from the heat and the smoke. Behind Sir Reginald they could see the metal armature of the crucifix, holding its shape but being absorbed into the incandescent heart of the conflagration. Those at the periphery took to their bare heels – it was clear this fire, with no sprinklers to stop it, would soon overtake the floor and then all the others it reached.

A couple of braver ones had gone for extinguishers, and now tried vainly spraying them through the doors.

With his congregation behind him, the High Priest set off to try and climb above the fire – which at least would gain them a little time. PC Dixon went happily with them.

All of this had been watched, silently, solemnly, by the Virgin in the security offices.

When they lit the pyre, she had hoped – for a very short instant – that Sir Reginald was going to call upon his followers to join him in auto-immolation. Her next thought was that the Chapel was on the 13th floor and she was almost directly below it on the 12th. The fire soon burned the cables to the cameras in the Chapel; bzzt – and no pictures. An alarm went off on her desk, startling her – although the door was locked and no-one could possibly get in to attack her.

As they ran along the corridor to put as much distance as they could between themselves and the fire, she saw the angelic congregation covering their ears.

The Virgin flicked a couple of switches, turned off the alarm and saw relief upon the pixel-faces on the screens.

The boy and Harold were out of her view – an area of Hospital without cameras. She could do nothing to warn them of the danger they might be heading towards.

'We believe you,' said the husband. 'Just do something about it.'

But the baby was half gone. It looked like a little cartoon genie – the torso solid but the legs dissolving into a misty wisp.

Steele said, 'There's nothing we can do –'

'No!' said the husband. 'You must –'

'– *this* time,' Steele completed his sentence. 'Please try not to be hysterical.' He looked at the husband when he said this. 'Please try to keep control.'

'Calm down?' Mary shouted. 'How can I be calm?'

Steele turned his full attention on her. 'Look,' he said, 'we're all trying to deal with massive changes.' How he wished Gemma were here; she would do everything so much better. 'It seems as if the only way your son can have a separate existence, according to our current knowledge, is if the two of you are in completely distinct airspaces. In other words,' he said, 'we would need to keep you apart until we can work out exactly what's happening.'

The baby had dissolved up to the arms. What remained of the placenta was being wound in like wool into a ball.

Mary waved her hands frantically through the blood-red mist, trying to chop it, disperse it; vainly, of course.

'I can almost feel him,' she said.

'Is this the only way?' the husband asked.

'No,' said Steele, 'the other way – which I would recommend – would be to keep the baby inside you for a few more days. He will be safe there, and we will be able to work out what exactly is going on. Once we're finished with these other operations, which are in some ways more pressing, I'll be able to devote more of my time to you. The fact is, many of the people don't need doctors any more – their bodies are healing themselves. What is terrible and frightening for you and your baby is a miracle to them.'

Mary held her baby's head, looking into the dazed brown eyes. The little boy tried to cry but had no lungs from which to produce air. He was like a putto from a Renaissance ceiling; wingless, though. In another minute, the reabsorption would be complete – and labour would begin again.

'Can you excuse us for just a second?' Steele asked, motioning to Fermier and Zandra Pandit.

The husband gave a defeated nod, keeping his full attention on his wife.

Once in the next-door theatre, Fermier said, 'I think they're taking it pretty well, considering.' He almost laughed at the understatement.

Steele said, 'Look, I need to deal with other cases. I know it's not surgery, but I'm going to leave this couple in your hands. Take care of them as best you can.'

Zandra Pandit said she would. Reluctantly, Iqbal nodded his consent.

They went back in to explain to the couple, only to find them gone.

Upstairs, the numbers of those attending the vigil at the bedside of the Unconscious One grew and grew. Many came simply because they had heard of the man's continuing critical status and wanted to see it for themselves. (Someone still ill? *Never.*) There were frequent attempts to remove His drips or, more violently, to kick and punch Him into life – to prove He was shamming it, playing dead for the benefits (sex was mentioned) it would bring Him when He finally did awake or pretend to awake.

Those worshipping at His bedside were vigilant in His defence, standing permanent guard beside His monitors and His drip. Despite what had happened, chaoswise, in the rest of Hospital, care for Him by Angela Dixon continued (somehow) undisturbed. The only person allowed within two metres of Him, apart from the loyal disciple of the earliest minutes (Nikki Froth), was His devoted nurse. She was treated by all the crowd as a handmaiden of the Lord; her slightest ministrations – the adjustment of His catheter, the renewal of His drip-bag – were noted and venerated. Small cults of side-worship grew up to honour Angela the Angelic; her nurses' station became itself an object of holy awe and a site of pilgrimage.

Whenever one of His alarms went off, as they did with reasonable and gratifying frequency, a thrill of morbid anticipation passed through the crowd. This was the first time most of them had seen what might be called 'religion-in-action'. Even the Christians among them, Catholic and Protestant, who regularly attended mass and witnessed the transformation of bread into body and wine into blood – even *these* were greatly more impressed by the diamond-white droplets within the Unconscious One's drip and the golden-glowing contents of His catheter bag.

Equipped with little more than the vision of Him asleep and directions as to where He could be found (Bed 2, ICU, north-west wing, 21st floor), evangelists set out from thence to convert the barbarous hordes, who by this time were very barbarous indeed.

Among the messengers was Akliku Lij, burned at a wedding.

'They can't have got far,' said Iqbal Fermier. 'I'll go and find them.'

'It's their choice – perhaps this is what they want. Perhaps they've just gone somewhere quiet to be on their own – wait for things to calm down.'

'They were hysterical,' Fermier said.

'All right,' said Steele. 'I'll stay here and deal with whatever comes along. But come back if you can't find them.'

Out in the corridor, Fermier looked left and right but couldn't see the couple among the agonized queuers – there was quite a bit of ghost-mist here, at trolley level.

Going on instinct, he turned right, towards the

window. He ran, knowing that he should be much faster than them.

Many of the doors to one side and the other were locked. Those rooms which were open, he quickly looked into. Most were dull offices, gray plastic and blue-patterned carpet.

He was about to give up and head straight for the stairs at the end when he glanced a figure beside an open window holding a chair – or what remained of a chair.

The first thing that Iqbal noticed about this particular office was that it contained much less furniture than the others – and, secondly, that the window wasn't open but broken, triangles of glass jagging in from the edges.

Approaching, he saw that the figure was a man, Joseph Trick, Munchausen's by proxy, and that he wasn't James the husband and that he was very thin and completely naked.

All that remained of the chair was the backrest. Whilst muttering quietly to himself, the man was slowly pushing this out the window and drawing it back. 'Oh yes, oh yes,' he said, 'very good very good.'

As Iqbal watched, the backrest was cut off further and further up its length. The young surgeon hadn't encountered this phenomenon before.

After chucking what remained out of the window, where it immediately disappeared, the naked man picked up another chair ready to hand.

Iqbal, still unseen, moved to one side and observed as this chair, too, was sliced into nothingness – whatever passed the vertical plane of the window being sheered off in a neat, laser-accurate cut.

'Every single time,' said the naked man, chucking and chuckling, 'every single time.'

It was only now that Iqbal noticed that the man was lacking all the fingers on each hand; he was picking up the chairs, clumsily, with palms and thumbs.

'What?' asked Iqbal, in a loud voice. If he intended to startle the man, he certainly succeeded: the whole of the second chair tumbled out into the fog.

'I wasn't,' said Joseph Trick. 'I wasn't. I didn't. I didn't.'

'I saw you,' said Iqbal. 'I saw you deliberately destroying Hospital property.'

This was a test, and the man failed it: he was a patient, not Hospital staff. If he'd been Hospital staff, he would have said, 'So what – so what?' Instead, he said, 'I was testing,' twice. 'It was experimental – mental.'

'What did you learn?' Iqbal asked. He came closer.

'That what goes out never comes back,' Joseph Trick said and re-said.

'Furniture,' said Iqbal. 'But what about people? You haven't tried with people, have you?'

Trick held up his hands. Iqbal could see the nubs of missing fingers – neatly healed over with pink skin, as if amputated years before.

'Never comes back,' he stated, '*never* comes back.'

Iqbal said, 'Thank you,' and began to walk away. He had hoped the man wouldn't be so obvious as to make a lunge for him, but he was disappointed – disappointed and ready.

Iqbal stepped aside, letting the man run into the hard edge of a desk. He swore a couple of times, then turned to face Iqbal down.

The man appeared to be in his early forties, but his posture suggested that at midnight he had been a much older man: he held himself a little coweringly, keeping his hands up in front of his chest as if he were knitting. On noting this, Iqbal felt a sudden physical confidence; being clothed, too, gave him a psychological advantage.

'I am a surgeon,' said Iqbal, 'I am trying to help people – to reduce their pain. I will not let you stop me doing this. Please get out of my way.'

The man stood his ground.

'If you don't get out of my way,' said Iqbal, 'I will throw you out the window.' Then he added, 'Throw you out the bloody window.'

For a few seconds it looked as if the man were determined to carry on his experiments – experiments (this time) with a human subject other than himself. Iqbal thought about adding, 'You can stay here – I won't report you to anyone.' But he knew this would be a weakening of his position: there was no longer anyone to report anyone to.

Hand ducking to cover his bollocks, Joseph Trick stepped aside.

Iqbal walked past him, ready for a second surprise-surprise attack – which didn't come.

When he got to the door, Iqbal turned to look back. Joseph had returned to his position beside the window.

Everything in the room looked just as it had when Iqbal first entered, except the two chairs.

Iqbal had a realization: this man wouldn't be able to resist the lure of the window; he would put himself out of it, bit by bit. His fascination was such . . .

The Chapel fire had by now spread rapidly throughout the 13th floor and was sending thick grey smoke up the staircases at the north-east end of the building.

The ceilings were lapped by an incoming tide

of flame. Although the speckled greyish tiles were fire-resistant, the blaze still found enough matter for combustion in the carpets and furniture below.

Most of the staff and patients ran in the opposite direction as soon as they saw the blaze: cuts and amputations might no longer have terrified them, but incessant burning certainly did.

Those below the fire continued down the stairs, those above reversed their direction – another way out, that's what was needed.

Even the mere smell of the fire sent some wards into a panic greater than any before. Some put their heads out the window to see what was going on down below, and were decapitated; others tried to calm the most hysterical, and were rewarded with curses or injuries.

Sir Reginald and his followers were able to ascend without too much difficulty, the smoke at their heels sweeping them along.

'Onwards and upwards,' Sir Reginald cried.

Iqbal didn't know what it was that made him turn and look back the way he'd come. Perhaps he was being extra-cautious in case the naked man had armed himself and was hunting him. Just opposite Steele's operating theatre he saw – among the doubled-over queuers-up – a distant but familiar figure, the husband, his top half.

The wife wasn't in view – probably she was still below the level of the mist.

Iqbal didn't shout at them. Instead, as quickly and quietly as he could, he began to run towards them.

This wasn't easy – the half-length surgical boots he was wearing gave a micey squeak every time they touched the lino.

Iqbal stayed close to the wall, though he knew if either of them looked up they'd certainly spot him.

He covered most of the distance between them at a sprint, then slowed to a rapid trot. He needed to catch his breath so he would be ready to explain his plan to them. (He was adapting himself quite rapidly to the new medicine – far faster than some of his more senior colleagues.)

'Wait,' he said, loudly, when the couple were just about outside Steele's operating-theatre door.

'Bugger,' he heard the husband say.

'I think I can help you,' said Iqbal. 'I think there's a way we can separate you and your son.'

Finally, Gemma and Sarah (who had taken turns pleading for passage and carrying the very much growing baby – or child) emerged onto the 7th floor, north-east wing.

'Let's hope the mother's here,' said Sarah, 'after all that.'

Gemma had her own hopes: that she would soon see Steele again, and know that he was alright. He was a surgeon, committed, intense, and at this moment either Trauma or the Surgical Unit was where he was most likely to be – doing what he did best; or, one of the things he did best.

It was too much to expect, in the circumstances, that they would be able to spend any quality time together, one on one. But a glance could say so much – a glance that reassured by lingering, that confirmed by caressing.

'How is the little one?' she asked, to distract herself from her reveries.

Sarah pulled the altar cloth off the child-baby's head – which was now covered in flaxen hair.

'Thriving,' she said. 'She looks about four years old.'

'Let's just try her with the milk,' said Gemma.

She wasn't interested, not one bit; it ran down her chin and dripped into the purple.

They set off down the corridor, the child-baby's legs dangling, and the closer they got to the unit, the more chickens they came across; pecking at the floor, pecking at one another's eyes.

'He's dead, isn't he? They've taken him away because he's dead. I want to see the body!'

'Please come back to theatre,' Iqbal said; 'we can help you there.'

Mary moved astonishingly fast – her hand-feet and feet-feet managing a semi-canter. Behind her head, her tied-up hair swished like the tail of an angry pony.

'Where is my baby?' she cried, her voice juddering unevenly with the jog-trot motion.

It would have been more appropriate, Iqbal felt, had this conversation been impossible – had Mary lost the power of speech, only wailed and wailed; her pain was so overwhelmingly great. But though animal-looking, Mary was still deducing a verbal logic to follow: emotional, grotesque, vocal, eloquent. If he were her – but his mind couldn't go quite that far; if *he* were her, he'd be wailing or maybe just whimpering. Too far, she had been forced, too much she had been asked, and still she went on: what a nightmare!

It was the husband who had failed; he spoke only to gibber and his gibber went like this: 'Oh Christ oh fucking Christ oh.' Brains, obviously, didn't fix themselves, despite the new laws of medical physics.

Iqbal wanted to sedate him, as the best help that could be offered.

He started to usher them into theatre.

Just then, a middle-aged man walked up to Iqbal; beside him was a young boy with a small tree growing out of his stomach.

Othniel had made rapid progress up to the 13th floor. But, from that point on, smoke was a problem.

He continued climbing for a while, aware that the air in the ventilation shaft was becoming hotter.

On the 16th floor, the smoke became too much – he could hardly see the next rung to grab it.

He found the slatted cover more by luck than anything else. Climbing a little above it, he got himself at an angle where he could kick it out.

A couple of good blows and the job was done.

After this, he just had to grab hold of the edge and – twenty floors of fall telescoping beneath him – pull himself through.

The fire hadn't reached here yet, but he knew very soon it would.

Othniel moved fast – through the office door and along the corridor to the fire staircase.

It wasn't as crowded as downstairs. Panic and whiffs of smoke had already swept the majority up to higher floors.

Othniel joined the stragglers, outpacing all of them.

The tree stood out a couple of feet, bright green leaves upon its branches. 'We're looking for a large pair of clippers,' said the man with the boy. 'Or better still, an electric saw.'

'I will help you,' said Iqbal, realizing this was another of the unusual cases that Steele had asked him to look out for. 'I will help you just as soon as I can, but right now I have to deal with something else.' Perhaps he should keep this case secret. Let Steele deal with Mary and the baby. 'Please, can you just wait out here? You're not in pain, are you?'

'No,' said the boy.

'Only when someone touches it,' said the man.

'Stay here,' said Iqbal. 'I'll be back very soon.'

He went into theatre, where the midwife was doing her best to console the wannabe-parents. 'It's not your fault,' she said.

'Two babies,' Mary wept. 'I can't believe it. What's so wrong with me?'

'Nothing,' said Zandra Pandit. 'Nothing at all.'

'He said he could help us,' James said. 'He said he had a way.'

'Did you?' asked Steele. If Iqbal was messing with their hopes, that was unforgivable.

'Yes,' said Iqbal. 'I think so.' And he explained what he'd seen of the man putting furniture out the window – how his fingers had been cut off, how they hadn't regrown. 'So I reckon –' he said.

'We do the same with the umbilical cord,' said Steele.

'Exactly,' said Iqbal, annoyed at having his moment of glory whipped away. He looked around the room, gauging the reaction: Steele stood square, head down, thinking in a very physical way; Zandra focused her attention on Mary, but Iqbal could tell she was a little freaked out – professionally and squeamishly; James was looking towards Steele, wanting to know whether he felt it worth trying; Mary needed no such confirmation: 'Yes,' she said. 'Anything. Anything to end this. Do it now.'

Steele appeared not to hear her. He was calculating the risks, the benefits, and all in a context of unremitting oddness.

'We have no idea what would happen,' he said to Mary and James.

'I want it,' said Mary.

'We do,' said Iqbal. 'We know it'll be like –'

Steele silenced him with a glance.

'It is our job to look after you in the best way we can. My advice,' said Steele, 'would be to do what I suggested before – wait until the situation normalizes.'

'Wait like *this*?' Mary screamed. 'This isn't waiting. I can't just sit around.' Her back arched in anger, her face still upside-down.

'We give you full permission,' said James, now out of his gibber. 'We're not going to sue you afterwards. If you've got forms, we'll sign them. Do what Mary wants.'

Steele looked again at Iqbal, annoyed at having been put in this impossible situation. He was aware of how many other patients were waiting to be helped while they had this discussion of medical ethics.

'Are you sure?' he asked, one final time.

'Oh, thank you,' said Mary.

While Gemma asked at each operating theatre, Sarah stood with the heavy child-baby in the corridor outside.

'No,' said the first surgeon. 'We're just dealing with bloody livestock at the moment. No time for babies.'

'Have you seen Steele?' Gemma asked.

'Get out,' was the reply.

The second surgeon was slightly more polite but equally unhelpful.

In the third theatre, it was the patient who spoke up. 'Yes, yes,' said the man, Andy Woods. 'I saw a woman with a baby sticking half out of her. I'll never forget it.'

Andy Woods' abdomen was slit from side to side, although sealing up quite rapidly. He spoke as if thanking a nurse for a cup of tea.

'Where were they?'

'Down the corridor,' he said. 'I saw them as I came in. I think they were trying to escape.'

'Which direction?'

'Thataway, I believe,' he said, and pointed.

Gemma thanked him then went to tell Sarah the sort-of good news.

They continued trying the theatres, one by one. In the next, Gemma found someone who had seen Steele only a few minutes ago – he had gone in to see if they had any spare scalpels.

Just to be sure they didn't miss anything, Gemma checked behind the next four or five doors they came across.

'Fuck off, fuck off, fuck off,' sang out one surgeon, Duncan Roodrest.

At last they arrived at the operating theatre where Steele had been – and it was empty.

Coming outside, drenched in disappointment, Gemma noticed for the first time the man and boy standing there.

'Don't ask me again,' said Mary. 'Just get on with it.'

Steele had the scissors poised around the umbilical cord, at the exact midpoint. His plan was clear in his mind.

Iqbal stood at his elbow, wishing to see everything. He would make a very fine surgeon one day. If this worked, it was quite brilliant. Steele doubted there would be any credit to be taken, but he would make sure Iqbal had his rightful share.

They had smashed a hole in one of the windows, careful to use something they could afford to lose – and to send the glass outwards. And just as Iqbal had explained, everything that passed beyond the plane of the pane was sheared off with laser-like precision. Then, they moved a desk until it was close up to the opening; Steele wanted as little delay as possible between making the cut and disposing of the umbilicus.

'I'm only going to make a small excision,' he explained.

Mary threw her head back, whether in pain or frustration wasn't clear.

'Be careful,' said her husband.

To begin with, Steele followed the same procedure as before: opening the bulging belly, lifting the baby out, handing it to the midwife.

Then, quickly but with no panic, Steele took the specially designed scissors from the midwife and made the first snip – through the familiar chewy texture of the cord; a second snip followed, about three centimetres further along.

As he lifted the excised section away, he could already see wisps of pink moving towards both the mother and the baby end of the cord.

'There,' he said, and neatly tossed the mutual flesh through the grey hole.

He wasn't careful enough – the latex-covered fingertips of his right hand went out the window.

When Steele drew them back, there were two oval holes on the fingertips of the surgical gloves, forefinger and middlefinger; yanking the latex off, he saw that he had lost part of the pads on both fingers. They did not regrow.

'Are you alright?' asked the midwife.

'Fine,' he said. 'That was a bit stupid.'

Iqbal was incredibly relieved – it would have been beyond tragic for this brilliant surgeon to lose one iota of manual dexterity.

All stood around to watch the remaining ends of the umbilical cord.

'That way,' said Harold. 'They went into one of the rooms on the left – third door along, I think.'

'Thank you,' said Sarah.

The boy was in pain, Gemma couldn't help but see that. She handed the baby to Sarah, and then squatted down so she wasn't looming over him like all the other adults.

'What is it?' she asked.

He showed her the shoot, now over two feet long.

'Oh dear,' she said. 'That does look painful.'

'We're going to have it cut off,' said the man. 'The young doctor is coming back in a moment.'

Gemma wondered for an instant whether, to this man in his forties, Steele would count as young.

'What's your name?' she asked.

And as soon as she said these words, the boy knew that he'd heard her voice before – and a second later, he remembered exactly where: Trauma, with his eyes closed, so no wonder he hadn't recognized her by sight.

'My name is Gemma,' she said, as if in confirmation, 'Gemma Swallow.'

'I don't know,' the boy said, relieved to be able to answer her at last. 'I don't know my name.'

'Oh dear,' she said.

'And I'm Harold,' said Harold.

'I've never seen anything like that before,' Gemma said to the boy. 'You must be very special.'

'I'm very bad,' he said.

'No, you're not,' said Gemma.

'I did something wrong.'

'We all do things wrong.'

'It was very bad. I ran away.'

'What did you do?'

The boy whispered quietly in her ear. He told her what he could remember, which wasn't very much: stealing, running, hiding, eating.

'I understand,' Gemma whispered back. 'She will forgive you but you should say sorry.'

Gemma took his hand, gave it a squeeze. A strong memory of his mother overtook him: she was so nice.

'I'm going home,' said the boy. 'I'm going out the front door, and then home. I almost got there once already.'

He said this loudly, with pride.

Sarah, her attention suddenly focused, looked down at the boy. She thought about telling him he shouldn't leave Hospital until the tree was sorted out, but what was the point? 'Come on,' she said to Gemma.

'I have to go now,' said Gemma. 'We're looking for this baby's mother.'

'Third on the left,' said Harold.

All the floors of Hospital were made of reinforced concrete, so the fire couldn't burn its way through, but once it had started up the stairwells it soon found a way into the 14th, 15th and 16th floors.

Those above, desperate to get clear, ran down the corridor towards the western fire escapes. Eventually, the fire doors were breached and flames began to lick out.

Along the way the blaze picked up the bonus points of exploding oxygen cylinders, highly flammable chemicals in glass bottles, the odd storeroom full of aerosols, toilet rolls, blankets, stationery. Computers burned surprisingly well, once they had caught, wodges of grey-khaki plastic turning black and gloopy, flaming like a car tyre, sending out-up complex molecules.

Upon reaching these floors of fire, Akliku Lij paused – but only for a few seconds. This was a test of his faith. And so he started matter-of-factly off into the flames, walking on until the flesh burned from his bones and his bones charred into ash. He fell where he stopped, unable to force non-existent muscle any further, and, like his saviour upstairs, he lay where he fell – lay barbecued on the melted lino and acridly smoking carpets of the floors immediately above the Chapel. The fire which consumed him in such explicit agony gave the atoms of his body little chance to reassemble, although they were constantly trying. And so despite burning like so many martyrs once had, he did not suffer like the damned in Hell. Disintegrated in body, he was hot matter incapable of voluntary movement or systematic thought. It was not that he had ceased to exist – he had ceased to be conscious of not being conscious of his own existence. But as the fires around him finished consuming everything flammable, the temperature began to sag and then dwindle. It was then that Akliku Lij was *truly* agonized – for his body was able to resurrect enough to form nerves; but these nerves were left with nothing to do but feel scorching, intolerable pain. When his flesh reassembled itself into something capable of animation, a skeleton of braised browned bones raggedly adorned with pinkly roasted flesh, he tried to stand up, to continue. And when the floor was cool enough, he mounted to his knees – and when these did not give way, he stood erect. He fell, he fell again and again, but as often as he did just as often did he try to stand. And when finally finally he succeeded, he continued to walk, what had come back together of him, walk through the smoke that attacked his lungs, and across the floor which scorched his feet. And when he arrived in a place that was below the burning, and when his flesh had fully regrown, Akliku Lij rejoiced, for he knew he had passed through the flames and been sanctified. This was the message he then brought: *If you want to get to Heaven, first you must make a pilgrimage through Hell – that is and has always been the secret purpose of Hell.*

Nothing happened – no wisps of pink or red extended from the two ends of the umbilicus; the baby felt just as solid as it had a minute before.

Mary's belly was sealing and shrinking, almost as if she had never been pregnant; not even stretchmarks.

The midwife handed her the little boy.

'Thank you,' said Mary.

James perched on the edge of the desk and put his arms around them both; a family.

They stayed like that, heads all together, for a good couple of minutes.

The midwife, Steele and Iqbal stood back and enjoyed the sight – all vibrating with emotion; Steele patted Iqbal on the back.

'Good work,' he said, hoarsely.

Just then, there was a gentle knock at the door, and Gemma's head appeared.

'Can we come in?' she asked, overjoyed at seeing her beloved man.

The midwife looked to Steele.

'Yes,' he said.

The Walker family were still in a huddle as Gemma approached, carrying their long-limbed baby girl.

Fireman Bob Packard had been touring the building, as far as he was able, ever since he got wind of the fire.

There didn't seem to be anyone in any kind of authority – no Security Guards, phones down – so, he had decided to take charge.

From one frightened patient, Billy Stickers, he heard about how the fire had started – a wildly exaggerated account of a devil appearing in the Chapel and causing fire to leap out of his fingertips.

Another person, Dr Norman LeStrange, stopped to correct this: actually, someone had started a fire in the Chapel, and then the Devil had been seen to walk out of the flames.

However, LeStrange also gave Bob Packard a crucial piece of information: the sprinklers had come on, worked for a few moments then died.

The first patient, Billy Stickers, began to argue that this was because the Devil had magicked them off – but Packard had hold of the salient fact:

Without any water inside, and without access to the building from outside (he already knew about the fog), there was no way this fire could be fought.

Evacuation seemed the only option – evacuation as speedily as possible.

'Make your way downstairs in as orderly a manner as possible,' he said to the arguing two.

'What do you think we're doing?' LeStrange said.

Bob Packard set off, singlehanded, to clear the building.

Spanner and Case had got bored with descending the stairs, step by painfully slow step. On the 4th floor, they'd pushed their way through the fire door. They were in search of entertainment, and they found it: Neo-Natal.

When they first walked in, the two of them completely freaked out. Here, they found themselves surrounded by strange humanoid creatures; the newborns of midnight who had by now grown into mature-bodied but still empty-headed young men and women.

Spanner could tell they were ex-babies even though their bodies were those of sixteen- or seventeen-year-olds; becoming hairier by the minute.

Most of them were completely naked – all except those with a scrap of torn, outgrown babygro still stretched around their wrist or neck. A few were trapped in their plastic cots, but the majority had managed to unbalance these by kicking and flailing around with their arms in a random but increasingly weighty way. Ending up on the floor had gained them nothing, though: it would have taken them months and months to learn how to walk, and they didn't have months (and who would teach them, anyway?) – they didn't even have hours. They lay there, waving their hands in the weird, meaningless non-semaphore of babies. The stronger ones lifted their arms more vigorously yet, as if conducting invisible orchestras stuck to the ceiling, Philharmonic. They lay, flopping about in their own blood – cut and re-cut by splintered plastic; going off occasionally into spasms. The eyes in their heads worked, even in the dimness, but their brains had not developed any greater cognitive skills than would be possessed by a two- or three-hour-old infant. Their muscle tone wasn't bad, so they were able to flail with some force. But it was the sounds the teen-babies made which had the greatest variety; they were capable of the whole spooky gamut of the involuntary – could breath-blow, air-taste, lip-smack, nose-whistle, mouth-pop, whoop, hiccup, cough, root'n'toot, snore, snort, snaffle, snuffle, sniffle, truffle, gurgle, grunt, quack, splutter, trickle, gibber, squeak, howl, sneeze-wheeze, rattle, honk.

'Would you look at these cunts?' said Case.

'Get up!' said Spanner, more disconcerted than ever in his life before. 'Get up, you stupid fucking idiots.'

Of course, the grownbabies did not react, apart from a slight shiver at the loud sound.

Spanner and Case looked around the room, and saw (and heard) more of what was going on: obeying their blind desire to suckle, the babies had attached themselves to one another in various ways – some obscene, though the term no longer had any meaning; most, however, had found some body part to suck. Groups of three or four had formed themselves into steady-state arrangements, her toe in his mouth, his fingers in his, his chin in her mouth, her nipple in his. Two adolescent female babies, bodies pointing in opposite directions, had their wide mouths around one another's big toes.

Spanner went up to one of the solo suckers and put his thumb in their mouth. It was immediately and vigorously clamped onto; saliva streamed past it on either side, down the throat; weed in riverwater.

When he tried to pull his thumb out, Spanner felt teeth gripping bone. It was at this point that he decided against a session of free, unconscious fellatio.

Instead, he arranged a male couple so they were in the 69 position – teasing inert cocks into erections; inserting. This made Case laugh, a lot.

Then Spanner went looking for more things to put in the babies' mouths.

Case, too, left the room.

Iqbal came towards them down the corridor. 'In here,' he said.

'What we really need,' Harold explained, 'is something to knock him out with while we pull this thing out of his stomach.'

They entered the empty operating theatre.

'Wait here,' said Iqbal, and went to gather some equipment from one of the storerooms.

The treetrunk hadn't looked too thick or too tough. He considered using bone shears. But it was wood, not bone. An amputation saw No. 10-a ought to do the job.

Even though it was dark, he managed to find one – shaped like a traditional hacksaw: straight steel blade held in tension by a rigid oblong frame.

The young surgeon turned back towards another instance of the unprecedented.

Mary was overjoyed – she cried and cried.

It didn't matter to her that her baby girl was so much bigger than her baby boy.

The twins, when laid alongside one another, seemed to be about six years apart, in terms of development.

'But they're alive,' she said, over and over again.

'And they're both fine,' said midwife Zandra Pandit, who had carefully checked.

James felt embarrassed by his own restraint. He, too, was crying, but he didn't feel that was enough; there was something else he should be doing, something more. But it wasn't handing out cigars and being masculine, it was something animal: whooping.

'Congratulations,' said Sarah.

Steele and Gemma stood off to one side, together.

'Well done,' she said.

'It was Iqbal Fermier, mostly. I'm very impressed with him.'

Gemma knew she had hoped for too much. Steele wasn't going to embrace her again – not here, not in front of everyone. (Down in Pathology it had been her that had run to him.) But even so, his manner was distressingly offhand. Didn't he care at all? Perhaps it was the bizarreness of what he had just witnessed. His noble face showed his agile mind to be elsewhere. This was one of the things she most admired about him: his ability to concentrate absolutely upon whatever he was doing. In some ways, it left him vulnerable – to scrutiny, to comment, to mockery. Yet it pained her to feel that he was capable of ignoring her. His wasn't the manner of a man in love; if he had felt for her what she did for him, he couldn't stand there so coldly.

'I wish –' he said, but went no further. 'I would like –'

His eyes were upon James Walker, taking his newborn son in his arms for the first time.

'Yes,' said Gemma, all her body tingly with expectation.

'I have to get back to work,' Steele said, abruptly. 'There are people who need my help.'

'Of course,' she said. How could she think of keeping him from them? Their need, if not greater, was far more pressing.

'What will you do now?' he asked, his voice very close.

'I don't think we can get back up to Trauma. The emergency lift fell down the shaft – just after we'd stepped out of it.' She laughed it off.

All of a sudden, she felt him take her gently but firmly by the arms – and, before she knew it, she was gazing up into his eggshell-blue eyes.

'You are an angel,' he said, 'truly. But you must look after yourself. I couldn't bear it –'

She had one final look at his face, radiant and strong, before he tore himself away.

'I'm sorry,' he said, over his shoulder.

Gemma watched him slam out the door. She *knew*.

Back in theatre, the boy was getting agitated.

'You'll be fine in a moment,' said Harold. 'We'll sort you out. You won't feel a thing. A whiff or two of laughing gas and you'll be laughing.'

Iqbal returned, and the boy looked straight at the hacksaw with its serrated blade – rather than scaring him, the sight helped him gain courage: it looked so mercilessly efficient; there was no way the appletree could resist the strong science and design of it.

The boy put his hands on either side of his tummy button, which had now been forced open to a diameter of about three centimetres. At his back he felt the tickle of the roots stirring in the air from the door.

'Right,' said Iqbal, 'let's see what we can do here.'

It was at this moment that Steele re-entered the OT. He had been examining his fingertips, to check that he'd still got his full sense of touch.

'What's this?' he asked.

Iqbal explained.

'Alright then,' said Steele, efficiently. 'You're the surgeon. You do what you think is right. I'll go and see if anyone needs relieving.'

He was gone before Iqbal could thank him. The young surgeon knew that he'd earned Steele's professional respect; nothing could be more important to him, and his vision went slightly blurry with the thought.

'Okay,' he said, to calm himself as much as anything.

With gentle hands he touched the boy's abdomen. He interlaced his forefingers and prodded. 'Tell me if it hurts,' he said.

When he approached within a few centimetres of the treetrunk, it hurt.

'Now could you turn on your side?'

It was more comfortable for the boy like this.

'I'm just going to try . . .'

Iqbal touched the roots, stroked them, and it was an almost entirely pleasant sensation. However, it still disturbed the boy to feel through nerve endings that weren't officially part of his body. The sensation wasn't unlike having a hand run through his hair – not unlike that, but more like running his own fingers through someone else's hair; it was different to when the Virgin had done it.

'Right-oh,' said Iqbal. 'We will have to remove this. You want me to, don't you?'

'Yes,' said Harold, 'and sharpish – before it grows too much more.'

The boy wasn't certain. Perhaps the tree was his punishment. But it would be far easier to get home without the burden and freakishness of it.

'Then we'll just have you take a few puffs of this. No need to count to ten or anything like that. Just relax – it'll soon make you sleepy.'

There was a mask of gray rubber which covered the boy's mouth and nose completely. He heard a hissing and knew he wanted this to happen – the touch of Iqbal's hands made him trustworthy. The boy could feel or thought he could feel that the young man was a good surgeon. He was less sure about Harold, though he had done nothing so far but try to help him.

Iqbal was relieved to see the boy's eyelids flutter shut. It didn't worry him, doing his own anaesthetics – he had seen it done enough times, and there was no chance this patient wouldn't come back up.

He lifted the boy's eyelids and checked his pupils – they were fully dilated and did not contract with exposure to his penlight. Good, he thought. This would be a difficult one – unprecedented in all the literature; but a little more interesting than just another chicken.

The young surgeon explained his plan to Harold, who was to assist by holding the trunk tight.

'Let's get to it,' said Harold.

Iqbal asked, 'Ready?' and then, almost before he'd got an answer, which was a nod, began vigorously to saw.

But the boy was awake.

The anaesthetic had distanced him from himself but not separated him completely; no velvet curtain was drawn across, only gauze. In fact, it seemed to the boy as if he were able to step out of himself, take a couple of paces to one side and watch what was being done.

He had heard about this: how people having operations had out-of-body experiences. Most of them said they rose up to the ceiling and looked down as the surgeons saved their lives. (Of course, those whose lives weren't saved never said anything.)

The boy was very keen to try flying – he wanted his point of view to be the classic whirly-from-above one. But to his disappointment he found he was resolutely floor-bound.

He tried jumping; he tried closing his eyes and concentrating on lightness, floatiness – neither tactic worked. So then he did the best he could: standing in between Iqbal and Harold.

The hacksaw was now halfway through the trunk – which was only about three times as wide as the blade.

So far, it had gone through the appletreetrunk without unnatural difficulty.

The wood puffed up in soft splinters around the edges – it was young, moist with sap.

The boy, to all appearances, had been completely knocked out by that dose of anaesthetic; from him, there came no murmur or movement.

But it was now that the problems began, for the wood behind the blade – the wood it had already severed – began to regrow.

Iqbal tried to speed up and after a minute brought the saw out the other side – only to stand and watch helpless as the second half of the incision closed up almost instantly; like a cut made in custard, not set.

When the healing had finished, no scar was left to show where the blade had passed through. It was a real sawing-the-lady-in-half trick, only the joining back together preceded any showing off of the separation.

The hacksaw was now stuck, with the trunk running through the oblong space between blade and frame.

Harold had been watching closely. 'Dammit,' he said. 'I thought that might happen. Give it another go – see if you can't separate it proper.'

When the first attempt failed, the boy was annoyed but also in a strange way relieved.

His first instinct had been right: the only way to solve this problem and cure himself had to be to get back home to his mother. A simple hacksaw was never going to be enough; he needed to make up for what he'd done wrong. The sensation of this was all around him, constantly; it altered the colours of the world, making them darker. Until he had said sorry, everywhere was a guilty place.

Yet he was proud of the tree – proud of the agony its growing caused him.

Everyone else in Hospital was different from him. He didn't feel freakish, he felt superior.

Iqbal first of all had to get the hacksaw back in position. To do this, he either had to detach the blade or pull the whole thing over and round the foliage.

Opting for the latter as faster and more direct, Iqbal found the side branches surprisingly resistant: they bent back but not far enough.

'Here, let me give you a hand,' said Harold, and started snapping them off.

He pulled a few branches away, throwing them – fresh and pliable – on the tiled floor behind him.

The saw was halfway free, and the remaining branches bent back easily enough – but Iqbal and Harold slowed down, distracted by the sight of the greeny-brown snakes reaching out from the tree to its severed branches, and vice versa. 'It's impossible,' said Iqbal, wrenching the hacksaw finally free. 'I'll just –'

'Let me have a go,' said Harold.

Iqbal handed him the saw, feeling defeated; annoyed, too. He was trying to work out the meaning of it all. Of course, he had seen other people wounding themselves, and those wounds healing up. That the boy's branches were behaving the same way was very intriguing; it suggested that the tree was an integral part of his body. If that were the case, all the older man's efforts, which turned out to be magnificent, were for nothing. Right now, he was going at it in a controlled almost-frenzy. The blade zipped back and forth twice as fast as when Iqbal, with all his caution of medico-surgical training, had been using it.

Harold got through in a very few seconds, triumphantly pulling the tree away from the boy and holding it above his head.

Trails of regrowth and reattachment began to ribbon out almost immediately.

The boy had watched Harold's more vigorous attempt to remove the appletree with greater anxiety – and there was a moment's real panic as the two halves separated.

He felt nothing physical, but the psychic pain of detachment and loss was immense.

And then the green snakes started to form and slither towards one another. Yes! thought the boy. 'I have to escape. They can't heal me.'

He made the decision to wake up, knowing he would have to fake ignorance: telling the truth would be too complicated.

Harold was disgusted at himself – the tree felt as if it were going floppy in his hands, or insubstantial, smoky. Out of pure annoyance, he pushed open the operating theatre's swing doors and chucked the rapidly wilting greenery into the corridor.

But the snake of brown and green made its way unnervingly through the gap at the bottom of the door.

At the same time, the boy began to show signs of waking up; he was burbling, and his hands were twitching – grabbing and relaxing, grabbing and relaxing.

'Did it work?' he mumbled, after a few moments more. If he had wanted to, he could have spoken more clearly but mumbling was more fitting to the moment he was trying to mimic.

'You wake up properly, Captain,' said Harold. 'Then we'll tell you all about it.' He wasn't looking forward to disappointing the lad; telling him how they'd let him down.

'It didn't, did it?' asked the boy, opening his eyes and at the same time grabbing for the appletreetrunk.

'No,' said Iqbal. 'I'm afraid that this time it didn't. But there's a way we can try again. It worked with –'

'No,' said the boy, now almost fully awake. 'It won't work. I need to get home – that's the only place they can help me.'

'I'm sure if we could just throw it out the window before it had a chance to –'

'No,' said the boy. 'I have to get to the front door. I'm going to the front door. If you don't want to help me, I will have to go on my own.'

But Iqbal, after his first success, wasn't to be thwarted. He grabbed a handful of leaves from the floor and ran out of the theatre.

Harold helped the boy off the bench; together they ran after Iqbal – who made it to Joseph Trick's smashed window before they could catch up. Joseph Trick was nowhere to be seen.

'Just watch,' Iqbal said, and threw the leaves out into the fog.

Again, the boy felt nothing. He had expected agony.

Then Iqbal said, 'My God, look –' For traces of snakelike green were coming back through the window towards the appletree. 'That's,' said Iqbal, 'that's impossible.'

The stolen leaves re-formed upon the branches of the boy's stomach; mended, grown.

'I'm sorry,' said Iqbal.

'We should go,' said the boy.

'I thought I could help.'

'I know,' said the boy. 'Don't worry about it. Go and help someone else.'

He and Harold walked out of the office.

Iqbal took only a minute before he returned, ashamed, to his operating theatre.

Gemma and Sarah stood in the corridor, looking at one another with some puzzlement: Sarah had seen Gemma's embrace with Steele, and thought that she understood; Gemma had just heard Sarah say she was going looking for Patricia.

'Why?' Gemma asked.

'She might be in danger.'

She might *be* a danger, thought Gemma. 'But she's

one of *them*, isn't she?' Gemma said. 'I mean, she was there when the baby was –'

'I know,' said Sarah. 'I need to ask her why. I need to find a reason.'

'You'd be more use down in A&E. That's where I'm going.'

'You're not staying here with Steele? I'm sure he'd want you to.'

'He doesn't,' said Gemma, with absolute certainty. 'He wants to be able to work undisturbed.'

Sarah smiled, and Gemma felt some of her old dislike returning. 'I never knew you *disturbed* him,' Sarah said, sarcastically.

'Why are you being like this?' Gemma asked. 'After all we've been through?'

'I'm sorry,' said Sarah, and seemed to become smaller as she retreated. 'I'm just jealous – I love Patricia so much, and it's so doomed.'

Gemma took a moment.

'*I* never knew *that*,' she said, when she felt herself capable of saying anything; astonished. How wrong she had been – all her jealousy of Sarah and Steele! How misdirected!

'I kept it pretty well hidden – for obvious reasons.'

'Yes,' said Gemma.

'I know she's not a good person,' said Sarah. 'That's probably why I find her so irresistible. I always did go for total bitches.'

A scream came, as if to underline this, from one of the patients being operated upon.

'It might be dangerous,' said Gemma, making her last attempt to dissuade Sarah.

'I don't care,' was the reply. 'I really don't care.'

With a terse hug, the two women parted.

*

Akliku Lij, who had walked through fire to bring the good news to the lower floors, arrived where the High Priest was.

Delighted by the prospect of an already-formed audience, and ignoring their somewhat unusual attire, he began to speak. He told them, without preamble, that the Messiah was alive and comatose on the 21st floor. The reaction, wow, was all he could have hoped for: the strangely dressed men and women were astonished. Alive? Really? His revelation had struck them like a lightning bolt. They were electrified.

Upon Sir Reginald's asking for a little more practical information, he described in some detail where the Messiah could be found.

'Thank you,' said the High Priest, and ordered his followers to throw Akliku Lij the evangelist out the nearest window.

This challenge to his authority – and through him to the authority of his proved master, Satan – was too much for Sir Reginald; opposition, even completely passive, was a threat.

Cropper and PC Dixon grabbed the evangelist's arms. Akliku Lij, feet first, did not struggle: for him, martyrdom was exquisite reward.

The High Priest gathered together as many of his people as he could and began to climb towards the ICU.

From what he learned upon the way, by inquiry and torture, there had already been several attempts to wake the man but he remained resolutely and some said divinely comatose. These believers, too, were defenestrated.

*

The singing was what he heard first: hymns from above.

When he reached the 21st floor, Othniel looked into the ICU and saw the calmest sight he'd seen since coming on shift.

The long room was crepuscular at the best of times; usually, there were only the lamps pointed to the wall and a little light from the monitors. Now, though, a dozen candles had been found to add to the seductive celestial atmosphere; ghost-mist mother-of-pearl glow.

Over a hundred people were sitting in neatly arranged circles round the bed of the very man he'd brought up here with Sarah Felt.

Othniel scratched his head. He wanted to continue up to the roof, but whatever this was, it needed to be understood.

He found some space for himself, beside the door, and waited to see if anything would happen.

With the fire staircases so overcrowded, Gemma went looking for an alternative route to A&E.

Following a couple of post-op patients, who seemed to know where they were going, she soon came to the trees – which seemed as good a way as any, so she began climbing down.

The maternity ward was deserted, all midwives, mothers and babies gone, but Children's Cancer was a total riot. Those who had been dying a couple of hours before were now violating bedtime in the most flagrant ways their undeveloped minds in adolescent bodies could think of.

Chemo was, of course, the ringleader – encouraging here, bullying there.

Earlier pillowfights had become fistfights which in turn had become experiments in cartoon physics and cartoon violence.

When Gemma climbed down into the room, she saw Ahmed throw open the fire door just as Chemo bent down to pick up a toy he'd pretend-dropped: slam, and his skull smashed – chortle chortle.

Further along the ward, a team of both boys and girls had pushed a line of beds close together, so they could bounce-bounce-bounce along them until – crunch – they hit the wall. Points were being vocally awarded for style and broken bones.

What made the sight even more grotesque was that the children didn't seem to have noticed that their bodies had lengthened and grown hairier; their shrieks of joy had lost their shrillness, and their fluty speaking voices had begun, now and again, to honk or bray.

Gemma knew there was no way she could restore order here, so she didn't even make the attempt – just kept going from branch to branch until she passed down out of sight.

The next floor would be Neo-Natal.

'Can you still walk?' Harold asked the boy when they got out into the corridor.

'Of course I can,' the boy said. 'It's not growing all *that* fast. I'll be fine. I can get to the door by myself if you want to go off and do something else.'

'No, I'll come with you,' replied Harold. 'But if I were you I'd –'

'You're not.'

'I'd find somewhere to sit tight till help comes.'

'Help isn't coming. This is the end. I need to see my mother again, before it's all over. I have to tell her I'm sorry for stealing and for running away. I want to know that she forgives me. I was so horrible to her – and now she will never know that I'm not horrible like that. I tried to be good but I was never good enough. She didn't notice when I did good things – it was only right after I'd done something bad that she'd catch me and think that that's what I was like. I wish she'd understood how hard I tried to be good.'

'I'm sure she does,' said Harold, who had been an uncle but never a father. This was one of the kinds of conversation, truth to tell, he'd been rather glad he had avoided. It seemed particularly uncanny coming from the mouth of what looked like a boy of eleven, especially one with a leafy green tree with tiny white and pink flowers appearing upon it growing out his front. 'We'll get you home to her,' he said. 'Don't you worry about that.'

The boy was determined that this would be the last time he gave any sign of weakness. 'Where shall we go next?' he asked.

'Back to the trees, I'd say.'

All this time the Virgin had been keeping watch over Sir Reginald – terrified that he might come back and try some new method of intercourse with her, or just have her carried to the nearest window and vengefully chucked out.

And now that he was heading away from her, she felt relieved (again) but also terrified. She had seen exactly what he and his followers were capable of; she also, by contrast, had observed the gentle development of events in the ICU.

If she could have been magically transported anywhere else in Hospital, that is where she would have chosen. The figure of the Comatose One drew her, just as it had so many.

Watching Sir Reginald's determined climb, she at first assumed he was merely heading away from the fire he'd started – perhaps intending to go out on the roof.

But as he ascended further and further, and got closer and closer to the ICU, she began to fear that he would happen upon that peaceful scene and destroy it, just as he had everything else; everything but her hymen.

The Virgin had watched the conversation with the evangelist Akliku Lij, but hadn't worked out its content.

Sir Reginald had continued to look wrathful, even after his orders were obeyed and the blissful-looking young man was defenestrated. And so the Virgin was in no doubt that, given the opportunity to do so, Sir Reginald would take his anger out upon the innocently sitting and watching crowd.

On another screen, the Virgin could see smoke starting to flow down the corridor towards the security offices, and behind it came fire.

Suck, suck, suck, sounded in the air.

Spanner had first of all found a mop, and given the handle end to one of the female grownbabies; it was a kindness, almost, to see her mouth clamp round it and her cheeks start pumping. He had wanted to show Case, but the stupid fucker wasn't around.

Next, from a nearby bathroom, he had fetched a soap dispenser – and one unlucky male babe was soon foaming pink choke-bubbles.

The adolescent gagged but kept sucking. They

were so stupid, Spanner thought; they would take anything.

Anything?

Then he went further afield, and found some industrial-strength bleach in a cleaning cupboard. He had taken a fancy to the pinky-mouth, and so chose him again for this next experiment.

Spanner cradled the young man's head in his lap, and got ready to pour the corrosive liquid down his throat.

'No,' said someone, 'you will not do that – you will stop.'

The shock of it made Spanner jump, spilling a splosh on the lino. His first thought was that one of the grownbabies had suddenly learned to talk.

'Put it down,' said the voice, female, young, sweet.

Spanner looked around through the gloom. A few feet away he saw the outline of a nurse, not Rubber.

The High Priest led his diabolic followers up the last few flights of stairs.

He had sent one of the patients, Holgate Washburn, ahead to check the lie of the land. It sounded, from the breathless young man's report, that given the element of surprise, they should be able to invade the Intensive Care Unit without encountering particularly fierce resistance. Sir Reginald was delighted: for the third time in a day he was getting the chance to desecrate a temple – although this latter would be a sadly improvised little one..

Firstly, it was necessary as much as possible to arm his followers; this would enhance yet further their advantage. Sir Reginald, when they reached the 19th floor, ordered them to turn aside – emerging out of the increasingly smoke-filled stairwell and into one of the overflow Geriatrics wards.

That, at least, was what it had been before; but of all the cured and re-energized and de-aged of Hospital, the formerly old had dealt worst with the transition. Despite the changes to their bodies, many still lay upon their beds and talked querulously or bitterly or bewilderedly to those on left and right about the inadequacy of Hospital, the cruelty of the nurses, the neglect of relatives, the pains they no longer suffered except in wishful imagination, and about events in the world outside. They pressed their buzzers, and were angered when no-one came to answer their call.

It would be a kindness, thought Sir Reginald, to throw all these bewildered middle-aged creatures out into the fog – a kindness and a complete waste of time.

Instead, the High Priest ordered his troops of Satan to spread out in search of anything that could be used as a weapon. Although no permanent injury could be inflicted, if they did enough temporary damage they would be able to achieve the hour's main objective, which was fighting their way through to the bedside of the unconscious messiah.

The children of darkness, as he liked to think of them, returned a few minutes later, armed with aluminium crutches, bedheads, lamp bases, the metal bits torn off the tops of clipboards (quite effective as an improvised dagger), syringes, the jagged necks of shattered flower vases, the femur from a plastic demonstration skeleton. PC Dixon had a nightstick. Pollard was still proudly brandishing his air-pistol.

Realizing morale was more important than ever, Sir Reginald praised their foraging skills (Hospital had sent him on many teambuilding courses, over the years) – then he laid out his evil plan.

The young man with the grownbaby in his lap had not moved, but he had not poured the liquid – whatever it was – down the poor thing's throat.

'What do you think you're doing?' Gemma said.

'Nothing,' he replied.

'Yes, you are,' said Gemma. 'You're intending to hurt that person.'

'They can't fucking *be* hurt,' he said. 'They mend as soon as you do anything to them.'

'Then you might as well not do it,' said Gemma, with perfect logic. 'Unless you're doing it simply to be cruel.'

He thought about this for a couple of moments. 'I suppose I am,' he said. 'Now, fuck off.'

Gemma stepped bravely forwards. 'Give me the bottle,' she said.

Suddenly, a strong arm went around her throat and she felt her feet lifting from the floor.

'What took you so fucking long?' said the young man.

'Sorry,' said a rough voice just behind her ear. 'I was just – you know . . .'

'You were, were you?' said the young man. 'You filthy sod.'

Gemma was choking, and because of this she couldn't speak; she needed to say that she was choking.

'What d'you want me to do with her?' asked the rough voice.

'You'll put her down immediately, that's what.'

It was another voice, from over by the base of the tree; Gemma couldn't see who was speaking.

'You'll put her down or you'll regret it.'

*

The Virgin knew she no longer had any choice: smoke was starting to seep under the door of the security offices.

And perhaps it was her heart, filling her body with adrenalized blood, or perhaps the room really *was* heating up.

One by one she had lost her eyes – lost the precious sight afforded her by the CCTV cameras.

Those in the north-west fire stairs were mostly long gone, either cloaked in smoke or burned to bits.

The last time she'd seen the boy and Harold, they had started climbing down the trees on the 7th floor; she could distantly assist them no longer.

But it was Sir Reginald who, of course, she had been watching most closely. And there now seemed little doubt what he was up to: the Satanists were arming themselves for an attack on those she thought of as the Holy Ones.

If she hadn't been able to do anything about it, this would have been merely tragic. However, in the past couple of minutes, what with the fire clearing so many floors, and people fleeing to the opposite end of the building, one of the regular lifts seemed to have started working again.

At least, from what she could see inside it, the numbers above the door kept changing as one or two brave or foolhardy souls used it to travel down to the ground floor.

But the person getting into it now, a long-haired blonde, was heading in the opposite direction: her slender fingers pressed the button for Trauma.

The attack by Sir Reginald wasn't an unpreventable tragedy – if she hurried, she might be able to warn the Holy Ones.

Perhaps if the fire hadn't been forcing her out of the room, she would have stayed there indefinitely; and perhaps if she hadn't seen the lift, she would have gone down instead of up. But from somewhere she found the bravery to confront the man she had been hiding from for so long.

Grabbing a piece of acrylic cloth to cover her mouth, the Virgin pulled open the door and sprinted off towards the lifts.

She might just make it.

The boy stood beside Harold, trying to make himself look as big as possible.

'What the fuck's that?' said the young man with the bottle in his hand: Spanner.

'I can't see,' said the ogre-looking man, his arm round Gemma Swallow's neck: Case. 'But it looks to me like he's got a fucking tree sticking out of him.'

Spanner laughed, harshly.

'A tree,' he said. 'How'd that get in there?'

'It's not him you've got to be worrying about,' said Harold. 'Put the nurse down. Now.'

'I'll take care of this,' said Spanner, and put the bottle on the floor.

He adopted a vaguely martial arts kind of stance, and approached Harold with crabwise feet.

Harold did not move.

Spanner aimed a couple of power-punches at Harold's head, which had moved by the time they arrived.

Disconcerted, Spanner retreated – not far enough.

Without hesitation but also without hurry, Harold took hold of the hand that was stretched out towards him, twisted it slightly one way, then a little more the other; Spanner gave a yelp. Harold moved smoothly forwards and grasped Spanner's wrist in both hands.

After that, things happened too fast for the boy to see.

In less than a second, Harold had Spanner on the floor, face down, half nelson, begging to be let go.

Case dropped Gemma and rushed forwards, attacking.

But the newly youthful Harold was too fast for him: he jinked to the side, and Case tripped stupidly over Spanner's outstretched body.

'Come on,' Harold said to the others. 'Muck in.'

The boy ran forwards and sat down on Spanner's back; Gemma came to join him, adding her weight.

Meanwhile, Harold had got hold of Case's right leg and twisted it until he was clawing at the floor and saying no, no, no.

'I will stop hurting you,' said Harold, 'if you stop wriggling around.'

Case went instantly still; Harold relaxed. 'Well,' he said, 'here we are – and things are a little different now, aren't they?'

'Let us go, you bastard,' said Spanner.

'Perhaps,' Harold said. 'What do you think?'

The boy realized he was the one being spoken to.

'We'll have to let them go, eventually,' he said.

'I was thinking more of tying them up and dumping them somewhere,' said Harold. 'In a cupboard.'

'We won't do anything,' said Spanner. 'We were just having fun.'

'It didn't feel like fun, him strangling me,' said Gemma. 'And it certainly wasn't going to be fun for that one over there.'

Pinky-mouth continued to flap around, ignorant of the battle he'd caused.

'That was him,' said Case, 'that wasn't me.'

'What you were doing was worse,' said Gemma, 'from the sound of it.'

'I think we should let them go,' said the boy. 'I don't want to waste any more time.'

'Fine,' said Harold, and dropped Case's foot. 'Now, scarper.'

Gemma and the boy got up, allowing Spanner to do so, too.

He and Case looked angrily at Harold but stalked off without having another go.

'Thank you,' said Gemma. 'I was in real trouble.'

'No problem,' said Harold. 'But I think you should probably come with us, now.'

'No,' she said, 'I'm going to stay here, and make these . . .' She didn't have the right words. 'I'm going to make them as comfortable as possible.'

'Suit yourself,' said Harold.

'Are you sure?' asked the boy.

'Yes,' said Gemma.

'Right-oh,' said Harold. 'I think the stairs are this way.'

Sarah Felt and the Virgin had never previously met; but under the circumstances, that didn't seem to matter.

Sarah was surprised when the lift stopped on the 12th floor – what if it was suddenly crowded with zombie-people, like before?

So when the Virgin, gasping, choking, staggered in, Sarah was immediately sympathetic.

But until she had pressed the button for the 21st floor, the Virgin wouldn't hear a thing.

'I said, "Are you alright?" '

'Yes,' said the Virgin, not wishing to go into all the ways she wasn't.

The fire had been travelling faster than she thought possible – even sprinting down the corridor she had almost been caught by it.

She took a few more deep breaths, then asked: 'Where are *you* going?'

'There's someone I have to see,' Sarah replied.

'It must be important,' said the Virgin.

'It is,' Sarah said, and then asked, 'Where are you going?'

The Virgin briefly described the situation: Satanists, Holy Ones, ambush. As she did so, she saw the floor change from 20 to 21. Almost there.

'And so I have to stop them,' the Virgin said.

'How do you know this?' Sarah asked.

'I was in the room with the security cameras. I saw it.'

'Was Patricia Parish with them?'

The Virgin paused, wondering whether or not to say what eventually came out. 'Of course she was. She's one of the worst of them.'

'No,' said Sarah. 'I don't believe it.'

'She's the High Priestess,' the Virgin said. 'After Sir Reginald, she's their leader.'

'Don't say that,' Sarah sobbed.

'I'm sorry,' said the Virgin. 'I'm sorry, but it's true.'

'They forced her,' Sarah said. 'She couldn't have.'

The Virgin looked Sarah straight in the eye. 'She did,' she said. 'I saw. I was in the room.'

But they were about to arrive on the floor of the ICU. There was no more time for discussion or comfort.

The Virgin got ready to run.

There had been warnings, earlier – some of the patients had come in smelling of smoke and talking of flames; but it was only once the fire came within sight of the Surgical Unit that Steele was forced to acknowledge its existence. Until then, he had been entirely focused upon his work.

Iqbal came in to see him. 'We can't stay any longer,' he said.

'Just one more,' replied Steele.

'No,' said Iqbal. 'We have to go *now*.'

Steele downed tools, his trusty CutmeisterPro-9 high-gloss blade, and thanked Nurse Wilson, who was about to leave.

'This way,' said Iqbal.

Steele went after him – shocked, even despite the young man's urgency, by the white-hot ferocity of the blaze at the far end of the corridor.

They ran, accompanied by many fleeing others – ran until they came to the trees.

Here, they looked up, saw fire above them, too; so began to descend, as fast as possible – jumping or climbing, helping the timid.

This only took them down three floors, into Neo-Natal.

'Steele,' said Gemma, who had looked up from one of her unfortunate charges to see the very figure she had tenderly been imagining.

'What are you doing here?' he asked. 'I thought you were going to A&E.'

With a hands-wide-fingers-spread gesture, Gemma indicated the grownbabies and their needs.

'You can't stay here,' said Steele. 'The building's on fire.'

'I don't want to abandon them.'

'You have to,' he said. 'You have to try and save yourself.'

Gemma hesitated.

Steele went to her. 'I'm not leaving you here,' he said. 'You're coming with me whether you like it or not.'

Faced with a will so much more powerful than her own, Gemma capitulated.

'Where are we going?' she asked.

'Down,' said Steele. 'Any way we can.'

The Virgin dashed down the corridor towards the ICU, Sarah a few paces behind her – but just before they got there, their path was blocked: where trees had plunged through from Sir Reginald's offices, huge holes had been left in the floor.

Leaning over to look down, the Virgin could see five or six storeys – then the orange of flames.

'We have to get across,' she said, and pointed to where the corridor continued.

There was nothing they could walk on – a yawning chasm – except, perhaps, part of the metal grid which had been buried in the concrete. But that wasn't below their feet, that was dangling above their heads.

Yet when the Virgin jumped up and took hold of it, she found her weight easily supported.

They could monkey-swing across the gap.

The Virgin wasted no time in preparation, but kicked her feet out in front of her to get her momentum up.

From one square of the grid to the next, like on a climbing-frame in a park – the Virgin was soon half-way across.

More tentative, Sarah took a few moments to gather her courage (Patricia, think of Patricia), then set off, too.

*

The first the worshippers knew of the attack was when Sir Reginald walked in through the fire-staircase doors and calmly announced that they should put up no resistance because they were completely surrounded and outnumbered. As he spoke, his followers stepped forwards and revealed whatever weapon it was they'd managed to improvise. A half-dozen more fanned out on either side of Sir Reginald, making a bolt for the door seem the least attractive option.

The High Priest's tone of posh authority coupled with his bizarre costume and full-frontal nudity silenced the hymn-singers almost instantaneously.

Whilst he created as huge a diversion as possible, four of the Security Guards – Cropper, Pollard, Shears, Cutmore – made quickly but inconspicuously for the Comatose One.

With all eyes upon the door and no-one raising a shout, they were able to reach his bedside and stand at its four corners. Sir Reginald had ensured that these stealth troops of his were equipped with the most fearsome weapons. Pollard's air-pistol was impossible to tell from a real gun.

'It is over,' Sir Reginald announced, when he saw that it was. 'You must do exactly what I say. If you don't, we will kill your precious god.'

All the worshippers now turned and saw their salvation surrounded by cunning enemies.

A riot started immediately – a riot rather than a fight. The motives involved were very varied: some wanted to rescue the Comatose One, some to kill Sir Reginald, some to get as far away as possible, some to liven things up with a good fight. Although the Satanists had the advantage of being armed, they were outnumbered four or five to one.

The angelic defenders attacked with fists. It didn't seem to matter to the defenders that they were clubbed or stabbed – this was their martyrdom, they had awaited it, become a bit bored awaiting it, and now they celebrated its arrival, with violence.

Of the four guards surrounding and aggressing the bed, one – Cutmore – was immediately grabbed and manhandled to the floor. Shears made a powerful lunge towards the sleeping figure, but two young women – Nikki Froth and Angela Dixon – had hold of his ankles. He tried hard, but wasn't able to kick them off. Instead, he toppled towards the bed – his knife stabbing the mattress, missing the man by centimetres. Pollard's air-pistol, it seemed, scared no-one – though he fired off several shots, some of which hit their targets. Many of the angels seemed to relish this chance to demonstrate they were no longer afraid of petty earthly dangers such as bullets. Chief among them was Othniel Calixte, who got Pollard in a choke-hold.

The Satanists, once overpowered, were kidney-punched, bitten, kneed in the groin, deadlegged and, in one case, decapitated with his own penknife.

Sir Reginald at first tried to regain control by continuing his speech, but when he realized this wasn't working he enthusiastically joined the fray: whoever won, the congregation was broken up.

What brought the riot to a halt was a loud cry of *stop!* And the turning of heads towards the centre of anger: the man.

He had been taken hostage; a knife was to his throat and the man holding it – Cropper – seemed more than willing to use it (though looking to Sir Reginald for guidance).

Fists paused after being drawn back; kicks stayed

buried in the flesh they were trying to damage; shouting ceased, replaced by a muttering, mostly of people to themselves; fear invaded the room far more effectively than had Sir Reginald and his band, whose name fell quite a long way short of amounting to legion.

'Stop,' said Cropper, unnecessarily, 'or I *will* cut his throat.'

All around him, bodies disentangled themselves from one another; the decapitated head began to snake its way back to its battered torso.

Watched by everyone, Sir Reginald began to make his way through the crowd. No-one else dared move, so his appearance at the bedside was quite an event.

'Well done,' he whispered to Cropper. Then he raised his sacrificial dagger high above his head and without further ado plunged it straight down into the comatose man's belly – the point of the blade slitting his belly-button in half.

'No!' screamed a voice from the door – it was the Virgin, arriving too late, much too late.

Behind her came Sarah Felt.

The boy doubled up, agonized.

If he had been able to think, he would have thought it felt just like when the stem of the tree had been broken, only a thousand times worse.

But he couldn't think. He was overtaken with bad sensation. He lost consciousness.

Harold caught him as he fell to the floor, preventing him from cracking his head.

'This is your god,' Sir Reginald said, ignoring the Virgin and turning to the crowd. 'And I have killed him in the name of –'

But no-one ever heard whose name it was in. A small *tfft* sound was heard and Sir Reginald seemed to choke on something. In actual fact, Othniel Calixte had used Pollard's air-pistol to shoot the High Priest in the head – the aim had been far more accurate than the porter could have hoped for, and the small shuttlecock-shaped piece of lead had gone straight into Sir Reginald's open mouth.

With everyone looking towards the High Priest, who had fallen into Cropper's arms, Othniel seized his opportunity – and Pollard's throat.

He pulled the Security Guard backwards from the room, towards where the trees stood, then he let him go.

'Now,' Othniel said, 'the time for insults is over – fight me.'

Pollard looked around for help which wasn't coming.

'You are a coward,' said Othniel.

This annoyed Pollard, who clumsily struck out at the righteous porter.

Othniel dodged the blow, but wasn't ready for the follow-up. Pollard went down into scrum-position and charged at Othniel's midriff.

The porter was driven backwards, towards the gaping hole in the floor. He was surprised by the Security Guard's strength.

Pollard kept pushing; Othniel resisted.

On the very brink of the precipice, they equalled one another out.

Othniel tried to swing Pollard round over the edge, but Pollard let go – and Othniel began to lose balance.

Pollard stepped closer, ready to give Othniel the

final shove he needed before he plunged down into empty space.

Othniel pivoted, saw the metal grid above his head and made a desperate leap – just as Pollard's hands made contact with his chest.

With fingertips, Othniel caught hold of the grid – dangling over the hole.

Pollard, with nothing left to push against, toppled forwards.

Othniel grabbed the grid with both hands and swung his legs up behind Pollard's head. Then, with the gentlest of backheels, he sent him down below; squealing.

Meanwhile, Sir Reginald's other troops had been doing their best to protect him – gathering round the bed in a tightening circle. Angela Dixon had spotted her ex-husband among the Satanists, and had been appalled but not surprised.

Surrounded by a widening circle of blood, the sacrificial dagger remained in the belly of the Comatose One. The monitors continued to register his heartbeat, but already it was starting to fail.

It took a few minutes for the boy to recover – or at least to wake up.

Harold's touch was the first thing he became aware of; Harold's dry hand on his forehead.

The boy groaned.

'I thought we'd lost you then,' said Harold.

'I'm okay,' said the boy, although he felt a lot weaker than before. 'Let's keep going.'

With help, he stood up; with faltering steps, he walked.

*

The fire on the 13th floor had now crossed to the side of the building where the forest was.

Although young and thriving, the pines with their green needles and fresh sap caught exceedingly easily and burned extremely rapidly.

Flames travelled upwards, a new floor every couple of minutes – and the black smoke went ahead, through the jump-holes.

More slowly but equally inexorably, the fire descended: hugging the bark, spitting malevolently.

The whole building was now girdled with a brightly incandescent band; top half and bottom half cut off from one another . . .

Explosions overhead did not distract the boy – he was getting close to the exit now.

The pain from the tree was getting worse and worse: for the boy, the world kept disappearing behind big black dots.

It did not help that people, patients *and* staff – though it had become impossible to tell them apart – were fascinated by his strange appearance.

Hands reached out to stroke the foliage, causing the boy to feel nauseous; a few even tried to grab a leaf, perhaps as a memento: at this, he would give a yell – and a snake of green would begin to steal back the stolen.

Harold and the boy arrived at the north-west fire staircase only to find crowds backed up all along the corridor.

'How long have you been waiting?' Harold shouted to someone he had picked out near the front.

Many voices answered: 'An hour and a half.' – 'Two hours.' – 'Haven't moved in ages.' – 'We try passing word down, to find out what's going on, but they never tell us anything.' – 'We hear rumours.' – 'I've lost all track of time.'

Harold knew what the answer would be but asked anyway. 'Is there another way down?'

'I heard that some people jumped down the lift shafts.' – 'I heard that, too.' – 'But that takes you down four floors underground, so you're closer to the way out here. You never know, it might start to move.' – 'We could be out in five minutes or we could be stuck here for ever.' – 'There's always a chance that the underground levels are less crowded. If you got down there, you might be able to climb out relatively quickly.' – 'But heaven knows what the fight for the exit is like if it's as bad as all this here.' – 'Just imagine if there'd been a fire.' – 'There is a fire – can't you smell it?' – 'I mean a fire when things were normal.' – 'Then there would have been police and fire engines and people in charge to organize us.' – 'The world's changed.'

'I know it's a silly question,' said Harold, 'but you wouldn't let us through, would you?'

The answer was no.

When the total power shutdown took place, the shutters to the ambulance bay had lowered automatically, as they were programmed to do. This meant that the door in A&E, already jam-packed, was the only exit from Hospital; some wannabe escapees had broken into offices, smashed windows and climbed out, but these were mostly solo efforts: they wouldn't solve the overall problem of outflow.

Bob Packard, seeing a way to improve matters, set to work opening the ambulance bay shutters manually. There was, he knew, a way of doing this: a handle that had to be fetched from a certain storeroom; luckily, when he got there, no-one had broken in and stolen it to use as a club.

Which is exactly what people assumed he was carrying it for, as he made his way back to the ambulance bay; they cowered against the walls or challenged him fair and square.

But when he reached the shutters again and tried to ratchet them up, he found he wasn't strong enough – or heavy enough, even leaning his whole weight on the lever.

'You look like you need some help, there,' said a voice; WPC Melanie Angel's.

Together, they got the shutters moving.

'Our victory is absolute!' As Othniel re-entered the ICU, Sir Reginald was speechifying. Somehow, the High Priest had managed to climb above the fray and onto the bed of the Comatose One. 'This man was the last hope of good – and now he is dying, unable to heal himself. We are all immortals! We are all free!'

'You're wrong,' said the Virgin, loud enough for everyone to hear. 'There's someone else – a boy.'

The crowd fell to muttering; a few of them had heard the rumours from downstairs.

'Tell us about him,' Nikki Froth shouted.

'He isn't growing older or younger,' the Virgin said. 'When he's injured, he doesn't heal. And he has leaves growing from his stomach – a whole tree, growing inside him. He is different from everyone else.'

'I've seen him,' interjected Cropper. 'I've seen the little bastard.'

'Where is he?' asked Sir Reginald, but his tone was one of command.

'I'm not going to tell you that,' said the Virgin. 'Not after what you tried to do to me.'

'*Tried*,' said Cropper.

'Has anyone else seen this *boy*?' Sir Reginald boomed, casting his eye around the room; hate – hate.

Othniel looked around. One or two hands went up, including (pointlessly) Cropper's meaty fist.

'Does anyone know where he is?'

There was silence; the room suspended as if falling infinitely. The Satanists looked angrily at the innocents all around them; the followers of the Unconscious One looked back, pitying.

Then a female voice spoke: 'I do.'

It was Sarah Felt.

'They're the only way down,' said Harold, meaning the lift shafts. 'Unless you want to jump out a ruddy window.'

The two of them had moved away from the fire staircase.

'Let's at least go and have a look,' said Harold, in answer to the silence.

'Alright,' said the boy. He was thinking about the cut from the cow's horn – if *that* hadn't healed then nothing else would. Other people might be able to jump from the top floor and walk away at the bottom five minutes later, not him.

'You've come a long way,' said Harold. 'It's not so far to go now. Keep your pecker up.'

The boy didn't appreciate the joke, though the encouragement was welcome: the nurse Gemma Swallow had been nice, too.

*

'What are you doing?' asked the Virgin.

'Telling them,' said Sarah; dull eyes, gray skin.

'Why?'

'Because nothing matters any more.'

'Doesn't it matter what they did to Steele, and to that baby?'

Sarah was dead-faced. 'No,' she said.

'You're right,' said Sir Reginald. 'It doesn't matter – so tell us.'

'They can probably guess, anyway,' Sarah said. 'And you were the one that told them about him.'

'I told *everyone*,' said the Virgin. 'I told them to give them hope, to let them know that *they* hadn't won.'

'Tell us,' said Patricia.

At the sound of her voice, Sarah changed completely; her back straightened, her head lifted: she gained purpose.

'For you,' she said, 'I will for you.'

'Go on,' Patricia said.

'He's –'

The Virgin put her hand over Sarah's mouth.

Straight away, another fight started; those who had defended the Unconscious One tried to gather round the Virgin, but they had a harder task than the Satanists.

Eventually, the whole crowd lost balance – and from the bottom of the pile, Sarah's voice was heard to shout: 'He's leaving! He's heading for the main exit! You can catch him in A&E!'

The Virgin tried to attack Sarah but only got a couple of muffed punches through; Sir Reginald's followers had dragged her away – and by the time the Virgin got to her feet, Sarah was standing alongside Patricia.

'Come on,' said Sir Reginald. 'No time to lose.'

*

Each of the lift shafts looked worse than the last, and the sounds coming up from below were incredible – as if two dozen werewolves were involved in the knockout stages of a howling competition.

'They jumped,' said Harold. 'I'm fairly sure they jumped. But if we climb . . .'

The pain wasn't so bad now; it came and went. If this was the only chance, the boy was prepared to give it a go.

Harold stuck his head into one of the shafts, looked up and down.

'There is a ladder,' he said. 'But it's a bit of a way off – on the far side. But there's a ledge here. I think we can shimmy round. What do you think?'

'Where?' he asked.

'There,' Harold pointed.

The boy turned his back on the drop and tried to take a step round the narrow ledge.

It was no use – the growth from his stomach stuck out much too far.

He turned sideways but almost overbalanced, and only Harold's grabbing hand stopped him tumbling down the shaft.

'I can't,' the boy said.

Harold immediately began to look for an alternative.

'Let me try carrying you on my back.'

The boy knew it would be agony – tried to ignore the first stabbing pangs.

A similar problem to before: he couldn't get close enough to Harold without being side-on.

'What if we jump?' he asked.

'Listen to them,' said Harold. 'I'm sure they jumped.'

It sounded like hell, at the bottom of the shaft.

'Then we're stuck,' said the boy.

'Hang on,' said Harold. 'Maybe . . .'

Sir Reginald wasn't messing around with stairs and queues – if the dangerous boy-messiah was on or near the ground-floor exit, then they were going to get there the fastest way possible: jumping.

Surrounded by his rugby-playing bruisers, he set off towards the central lift lobby.

However, pretty soon they were halted by the huge holes in the floor made by the trees, crashing down from his office directly above.

Smoke billowed upwards out of these great inward gashes; and a dim red glow could be sighted far below.

At this, some of his followers showed signs of dismay – they were weak and easily upset, but Sir Reginald was undaunted.

'I'm sure there's a way,' he said.

Sarah Felt spoke up. 'We got across like so . . .' And she demonstrated.

The others, led by Patricia, were not slow to follow.

They reached the lifts in less than five minutes – only two had lost their grip and fallen.

What Harold had seen was a single lift cable, dangling down the middle of the shaft.

'With a bit of a run-up,' he said. 'And a bit of luck.'

'But I can't do that,' said the boy, though he was more than willing to give it a go if it was his only chance.

'No, maybe not,' said Harold. 'But I could try and swing it back and forth. Then you could just grab ahold.'

The boy looked doubtful. 'What if it's still attached at the bottom?'

'Doesn't look under tension to me. I used to do this all the time, when I was in the Navy – like a frigging monkey I was, pardon my French. Up and down the rigging. And now I'm feeling a little more myself . . .'

It was true: Harold, if the boy could have got a clear sight of him, was now about forty years old.

'If you fall,' said the boy, 'I'll come after you.'

'Of course you will,' said Harold. 'And we've lost nothing in trying.'

He measured several steps back from the lift shaft door.

'Stand aside,' he said. 'And keep your fingers crossed.'

Harold ran, jumped.

Defeated, and with nothing better to do, Spanner and Case had wandered desultorily through empty corridors, crossing the building from side to side – and eventually they found themselves at an edge, looking down.

Ten floors below them, a huge pile of animals writhed; the bolus fallen from the kitchen. But this was almost impossible to see, through layer after layer of ghost-mist. What light there was was luridly orange, and flickered from above.

'The fuck is that?' asked Case.

'It's moving,' said Spanner. 'Isn't it? It's moving.'

'Is it water?'

'Fuck, no,' said Spanner. 'It's like a pile of stuff.'

He looked upwards, at the bitten-through edges of rooms: here, a desk hung halfway out into the void; there, papers fluttered down.

A burning figure, human, fell past, screaming.

Their eyes followed it down. No sound reached them when the crump of landing happened.

'That's gotta sting,' said Case.

They both laughed

Then Spanner grabbed Case by the arm and tried to shove him off the edge.

'Fuck off,' shouted Case, but he was unbalanced – not going to stay on his feet.

Spanner had hold of his friend's muscular arm.

Case, toppling now, grabbed Spanner's wrist.

'Let go,' said Spanner.

'Bastard,' said Case, and yanked at the wrist.

Spanner's weight and will offered just enough resistance: Case pulled himself towards safety – at the same time, sending Spanner out into empty air. The two changed places, almost like a dance move; rock'n'roll.

Spanner couldn't believe that he was falling.

Case found himself tip-toe, back to the void, arms wildly windmilling.

He wobbled, twisted, fell.

Harold grabbed, slipped and then gripped.

He was swinging from the cable, and the cable itself was swinging – over towards the far wall, where Harold managed to get his feet in place for a *push* away.

Once, twice, several times, and Harold was holding his free hand out to the boy.

'Come on,' he said. 'It's easy now.'

Another swing – the boy waited another swing, just to get his timing right, then jumped.

And fell down until, at the last moment, Harold caught him – not by the hand (which had slipped past) but by the trunk of the appletree.

The boy hung horizontal, almost paralysed by pain.

'Grab ahold of something,' shouted Harold. 'I can't keep you like this for much longer.'

As if to confirm this, the boy slipped further down – and the shaft in Harold's hand narrowed, weakened.

With his fingers, the boy felt around for the cable – where was it?

Bob Packard's efforts in re-opening the ambulance bay were not in vain: almost as soon as Harold and the boy gave up on that way down, the crowd on the north-west staircase had begun to move. A steady flow, anything up to twelve abreast, was now leaving Hospital via the bay door.

From the 3rd floor, Steele and Gemma moved fairly rapidly down past the 1st and 2nd – the fire catching up with them all the time.

Conversation would have been easy in the stairwell but hardly private. It was only when they reached the ground floor that Steele grabbed Gemma's hand and pulled her forcefully in the opposite direction to the crowds.

The corridors down which they passed were soon entirely deserted: quieter, even, than at this time on a normal night.

Still, Steele wasn't satisfied before he'd found an empty consulting room and locked the door behind them.

There was an outside window, and yellow light came in from the fog: it was by this that Steele examined Gemma, pushing the hair gently back from her forehead.

*

The Virgin approached the Comatose One – she came tenderly, and Angela Dixon, now back at his side, knew she meant no harm.

'How soon will he die?' the Virgin asked.

Angela checked the monitors and thought for a second. 'I don't know what kind of damage that blade did,' she said. 'Within the hour, probably.'

'Then there might still be time,' said the Virgin, and turned towards the crowd. 'We can still stop them – still get to the boy first.'

'What does that matter?' asked Johannes Fast, thoroughly depressed.

'I don't know,' said the Virgin. 'But Sir Reginald obviously wants to kill him. Isn't that a good enough reason for us to want to do the opposite?'

There were stirrings of support; the naked young woman had a point.

Nikki Froth, who many respected as the Comatose One's first female worshipper, came forward to give her support. 'No-one's forcing you to go,' she said. 'And a few people should stay here for, like, when he dies. But if we can make a difference, then we should, you know.'

'I agree,' said Othniel Calixte.

More came to join them; the Virgin greeting each with joy. At first there were only a few, then it seemed the whole room was moving to their side. Johannes Fast came, too.

'Now, follow me,' she said, and led them towards the holes in the floor.

After assessing each of the shafts in turn, most of their doors already forced open, Sir Reginald ordered his followers to divide into six equal groups – one for each shaft.

'Now, jump,' ordered Sir Reginald. 'We'll meet up again at the bottom.'

Patricia led the way, loyal to the last, closely followed by Zapper – he had always wanted to try flying without a helicopter; now was the best chance he was ever going to get.

They jumped, naked, and fell at first through the air – 21st, 20th, 19th – and then through the flames – 15th, 14th, 13th floors – and then, not too charred, through air clearer still.

Sir Reginald went last: he wasn't going to be unnecessarily crushed by anyone. Although it wouldn't be permanent, having Cropper land on you from twenty storeys up was to be avoided (even a more youthful, slightly slimmed-down Cropper).

When they were all gone, Sir Reginald walked round to the emergency lift shaft and entrusted himself to its silent darkness.

There were casualties of the fall: Zapper's downward trajectory took him straight onto the jagged top of a shattered fir-tree. The point pierced him through the stomach and, with his built-up momentum, he carried on for a good couple of metres before the wedge brought him to a stop.

Zapper was a floor or two past the fire; but he was caught there with no hope of rescue: held up, like something to be kebabed, Zapper would in some ways have found death preferable to what was coming – crackly-coming.

Others fell past him (including PC Dixon) with shrieks of delight or shrieks of terror, a few even slapped into his side – narrowly missing the same fate.

He closed his eyes and tried as hard as he could to lose consciousness from pain; failed.

*

Spanner's shattered body was halfway through a cow. But he was better off than Case, who had fallen head first into an area of mostly pigs.

At first, there was too much pain for looking. Then Spanner saw where he was: a wilderness of writhing meat.

Case tried to find something secure to stand on, but bristly pink panic, muscular beyond his strength, was all around him.

He began to slip down, into the brief gaps. It was dark down there, and things were kicking and biting and pecking.

Spanner got hold of the tail of another cow, grasped it and pulled. Wet entrails were against his stomach. He needed to get out – the cow he had punctured was healing.

Shit came out of the second cow's arse, coating the tail in dark brown slippiness.

This began immediately to turn to snaky vapour, but that didn't help Spanner, whose good grip was lost.

Some strange force was sucking him into the cow's belly.

His knees were forced up into his chest, his head pushed down into his gut.

As his hand finally let go of the tail, the hairy black and white skin closed round it.

The first of the diabolic fallers brushed the boy's outstretched feet, making him judder up and down.

Harold's grip loosened, and a second jumper brushed past his shoulder.

A third, forth and fifth body fell past, missing them both; air-whistling.

The boy's flailing hands felt the harsh metal of the

cable (scrape), teasingly it touched them then moved away.

When the sixth jumper glanced off his shoulder, Harold momentarily lost his grip; the boy fell, turning, and the change in position brought the cable beautifully into his palms.

He clung on, just as when up a rope in the exercise hall at school – some bully jerking it about from below while teacher is away.

Another jumper brushed through the sticking-out leaves of the appletree.

'Bugger me,' cursed Harold.

The boy wrapped his legs around the cable and felt, for the first time, almost safe. Harold above him took a couple more impacts but held on for grim death, as he would have said.

After five or six more prangs, the rush seemed to have stopped.

Loud cries came up (fresh) out of the dark – injuries still being felt.

'You alright?' asked Harold.

'Yes,' said the boy.

'Don't need to catch your breath?'

'No,' he said, then began to climb down, hand over hand.

'The holes go almost to the ground floor,' said the Virgin, standing on the very edge. 'If we're lucky, we'll fall through the fire without even feeling it.'

'And if we're not lucky?' asked Johannes Fast, who had come along without really knowing why.

'At least we'll have tried,' the Virgin said, then spoke to all who had come with her: 'When you get as far down as you can, go to the stairs. Make your way to A&E. Tell the people there – tell them to protect the boy. He must get to the door. It's our only chance.'

'I will,' said Othniel Calixte.

'Good luck,' said Nikki Froth.

'There's no time for anything else,' the Virgin said.

Everyone's eyes were down into the hole, out of which came a fierce red glow and the gagging smell of smoke.

'I'll go first,' said the Virgin, and jumped.

Hand over hand, yard after yard, the boy climbed down the dangling cable; Harold above, also.

The twisted metal threads of it were harsh against the palms of his hands, which did not heal when blistered or scraped.

Tough, he kept the cable gripped between his knees and ankles, so was able to hold on sometimes with only one hand.

A half-dozen more jumpers whooshed past, yelling, but they didn't hit either him or Harold –

– Harold, who gave constant encouragement: *Not too far to go, I'm sure* and *Getting on very well now* and *Take a bit of a breather, if you feel like you need it.*

One or two of the lift doors were open, but they hadn't yet reached the ground floor.

There were quite a few bits of ghost-mist in the shaft, and they often appeared as lines rather than points; deaths-in-motion.

Every time they reached a floor, where the lift would often have been stationary, there was a thickish layer of glowing white – not too thick to see through.

When he looked down, which he mostly tried to avoid, the boy could see four or maybe five different lower layers.

They neither of them had any sense of time; the

descent might have been anything between five minutes and half an hour.

Harold felt no fatigue whatsoever – if anything, his fettle was improving by the minute.

The boy, however, was becoming exhausted; coming on top of all his other efforts to leave Hospital, this holding-on-and-never-letting-go was almost too much.

He felt his hands lose their grip, and it was only by tensing his legs as much as he could that he stopped himself sliding down to the very bottom – louder now; screamy.

'I can't,' he said, when his breath was back. 'My arms feel like they're about to drop off.'

'Only another couple of floors,' Harold said – which was a white lie: there were three more to go.

The boy's fingers seemed to have locked solid on the cable, and if he opened them to move them, there was no guarantee they would ever close again.

And he could hear nothing now but his own breathing, and the echo of his breaths off the walls, which seemed also to be breathing, pounding in.

Another uncontrolled slide began, and he just managed to stop it: if it happened again, he wouldn't have the strength; tattered-hands, with blood.

'I've been a fool – a total and utter fool,' Steele said. 'I've waited too long, and now, perhaps, it's too late.'

'Too late for what?' asked Gemma, confident enough to flirt a little: what did she care, at this moment, that Hospital was collapsing in forest and fire? She had her man. Or did she?

'You know damn well,' Steele said. 'Ever since I saw you that first time, in the carpark, I've hardly been able to think of anything else.'

'But you told me then that I wouldn't even last a couple of weeks.'

'I did *not*,' he said, offended, shocked.

'You said those exact words,' said Gemma, feeling the sting anew.

His handsome face showed puzzlement, until the memory came back to him – almost causing him to laugh. 'No, no,' he cried, 'I said, "You'll feel right at home in a couple of weeks."'

'Did you?' asked Gemma, all trust.

'Do you think I'd treat anyone so badly as to say that? That I hoped they'd fail.'

'I thought you hated me,' said Gemma. 'Especially yesterday, when I made you look so foolish.'

For the first time, he looked embarrassed.

'You see how distracted I was?'

All their misunderstandings were over! It only remained for them to kiss, which – with the greatest tenderness (hers) and the greatest passion (his) – they slowly did.

Somehow they made it, the boy and Harold, but the lift doors on the ground floor were shut: obviously, no-one had felt the need to jump from here – not if what they wanted to do was escape; main exit!

The ghost-mist was thick around them, thicker here than on any other floor; it tingled sharply within the boy's limbs and head, helping him stay alert.

'Let's try swinging,' said Harold. 'If I can make it to the ladder, I can shuffle round, maybe get the blighter open.'

The boy freed one of his legs, and felt his grip on safety weaken.

'On three,' said Harold.

Scream from below, right on cue.

Together they kicked out, and again, and again – and the cable began to sway slightly but they were trying to get energy into a huge dead weight; when Harold got it moving before, he'd had the initial momentum of his jump.

All the sideways movement did for the boy was increase the agony in his hands. Even though he didn't want to, he knew he would let go soon. In the instant before he fell, the relief (bloody hands) would be extraordinary; almost worth it.

'I can't hold on any more,' he said.

'I've got an idea,' said Harold, and started to manoeuvre himself until he was upside-down, the cable locked between his legs.

'Give me your left wrist,' he said, with authority. 'I'm going to swing you. Don't worry, I'll hold on tight.'

In only a moment, the boy was hanging in Harold's grip – and immediately after that, he felt himself being thrown out to one side then (after a slight swing) the other.

At first it seemed like they wouldn't succeed this way either, but with the whole of the boy's weight being swung around, the cable too began to swing – swing a few centimetres – swing a metre.

The boy kicked his feet as he'd seen acrobats do on the high-wire, and as he himself had done on the swings in the park.

'Good-oh,' said Harold, hardly puffed. 'Keep that up.'

By now they were almost touching the walls; each time they swung close, the boy could see the rungs of the ladder.

But the blood leaking from the boy's palms was making their grip slick; perhaps he'd drop.

'Can you grab it?' asked Harold. 'I need you to grab it.'

On the first swing, the boy touched one of the rungs with his toes – on the second, it bashed hard against his ankles –

'Let go of my right hand,' he said.

Harold did, and on the next swing the boy transferred himself very elegantly onto the ladder.

'Brilliant,' said Harold, turning right-way-up.

There was a shriek from above, a blaze of falling fire, a soft thud and, as the boy looked up to see what it was, Harold (hit whammingly hard) lost his grip on the cable and fell away through the ghost-mist.

The press of bodies at the bottom of the emergency lift shaft wasn't as great as in the museum, but it went two storeys deep, and was extremely dark.

A few flickers of reddish light reached down from burning floors above, and it was by these that Sir Reginald was able to look around (after re-forming) and take stock.

The fleshly writhe all about him wasn't unlike that of an orgy; he felt himself to be on the bubbling top of some coming-to-the-boil liquid. Sometimes, beneath his buttocks, he felt uncomfortable elbows and sometimes pillowy buttocks. But at points it seemed as if the noise itself might buoy him up – for every human sound was there, from click and grunt to scream and screech.

Perhaps his solo leap had been a mistake; at least in one of the other shafts he would have had some willing slaves to do his bidding. Whilst he was trapped down here – and for how long? – the boy was getting closer to the exit. Maybe he'd escaped already, but somehow Sir Reginald doubted it. If that had happened, something within Hospital would have changed; the atmosphere would have become more certain. Sir Reginald sixth-sensed an intimate connection between the two – which he wanted to control or be seen to destroy.

Then a dim oblong of light appeared above his head, accompanied by a creaking-wrenching sound.

A voice called his name – a female voice – Patricia's; loyal.

'I'm here,' he cried. 'I'm here.'

The noise around and beneath him quietened a moment.

'Hold on,' Patricia shouted. 'We'll get you out!'

For a second or two, Sir Reginald could have sworn he hovered on a bed of screams; the sensation, he discovered, wasn't unpleasant.

It must have been a jumper-faller – jumping down from one of the burning floors; struck Harold full on and knocked him off.

Nothing else to do now but carry on alone.

But how?

The boy remembered trying to edge round the ledge before, how the treetrunk had got in the way.

He tried to sit on it, the ledge, thinking he might shuffle sideways on his bum, but it was too narrow for that; he would slip off.

The roots sticking out of his back were softer and more flexible than the branches. There was a chance that, if he kept his torso at an angle, he could go upright round the ledge with his back to the wall.

He tried it, still holding on to the ladder with one hand; it seemed to work – temporarily.

At the same time, he listened for Harold's voice, trying to pick it out from the many cries down below.

But they were all much the same: aghast with pain and panic.

Yes, it seemed to work – and the boy had no other chance, so he (brave) let go of the ladder; and almost immediately toppled forwards: it was only the balancing weight of the roots behind that prevented him.

Keeping his head far back, knocking against the concrete, the boy took a tentative step, then another.

He had mastered, just about, the straight-line shuffle when he came to the first corner; some cables ran down it, forcing him away from the wall but also giving his behind-back hands something to hold on to.

The boy made it round the angle, then continued across the side way. He felt dizzy, as if he might faint, but he kept going.

The Virgin's angels (most of them) had fallen as far as they could, the 2nd floor, and were now re-forming. Burns had been suffered by those (including Othniel) whose trajectory landed them, until they could crawl off an edge, on the floors aflame – these healed, but seemed to leave worse memories than mere self-inflicted cuts.

'To the stairs!' the Virgin cried, and the call was widely taken up.

But when they got there, they found them freshly impassable: a massive draught, caused by the ambulance bay doors, had gradually built up and was now sucking the flames downwards.

'Back to the lifts!'

It took them no time at all; they were almost directly above the main exit.

They carried on, to the lift shafts; but the fire was there, too.

'Back!' went the cry. 'Back to the trees!'

And in fact the biggest of the pines, as the Virgin had already noticed, was halfway through to the 1st floor. It seemed that only a few strands of metal grid held it suspended – and maybe something could be done about that. (She was not sure where all her new certainties were coming from; never before had she felt this giddy and yet this in control.)

'We can use it as a battering-ram,' she said. 'We can go straight down.'

'How?' asked Nikki Froth, speaking for the hundred.

To the Virgin, it seemed terribly obvious. 'We climb onto the branches,' she said, 'and then all jump up and down together. I'm sure it won't take much.'

She went first, taking one of the lower boughs; the others, trusting her, copied.

Soon they were like baubles on a Christmas tree; naked and optimistic and sparkly each in their own way.

And already one of the metal threads had pinged loose, the trunk dropping a few hopeful inches.

'Everyone ready?' the Virgin called.

The response was immediate and positive.

'After three!' she cried.

And they counted down together.

By assisting one another, the Satanists had managed (most of them) to climb their way out of the lift shafts: doors were wrenched open, fire hoses used as ropes. But in the dark, it was difficult to tell who was who – and a few of the braver others were able to escape, claiming kinship.

Among these, of course, was Harold. He had overheard some agonized conversations, and gathered enough to know that a cry of 'Sir Reginald! Sir Reginald!' would work as password.

The only problem was that, having been helped out of the shaft, he couldn't just excuse himself and go looking for the boy – who, a further bit of eaves-dropping told him, was *exactly* the person this strange bunch were after.

And so, as they reconvened on the minus 2nd floor, Harold did his best to remain inconspicuous.

'There is no time for speeches,' shouted the High Priest. 'We must take the ground floor by force! We must guard all the exits! The boy must not be allowed to leave! Follow me!'

And after him they loyally went; Harold doing his best to look eager and dawdle as much as possible.

By the time they reached the stairs, there were about a hundred of the devils around him.

When he got to them, the lift doors were slightly open – but not enough to squeeze through, and the boy wasn't strong enough (on his own) to push them further apart.

It would be a risk to stick his arm through the gap and wave it – who knew what sadist might come along? But, again, he had no choice.

He shouted, as well – shouted, 'Help! Help!'

No-one came.

The man was dying, definitely – if not from the subarachnoid haemorrhage then from the knife wound to his gut and if not from that, from the fire that by now had almost reached the ICU. Smoke was there already, and Nurse Angela Dixon read the bright digits of his decline through a greyish air; coughing, when she had to.

The Virgin's call-to-action had been so successful that every single one of the worshippers had gone with her, leaving Angela alone to witness the Comatose One's final moments.

But she was not to remain alone – for out of the wind-tunnel of the fire staircase stepped a strange tall figure, reeking of burned rubber.

Like everyone but the boy and the man, she healed – her outline returning to injection-moulded perfection; however, before this happened, Angela was afforded an unprecedented glimpse into the Rubber Nurse's innards – or, rather, the lack of them. A chunk missing out of her side showed no entrails, only a gooey mess: the woman (woman?) truly was rubber through and through. If she had jumped down one of the tree-holes, on hitting the final floor she would probably have bounced a considerable way back.

'I've come to help,' said the Rubber Nurse.

'Thank you,' said Angela, still in control of herself. 'But there's really nothing much to do.'

'I want to care for somebody. I've spent all my time punishing people, and now . . .'

It seemed as if the Rubber Nurse was trying to cry, but lacked the tears.

'Of course,' said Angela. 'Come over here.'

The Rubber Nurse teetered closer: with narrowed eyes, as if she were short-sighted, she inspected the face of the Unconscious One.

'He isn't naughty,' she said. 'Everyone else is – you certainly are. But he hasn't done anything.'

Angela, for a minute, was unable to speak for coughing – coughing which was crying and also choking. She didn't know why she had decided to stay with the man. Perhaps it was something to do with PC Peter Dixon; she had been such a bitch to him. And now he had turned to the bad. Was she trying to make up, going completely over the top?

'I'm sure he's just as bad as everyone else,' she said.

The Rubber Nurse shook her head but the words she spoke were: 'Maybe. You could be right. We'll never know.'

There was an explosion down the corridor, as a cupboard full of oxygen tanks went up; the fire would be with them in a few moments.

'We could do something else,' said Angela. 'We could all go out the window – or onto the roof.'

'No,' said the Rubber Nurse. 'Let's just wait here.'

For a while their passion and tenderness had been overwhelming, and delectable, but now, for Gemma and Steele, duty called.

'We should –' he said, gruffly.

'Yes,' she replied, reading his thoughts without them needing to be uttered; it was ever thus.

'If we don't –'

'Who will?' she completed.

'And when we can't do anything else –'

'Then we'll leave,' she said. 'But only then.'

Once again, Steele held her in his arms and looked over her face as if it were the greatest, most precious object in the world – which, for him, it was.

'If only there had been more time,' he said. 'There are so many things I want to ask you – to find out.'

'You know,' she said. 'You know already.'

He smiled, ruefully. 'Perhaps I do,' he said.

'I love you, Mr Steele,' Gemma said. 'That's all I need to say.'

'And I love you, Nurse Swallow,' said Steele. 'I love you.'

Once more, they embraced – muscles tensed as if

to hold back time; and, for a moment or two, it seemed to them, they achieved a kind of eternity: eternity of unity.

With Cropper to his left and Patricia to his right, the High Priest strode stormily into A&E.

The satanic forces had encountered no opposition on the stairs – and what faced them now was more like a big fat queue than anything else. They were opposed in their will, but only by inertia and stupidity; it was necessary to get to the exit. On the way, they could check for the boy, but the door was their first goal.

The queue, however, reacted with wrath: no-one had been allowed to push in – right from the beginning the exodus had been English and orderly.

'Hey,' said Herbert Hoof.

Bob Packard and Melanie Angel had been standing on the reception desk, supervising, as far as they could, the departure lounge. Sister Agnes Day, after handing over authority to them, had finally decided to leave, and was by now halfway to the door.

Cropper began brutally to shove people aside.

Melanie spotted Cropper, pointed him out to Bob; they conferred.

'Stay where you are,' shouted Melanie, over the heads of the crowd.

The Satanists continued to push onwards.

And a word that had been floating over the room for some time suddenly coalesced: it wasn't panic, it was fury.

A catalyst had been introduced, and within a couple of instants the atmosphere of the room had been changed entirely.

Riot!

*

Someone grabbed the boy's hand.

For a terrified second, he thought they were going to cut it off; but then he felt it being shaken.

A familiar voice said, 'Stuck, I see.' Then added, 'Don't worry.'

The boy could hear Harold issuing orders, and within a couple of minutes the fingers of several hands appeared in the crack of the lift doors.

'Put a bit of backbone into it, lads,' said Harold. 'That's the spirit.'

And inch by inch the doors began to move apart – until the gap was wide enough for the boy to pass through, shoulders square (with the tree sticking so far out, there was no more efficient angle).

Harold knew better than to give him a hug. Instead, he thanked the helpers, who carried on their way towards the door.

'Are you alright?' Harold asked when they were gone.

'Fine,' said the boy, though in truth he was as exhausted as he had ever been. Stuck in the lift shaft, balanced on the ledge, he had several times thought he was going to faint from sheer tiredness.

'Let's push on, then,' said Harold. 'If I'm not mistaken, we're almost there.'

They followed the helpers down one final corridor – towards A&E.

It was harder than she thought, the Virgin: each thump seemed to promise a breakthrough, but none of them – so far – had delivered.

A few stragglers fell past, then got the gist and joined in, increasing the overall weight.

But what would eventually make the difference was happening ten floors above their heads: as the fire burned itself out, upwards and downwards, it allowed the left-behind trees to put on slightly more needly foliage.

The grid began to sag – the lowest roots were now touching the 1st floor, dangling all the way down.

'Harder!' cried the Virgin, and an involuntary memory struck her: of earlier, of Sir Reginald, of his own attempt to break through. She was horrified all over again, but converted this into a greater intensity; useful. 'Together,' she shouted. 'We need to work together!'

With a giant twang, another of the wires gave way.

The angels on their giant fragrant pogo-stick lurched downwards, lost balance for a moment then regrouped in the knowledge that one more good thump would take them through.

A&E: eyes staring or glaring; each mouth the glistening cave of an O; arms no longer down by sides but at radical diagonals, hitting; torsos tensed as if new muscles had threaded their way obliquely through them; knuckles a seasick white; the lines along edges of forms whipping back upon themselves – *the crowd*, this is, seen thus, in an instant of fight; paused.

And then the screaming when time is introduced: the roar of attack and the screech of severe injury. The noises that upper teeth make against lower, and bones make beneath feet. All of it combining to a kind of cloth-twisting of the air; the whole painful room having all the memory and all the life it contains wrung out of it.

Down here, midwife Honey Hopeful cowering in the space beneath a waiting-room chair; there, Digby Rutter engaged in yet another rape; over there, like anger personified, Matron Kettle using her fingernails upon anonymous eyes; and in the middle, Lady Grace Jansen, biting as if she had twenty mouths.

For some, a growing feeling of rightness in this; human-animal vocation finally fulfilled: all meetings, all parties, all sex from masturbation to orgy; all politics – everything social was always a failure to be *this*, and now it's happening and you are causing it to happen and those around you are magnifying in horror everything you feel. You want to rip the substance of the room into tatters – wring the cloth until it shreds, becomes fibres which split into unravelling threads and these, still under intense torsion, vaporize to molecules, atoms, quarks, strings; strings still spiralling and fraying into some smaller unknown.

Everyone feels this, even those aghast with terror, even those hiding from themselves, for their terror is murderous in energy and essence.

The ugliness of what is seen by each eye becomes the only beauty.

As identities begin to meld, everyone is able to act upon themselves as before they wanted but feared to act upon others, and have others act upon them: now desire is fulfilment and lack *of any sort* is abolished.

There is no language to space this room out, no struts of speech; the thought in one mind does not merely belong, it pluralizes, foams; the wound inflicted over by the reception desk is delivered without insult by the slash near the doors.

It happens in the smallest details too – abrasions of skin, plucking of hairs from follicles – these are without proximate cause.

No-one is guilty of act; no-one is dimensional

enough for guilt – all is collapse into mash of mush of happening-lost and you-them.

What is physical expresses perfectly every other thing, external yearnings, external from the physical, from the human – expresses them not in shape or slicing direction but in *moment*: for the first time, this really is an end; truly vulgar, utterly null.

Above it, the building collapses with growth and fire; and into this come Harold and the boy.

As they fell down, clinging on to the branches around them, the angels felt victorious but panicked: control was gone, the only thing left was a second or two of trust – trust to whatever.

And, slam, the hard part of the trunk sledgehammered the 1st floor, damaging it massively.

Again, the Virgin could see through a couple of small holes to the floor below.

There was fire close above them, now – and fire on both sides, flowing down the staircase and the lift shafts.

Another breakthrough was their only hope: they were so close to the door.

Once there, they could make sure the boy got through.

'Again!' cried the Virgin. 'We can do it!'

The room seems impassable; with enough time, maybe – with a day. But that isn't here to be had, and the boy has been thinking for some time now of his third wish. He will phrase it carefully, when he makes it; the words shall be made to express the *exact* thing he needs to happen.

Harold tries to clear a path through the people,

most of whom are naked. When he touches them, they try to fight him: only for a second, then they try to fight someone else.

The boy gives up. He knows they can't do this physically. So, he goes down on his knees, amid the kicking feet, and he pulls himself into a ball as tight as the seed he swallowed.

I wish, he thinks, *I wish that nothing could stop me getting home to my mother*.

And at that, something does happen. Harold pushes against a body and it gives way very easily. He continues past it, and it doesn't re-enter the space behind him.

When the boy opens his eyes, hopefully, he sees a path forming behind Harold – through the crowd.

He stands up, and the people part so that the boy can walk between them without him touching them with his leaves; they avoid even his furthest, featheriest branches.

Some of them look at the boy in awe: they have heard of him; they are fascinated by the appletree but even more by the unhealed wound in his arm. Their hands jerk, as if wanting to touch it.

Harold leads on, and now the crowd dissolves before he gets to it. The path opens all the way from his feet to the main exit – clear floor, unfighting space.

And other parts of the room are learning to be still; they are beginning to crane to watch.

It's him, is the thought in all their heads.

In the path, the boy sees his third wish coming true; he accepts it and begins to hurry.

But someone shouts out. It is a policewoman, WPC Melanie Angel.

'I've found you,' she says. 'At last!'

The boy remembers what the Virgin said. How a policewoman came looking for him.

'Your father – he's upstairs,' says Melanie. 'He's very ill but he's still alive. He's in a coma.'

'No,' says the boy.

'You should go and see him.'

The boy ignores her. It is his mother he needs.

He keeps going, following Harold.

But then someone steps out of the crowd to stand in their way, and another person, and another: Patricia, and behind her Cropper, and behind him Sir Reginald.

Sarah emerges from the satanic crowd. 'Let him go,' she says.

'Keep out of this,' Patricia replies.

'You'll never love me!' Sarah shrieks, and lunges towards the woman she so desires.

Caught off balance, Patricia falls to the floor, Sarah on top of her.

As they fight viciously, the boy steps past them.

Then Harold asks Cropper to please move. But he stays where he is – he looks through Harold and at the boy. His fingers are curled to grab and his breathing describes violence.

'Come on,' he says.

The boy is confident Cropper won't be able to stop him: he believes in the power of his wish; it helped him disappear from Cropper before, and it will do so again.

Harold takes a step closer to Cropper, within range of the punches that come.

An ugly fight begins; grabbing of legs to up-end and scragging of eyes. First Harold is down, then Cropper.

The boy waits, as if this is irrelevant. He wants to

give Harold his chance to help one final time, after their long and difficult journey down.

Sir Reginald kicks Harold in the teeth, knocking him back away from Cropper – who stands up and follows through with a roaring charge.

Harold is down, held, punched, strangled.

The boy walks towards Cropper, as if to walk through him – and then does walk through him.

Each leaf-edge cuts as precisely as the plane of the fog, moving forwards with the boy: Cropper has a tree shape appearing in the density of his body.

Unconnected slices of him start dropping towards the floor – but when they come across leaves, they disappear into them. If they touch one of them, they drip as meat-fragments.

Cropper's head is above the level of the top of the foliage; the boy walks on, and, unsupported by gone spine, the face drops through the irregular lattice of the tree – an expression of uncomprehending fury cut to slivers and then to nothing at all.

Above them, the building starts to rumble with huge internal blows; a thump-thump-thump.

The boy steps over Harold, who is unharmed even when the leaves brush against his forehead.

Now only Sir Reginald stands between him and the door.

Another blow lands; the room trembles.

The crowd are astonished at what those close enough or tall enough to see have seen: the boy acting as fog. No-one is fighting any longer – they want to know what happens.

'You shall not pass,' says Sir Reginald, his voice audible even over the thumping.

In the boy's wake, Harold stands up. He looks down at what remains of Cropper, and sees that the pieces are still moving, still alive, although showing no signs of re-forming; they will continue as the fragmented edges of wounds, pain-feeling and unhealed.

'I am going home,' says the boy. 'You can't stop me.'

'I can,' says Sir Reginald, and reaches out to touch the nearest leaf to him.

Thump.

His finger remains intact.

Encouraged, he grabs the leaf and pulls it off.

Thump!

The boy feels a distant sting of pain.

Sir Reginald holds the leaf up for all to see.

'I am too strong for him,' he says.

Tiles are falling from the ceiling. Above Sir Reginald's head, a strip peels off like sticking-plaster.

The boy steps back, because he knows what is going to happen.

Another thump, and concrete begins to fall.

Sir Reginald stands his ground, the exit immediately behind him.

He does not look up and so he doesn't see the roots dangling, or the trunk emerging, or the pine tree falling through to crush him *flat.*

Angels fall off to either side, in dozens – the Virgin tumbles through, uninjured; Othniel and Nikki, who added their weight also, land together.

And with them comes the crimson light of the fire, burning the upper branches of the tree, burning all the way up through the pharmacy, the Urogenital clinic, Gynaecology, Neo-Natal, the Children's Cancer Ward, Maternity, the Surgical Unit, Radiology, Tropical Medicine, the Security Offices, the Chapel, the administrative floors, Oncology/Haematology,

Cardiology, Pink and Blue Elephant wards, Geriatrics, the Burns Unit, Intensive Care – where the man is a very few seconds from death: his heart about to stop even as the heat from the fire begins to overwhelm the room. Angela holds his right hand, the Rubber Nurse his left. As they feel the scorch of the flames, their grip tightens; they will die a tableaux of care. And then the man opens his eyes, and impossibly sees:

Faggots all aflame falling onto the heads of the ground-floor crowd, who cower; blackened chunks of concrete rain down; a breath of heat passes over them – a lick of fire-tongue.

The boy isn't discouraged by the tree that blocks his path, Sir Reginald beneath it: he walks towards it and when the leaves of the appletree touch it, they dissolve into it; accepted. They are the same substance, appearing solid but intermingling. Unlike Cropper, the trunk is not cut. But the boy can walk forwards unimpeded. Nothing can stop him, and this is the way he is being allowed to leave.

He goes all the way inside the tree; white roots disappearing after him – gone.

And then something unexpected: the boy comes back – not all of him, just his face, sticking out of the bark of the tree as if it were the surface of a pond.

He looks around – at Gemma, at Steele, at Iqbal, at the Virgin, at Othniel, at Bob Packard, at Harold, at the crowd.

'Thank you,' he says, being polite.

And then the face is pulled back inside the tree.

There is a moment when nothing happens; the boy is turning round; preparing himself for the whatever or nothing of the fog.

*

And then it happens:

The boy walks through the exit and out of the hospital. And the exit walks through the hospital and out of the man. And the hospital walks through the man and out of the boy. And the man walks through the boy and out of the exit.

And there is a world there.

And a mother.